ASHUR'S TEARS

CYPHER 1.0

ASHUR'S TEARS

BILL RILEY

BROWN BOOKS KIDS

Ashur's Tears

Brown Books Kids
Dallas / New York
www.BrownBooksKids.com
(972) 381-0009

A New Era in Publishing®

Publisher's Cataloging-In-Publication Data

Names: Riley, Bill, 1965- author.
Title: Ashur's tears / Bill Riley.
Description: Dallas ; New York : Brown Books Kids, [2022] | Series: Cypher ; 1.0 | Interest age level: 011-015. | Summary: "Toby Cypher has it pretty good. He's on the cusp of success with his mimics, programmable morphing robots advanced enough to be indistinguishable from humans ... Toby's world falls apart when he learns that his father, Dr. Erasmus Cypher, a scientist who does classified work for the government, has gone down in a plane crash in the contested border between Turkey and Iraq. But then Toby's sister, Katie, uncovers a secret message in the last song on their dad's smart phone-one sent after the plane crash. Toby and Katie are drawn into the dizzying world of their father's secret work, government lies, and magic ..." —Provided by publisher.
Identifiers: ISBN 9781612545349 (paperback)
Subjects: LCSH: Brothers and sisters--Juvenile fiction. | Fathers--Juvenile fiction. | Official secrets--Juvenile fiction. | Aircraft accidents--Juvenile fiction. | Magic--Juvenile fiction. | Artificial intelligence--Juvenile fiction. | CYAC: Brothers and sisters--Fiction. | Fathers--Fiction. | Secrets--Fiction. | Aircraft accidents--Fiction. | Magic--Fiction. | Artificial intelligence--Fiction.
Classification: LCC PZ7.1.R548 As 2022 | DDC [Fic]--dc23

ISBN 978-1-61254-534-9
LCCN 2021908781

Printed in the United States
10 9 8 7 6 5 4 3 2 1

For more information or to contact the author, please go to www.BillRileyAuthor.com.

For Jo, Xander, and Sam

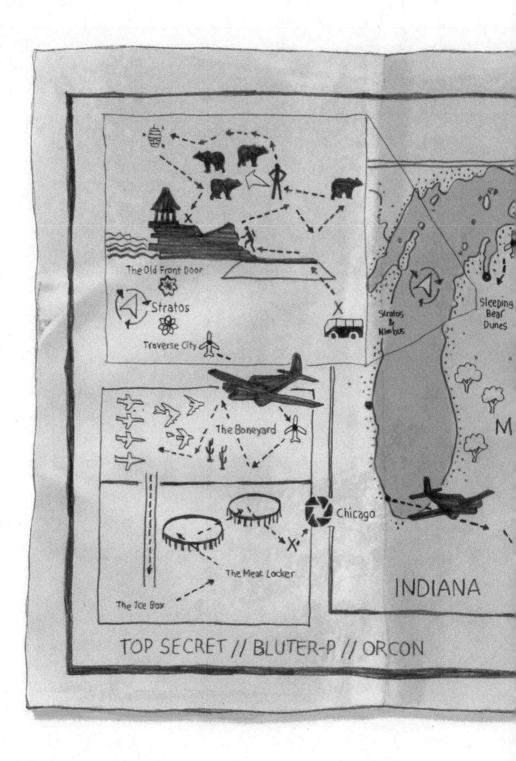

The Old Front Door

Stratos

Traverse City

Stratos & Nimbus

Sleeping Bear Dunes

M

The Boneyard

Chicago

The Meat Locker

The Ice Box

INDIANA

TOP SECRET // BLUTER-P // ORCON

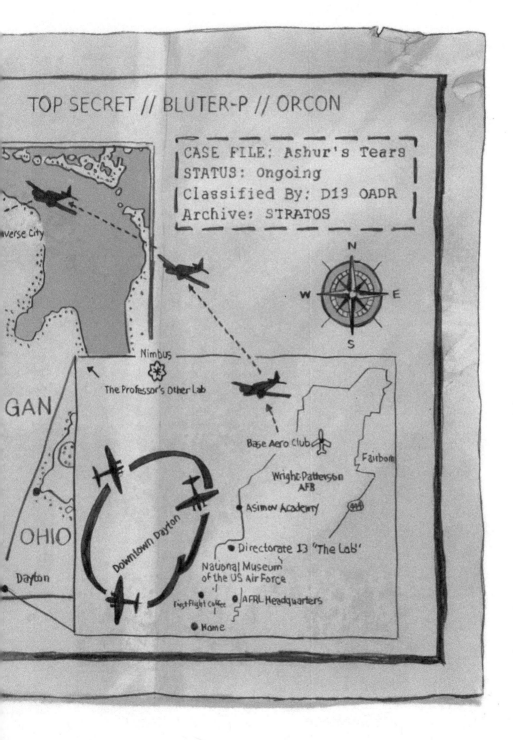

TABLE OF CONTENTS

CHAPTER 1

MIMICS

Toby Cypher climbed the steps and crossed the assembly hall stage like a lion stalking his prey. Toby was fourteen. He'd skipped two grades and hated being the shortest junior guy at Asimov Academy, but he loved how the jumbotron monitors behind him made him look like a giant. He stopped at the podium and swept a lock of dark brown hair from his eyes. Toby had hazel-colored eyes, and the stage lights changed them from brown and gold to a fierce turquoise as he scanned the audience.

Most of the school had come. The auditorium sat three hundred, and people were standing in the back to watch. He could see his twelve-year-old sister Katie near the other middle schoolers, but the seat reserved for his dad, with the other parents, was empty yet again.

Don't know why I even bother to look, Toby thought as he pulled the microphone down to his mouth. *Relax.* He stopped grinding his teeth, let his anger fade to disappointment, and switched on the mic. *Dad hasn't shown up once. Why would this time be any different?*

Toby nodded to the scientists. They were the geek version of pro football recruiters vying for talent, and they filled the first two rows, scheming and side-eyeing the competition. Scientists might be unusual at other school presentations, but this was Asimov Academy—a K–12 private boarding school for students with the potential to change the world. The best colleges and tech companies fought over Asimov students, even for summer jobs.

Toby was what magazines called "a prodigy obsessed with flying, fixing old airplanes, nanotechnology, and building better robots." And his creations had made big bucks since grade school. So, the scientists gawked and plotted. Each had a use for Toby's talent to better humanity, and all of them had plans to help him spend his money.

The auditorium was an old military command center, whose ancient blue and green metal computer banks were repurposed as art and to hold up the stage. Before it was Asimov Academy in Dayton, Ohio, the campus was a part of Wright-Patterson Air Force Base. No one knew what was done there, but there were wild rumors of UFOs, alien experiments, and strange-colored lights that glowed in the buildings at night. Aliens were urban legends at Asimov, around the base, and in the Dayton suburbs, but whatever secrets the campus held were either long gone or good at hiding.

It'll work. I fixed every major bug. Well . . . mostly.

Toby cleared his throat and tapped his phone. Blinds closed over the windowed walls like waves of falling dominoes, and the auditorium was blanketed in darkness.

Holographic images formed on the stage. An old man wearing black-rimmed glasses in a linen suit materialized in front of the churning plasma of the sun. He walked through the solar system, Mercury to Pluto, spinning planets as he went, and Toby began, "Sir Arthur C. Clarke, a British sci-fi writer, once said, 'Any sufficiently advanced technology is indistinguishable from magic.'

"And that means magic, if it exists, is just science we don't understand yet. Clarke imagined a future of space travel. He wondered where we would go or what we might do, and he dreamed of a world where all of us could talk to anyone, anywhere," Toby said as Clarke ran across the stage, smacking spinning planets into the audience. Just before they hit, the solar system faded with Clarke, and Toby spread his arms dramatically wide, gesturing to both sides of the stage where images of rockets formed and launched with a roar.

Toby smiled and tried to make his voice sound dramatic as rocket stages fell away and satellites deployed around the Earth turning above the students. "Not long ago, communicating around the world was impossible. But Clarke believed that with just three geosynchronous satellites—one each over the Atlantic, Pacific, and Indian oceans—everyone could talk and share their stories. Today, we call those satellite orbits the Clarke Belt, named after him. His dream is our reality. Check out the data on the monitors. This is one of my dreams. I've made autonomous robots that are indistinguishable from people. I call it *mimic tech*, and it will change entertainment, espionage, and maybe even the world."

Toby paused for effect, making eye contact with scientists and students, but his gaze stopped again at the one empty chair. He felt his heart drop and his face go grim. "More importantly," Toby said, slipping back on his best showman smile, "mimics are reliable, and no one will have to be alone ever again. So, let me take you through the concept. Then my demo's gonna blow you away . . ."

Axel Suarez glared at Toby, up on the stage, blah-blahing about how his robots worked and changed to copy and act like people. Then he looked at the scientists smiling and nodding, and he wanted to puke. You could count the number of scientists on one hand who came to see everyone else's projects, but that smug, little Toby Cypher got a full house? It didn't make sense. Cypher was smart, but he wasn't that smart.

Axel still didn't have a summer job lined up, even after his presentation got three military scientists interested in how he could target and destroy computers from miles away. None of them had texted him back yet, and he frowned. Then, he thought about what came next, and Axel felt better. Toby Cypher's time as Asimov Academy's number one was about to end. It had taken a month to program the virus and source the hardware and another week to get everything in place.

Toby's right about one thing, Axel thought. *His demo will blow.*

If you squinted, Axel looked like a viking. He was the MVP of the lacrosse team, and his two most loyal minions, Zig and Ruck, sat to his left and right. They were an-hour-a-day-lifting-in-the-gym swole, and both looked like less-developed versions of Axel. Zig and Ruck could have been twins except Zig had buck teeth, and Ruck had more freckles than face.

Axel leaned toward Zig. "EMP status?"

Zig chortled, "Super magnets charging now. They start messin' with Cypher's demo in fifteen seconds. Your electromagnetic pulse generator is set to fry only his mimics. No one else is gonna notice."

Axel grinned, leaned to his right, and asked Ruck, "Virus active?"

Ruck showed Axel the lines of code running down his tablet. "It is, and it nasty. Between jamming and the virus, Cypher's gettin' owned."

Axel slapped Ruck on the back and settled in to enjoy the show.

Light beams swung through the crowd, converging on what looked like a giant steel rolltop bread box rising from the floor at center stage. "That was the technical part of my presentation," said Toby. "Theory's important, but let's make it real."

Toby hit "play" on his phone, and Japanese taiko drumbeats filled the auditorium. The front of the bread box rolled back to expose five thick silver cylinders, taller than Toby.

Everyone in the audience leaned forward with expectation. The drumbeats were powerful enough to feel in your chest, but the five big, shiny tubes just sat there.

As the audience took a deep, collective breath to laugh and boo, fine, oddly shaped lines suddenly spread like fire across each cylinder until they looked like crimson, backlit puzzle pieces. Then the pieces twisted, expanded, and combined until each cylinder was a crude chrome body with a head, torso, arms, and legs.

The mimics started shaking their hips to the drumbeat and snapping their fat sausage fingers. Their arms struck ballet and martial arts poses as they bopped and changed.

Toby still wore his ringmaster smile, but he was sweating. The mimics were slow to start. *Why?* was Toby's first thought as he clicked through apps on his phone. *What the . . . no way.* Then he understood. *It's an attack. The stage is a minefield, and my demo's a battleground. Great.* Toby's fingers raced across the touchscreen. *Just great.*

When all five mimics looked like people-sized mirrored skeletons wrapped in translucent membranes, Toby had to make a decision: either end the demo quickly, or pull all the safeties and power reserves to fight the crushing electromagnetic fields and show everyone what his mimics could do. Toby blew past the orange, flashing "Disable Safety Protocol— Are You Sure?" warning, hit "YES," and his mimics sprang high into the air as their bread box sank back into the stage.

The audience *oohed* and *aahed* as the mimics spun and tumbled in the strobe lights. Then they changed again with the music, until they were a perfect five-man boy band strutting down the stage, singing about love and longing for the girl who got away. It was like magic, and the audience clapped and cheered.

Toby would have cursed, but the mic was on, and he was too busy. He'd just finished increasing the mimic's strength and shielding to stop them from getting pulled to the stage floor and ripped apart by the magnetic fields or completely fried by EMP—electromagnetic pulses—when red pop-up alarms covered his phone as malicious code hammered his mimics. Toby was grinding his teeth again when he heard the applause and looked up. *Yeah, there are problems, but the audience hasn't noticed,* he thought. *I can't stop the virus, but maybe I can slow it down to buy just enough time.*

Toby bit his lip as he worked it out. His happy face was hard to slip back on, but he wasn't going to fail.

The boy band reached their big finale. They slid on their knees, stopping arms out on the edge of the stage, at the song's last note. "Thank you for letting us play for you," the mimic boys said, as they smiled, waved, and held their hands to their ears, listening for the applause, which was deafening.

"You like that?" Toby said, taking a half bow. "That's just the beginning." He searched the crowd again. This time he locked eyes with Axel, laughing with his crew. Zig patted his tablet. Ruck pointed at Toby with an exaggerated boo-hoo crying face.

5

Axel made a throat-cut motion as he and Toby stared each other down. Then Axel waved "buh-bye," huddled his pals, and reattacked. *Nice try, Axel. You and your goons won't shut me down.*

"Shouldn't we see what happens," Toby asked the crowd, "if we dial up the mimics and turn them loose?"

The crowd whooped and clapped. Toby engaged full mimic mode, and they shimmered and shrank and grew in places as the next song started. Four mimics became stunning backup singers, surrounding musical sensation FUBAR, who was rapping, "Snitches and twitches, clown. Retribution, LA style. Sneaches and peaches, all around, lost and found, can't keep me down. Sky ain't the limit no more, footprints on the moon make me want so much more . . ."

It wasn't just a perfect likeness of FUBAR, it *was* FUBAR. His look, his moves, that charisma, his voice.

The backup singers jumped from the stage and moved through the audience. Mimics coaxed students from their seats, and they danced. Every time a mimic touched a student, the robot copied that student, and it was so much more than looking in a mirror. It was a twin. The crowd went crazy. Everyone, wanting to be next to dance with their twinsies, reached for a mimic.

Toby hadn't wanted to bite his nails since grade school. Now he wanted to chew off his hands. After each mimic had successfully copied dozens of students and scientists, Toby's problem got worse. The magnets and targeted EMP bursts were weakening the mimics, and the virus was relentlessly drilling its way into their systems. Toby overclocked his mimic's processors and isolated their most critical functions from the network. That slowed the attack, but it still wasn't enough.

First, the glitches were small. Crayon-colored hair, wild costumes, a few animal ears, and crazy tattoos that randomly appeared.

But the glitches only made the game more fun. The cheering got louder as the show got wilder. FUBAR's rap changed to country music, then from metal to opera.

The music turned back to rap, and Toby lost control.

The mimics left their dancing twins, cartwheeling and jumping back to the stage. When they landed, they changed again. A guy with crazy Einstein hair massaged the keys of a holographic piano. A baby-faced, ebony man wearing purple glasses ghost-beat a phantom set of drums. Two short-haired girls in bell-bottom jeans windmilled power chords on their electric guitars.

While the band rocked on, Toby plugged directly into the piano man and uploaded an anti-virus to try to regain control. Toby had just disconnected when FUBAR stopped singing, turned to him, and morphed. FUBAR greyed out and shrank until he was a greenish alien with tiny limbs, and glowing avocado-shaped eyes, in a face that was mostly forehead.

Toby's stomach dropped. He glanced at the audience. *Good.* They were mostly smiling and banging their heads to the beat. *Okay. I can make this work.* Toby grabbed the mic off the podium and sashayed to the music and toward the alien. "We've all heard the urban-legend. Now you get to see it live. I present to you the alien of Wright-Patterson Air Force Base." The alien looked up at Toby, its dark eyes glittering. He put the mic to the alien's mouth and said a little prayer. *Please follow your programming and sing.*

The little alien took a deep breath, and Toby sighed with relief. Then its arms and legs sprouted, and it grew. In an instant, the alien towered over Toby, made a huge fist, and swung at his head.

The audience gasped, just as Toby's anti-virus hack took effect.

The piano man mimic evaluated the situation, prioritized Toby's safety, and acted. The music stopped. The piano player flew across the stage, picked up the alien, and flung it across the room.

It crashed into the wall and shattered the windows. Before the crowd could react, the band started again with a wild beat of drums. The gangly alien mimic slowly stood and swelled into an enormous, armored ape that bellowed and beat its metal covered chest. But then, its angry face grew afraid, and it ran away through the broken windows.

Everyone looked back to the stage. The piano player had transformed into a petite blond middle schooler, revving a chainsaw. It was a flawless copy of Toby's sister Katie that jumped from the stage, chasing the ape. She was laughing as she bounded away, her French braid trailing behind her.

Toby checked the countdown on his phone. *Fifteen seconds of battery left.* He had just enough control for the finale.

The audience still looked amused, except for Katie. Most days Katie acted twelve-going-on-twenty. Mean one moment, sweet the next, but she was mortified by her mimic fighting an ape in front of everyone. Her face was red, and her glare burned into Toby like sunlight focused at an ant through a magnifying glass.

The three mimics on the stage became perfect Toby clones. He raised a hand, they raised a hand, but the last mimic was a little off. Toby stepped forward, two stepped forward, and one stepped back. The music ended in one echoing guitar note, and the Toby mimics waved good-bye. That was supposed to be the end, but then the Toby mimics smiled big for the audience and exploded. There was a hot flash, a burnt wire stench, and a clatter of falling parts.

The room fell silent. Everyone not close enough to see it directly watched on the jumbotron as the ape's head—in a red-plumed Roman helmet, neck wires still crackling—bounced into the room and rolled to a stop in front of the stage.

Toby Cypher tapped his phone, and the lights came up. He stood on the stage in a cloud of grey smoke, with singed hair and scorched clothes. His wide turquoise eyes looked out at the audience from his smudged face. His heart pounded. It was finally over.

Toby said, "And that's my presentation."

The stunned crowd erupted into a standing ovation.

Axel and his minions were falling out of their chairs, laughing.

Toby took his bow, exited the stage, and handed the microphone to his teacher.

"It goes without saying," said Mr. Carpenter. "You're paying to repair the damage and replace those windows. And you will get this mess cleaned up."

"It wasn't my fault. You know I—"

"Mr. Cypher. Consider a moment before you say another word."

"Yes, sir," Toby said, through his teeth. "I'll take care of it."

Mr. Carpenter turned on the mic. "That concludes our last science project. Thank you for coming out this afternoon. Mr. Cypher and Ms. Rachel Majeski, see me at the stage."

Toby groaned as he watched Axel say goodbye to Rachel, point at him, and leave laughing. He wasn't sure what to expect after all the drama and destruction, but the scientists queued up to shake his hand and said things like, "Still a few issues, but very impressive, Mr. Cypher," and, "We look forward to working with you. We'll be in touch soon."

When the last scientist was gone, Toby dropped his showman smile and climbed back on stage. *I spent three months of nights and weekends getting this demo right.* He wanted to scream, but instead he followed his nose past Mr. Carpenter to where the smell of high-voltage ozone was the strongest. He brushed away mimic remains, opened a trap door in the stage, poked his head inside—and there they were. Axel's EMP generator in the middle of a web of military-grade magnets, but they were dissolving away.

Smart. They used a fast-acting bacteria that only eats the kind of metal they used in their equipment to cover their tracks. But it was a big web, and Toby hauled up a string of magnets the bacteria hadn't reached and broke their connection.

They put this much effort into taking me down, and I still won.

Toby took a few breaths to calm himself and started plotting his revenge. Asimov had strict rules about interfering with another student's work, as well as excellent surveillance and security systems, so Axel and crew were probably already busted—they were just too stupid to realize it. *If not, I will make them pay.*

Mr. Carpenter was standing next to Toby, frowning at the pile of magnets, then looked up. "Nice of you to join us, Ms. Majeski."

Rachel Majeski. Fifteen. Transferred in last year from . . . Nevada. We're both Juniors. She's brilliant and nice and in trouble again. Their eyes met, and she waved. *Well, that makes two of us.* Toby smiled. *I'd talk to her more, but she's with Axel, and Axel is—Axel.*

"You wanted to see me?" asked Rachel.

Toby waited as she talked to Mr. Carpenter. He couldn't remember ever seeing anyone with steel-grey eyes before, and her hair was always a shade of purple. Sometimes with pink and red highlights. Today, it was amethyst and plum.

"Yes, Ms. Majeski. I want Toby to tutor you in math and science. You don't have much time left before finals. If you don't bring up your grades, you won't be able to stay at Asimov—"

"I don't have time for tutoring."

"If you don't make time, you're going to fail," said Mr. Carpenter. "Or do you wish to attend another school?"

Rachel growled. "No, fine."

Then Mr. Carpenter turned to Toby. "A chainsaw, Mr. Cypher. Really? And mimics thrown from the stage and breaking glass walls. Your demonstration could have hurt someone."

"It didn't," Toby said, gritting his teeth as he kicked a magnet toward Mr. Carpenter, wondering if it was the tooth grinding or all the fake smiling that was making his face hurt.

"And while it does appear that someone tried to ruin your presentation, and *we* will attend to that, you could have made your point *and* limited the risk. But you elected to remove required safeguards to make a big, showy splash . . ."

Toby grew angrier as he half listened, thinking, *Yeah, and if Axel hadn't broken into your school and set a trap for* me *under* your *nose, this wouldn't even be an issue.* But that changed when Mr. Carpenter said, "Reflect on what might have happened while you tutor Ms. Majeski."

Without thinking, Toby said, "Yes!" Flustered, he added, "I mean, I will if I have to."

"I'll have to check my schedule," said Rachel.

That made Toby think about his schedule: *Get my mimics and parts back, then rebuild them, let the guys at the museum know I won't be able to help for a few days . . .*

Toby smiled. He was looking forward to tutoring Rachel.

"Ms. Majeski, your tutoring begins now."

Rachel rolled her eyes in disgust. "Fine."

Toby rebooted his one surviving mimic and set it to work cleaning the auditorium. Before he and Rachel left, Mr. Carpenter pressed a thick folder full of Rachel's exams into his hands.

Principal Jackson arrived as the two students left. "So what do you think?" he asked Mr. Carpenter.

"Cypher's presentation was impressive, but he lacks patience, restraint and, today, common sense. I'm also taking care of a disciplinary issue that will require your attention shortly. And then there's the matter of your ward. Her talent is undeniable, but I'm still not convinced she's Asimov material. Her teachers are following your instructions, but—"

"Well," said Principal Jackson, "this will be an interesting experiment, then. Ms. Majeski is still a bit feral, but I believe in her, and want to see her achieve her potential."

"If that's the case, aren't you making this harder on her than necessary? With her history you could grant an exception and give her time to address her grades."

"I could," said Principal Jackson, "but she made a deal, and it's in her nature to honor it. Grading her against a different standard would be the same as telling her she isn't as good as everyone else, and that is simply not true. I respect her too much to do that. No one can do everything by themselves. She's smart, and she's a survivor. Now she needs to figure out how to work with others to solve problems, particularly her most pressing one, and those two will complement each other nicely."

"Why do you say that?"

"Mr. Cypher needs to learn to see the world for what it really is, and Ms. Majeski needs to finally learn how to trust someone worthy of her trust."

CHAPTER 2

ASHUR'S TEARS

The story was written in burning white script on five metal sheets that floated in the air around Doctor Erasmus Cypher. The symbols gave off a flickering light that, in the otherwise dark room, made his eyes shimmer and his short blond hair and goatee look white.

Doctor Cypher sat alone at a big, round table in his office in Air Force Research Lab Directorate 13. The people who worked for him just called it the Lab, and officially, D13 didn't exist. It was a secret hidden in plain site on Wright-Patterson AFB. Outside of the Lab, only three other people in the Air Force really knew what they did. Magic was dangerous. The fewer who knew the truth the better.

He had been struggling to figure out the strange, burning script circling around him for hours. When he finally cracked the code, he grew lost in the story of the fall of the ancient kingdom of Aquabah—until Professor Lawrence Urbanex walked in without knocking.

"Where did these come from?" the Professor asked, his head bobbing to the left as he examined the floating story sheets. His complexion was deep brown, and he was clean shaven except for a precisely trimmed, silver-streaked black beard. "This is living metal. So rare it's not supposed to exist." His brown eyes narrowed when Doctor Cypher grinned and gestured, and the foil sheets darted around the Professor like battling kites.

"The lost temple rumored to house the relic Ashur's Tears may have been found and destroyed," said Doctor Cypher. "Supposedly, they came from there, Lawrence."

"Don't be juvenile, Raz," the Professor said, banging the tip of the old umbrella he used as a cane against the floor. It made a louder *boom* than expected, and the foil sheets fled and hid behind Doctor Cypher. "What do they say?"

"They document a battle of good versus evil," Doctor Cypher said, sagging in his chair and closing his eyes. "You know, the usual." Then he looked sidelong at the Professor. "It starts, 'Leave nothing alive. You are death and blight. Poison her wells. Salt her earth. Topple her stones.' Those were the orders Sin-Assa-Verata issued to his forces. He was known as the Dark Emperor of Shadow, and he wielded Ashur's Tears to bring forth what we fear in the dark."

"As I recall," the Professor said, leaning on his umbrella, "Ashur's Tears was described in some references as a magical flower of creation, and in others as a weapon of legend that destroyed civilizations."

"Couldn't it be both? We've seen artifacts change to become what their user needed them to be. Records in the archives also call it the Dark Bridge, Ender of Worlds, and, curiously, Ashur's Gift. The story engraved here," Doctor Cypher said, gesturing to the foil sheets still cowering behind him, "says that Ashur, the Mesopotamian god of sky and creation, left a great power for mankind when he left our realm. Then this Dark Emperor stole Ashur's Tears, summoned an army of demons, and destroyed the ancient kingdom of Aquabah. But he was tricked by a boy king who sacrificed his life to stop the invading Emperor. In the end, Ashur's Tears was so dangerous the goddess A'nana and her daughter Tansiluros took it and hid it from man."

"So, you believe these are from where Ashur's Tears was kept," the Professor said, his head bobbing toward the burning script on the metal sheets keeping their distance from him, "and that this story is true?"

"Not sure yet, Lawrence, but I have a bad feeling it is. The alt-tech the scribe used to record this is sophisticated, and it tracks with what little we know about Ashur's Tears. But first, I need to research a few things and confirm the reports." Doctor Cypher pointed to the five floating foil sheets and made a fist. Then he held out his right hand and the white-flame writing extinguished, and the sheets folded up until each was the size of a large silver coin that stacked itself in his palm.

He sealed the folded metal story discs in a large black-and-purple envelope labeled "TOP SECRET//BLUTER-P. Classified by Directorate 13" and handed it to the Professor. "Lawrence, get this to Stratos. Highest priority."

"Certainly. What are you going to do?"

"If Ashur's Tears is loose in the world? Find it. Before it's too late."

CHAPTER 3

TUTORING RACHEL

The library was a glass and steel building built around an old air traffic control tower. From outside, the library resembled a rocket ship. From the top floor study room, Asimov looked like a park with aircraft displays, shade trees, and beds of flowers. A flagpole set between two giant missiles marked the center of campus, and crenellated stone buildings surrounded the park like castle walls.

They reached the library in silence. What followed was a miserable hour of trying to help Rachel prepare for her finals. She sat arms crossed and wouldn't even look at Toby, except to glance at what he wrote on the board. Then she'd spit out an answer and say, "Next."

Each problem made her angrier. *What am I missing?* Toby hung his head. *She says she wants to stay at Asimov, but she definitely doesn't want this, or to be here with me.* He didn't get even half of the next problem on the board. Rachel answered it and said, "Next."

Toby loosened his blue uniform tie, undid his top button, and sighed. *This isn't going anywhere.* He snatched Rachel's exams from the table and flipped through them. They were marked with so much red ink they looked bloodstained, but none of her answers were wrong. They weren't right either because showing your work counts for most of the grade. Not only was there no work, but her answers read like insults: *3.14, duh. Don't waste my time. There is no positive integer for x, y, z. Really? The lines obviously intersect at x in 5.8 meters. Was the Easter egg hunt to find angles fun for you?*

Toby sighed again. "Grades and projects are everything at Asimov. You need to pass to stay, right? Why keep fighting your teachers?"

"I don't know. Their attitude just sets me off."

Toby crossed his arms, and they glared at each other.

"Okay, fine. I thought I finally caught a break, but instead I get treated like I'm stupid. I never asked to come here. They found me. They brought me to Asimov. I went to seven schools in the last three years, and somehow that made it cool to move me up a grade? And our teachers think they're all so smart," Rachel said.

"You know, I saw your presentation on quantum computing."

"Yeah, what about it?"

"I don't think anyone ever looked at it like that before. It blew me away, and you really made me think." Rachel began to smile, then Toby said, "But," and it turned into a withering look. "But it ended in a shouting match between you and two of the best quantum theorists in the world."

"They're wrong. What's next?"

I'm doing the same thing her teachers did, and it won't help her pass. He thought about what might work and felt his stomach drop. *If she doesn't like me now, she's gonna love me after this.*

Toby slapped down the tests in front of her. Rachel was slumped in her chair, playing with a rope of plum-colored hair she had pulled over her right shoulder and twisted.

Rachel narrowed her smoke-grey eyes at the exams and scowled.

"Your problem," said Toby, "is you don't seem to understand basic logic or math."

Rachel swept the papers into her bag. "Another waste of time. Conceited teachers lecture me enough." Rachel stood, knocking over her chair.

"You don't know the basics," repeated Toby. "And—"

"And what? I don't belong here?" Rachel whispered, staring out the window, struggling to compose herself. "I've heard teachers say it. Maybe they're right. No matter how hard I try, I don't get it, and now they're throwing me out like trash. Goodbye, Asimov, and if that happens, I . . ." Rachel looked away. "I don't know why I'm telling you. You just got stuck with me," Rachel said as she fled out the door.

Toby gnashed his teeth. *This is it. This is where she either lets me help, or she bolts and hates me forever.* "I'm not done with you yet," Toby said to her back. "Or do you always run when things get hard?"

"What?" yelled Rachel, spinning around, her plaid skirt fluttering. "You don't know me!"

"I know you don't understand logic or math."

"That again . . ."

"*But* you have great instincts. And you *can* do this."

"So, what's wrong with me? I feel like a freak."

"Nothing," said Toby. "Near as I can tell, before you got here, you didn't learn a lot about math. You lack fundamentals. That's all. It's why you can't show your work, but we can fix that."

"How can I learn calculus in a couple of weeks?"

"You can't. But you can already figure out the right answers, and if you can do that, you can learn enough to pass. The rest you can pick up this summer. That is, if you stay, and you're willing to work. If not, don't waste my time. The Air Force Museum across town is restoring a bunch of rare aircraft. I like volunteering there. Not tutoring you opens my schedule. But, for what it's worth, you can do this. Let me help."

"What's in it for you?" Rachel asked, crossing her arms again.

"Aside from Mr. Carpenter saying I have to," Toby said, looking away, "you're not the only freak here."

"You're Toby Cypher. A lot of people would kill to be you."

"Still a freak though, or a prize. Or someone people suck up to because they want something. Don't get me wrong, most days being me is great," Toby said with a grin. Then his heart raced as he looked into her steel-colored eyes. "But I want to be friends."

"That's it?" Rachel asked.

"That's it. I mean, like you said, I don't even know you," Toby said with a smirk.

"And you have no other terms or conditions?"

"Nope," said Toby. "Just give it your all, and don't waste my time."

"Fine." Rachel took a deep breath and shut the study room door. "What do I have to do?"

Toby stood up her chair. "Show your work. And it'll really help if you stop treating your teachers like morons."

Rachel sat with a groan and scowled at Toby like he was an idiot. "Why does one plus one equal two?" Rachel asked, taking a black scrunchie from her bag and gathering her hair.

"It's additive," Toby said, distracted by what she was doing. "It's obvious. It just does."

"Mmhmm. That's how games, probability . . . anything with calculations are for me," she said, working her hair through the scrunchie. "Once I know the starting point, it's like following a string until I reach the answer. Simple as one plus one equals two." Rachel seemed pleased as she checked her pulled back hair with her phone. "The outcome is obvious. The answer's the answer. It just is."

"But if you don't show the work, and you treat your teachers like schlubs," said Toby, shrugging, "are you really surprised they think you're cheating and want you out?"

"All *they* ever do is argue over the 'why,' and why you got there doesn't matter if you're right. What matters is what you do with the answer. But they don't get it. The answer is what it is, and when answers are complicated, like in real life, by the time *they* figure out their precious 'why,' the outcome is already changed."

"I believe you," said Toby, erasing the board and looking back at her. "You're pretty . . . impressive. But most people can't get from A to D without going through the B and C first."

"Not my problem," said Rachel, fiddling with the blue, floppy bow tie that identified her as a junior. "My answers are right."

"So . . . what does not showing your work in math and physics equal?"

She glowered at him. "It equals screw you."

"No, it equals you're screwed," said Toby. "I thought you wanted to stay."

"Fine," Rachel said, opening her notebook.

CHAPTER 4

BACK AT THE RANCH

It was dark when Toby got home. The lights were on, but he still caught his foot on the top step, stumbled over the porch, and banged into the front door hard. "Stupid step," Toby mumbled. "Stupid door."

Pro: I hung out with Rachel. Con: we mostly argued. Toby was spent. *At least she doesn't hate me, probably.*

Toby was still leaning on the door, thinking, when it opened. He grabbed the doorjamb and stopped face-to-face with his sister.

Katie pinched her nose. "You smell like a dumpster fire."

"Great, thanks. Exaggerate much? Now, let me in." Katie was no linebacker. She had a slight build, but for some reason, no one could ever get past her if she didn't want them to. No matter how hard they pushed. It was like they weren't even there.

Katie's blue eyes pierced him. "Don't ever drag me into your freak show again. How could you make a such a stupid version of me? I already stand out. Now tomorrow, everyone will be talking about you and laughing at me."

"I got hacked and worse. It wasn't my fault," Toby snapped. All he wanted was to shower and sleep, but Katie was standing in his way, and there were big tears in her eyes.

No fair. I didn't do anything wrong. But Toby melted. Ever since he was little, he couldn't stand to see Katie cry. "I . . . I'm sorry, Katie. I would never—"

"Then who did?" Katie asked with a sniffle.

Toby sighed. "Axel Suarez and his crew, and things went crazy."

"How could you let this happen?" Katie said, wiping her face with her sleeve.

"Mr. Carpenter already caught them, and Asimov doesn't let things slide," Toby said, holding up his phone. Displayed was a one-word text from Axel that read,

SORRY

"Can you imagine what they did to get him to send this?" he gloated. "Justice is sweet."

"Good for you, Toby," Katie said, patting his shoulder. "But you trust the system way too much. How will you make this up to me?"

"What do you want?"

"For starters, food. When you see Dad, I vote Chinese," Katie said, holding up both hands to double her vote.

"Is he making dinner?"

"He says he is, but he's holed up in his office, and I'm starving." Katie had a devious look on her face. "Now's the time for takeout."

"What's he doing that's so important he didn't show, again?"

"You can ask him when you see him."

"What makes you think I'll see him?" Toby said, closing the front door hard.

"It's always some secret," Katie said, dragging him from the entry through the living room to the lower-level stairs. "He only talks to you when he gets like this, and you need to tell him how you feel. Plus, you owe me."

Toby stopped.

Katie huffed and pushed. Toby was still raw about the no-show.

Can't wait to hear what it was this time.

Then he looked at Katie, remembered her tears, and started down the carpeted stairs.

Katie hung over the railing, calling after him, "Don't forget. Nothing makes you feel better faster than dim sum dumplings."

One wall of the finished basement had windows and French doors that opened to a patio where Katie had set up a big telescope. There was a stacked stone fireplace, a TV, and thick sofas for movie night. Past a kitchenette was Dad's office. His door had a veneer that made it look like the other wood-paneled doors, but it was made of steel. A palm reader and keypad were mounted on the wall. The door was open.

There were no windows in his dad's office. Past the rectangle of cheery light intruding from the rest of the basement, a few odd table lamps illuminated things in the gloom.

Toby knocked. His father looked up and waved him in.

Bookcases had overflowed into book piles on the floor, stacks teetered on every table, and a big closet was sealed by a vault door.

Stone statues of old gods and lab equipment were mostly covered by the cartoon character bedsheets Toby and Katie had outgrown. Lights moved under some of the sheets, and the room smelled like paper, old leather, and coffee. Toby passed a picture of himself in the cockpit of Dad's plane after his solo flight, and his father's silver astronaut wings were on display next to a picture of Dad in an orange spacesuit shaking hands with the president who retired him from the Air Force. He still wore his blond hair cut short, only now he had a mustache and goatee and reading glasses over his sky-blue eyes.

Behind his large desk hung more pictures from way back: a younger Toby, laughing and sitting on the shoulders of the first two robots he sold, his mom kissing his dad in his flight suit from before the accident, and Katie holding a huge pumpkin with a triumphant look on her face. Models of rockets and aircraft were arranged on his desk, and behind them sat the chunky, plastic phone Dad used to make secret calls. His father was working on something shiny.

Toby sat in one of the red leather chairs across from the desk and waited impatiently. He lost it when his father went back to polishing a ring. "In case you forgot, today was the big presentation. You promised you'd be there this time!" Before Toby realized it, he was standing at the edge of the desk, yelling. "And you didn't show again. There was one open seat in the whole auditorium, and it was yours."

Doctor Cypher set down the ring, took off his glasses, and sat back. "You know I would have been there if I could have."

"So, what happened this time?" growled Toby.

"I didn't want to miss it, but something came up, and I got called back to the lab."

"For what?"

"Toby, I wish I could tell you, but—"

"It's classified," they both said together.

Doctor Cypher's voice hardened. "It is, and that's the job." Then he took a deep breath and his voice softened, "I wish I could say more. You know how proud I am of you."

"But you're never here when it matters," Toby shouted. "I'm sick of all the secrets."

"I was there when you were building the mimics," said his dad, his voice growing louder. "How many nights did I spend with you out in the workshop watching them come together, and how many weekends did we spend together flying?"

"This was important, Dad."

"Understood, and I am sorry." Doctor Cypher sighed, ran his hand through his hair, and groaned. "For what it's worth, I'm tired of all the secrets too. I have one more trip, then things will be different."

"Heard that before."

"I know. But this time it will. Jack will be here while I'm away."

"Well, that's great," said Toby. "So, Uncle Jack can do special forces missions around the world, and still make time for us."

"Toby!" snarled Doctor Cypher, standing. They glared at each other across the desk. His dad took a deep breath and sat. "I have to do this. As soon as I'm back we'll talk."

"Don't take too long," Toby said sharply, but he was suddenly more tired than angry.

"I won't," said his dad. "And I did want to see your presentation. How was it?"

Toby sat on the edge of the chair. "Well . . . there was more drama than expected. And I'll, uh, be home late all this week," said Toby, suddenly feeling uncomfortable. *I am not talking about her with him.* "But I got a standing ovation."

"Way to go, Toby! How'd the nanoshifters and new optics and servos hold up?"

Toby thought about how excited he was when his dad came home early from his last trip and surprised him in the workshop. Lately, he was always gone. *I was stuck on how to make the mimics move while they changed, and there he was with coffee and donuts asking me what I was working on. I was two Krispy Kremes in when I figured it out.* "They worked great until they didn't," Toby said, rubbing his jaw. "I'm going to have to harden them and the core against EMP and powerful magnets."

"Magnets?"

"And malicious code," said Toby. "And add new safety shutdown protocols—long story."

"Sabotage?"

"Big time," said Toby.

"Do I need to get involved?"

"No. I worked it out," Toby said, thinking about the applause and apology text Asimov squeezed out of Axel.

"Well, congratulations then," said Doctor Cypher. "Let me know if you get in over your head. So . . . what's Katie want for dinner?"

"Dim sum dumplings."

"Dim sum, hmm? Well, whatever she picks always winds up being the best thing on the menu anyway. Okay, and the usual for you?"

Toby nodded.

"That covers dinner. So . . . who's the girl you'll be out late with all this week?"

"How did you?—"

"Is she pretty?"

"Dad!" Toby fell back in his chair and moaned.

"So, what's she like? Do we need a refresher on the special talk?"

"No, God. Dad, stop! Her name is Rachel. It's just tutoring."

"But you like her, right?"

"You never know when to quit. You're such a child," Toby said.

"And isn't it good that you're so mature, we balance each other out?" Doctor Cypher said as he set his wedding ring down to rub his temples. Toby fixated on the ring. He had never seen another like it. Instead of a plain gold band, it was a rectangular, flat-cut topaz stone attached to an antique ring shaped like entwined vines with tiny flowers.

Doctor Cypher grinned. Then he held up the ring. "I picked this stone because it's the same color as your mother's eyes."

Toby sat up. *Dad never talks about Mom anymore.* He was in grade school, and his parents were going out of town for work. Uncle Jack was looking after them, and his mom drove him to school. Toby still remembered her hug and kiss goodbye. A few days later he got called into the principal's office. Uncle Jack was there with Katie. *Dad was hurt bad. I cried, Katie cried, and then we looked around for Mom.*

Toby always admired his father's wedding ring. The topaz had bright, deep colors that ranged from blue and green to gold and brown, depending on the light.

"Mom's eyes were . . . hazel, right?"

"Brilliant hazel," said his father, turning the picture of Ariana Cypher on his desk around so Toby could see it. "Just like yours. Her eyes changed color with her mood. I never saw eyes so beautiful before."

"You think she's still out there?" It hurt to ask. Toby wanted to believe. *Mom was studying the remains of a civilization in a cave on some island. Dad was on his way to see her when the earthquake hit, but Mom was underground,* he remembered. He hoped that one day, he would get called out of class, and she would be there. But years had passed.

"I don't know, Toby. We searched a long time," Doctor Cypher said, looking away. "She loved us very much." Then he set the ring down on the edge of his desk.

Toby picked it up and turned it over in his hands. *It's not as heavy as when I was a kid*, he thought, but when he tried the ring on, it still didn't fit. *They never found her body.*

"I can share one secret, if you can keep it secret," Dad said, interrupting Toby's thoughts.

Toby nodded his head.

"Good. That ring has a hidden compartment."

"No way," said Toby, unsure if his father was teasing him or not.

"Way," said his father. "Press and hold the flowers on both sides of the ring at the same time. When you get it right, you'll hear a chime. When you do, say 'Melianthus.'"

The gold flowers were tiny, and they only moved if Toby touched the right place, with the right amount of force. It took some fumbling to figure out, but when all four flowers clicked in, nothing happened. Toby looked up at his father.

Then there was the soft peal of a glass bell, Toby said, "Melianthus," and the rectangular gem swung open on its long side.

Toby set the ring on the desk. Between the gem and the band was a secret space with a small, folded bit of foil, like a gum wrapper, tucked inside.

"How did you figure this out? Wait, did you make it? Or—"

"Poke the foil and see what happens," said Doctor Cypher.

Toby nudged the grey foil with his finger, and a ripple spread across it. Then it shimmered and unfolded as it rose into the air.

The metal opened into a notebook-sized rectangle that hovered at eye level, and purple script appeared like plants sprouting from seeds and growing. The writing looked like calligraphy and a star chart at the same time. Toby couldn't read any of it.

He flinched when the text ignited. It burned with white fire. Then the foil floated down to the desk, the flames went out, and the writing faded away.

"What is this?" Toby asked as he touched it. "The metal, it's amazing, and the writing—"

"Pretty cool, huh? The only other living person who knows is Lawrence."

"So just you, me, and the Professor? It's awesome. What is it? What does it mean?"

"It stays between us, right?"

"Yes," said Toby.

"If I had to guess, I'd say it's a warning. Maybe even a key."

"It's an unknown language, and that metal has memory and flight properties that shouldn't exist," Toby said. "Where did you find it? How'd you figure it out? What do we know for sure?"

"Well," said Doctor Cypher, smiling as he ran his finger down the middle of the foil, which folded itself back into a tiny rectangle he replaced in his wedding ring. "We know we'll never hear the end of it, if we don't get Katie dim sum."

"You can't just show me something like this and then stop. I have questions. Think of the applications for—"

"That's the thing about secrets, Toby. One inevitably leads to another. Eventually, they weigh you down, and they only get heavier with time."

"Dad!"

"It's getting late. If we want Chinese, I gotta go now. Don't forget, Toby," his dad said, standing. "This conversation stays between you and me." Doctor Cypher held up his ring, then slid it on. "I'll be in the Middle East for a few weeks. When I fly back, we'll talk."

CHAPTER 5

FRIENDS

Axel raged every time Rachel smiled at Toby Cypher. When tutoring started, Rachel walked fast, and Cypher had to almost run his stumpy legs off, chasing her. *That was funny.* Now, she and geek-boy were inseparable. She even grabbed Cypher's hand to keep them together in a dismissal-bell flood of students. Axel pushed through the crowd when he saw it to thump Cypher good, but he collided with the lacrosse coach, who made him run laps.

Axel and Rachel had been together, off and on, but with his detention—*Cypher's fault*—and her tutoring—*Cypher's fault*—Axel barely got to see Rachel anymore. She used to come watch him play lacrosse. Now, when they hung out, all Rachel talked about was finals and freaking Toby Cypher.

Rachel waved instead of stopping for lunch. Cypher was telling her some story about some bomber he was fixing at some museum, and every time Rachel laughed, Axel wanted to beat the grin off Cypher's stupid face. *Who does he think he is? He's just a brainiac with a big mouth. I could tutor her, but she never wants help from me.* The plastic fork snapped in Axel's white-knuckle fist as he watched them walk away. *Cypher. You're done.*

Summer break was within reach. Toby stood at the study room window, watching a distant line of black clouds move toward them. But it was two o'clock, the sun was bright, and the light flooding the room backlit

Rachel. "Finals start tomorrow," Toby said, reaching over to close the blinds. "How do you feel?" After blinking, Toby realized his face was close to hers.

She smiled. Toby startled, stepped back, and fell into his chair. "I feel awful," said Rachel, sitting next to him.

Toby tried to be cool, but he was super aware Rachel was next to him. *She smells nice.* As soon as he noticed, his heart raced. He looked forward to seeing Rachel, and the more time they spent together, the more he liked her. He cleared his throat. "Awful? How can you be so close to your goal and feel awful? You worked hard."

"What if it's not enough?"

Toby set the practice exams on the table. "You got this."

After Rachel finished the first practice test, they reviewed and took a break. She did okay, showing some work with less snark. *Almost there. But she knows this stuff. Why's she holding back?* Toby went to the vending machine two floors down to get snacks he knew she would like, and while he was out, Rachel stretched and opened the blinds. The sky was black. It was only four o' clock, but it was darker than midnight.

When Toby returned with sodas and Rachel's favorite mini donuts, she was sitting at the table, staring at her practice test with her head in her hands. She looked like she was about to cry. "What happened?" He set the snacks down. "What's wrong?"

"I'm not gonna pull this off," said Rachel. "I'll have to leave."

"You know your stuff," he said. "Trust yourself a little more."

Rachel looked up, and Toby saw the frustration in her eyes. He squeezed her shoulder to comfort her, then handed her a soda.

"You can do this. I don't get why you're stressing so hard."

Rachel put down her drink and started twisting her hair. After a while she let out a long sigh. "Okay, you might actually get it. So, here goes. I'll tell you, then we *never* talk about it again. This stays between us, agreed?"

"Yes," said Toby.

"Promise?"

"You have my word."

"Fine," said Rachel. Then she dug her nails into her arm and took a deep breath. "Remember when you said it was nice to be treated like everyone else for a change, because you're always treated different, or used?"

Toby nodded.

"It's the same for me. I don't love everything about Asimov, and I know this sounds stupid, but I think if I stay here, I can actually be someone I'm proud of. For me, that's a big deal. I've been passed around by adults since I was little, and I couldn't do anything, except what I was told or . . . well, there were consequences. But people here are nice. Cars are shiny. Clothes are straight out of magazines. Instead of scratching to get by, you're all trying to make the world a better place, get rich, or both. You don't know how good you have it," Rachel said, shaking her head. "Now that I've seen what's possible, I won't go back to what I was."

"Why is someone like you with Axel?" The words were out before Toby even realized he said them. "I mean—"

"That is really none of your business, Toby Cypher," Rachel snapped. "Axel can be really sweet once you separate the alpha from his pack. So, do I stop here? Friends listen, right? And you were the one who asked."

"Sorry, Rachel." Hearing her talk about Axel stung.

"Okay, then shut up. This is hard." Rachel took another deep breath. "I love games. Ever since I was a little girl, I loved playing them, but the other kids always quit on me because I won all the time. I cried when they called me a cheater, but that's what I am. I didn't mean to. I didn't know I was doing it. My dad figured it out and put me to work after he lost his job.

"I remember he and my mom argued all night. The next morning, she made me French toast. A man I didn't know picked her up after breakfast, and I never saw her again.

"I cried for days, but she didn't come back, and crying only made Dad mad. So, I stopped, and I learned how to make my own French toast. Looking back, I knew I could do something other people can't. I can calculate faster and better than any computer. I could have helped put a woman on Mars, or decrypted enemy messages, or helped scientists figure out how to feed starving people. But my dad looked at all the possibilities of what I could do and decided the best use for my talent was cheating at gambling for him.

"Sounds chill, right? Win big, beat the house at their own game—easy money. We were always on the move, until Vegas."

"What did you have to do?"

"Believe it or not, I can sit in a casino, listen to people playing and slot machine sounds, and after a few hours, I can tell you which machines are ready to hit. We got by with that trick for a while, but Dad started drinking even more and never went back to work.

"We moved on to table games. I would figure out what to do, and he would place the bets. That was harder, but casinos wanna be family friendly, so kids are allowed to walk through the gambling floors, but you're not allowed to stop for anything. If you do, security moves you along. If they move you along, they watch you close, and that's a problem when you're trying to cheat."

"Don't they use tech to make cheating impossible?" asked Toby.

"It's not impossible. We had a system. It was hard, but fun. Roulette was easier to figure out and signal than cards. With card games, you're lucky if you can see a few hands dealt by the time you cross the floor, but Daddy wanted to be a poker champion, and we almost pulled it off. I'll never forget the night we won so big he had to cash out with the casino manager. We went to the office, thinking he was gonna comp us a high roller suite, but they dragged us away.

"We ended up in the back of a refrigerator as big as a house. They pushed me against a rack full of ears of corn and giant salad dressing containers, and they told me to sit and stay, like a dog."

Toby didn't know what to do. He took Rachel's hand, and she entwined her fingers with his. Her hand was cool and soft. Rachel had held his hand before, but his taking hers felt different. Then her fingers tightened.

"Three guys took turns beating my dad. All I could do was watch and cry, until one of them told me to shut up or I'd be next. So, I did, and I quiet-cried in the cold." Rachel pulled a tissue from her bag.

"After forever, some suit showed, and I recognized him. He was the same guy my mom went away with, after she made me French toast. The guy in the suit said something to Dad, and my father curled up and cried like a baby. Then that guy told me, 'You look just like your mother. So, for old times, I'm letting you go.'

"They dumped us near where we lived. We were banned from every casino, bingo parlor, and cruise ship—everywhere."

"What happened to your dad?" Toby asked softly.

"We had a neighbor who used to be a doctor," Rachel said, getting a fresh tissue. "He looked after Dad for a couple of weeks, then stole a bunch of stuff and disappeared.

"One morning, Dad was already showered and dressed when I got up. He was bandaged and covered in bruises, but he was clean and shaven and in a nice suit. With his sunglasses on, he even looked cool. Said he found a regular job. Didn't pay a lot, but it paid enough, and he promised he'd make things right. He hugged me and kissed me, and I was so happy.

"A few days later, the police came and took me away. A woman who looked like she cut her own hair with her eyes closed pushed me into an interview room, just us, two chairs, and a metal table.

"I looked for it, but there was no two-way mirror like in the movies. I remember being disappointed. I studied everything—anything—to avoid what I knew was coming. It was obvious. It was A to D, without the B and C. One plus one equals two.

"She slathered her hands with sanitizer and told me my dad was dead. He did it himself. They found him in a park.

"I sobbed through her questions, they signed me over to relatives I didn't know, and things went downhill from there. I could go on, but, looking at your face, we'd both start crying."

"I'm so sorry," said Toby. "About your dad, and what you—"

"Thanks. It was a while ago, but thanks."

Toby wasn't sure what to say. "How'd you wind up at Asimov?"

"Let's just say I didn't have a lot of luck with foster care, and adults won't believe what they don't wanna believe. I got in enough trouble to become a ward of the state, and that's bad. I was in the middle of court, waiting for a judge to tell me where they were sending me next. Then Principal Jackson turned up."

"Principal Jackson?" Toby looked confused. "Our principal?"

"I know, right? It was total drama. He walked in with lawyers. Said he was there to recruit me, told the judge I had talent, and that he would guarantee me a full scholarship to Asimov Academy and be my guardian. I never heard of the place, but it impressed the judge. He said Jackson was legit, and if I stayed out of trouble, passed my classes, and graduated, I could do whatever I wanted. So, I took the deal."

"If you didn't know about Asimov," Toby asked, "how did Jackson—"

"You know what our principal did before opening Asimov?"

"He was in tech. He's still on some government advisory boards."

Rachel smiled. "He told me on the plane ride here. His first company made advanced security and surveillance software for NASA, the NSA, and every major casino. He saw some old footage of me, and it interested him. Said he tracked me down because I was special. But you know special isn't always good. Sometimes it brings out the worst in people. I like myself at Asimov. I can be a new me. But if I fail, I get sent back. That was my deal."

Toby noticed Rachel's hands were finally warm. She blushed and let him go. "TMI. Sorry."

"Don't be, we're friends," said Toby. "I get it now."

"We're really friends?"

"Ever tell anyone else what you just told me?"

"No. Never," said Rachel. "You're the first."

"Then we're definitely friends. You know," he said, suddenly feeling awkward, "my birthday's coming up. I'm having a party. You should come. We have a pool. You can even bring Axel if you have to."

"That would be . . . difficult," said Rachel, "but I'll see what I can do."

"Okay, ready for the last practice test?"

"Bring it."

Rachel smacked him with her finished test when she was done.

Toby slowly flipped through the answers, then sighed.

"Tell me already." She couldn't stand it anymore. "Well?"

"That's an A. You did—"

Rachel squealed and hugged him tight. It happened so fast Toby turned red.

"Yes!" she said. Then she pushed him away, embarrassed. "I mean, thanks."

"Don't forget," Toby managed to say, "my party. After finals. Come swim." His thoughts were usually a swirl of fixing old things and making new things, but Toby's head was full of Rachel.

Then the lights flickered, the library's closing was announced, and it was time to go.

CHAPTER 6

CAT IN A TREE

Thick dark clouds circled Asimov. Trees groaned, and gusts tore at the gardens. The wind buffeted Rachel and Toby as they pulled each other across the empty campus.

In the center courtyard, a large flag flapped, but the Atlas missiles flanking the flagpole blocked the worst of the wind. One Atlas rocket had launched interplanetary probes; the other was configured as an ICBM, a nuclear ballistic relic from the Cold War. They were eight-story-tall reminders that technology could both inspire and terrify.

"This is bad," said Rachel. She realized she was still holding Toby's hand and let it go. "How did you get here?"

"Bike," said Toby.

"Hmm," Rachel said, looking at the sky. "It's going to pour. I'll drive you home."

"How'd you get a license?" Toby said, impressed. "I thought you had to be sixteen."

"My guardians weren't great adults, and even though I was banned from casinos, there are a ton of ways to gamble in Vegas. So, I learned how to hold onto my own money and scraped by. I bought an old car and got a hardship license to go to school and get around. My deal with Asimov and the court let me keep it."

They turned toward the parking lot when Axel and his crew stepped out from behind the flagpole ICBM. Rachel waved and took a step toward Axel but stopped. He didn't have a friendly look on his face, and Zig and Ruck followed him.

Axel walked past Rachel. Without a word, he jabbed Toby in the gut with his lacrosse stick. As Toby hunched, trying to catch his breath, Axel lifted Toby's face and said, "See what happens when you hit on my girl?"

"Axel, what the hell?" Rachel shouted. "Stop!"

"I saw you with him. You didn't think I'd notice? You're always holding hands."

As Axel argued with Rachel, Zig and Ruck fist-bumped and hauled Toby away. They laughed as they threw Toby face-first into the flagpole.

Their laughing stopped when Toby swung around the pole and donkey-kicked a surprised Ruck square in the crotch.

Toby raised his fists, but Ruck face-planted on the ground with a crunch. Then Axel and Zig barreled into Toby, and the flagpole clanged as they hit him.

Rachel rushed in to pull them apart.

And Zig belted her so hard it knocked Rachel down.

Axel stopped hitting Toby. "What did you do?" he yelled, punching Zig with everything he had.

Zig fell backward, taking Ruck down again with him.

Rachel got to her feet, holding the side of her face. "I am not some prize to fight over!"

"Rachel, I—" Axel looked around, trying to figure out what had gone so wrong.

"No. Shut up, Axel. He was helping me pass finals. And you do this?"

Axel grabbed Rachel's arm and forced her back, saying, "Listen, I—" That was when Toby went ballistic. Axel shouldn't have ignored Toby, and he especially shouldn't have grabbed Rachel.

Toby landed jabs in quick succession before Axel even knew what hit him. Axel swung a wide right hook, but Toby caught his arm and used Axel's momentum to throw him at Zig and Ruck. When Axel hit them, they went down again like bowling pins.

Toby didn't have a lot of mass compared to them, but Uncle Jack had taught Toby and Katie martial arts since they were little. He trained special forces, and fighting one-on-one was a different story than three-on-one after a sucker punch.

Zig jumped up and thrust his lacrosse stick at Toby like a spear, but Toby grabbed it and beat him back with a flurry of strikes. Zig hit the ground hard. Ruck was still kneeling and nursing his nuts, but Axel was up and on Toby with a scream.

Axel was a good athlete and great bully, but he wasn't much of a fighter. Toby was fast and precise and was done holding back. Axel swung his stick, and Toby knocked it from his hands. Axel came in swinging, and Toby used Zig's lacrosse stick to fell Axel like a tree.

When he was sure it was over, Toby pointed the lacrosse stick at Axel's head and said, "We're done."

Axel groaned and got up. He knew he couldn't win, and it was unbearable. Toby tightened his grip on the stick as Axel limped over to Rachel. "I'm sorry. You got hurt. Let's get out of—"

Rachel's fist moved fast. She punched over her head and connected with Axel's jaw, hard. He fell back and hit the ground, stunned. "No, Axel," she said, standing over him. "We're over. This is goodbye. Just go."

That was the blow that broke Axel. He pulled up his friends, and they left.

Toby nodded approvingly, and when Axel and his crew were far enough away, he dropped the lacrosse stick, and Rachel shook out her hand. "That really hurts."

"Well, it turned out better than it could have," Toby said. He ached all over, but he also felt strangely satisfied. "Nice uppercut, by the way." Toby could see where her face was red and swelling. "He shouldn't have hit you."

"I'm so sorry," Rachel said, pulling her plum-colored hair over her face. "I got you involved in all of this."

"You didn't do anything wrong," he said with a mangled smile.

"You really stood up to them," said Rachel. "How'd you know how to fight like that?"

"My uncle taught me, and well, physics. Every action has an equal and opposite—ow!" Toby said, as Rachel wiped the blood off his mouth with her sleeve.

"You're a mess, Toby Cypher."

"Well, there were three of them."

Doctor Cypher locked his door and logged into his computer. A banner scrolled across the top and bottom of his screen. It read: "TOP SECRET. TIER-1 Classified. AFRL-13 Terminal Active."

"Good evening, Doctor Cypher," said a girl's voice through his computer. "Director Frost is only an hour away from dinner at your home. Shouldn't you be getting ready?"

"I'm already ready, Ai." He said, pronouncing *Ai* as *eye*.

"Humph." Then there was a long pause. Doctor Cypher could almost see Ai frowning at him over crossed arms.

"Okay, you win. It's last-minute research on the Ashur's Tears matter. It's just one video, a quick update, and I'm done."

Ai sighed. "Doctor Cypher, you have fifty-eight minutes remaining until Director Frost's arrival. How much preparation remains?"

"Wine's open and breathing, a lot of it. Katie's on the food, and I just need to change." There was another pause. "Come on, Ai, you work for me."

"I work to enable your research, manage Directorate 13 assets, assist you as Directorate 13 leader, and keep you and your tasks on track."

"Wait," said Doctor Cypher. "Who added that last part?"

"The Professor. Last week."

"Ai!"

"This would not be necessary if you came to your own meetings on time. You may discuss my parameters with Professor Urbanex when he arrives in forty-two minutes."

"I will have a talk with Lawrence. For now, please set a countdown timer and end this session ten minutes prior to the Director's arrival."

"Thank you, sir," said Ai. "Accessing specified mission video." A summary of the incident was displayed:

Ottoman Air Cargo Flight 470, en route from Ankara, Turkey, to

Baltimore experienced an explosive decompression at 27,000 feet

above the Chesapeake Bay. The crew regained control. Aircraft

diverted to Norfolk Naval Station and secured. Crew detained

for medical treatment and debriefing. Flagged: **Suspicious**

Activity. Flagged: **Potential use of Alternative Technology.**

Flagged: **BLUTER-P** Per Air Force Research Laboratory (AFRL)

Directorate 13 order.

It still gave him a rush. Alternative Technology was what governments called magic, magical technologies, and artifacts. *It's unfortunate we have to suppress public awareness of real magic and paranormal activity, but most of what's survived is dangerous, and the BLUTER-P has saved lives.*

BLUTER-P. Doctor Cypher grinned. *Who comes up with the names for this stuff?* It stood for Bluebook Termination Protocol, named after the old Air Force program that investigated reports of UFOs and strange phenomena. In the 1960s and 1970s, the Air Force had successfully blamed the aftermath of magical events on UFOs. It raised enough doubt, and hopeful speculation, about aliens that the Bluebook program was canceled, and BLUTER-P went into effect, so Directorate 13 could more seriously study and capture Alt Tech in secret, since the public had mostly moved on. The video began:

Chief Petty Officer (CPO) Roland, the special response team (SRT) leader, gave the sign to move out. Red laser beams and white gun lights swept the darkness of the nearly empty aircraft cargo hold, looking for threats.

"Left?"

"Clear."

"Right?"

"Clear."

"Advance."

They fanned out four abreast. Their lights illuminated thick, shiny gouges in the floor and across the fuselage, like claw marks.

A thin, dark fog filled the hold.

"What the—halt!" ordered CPO Roland. The squad's movement had parted the low, black mist.

"Cut the chatter," said their lieutenant over the radio. "What do you see?"

"Something's not right here, sir. There was a fight. There's a lot of blood under some kind of fog. Maybe residue from the blast. No enemy contact, no bodies, but nearly all the cargo's gone. The cargo door was melted clean away, and there's a deformation in the deck from the point of ignition to where the door used to be, but damage is minimal. It's a perfect isosceles triangle, maybe a cone. I've never seen anything like it."

The team advanced.

They searched to the aft bulkhead at the end of the cargo bay, then turned around. "Anyone got anything?" said CPO Roland. Everyone replied negative. "Lieutenant, aircraft sec—son of a . . . standby."

CPO Roland shined his light down. The other gun lights and lasers converged around his foot. He was stepping on an arm sticking out from cargo netting attached to one of the last pieces of cargo still in the hold.

"How the hell did we miss this?" He keyed his mic and pushed his hand through the netting to check for a pulse. "Sir, we have one casualty. Twenty to thirty years old, male. Deceased. Sir, this isn't right either."

"Clarify?"

"Chunks of him are missing, but there's only blood, no other remains. He's still warm. Could be an explosive hit him, but his wounds and the aircraft damage just don't add up."

"Copy. Aircraft secure," said the lieutenant. "Rally on me for debrief."

The screen faded to black.

"Ai, what else do we know about the victim?"

"The deceased was identified as Luc-Jean Haddad, a twenty-eight-year-old male and US citizen. Dr. Haddad was an archeologist and talented linguist. He was covered in lacerations we identified as animal bites. His cause of death was blood loss."

"What kind of animal?" Doctor Cypher asked as he typed his report.

"The closest relevant bite match," said Ai, "is produced by the tiger shark."

"Interesting. Any other pertinent data?"

"A worn leather bag was found on the victim. It contained the five transforming metal discs you've been studying and a journal. Carbon dating and spectral analysis suggest the discs were created 8,000 years ago in the Middle East. To put this in perspective, Egypt's Great Pyramid of Giza was built 4,500 years ago."

"Ai, why didn't I receive the journal with the disks?"

"I am unsure. I will launch an inquiry."

"Do we have a transcript of the journal?"

"Yes, sir. Dr. Haddad's notes indicate he had uncovered Ashur's Tears at a previously unknown archeological site northeast of Akre, in the contested border between Turkey and Iraq. He claims to have escaped when an unknown force seized the artifact and executed his team. His notes contain a map to the site."

"Bingo! Compile a virtual model of the incident scene, discs, and translation. Upload everything to Stratos and incorporate the data into my report to the other AT Directors at CIA, DARPA, DOE, JCS, NSA, and the Smithsonian," Doctor Cypher said.

"Anything else, boss?"

"Add this closing: *I fly out in eight days to confirm the notes we recovered from the Flight 470 incident. I have arranged in-country special operations support in Turkey and Iraq to assist with this mission and to secure the remains of Dr. Haddad's excavation site. The destruction associated with this apocalypse-class relic makes Ashur's Tears, if it has in fact been unearthed, a national security retrieval priority.* Signed, Erasmus T. Cypher, Director, AFRL-13—and send. How am I doing on time, Ai?"

"Your stock is rising, sir. You have fourteen minutes until Director Frost's arrival."

Rachel glanced at Toby's cut and swollen face as they followed the path to the parking lot. "You're really not mad?"

The wind whipped up, the temperature shot down, and Toby stopped. "At you?"

Rachel nodded.

Toby took off his school blazer. It was still warm as he wrapped it around her shoulders. "No." Then he flashed a jack-o'-lantern-looking smile, pulled on a hoodie from his pack, and took her hand.

They passed under the sprawling oak tree that marked the edge of campus. It had a fat trunk that wore a wide girdle of moss with thick limbs that grew up and over, then down to rest their weight on the ground before its branches grew skyward again. Every Asimov Academy elementary school class took pictures there with students hanging from its branches.

Rachel stopped. She heard a deep growl. "What was that?"

"It's the wind," said Toby. "We need to keep going, or I'll be late, and my dad will have a conniption. His new boss is coming to dinner, and I look like I was in a fight."

"You were in a fight," said Rachel. "Wait, do you hear a cat?"

He did. Their eyes followed the rough tree trunk thirty feet up to where a big, tawny cat clung to a swaying branch, its coat bristling as it clawed and hissed at the sky.

"You gotta be kidding," said Toby, shielding his eyes from the rain of acorns. He took Rachel's hand, but she wouldn't budge. "You can't get it down in this storm. There's no way."

"Toby."

"Rachel, it was clever enough to climb the tree. It can get itself down."

"We can't just leave it there."

Toby sighed and searched for anything they might use to save the cat, short of climbing up after it. Then three things happened in quick succession: the swirl of the fluorescent green and black clouds sped up, a nasty darkness oozed down from the sky that seemed to turn everything it touched black and white, and a golden blur of a cat dove from the tree and landed on Toby's back. It hit him so hard it knocked him face down in the mud with an indignant yowl before it leapt into Rachel's arms. It was warm and heavy, and its purrs vibrated deep in Rachel's chest as they stared at each other.

It was an exotic cat with big almond-shaped amber eyes, tan fur with brown stripes, big white paws, and jewelry. Rachel had never seen a cat

with real jewelry, but it wore a thick gold collar full of sparkling blue stones and gold earrings carved with odd patterns.

Toby stood, cursing, and Rachel chuckled as she knocked off acorns stuck to his hoodie.

"You were right," said Rachel. "It was smart enough to get itself down."

Toby muttered something about the stupid cat, and it jumped from Rachel, back to Toby, wrapping its forepaws around his head and sinking its back claws into his sides. Toby staggered as the cat held his face like a vice, and it licked the place where his lip was split and still bleeding. Toby stiffened. "Let go. Stop." The cat's tongue felt like a rasp working his raw skin.

He tried to pull the cat off, but suddenly, Toby's face felt better. The pain from the fight was gone. As soon as he realized he didn't hurt anymore, the big cat scaled him, and it didn't stop climbing until it was perched on his head.

Toby grabbed the cat. It caterwauled. Toby saw something in the sky, and he was enveloped in a blinding light.

He felt like his arms and legs had been asleep and were waking up all pins and needles. Then the ground was so close.

Before everything went black, his last thought was, *Burnt fur smells awful.*

Toby awoke wet and cold. It was raining, and he saw a crazy flickering image of Rachel shaking him. Toby groaned, and Rachel helped pull him up. "What happened?" he asked.

"Lightning," said Rachel. All that remained of the ancient tree was an eight-foot stump that crackled and burned like a giant matchstick. "We're lucky to be alive."

It took Toby time to get his bearings. Everywhere was covered with leaves, smoking bark, shredded branches, and little fires that sizzled in the rain.

Some of the acorns had popped like popcorn. "You okay?" Toby asked, as he checked himself.

"Yes," said Rachel, still surveying the destruction.

Toby looked through the debris until he found the cat they had "rescued." It was unconscious and smoldering but still breathing. He collected the cat, and they made it to Rachel's blue hatchback as the rain began to pour.

Toby hoped the cat was okay and that he still had eyebrows.

When they got to his house, Rachel had to park on the street. A long black Mercedes-Benz was blocking the driveway, and Toby wondered how late he was. He tried to call, but mud smeared his phone, and he gave up. *Dad will understand, probably.*

Toby gently lifted the big, motionless cat. It had long ears that were black at the back, with tassels at the tips and white tufts in the front. He placed its head on his shoulder and rested its weight in the crook of his arm. He felt its claws dig through his shirt and into his back and chest, but he also felt its breath against his neck and its warmth. Despite the discomfort, it made the strangely heavy cat easier to carry.

"I gotta go," Toby said, reluctantly, as he and Rachel said their goodbyes. Toby watched Rachel drive away, and he tried to remember what he had seen in the tree as he walked to the house, but everything was a blur, like something from a dream. *More like the lightning's still messing with my head.* The harder he tried to remember what was above the tree, the deeper the cat's claws dug into him. *Stupid cat.*

The front door had barely opened when Katie blocked it. She was in a sparkly dinner dress, with her hair up. She took one look at Toby and smiled like he'd just made her year.

"Daddy's just going to love this. Late *and* dirty. Oh, reminder, Dad's new boss is here for dinner. Plus a few other guests, and we've all been waiting for you."

Toby was tired, beat up, covered in mud, and recently struck by lightning. He was in no mood.

"Shut up, Katie," Toby said.

Katie stood her ground, imperious, despite her blond ringlets and being a foot shorter than him. "Make me," she said, putting her hands on her hips. Then she took a deep breath and announced in a loud voice, "Daddy, it's him!" Those three words, under normal circumstances, wouldn't have made Toby's stomach drop, but Katie pronounced every syllable, even finding a few extra. "DAAH-DYYY, IIIITT'S HIII-IIM!"

"You could have let me clean up first," said Toby.

"Nope."

Great. Dirty and carrying a wet cat. He'll think I blew this off. Toby slipped his muddy shoes off on the porch. "Katie, just let me in," he said pushing the door.

"So, is it true you got in a fight with Axel Suarez and two of his goons?"

Toby froze. "Where'd you hear that?"

"Girls know things."

"Okay, how?"

"Duh. I'm in the school directory. Rachel texted me deets because your phone broke. Your turn," Katie said, slyly. "Why would Rachel Majeski even care to let us know you were okay?"

Toby tried to remember Rachel texting, but everything was still foggy. Then his father and his guests were standing in the entry.

"Well, well, hello, Daddy," Katie said, throwing open the door and gesturing to Toby with both hands as she continued. "I present your lost boy, the one you held dinner for, while your new boss waited . . . hey, is that a cat? Hey, it is. You got a cat!" Katie said, switching to nice little sister mode. "Let me see it, Toby. Pleeease!"

Toby lifted the still cat off his shoulder. It was surprisingly clean, and he eased it into Katie's arms so she could hold it like a baby.

"Oh my God," Katie said, looking at the limp cat. "You killed it."

"It's alive," Toby grumbled. "It had a scary night. Maybe you could fix it some tuna."

At that, the cat opened one bright amber eye and purred.

"Not it—she! Look, she's accessorized." Katie squealed as she rocked the cat, and her collar sparkled. "Can we keep her, Daddy? Pleeease?"

"We'll discuss it in the morning, pumpkin," said Doctor Cypher. "For now, dry her off and see if she'll eat. After that, she can sleep in the garage."

Doctor Cypher turned to Toby. "Katie said you were in a fight. You okay?"

"Yes," said Toby. "Sorry I'm late."

"I'm just glad you're all right. Don't sweat it—hit the shower, we'll talk later."

The cat hissed at Mr. Frost, then reversed herself and climbed over Katie's shoulders until she hung from her neck like a cat-scarf.

Everyone wore a different expression as they watched Katie and the cat depart. Toby looked tired and relieved. Doctor Cypher smiled as his daughter made plans for the cat's future. Mr. Frost frowned.

"Not a cat person, Mr. Frost?" asked Doctor Cypher.

Frost narrowed his eyes. "Let's just say I'm deathly allergic to animals."

"In that case, we'll keep her away."

Doctor Cypher returned to the kitchen with Mr. Frost and poured wine from a dusty old bottle into big glasses. He handed one to Mr. Frost, who grunted approvingly and slurped it like he was gargling. As an afterthought, Doctor Cypher called out, "Katie, the garage."

"The garage," echoed Katie, turning and climbing down from the stairs to her bedroom.

CHAPTER 7

KATIE'S CAT

It was Saturday morning. Doctor Cypher had already left for the lab, Toby was in the workshop building new mimics, and Katie was in pj's sitting in bed. She had slept in. It had been a rare, clear night in Dayton, and before she knew it—it was four in the morning. But she had to try out the new mods she'd made to her telescope, and she had taken pictures of the canals on Mars and gotten great shots of Saturn's rings and tracked a comet that other astronomers wouldn't see for another week. Now, she was chatting as she brushed the big cat that looked like a bejeweled caracal snoozing in her lap.

"Daddy can be such a boy sometimes, don't even get me started. He doesn't get I'm not a kid anymore. He still brings me back stuffed animals from his trips," Katie said, looking at the double-packed row of them on top of her bookcase, and the cute, oversized plushies in and around her chair. "Now, Uncle Jack gets me," Katie said, pulling her blond hair back to show the cat her silver and blue lapis earrings and bracelet. "He bought these last year in the Medina street market in Morocco." The sleeping cat alternated between purring and adorable snores as Katie carefully brushed her paws and tail. "You'll like him. He's an Air Force colonel, like dad was. He does special operations and looks after us when Dad's away."

Katie paused to clean the metal bristles. The brush wasn't removing much hair, but the cat's coat was getting softer and shinier. "When I moved up two grades, Daddy was away on a long trip. I really missed him, and it was the first time everyone in class was so much bigger than me. I was small, kind of a spaz, and I had the best grades, so I got teased about everything. I hated being different, and one day I just couldn't stand it anymore. Uncle Jack asked me how my day was, and it just all sort of came out. I sobbed, then I was hungry, and he took me to try out this new burger joint to cheer me up.

"It had an indoor playground built like a castle with ladders and slides and a ball pit moat. Mostly you crawled around inside. I *was* a kid back then and playing there *did* make me feel better, but when I came out of the playground, my shoes were gone. A teenager had them and wouldn't give them back. He laughed, held them over my head, and I cried myself all the way to Uncle Jack. He told me not to worry, he'd talk to the boy's dad, but when Uncle Jack explained what happened, the dad got in his face, cursing and grabbing his shirt. Uncle Jack just sighed, then took the dad's hand and twisted it. Then Uncle Jack said something I couldn't hear, the dad yelled at the teenager, and I got my shoes back.

"It didn't end there. Uncle Jack made them give me their shoes too. When Uncle Jack let the dad go, they fled, cursing. I was in shock and kinda impressed, but after their car peeled away, Kyle, the manager, told us we had to leave. I didn't think it was fair, but Uncle Jack nodded and handed Kyle their shoes.

"The restaurant was on the other side of Dayton, so it was a long silent drive. Until Uncle Jack said," and Katie growled it in her best Uncle Jack voice, "'Bullies are everywhere, pumpkin. I can show you how to make them not pick on you, if you want.' That made me so happy. I asked him how he did that thing with the bad dad's hand.

"We got home, Toby was in the workshop, and Uncle Jack and I sat on the floor, right there by mom's old mirror," Katie said, pointing. "We braided each other's hair while I tried out the funny comebacks he taught me. That was when he started teaching me and Toby how to fight. I did Uncle Jack's hair in Dutch double braids, but they weren't very good, and I braided his entire beard. Not many men can work that look. Uncle Jack did."

The cat was listening. Her strength was slowly returning, but she could barely move.

Katie set down the brush and rubbed the cat's belly, and she giggled when it produced a loud rumbly purr. "Poor girl, I wish I could do more." Her hands lingered in its warm fur. Katie could feel the cat's rapid heartbeat. Then it happened. Katie's own heart raced. Her eyes glowed

Christmas-bulb blue. Auroras danced around her like rippling streamers of perfect sky. Energy crackled as it surged down Katie's arms. It poured into the cat, jolting her awake, and her eyes and claws blazed with golden light.

Katie felt connected to the cat, like she was flowing into her, and thoughts and images that were not her own filled Katie's head. Their minds drifted closer. Katie wrapped the cat's body in fluttering, sky-blue ribbons, and Katie's touch mended the big cat's internal wounds. Healing her felt like the air against Katie's hand flying in the wind outside the window of a moving car. And just as her hand knew how to flex and bend in the breeze to go up and down, Katie could feel where she needed to touch to heal the cat. *I'm doing this.* Katie was lost in the new sensation. *If I do this, she gets better. It just feels right.* Each wound Katie healed felt like winning a race.

Katie sweat through her pj's, then shivered with chill. She could feel the cat getting better.

The power circulating through her was real, and scary, but even more, it was exciting. It felt like her arms had come out of casts, and she could move them again after living without them.

With every heartbeat Katie felt emptier. The cat grew hot in her hands, and for Katie, it was like she was in two places at once. She knew she was in her room on her bed with her hands buried deep in the belly fur of a tawny cat, but at the same time, it was cold in the desert as Katie descended from the starry night sky. The Milky Way was a broad, bright river above her, and when her feet touched the warm stone at the top of a ziggurat as big as a mountain, she paused. The huts along the two long rivers had become stone and grown as humans flourished and left that fertile crescent of land. Katie was unsure how she felt about that. Humans were weak, but they had made tools and imposed their will on nature. Katie felt herself still flowing into the cat, and at the same time, she felt each warm stone step under her paws as she descended, and the people gathered there venerated her with songs and prayers. Then and now. That ancient land and Dayton. Katie was connected to it.

I'm a part of it all. We're a part of it all.

She was Katie, and she was a goddess.

The images in Katie's head overwhelmed her. There were Katie's thoughts and the layered thoughts of a cat goddess, and they were coming together. Katie was the moon passing in front of the goddess's sun, and it felt like she was reliving someone else's yesterday.

There was a total eclipse, and for an instant, Katie and the goddess's mind were one.

Then, they were each other again.

Katie fell back on the bed. Her arms and head were heavy, but her heart had calmed, and she felt more relaxed than ever before. Her head was full of things she knew but had never thought or seen, and it was hard to stay awake.

The cat stretched, stepped over her leg, then sat so they were face to face.

"I know what you are," Katie said, "and your name is Tansy."

"I am," Tansy said, nuzzling her, "and you, Katie Cypher, are a very special girl."

Katie woke, bolted upright, and looked around wide-eyed. Her breath was fast and shallow. "Where am I?" Katie asked, trembling and clutching the bed quilt.

"Welcome back from your nap," Tansy said from the window seat across from the bed. The sun was setting behind her, making the rippled clouds look like tangerine segments.

Tansy hopped on the bed and leaned into Katie. Katie was afraid and shuddering. She wrapped her arms around Tansy, and Tansy allowed it.

"There was a war," Katie said, reliving Tansy's memories as her own. She dried her tears in Tansy's fur. "It was horrible. There were monsters. And a man did terrible things, but a boy king tricked him. Then the demons came back. They ate the bad man," Katie panted, squeezing the little goddess.

"People settled around me. They built my temple, stone by stone, on a mountain at the edge of the desert, until it was a fortress protecting an oasis. It grew like a movie on fast-forward—because decades were only moments.

"They worshipped me. I did what I could for them, and their children, and their children's children—so many lives, for so long." Katie smiled proudly, caught her breath, and let Tansy go. Then her face twisted with rage. "Until men from Minotaur came. They stole my uncle's remains. Mother said Ashur's Gift had become Ashur's Tears, and this power must never again fall into the hands of man. The duty was mine.

"I hunted them. My temple exploded. I was buried alive.

"I failed my task. I should have died. It felt like I did.

"Mother made me like this," Katie said, running her hands over her body, looking at her hands, confused that they didn't match the paws in her memory. "Then she cast me out, and I fell." Tears streamed down Katie's face. "She was so disappointed in me, it hurt so much more than my shame." Katie hugged Tansy again and her throat tightened as she choked on the words, "A . . . demon, like a spider, followed us onto the plane when we left Ankara in Turkey. My friend, Luc, used the last of his life to drive it away with his blue flames, and we tumbled from the sky. I opened a gate and followed the trail of Ashur's Tears to here. From a great tree, I battled the storm demon, and with a taste of Toby's blood, I won.

"They know I'm alive. They want what I know. I have to get Ashur's Tears, or—"

"Shh, kitten," said Tansy. "That's enough. You are safe in your house, and I—"

"This is crazy. I remember. It happened. I was there, but I wasn't."

"Those are my memories, Katie Cypher. Now, they are also yours."

"How's that even possible?" Katie snapped.

"I was wounded and vulnerable," Tansy said, putting her forepaws on Katie's shoulders and gazing into her eyes. "I do not yet understand how you know what weighed on my mind when you cast your spell, but as you healed me your magic passed into me. In that moment, you lived some of my memories as I lived some of yours." Tansy sat. "This has not happened before."

"Ahhhh!" Katie moaned. "You *are* a talking cat. I *could* still be dreaming."

"You know in your heart that is not true," Tansy said, baring her fangs in a kind of smile. "If you like, I can scratch you and prove you are awake." Her gold and blue gem necklace tinkled, and her earrings glinted as she groomed her face with her paw. "You are surprisingly composed. Typically, humans react to me with awe or disbelief. Sometimes fanatically, often violently. 'Tis a nice change."

"Well, I was you," Katie said, like she might say *today is Saturday, or I love strawberry shortcake with whipped cream on top*, but as she pulled her hair into a French braid, the enormity of it hit her. "Whoa, I was a goddess. Wait, I did magic?"

"You have a rare gift, Katie Cypher."

"But what did I do, specifically?"

"Specifically, you accidentally cast a spell."

"Parts are fuzzy. I remember how it felt more than what I did," Katie said, absently rubbing her fingers with her thumbs. Her fingertips still tingled. "Then I blacked out."

"Simply put, you tended my wounds but did not know how to regulate your power, and you discharged all your magic into me at once. To use human expressions, you put gas in my tank. Few humans, in all your history, could jump-start a goddess, and the price you paid was every bit of excess magic and spirit energy you had."

"Is that why I feel so woozy?" Katie asked, yawning despite her excitement that she had cast a spell. "You keep telling me I'm special and talking about my power, and it's so weird that I'm not weirded out. Everything feels right. I want to use magic again." Katie dramatically flexed her arms, and immediately regretted it. "Oww, OWW, oww!" Then she looked betrayed.

Tansy snorted at Katie's pout. "You feel good because your mind and body were probably always aware you were missing something, but you did not know it was magic until now. Your body hurts because you overdid it your first time, and now, muscles you didn't know you had will ache for days. But this shall pass, and as you rest, your power will replenish."

Katie raised an eyebrow and shot Tansy a dirty look, and Tansy swatted Katie's leg with her tail. "Hey! Not nice." Katie sighed, still massaging her arms.

"This is important," Tansy said, allowing Katie to pet her. "The more you use your gifts, the better you will control them, the better you control magic, the greater your power will grow."

Katie scratched under Tansy's chin. "And how do I do that?"

"I will teach you the basics before I go."

Katie giddily bounced out of bed and turned on the lights. "How long was I asleep?" she asked, looking at the streetlamps, then her stomach growled. "I'm so hungry."

"When you did not wake for dinner, your father left a drink and a plate of tacos on your desk. He said today was the makeup day for something called Taco Tuesday."

"And you're a goddess and a guardian?" Katie asked, confirming what she remembered.

"I was the guardian tasked to keep Ashur's Tears from man. I failed," snarled Tansy.

"So, you're like a sphinx?"

This time, Tansy sighed. "My task was not to judge a trial like a sphinx, when after answering a riddle, you are either eaten if you fail or allowed to pass if you answer correctly. A sphinx simply provides traffic control. It is little more than a mean, hungry stoplight. A guardian exists to protect something that cannot be lost."

"Then how did Ashur's Tears get taken? My dad does research— maybe he can help."

"It should not have been possible," Tansy grumbled, growing angry. "But the thieves who stole the relic will not stop chasing me, until I am locked in a cage, and everyone who helped me is dead. I cannot stay. I must get Ashur's Tears and—"

"Wait, what about your mother? She could—"

Tansy pinned her ears and hissed. "You know my feelings on this. I am indebted to you, but I will not embroil you or your family in this task." Tansy knew all too well that even after Katie's help, she was still a poor copy of herself. The form Mother had given her could never contain her true power, and Tansy was not yet sure how to deal with that problem. "I will not dwell on my failure, or talk of her," Tansy growled, walking away with her tail puffed up.

"At least you still have a mother," snapped Katie.

Tansy growled again. When she reached the foot of the bed, it hit her, and Katie's memories devastated Tansy. *Mom's dead, she's gone.* Katie's grief and loss, the constant hollow ache that followed. Praying she was alive, but never knowing. *She's gone, Mom's dead.* It was the first time Tansy felt mortality, the sadness of trying to keep Mom's memory alive and hating herself for knowing that she had already let her mother go. Tansy yowled and shook as she cried, reliving every bit of Katie's loss.

Katie never meant to make her cry. She crawled over to Tansy and curled up with her. They stayed like that, Tansy sobbing in soft howls with big tears, and Katie petting her. Katie knew all too well how much it hurt.

When Tansy settled down, she said, "I apologize, Katie Cypher. Part of us now lives within the other, and I understand. You loved your mom, and I will make peace with my mother, eventually." Katie scratched Tansy and gently pulled the black tufts on the tips of her ears.

"S'okay," Katie said. "Been a crazy week for both of us."

Then Katie's stomach growled again, and she rolled off the bed and walked to her desk.

Katie reached for a taco. "Ugh, they're cold." The ice was melted, and her cola was watered down and flat. It didn't help that Katie was tired, sore all over, and hangry.

"Lesson one," said Tansy, hopping up to the desk. "I shall show you how to warm them."

"I don't want my first spell to be heating up tacos when I can just use the microwave."

"Your first spell was restoring a goddess and learning her mind, and never underestimate the value of practical magic. The same technique for heating a taco, with a twist, can keep you warm in a blizzard, help you survive in freezing water, or make fire when you need it most." Tansy held her paw over the plate with three tacos, extended one claw, and with a flick she carved a silver U and something that looked like a cursive Z into the air. Then she touched the plate. When Tansy raised her paw, the symbols faded, and the tacos multiplied, following her paw until the taco stack was so high you couldn't even see her ears when Tansy circled around it. "Magic is just another way to fulfill a need or desire, for a price."

"You can use magic to make tacos! This just gets better and better," Katie said, taking a taco off the top of the stack. "Still cold though," she said, putting it back.

"That is where you come in, kitten."

"What do I do?"

"The first rule of magic is to know what you want. What makes a taco perfect to you?"

"Warm meat, the right spices and herbs, farm fresh toppings, and salsa. Melty cheese—no, crumbled cheese. All wrapped in a grilled fresh tortilla that's hot and crisp and chewy." Katie was starting to drool just thinking about it.

"Now, take a cold taco in your hand, close your eyes, and imagine your perfect taco."

"Got it."

"Draw a circle around it. Circles are important. They are simple yet powerful spaces to focus your mind and harness your power. Feel the taco in your hand, and feel the connection between it and the perfect taco in your mind. Remember the connection you had to me and what it felt like when your magic flowed. Visualize what should be hot and cold."

"I've got it, Tansy. I can feel it."

"Excellent. Now move that perfect image to the taco in your hand, and add a little of that power you feel to the taco, until it begins to change into the form you desire."

Katie could feel the taco starting to warm up and change in her hand. "It's working!"

"Words and gestures can also help channel and strengthen your magic, as can other things. They are helpful, and they are where incantations and spells, as you know them, come from; however, they will not be needed today."

The taco in Katie's hand smelled delicious. Tendrils of steam rose from it. Grill marks appeared on the tortilla, ground beef became steak, and the toppings grew fresh and crisp.

"You're almost there, kitten. Don't worry, I've set up a barrier so no one will get hurt or hear if the taco explodes."

"What?!" Katie said, snapping open her eyes. The framework she had built in her mind of taco perfection in a magic circle crumbled, and the taco broke in half and fell from her hand. One half caught fire—which Tansy extinguished. The other half hit the ground hard in a bluish sphere of ice that bounced once and rolled away.

"What did you do that for?" shouted Katie.

"The second rule is, if you begin a thing using magic, you must either completely stop it—which is difficult once you've begun—or finish what you started. If you get distracted, the consequences may be severe."

Katie huffed. "You wasted a perfectly good taco."

"And for that sacrifice you gained understanding and an idea of how to also make fire and ice. Now, again."

Katie inhaled deeply, took another taco from the stack, and closed her eyes. She practiced enhancing tacos, and inadvertently learned more about creating fire and ice, until she was exhausted and could barely lift her arms but had made the best tacos ever.

"That is enough for today. Once you master the fundamentals, you can make your own magic. You can also contract with elemental spirits and more powerful beings to use their power, but never forget, there is always a cost. I'll teach you about contracts after you rest."

"But Taansyyy—"

Katie was cleaned up, in fresh pj's, under her quilt, and hugging her pillow. She was exhausted, but she still couldn't sleep. *I was a goddess. I saved my friend. And I can do magic.* Tansy was warm against her back, breathing softly. Katie buried her face in her pillow and giggled loudly enough for Tansy to open an eye before returning to sleep. *Dad and Toby always have secrets, now I have a secret of my own—and it's a good one.*

CHAPTER 8

TOBY'S BIRTHDAY

Toby took a break from the pool to get his phone from the charger. *No new messages.* Well, no new messages from Rachel. He sighed. He had three sad blue text bubbles that said she had read them, but no reply. *Deep breath.* He sent one last text:

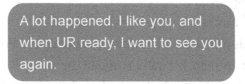

A lot happened. I like you, and when UR ready, I want to see you again.

Then he added his schedule at the museum. *Send.* Then he panicked about sending his schedule, but he didn't know what else to say. Any more would be stalking. Toby groaned. The text went from *Delivered* to *Read* 4:04 p.m., but there was no reply.

The doorbell rang, but his sister beat him to it.

"Hello, Katie, Toby. Where's your father?" Mr. Frost asked when Katie let him in. Then he saw the cat in her arms and sneezed.

"Everyone's out back by the pool," Katie said, scratching the purring cat behind her ears. "Tansy doesn't like getting splashed, so we came inside to play."

Mr. Frost's lip curled, and he looked at Tansy the way a toddler might look at liver and onions in a broccoli burrito.

Katie grinned, taking slow, deliberate steps toward him. "Would you like to play a game with us?"

"I've got to see your father," Frost said, skirting around her.

"See you later, Mr. Frost," Katie said sweetly.

Doctor Cypher was under the palapa by the pool talking to the Professor and pushing large candles into a huge cake, and Toby and Katie watched Frost rush away through the sliding glass door.

"You're just pure evil, aren't you?" Toby said, patting Katie's head. "You freaked him out. Well played."

Tansy jumped down and Katie smiled brightly and slapped Toby's hand off her head. "Do you remember any of Dad's other bosses hanging around so much? When the lab was run by generals, we knew them, but Frost seems different."

"Different how?" Toby asked.

"I'm not sure yet," said Katie. "He's more . . . clingy."

"He's new, and it's the first time a civilian's ever run the lab. Could that be it?"

"I don't know. Does that mean he always has to be so fake and condescending?"

"I don't know," said Toby. "Maybe it does."

"I really don't like him," Katie said, frowning at Frost.

Katie left to help her father under the palapa, and Toby had just slipped back into the pool when he heard, "Coming for you, dude!" He turned too late and got knocked underwater by Bobby Stevens' cannon-balling butt.

Toby's friends converged. The water churned like a piranha feeding frenzy, and Toby fought, but everyone grabbed one of his arms or legs. They carried him to the head of the table like a human sacrifice, while everyone else snapped photos like paparazzi.

"Now for the mandatory fun," Dad said, as Toby's friends dumped him into a chair.

"Happy birthday, bro," Katie said. "I ordered a cake filled with all the stuff we like."

"Happy birthday, Toby," said his father. He pointed his phone at the cake, tapped the screen, and fifteen fountains of silver and blue sparks shot from the candles.

Toby tried to stand to blow them out, but his dad stopped him. "There's more." His father backed away. Then Toby noticed the fire extinguisher in his other hand.

Toby pushed back from the table as the fountain of sparks collapsed, the candles opened, and fifteen miniature suns ignited over the crème and chocolate surface. Rocket ships orbited each sun, each with at least one hot, burning engine.

"Make a wish," his dad shouted over the rocket roar. "Everyone, help Toby blow out the candles before the cake catches fire."

By the time the last sun was blown out, Toby couldn't remember what he wished for, and his bathing suit was itchily damp. Except for the charred spots, the cake was delicious.

"Dude, spill already," Raul said, and Toby looked up. He'd buried himself in repairs at the museum and locked himself away in the workshop all week building next generation mimics, and now, his friends expected details.

Toby sighed. "I haven't talked to Rachel since we got called into the principal's office."

"Did you really fight all three of them?" asked John.

"Because, no offense, you don't look like you got your butt kicked last week," said Raul.

"Yeah, they used my head like a punching bag." But the bruises on Toby's face were mostly faded, and the swelling was gone.

"I don't know, dude," said John. "It looks like you fell shaving."

"Axel, Zig, and Ruck jumped me and went to town. Maybe it wasn't as bad as it felt."

"They looked way worse than you at finals," said John. "Respect."

"Sooo, you're spending a lot of time with Rachel," said Raul.

"I was tutoring her," Toby said, frowning. "Axel had a problem with it."

"With you and Rachel?" asked Raul with a smirk.

"With me and anything. He also tried to ruin my mimic demo."

"True, but all's fair in love and war, right?" said John.

"It's not like that, guys."

"So, you're not going out with her?" asked Bobby.

I wish. "We're friends."

"But you like her?" Bobby asked.

"What's not to like?" Toby opened and closed his fist, missing the feeling of her hand.

"So, since the fight," said Raul, "you two haven't talked?"

"She gave me a ride home, and everything was good, until we got called into Principal Jackson's office with our parents. Rachel was so embarrassed she wouldn't even look at me. Axel's dad said I assaulted his son and his friends, and he was pressing charges."

"That's messed up," said John.

"It got nasty. Axel's dad demanded an apology. I laughed. He lost it, then our dads got into it until Principal Jackson played the security footage. After that, everyone knew what happened. We took our finals, and Axel and his crew got summer school."

"You haven't seen her since?" asked Bobby.

"Nope," Toby said, staring at the palapa's wood and thatched palm leaf ceiling. "And it's been more than a week. She did send me a thank you—slash—I passed—slash—happy birthday text."

"That's it?" Raul asked. "After all that?"

"That's just sad," said John.

Toby had to agree. "Katie said it means she likes me, but with all that happened, she needs space."

"You get dating advice from your little sister?" said Bobby.

"Yeah," said Toby. "What girls do you know?"

"Hey," Bobby said. "I—"

"Who's not your mom or big sister?"

"Well—"

The Professor stopped and slipped off his dark, round sunglasses that looked like welding goggles. He had intense brown eyes, and he looked the boys over.

"Pity to interrupt such a fascinating conversation," said the Professor, his head bobbing front to back. The Professor spoke with a guttural South African accent, and he did not always use his university words.

"As I am leaving," continued the Professor, "I must present Toby with his gift. So, all of you, shut it." The Professor handed Toby a bubble-wrapped ruler-sized rectangle. "Listen well, or the giant robots you must pilot will fail to save this troubled world."

Professor Lawrence Urbanex and Dad were friends. Dad said the Professor had lived through a rare tropical disease when he was a kid in Namibia, but after he recovered, his head would bob front to back or side to side.

Toby was nine when they met the Professor. Katie was fearless, and even she hid behind Toby when the Professor tried to talk to her. Then the Professor sat on the floor and said, "It's okay. I am different, but try to look past this shambling and shaking and see who I am, not how I look. I like working with your father. I would like it very much if you weren't afraid of me."

Katie stepped from behind Toby and touched the Professor's face. She held it with both hands, and his head stopped moving. It surprised him, and Katie smiled. Then, his eyes teared up. He looked away, head bobbing again, and said, "Wash your hands before you touch people."

Everyone laughed, then the Professor had Toby and Katie follow him, bobbing their heads to see what it was like being him. They marched around like a line of quail. Now he was family.

The Professor had made Toby a virtual reality rig for his last birthday. Using it was like waking up in another world, but the VR content was limited to battles between elves and orcs. That was about to change.

"You'll find the maintenance, armament, and research functions useful. Mission profiles include giant robot versus conventional forces, robot on robot, and a mech versus giant monster mode," the Professor said, narrowing his eyes. "There's only one level, and it's so real it hurts. Pilot your mech well, and don't be stupid. Max pain is set to what a stubbed toe feels like."

Toby hugged the Professor. "Thank you. I can't wait."

The Professor gently tapped Toby's back. "I'm glad. Now get off."

After Doctor Cypher walked the Professor and Mr. Frost out, he returned, ready to leave. He sank into the chair between Toby and Katie and put his arms around them. "Happy birthday, Toby. And Katie, the food and cake were perfect. I gotta go. Everything's taken care of, and Toby's in charge. I'll be back before you know it, two weeks tops. And Jack will be here in a few days."

"Have a safe trip," said Katie. "Don't forget, nice souvenirs are always appreciated."

"Got it," said Toby. "Thanks for the party."

He looked at Toby. "Don't worry. I won't forget. When I'm back we'll talk. I'll be flying overseas, so if you need to reach me, call Director Frost or the command post, and I'll check in when I can." Then he kissed Katie on the head. "See you soon, pumpkin."

Toby and his friends left soon after, eager to pilot giant robots.

When everyone was gone, Katie picked up Tansy. She wore a forlorn expression. "Do you really have to leave? Once you go, I'll be all alone, and I'll miss you."

"Yes," Tansy said, too quickly for Katie's liking, and it crushed her. "I shall miss you, Katie Cypher. You nursed me back to health, and I am grateful, but my search must continue. Ashur's Tears has already killed." Tansy paused, and she felt her claws extend, thinking of Luc and her temple. Then she took a deep breath and retracted them. "More will die if I do not get it back. There are rumors of creatures in Dayton that should not be here. I must check them out."

Katie clung tighter. "Why wouldn't you talk to my dad or Toby? They could help."

"You are in danger with me here, and I will not further involve your family." Tansy didn't say that before Mr. Frost and Doctor Cypher left, she smelled the bitter tang of Ashur's Tears on both men. *But it was faint, its scent is everywhere, and my best leads point to Dayton.* "And you are not alone, kitten. Your brother is here."

"Pfft, Toby's like Dad," Katie said, narrowing her sky-blue eyes, "always chasing something new, the next mystery to solve. We used to be close, but we hardly do anything anymore. He'll be away in college soon, and I'm an elementary schooler who just finished junior high. Even at school, the other girls don't see me as an equal. I get treated like a doll, or worse—" Katie said, scratching Tansy's ears, "a pet that does tricks."

Tansy bared her fangs in a smile. "You wound me, Katie Cypher."

"I'm just sad," Katie said, wrapping her arms around Tansy, who allowed it.

"You have a rare gift for magic, kitten. Keep practicing what I have taught you. When you truly need me, I shall return."

CHAPTER 9

UNCLE JACK

Katie ran to meet Uncle Jack at the door.

"Hey, Katie. You're getting big."

The last time she had seen her uncle, his blond hair was tied back, and his grizzled beard reached his chest. Now, he was clean shaven, and his hair was pruned back to a thick flat-top. He looked a little older, but his sapphire eyes were cheerful despite his scowl.

"I come bearing steaks, brats, and ribs for the grill," Uncle Jack said, holding up a bag.

Katie rolled her eyes and started to close the door, but Jack put his foot in the way to stop her. "Guess you're not interested in what I brought from that pastry shop by my house then?" Jack said, holding up the other bag. "You know, the famous one you're always whining about?"

Katie squealed, threw open the door, and jumped into Jack's bag-laden arms, wrapping herself around him in a tight hug. Her love would have knocked a lesser man to the ground. "Why didn't you say so? Did I mention how much I missed the best uncle ever?"

"Never leave loose ends," Uncle Jack said between mouthfuls of meat. "They always come back to bite you."

"It can't be as simple as that," Toby said.

Uncle Jack pulled the rib platter closer and reloaded his plate. "I never said war was simple, I said never leave loose ends, but since you brought it up—sometimes, the simple things are the hardest things we have to do."

"You kinda pounded that into us when you were teaching us martial arts," Toby said, and Katie nodded.

"Ha! Well, it's true. Everyone starts with a stance, and that's just a way to stand. Simple, right? Then you add a kick, block, and punch. You master each movement. After that, you put them together, one motion, one form at a time," Jack said, reaching for the paper towel roll. "Same can be said for anything in life."

"Hmph." Toby had a faraway look in his eyes.

"Or when a form was too hard, did you stop?"

Or do you just give up when things get hard? I said almost the same thing to Rachel. "No," Toby said, "I—"

"You what?"

"I kept at it until each strike and movement was like breathing."

"Let me see your hands," Uncle Jack said, examining them. "Did you get these scars and calluses because you couldn't break all those blocks and boards?"

"No, I—"

"Get it?"

Toby nodded. "I got them one at a time until I could bust bricks and boards."

Uncle Jack grunted approvingly. "And because you guys are stubborn, in a good way."

"Don't you mean disciplined and persistent?" Katie said with a pout.

"I do. Let's go with that," said Uncle Jack, smiling at Katie then glancing at Toby. "Speaking of stubborn, how are you and your dad getting along?"

"Well, he's gone again, and until you got here, I was stuck taking care of everything."

"I'm pretty self-sufficient, Toby," Katie chided.

"Yeah, now. But it wasn't always like that, was it? He retired from the military to spend more time with us. Instead, he's constantly working, or gone, and it's always classified."

"Your dad's the best in the world at what he does," said Jack.

"So, what does he do?"

"That's—"

71

"Classified, right?" said Toby.

Jack smiled. "Right. But you're getting stuck on the details and missing the big picture."

"What's that?"

"You already know. He runs a specialized team that studies and applies new and exotic technologies for national defense. It's the truth. My question to you is, why isn't that enough?" Jack asked.

"Aside from the fact he's missed every graduation, project, recital, and holiday for the last three years? He could be doing so much more. I could deal when he was defending us in the Air Force. He was a hero, like you. But now he hides behind 'classified' like a coward."

Katie snarled, "Toby—"

Uncle Jack banged his fist on the table, and everyone stopped.

"Your dad's a lot of things, but he's no coward. He was a great test pilot. Hell, he was an astronaut, but your mother was his world. After she disappeared, he—"

"I'm sorry, all right? Can we change the subject?"

"Sure," said Jack. "But you need to cut your old man some slack. He may not have always been there, but he loves you, and by any definition, you got a pretty sweet life."

"We're supposed to talk things out when he gets back. Maybe this time we really will."

"General Mattis liked to say, 'The most important six inches a man carries into battle is between his ears.' I always took you for an eight-inch brain. If you try, you'll work it out."

"Boys sure do like measuring things in inches," Katie said, shaking her head.

Jack cleared his throat. "Your dad mentioned a cat, but I haven't seen one around."

"Toby found a hurt stray, but when she got better, she ran away," Katie said, taking her plates and leaving.

"We looked for her and put up missing cat signs. I thought Katie would be more upset, but she hasn't mentioned that stupid cat even once," Toby told his uncle.

Katie returned wearing a blue-and-white tankini top with board shorts, her French braid draped over her shoulder.

She glared at Toby. "It's hot. Come with me. I'm going for a swim."

"I'm good."

Katie put her hands on her hips. "You've been playing virtual Rock'em Sock'em Robots nonstop for three straight days."

Toby shook his head. "It's a sophisticated future-combat simulator."

"You've been locked in your room. You need to get out of the house, and you smell."

"I don't smell."

Katie stomped off to the pool.

After she left, Toby sniffed his shirt. "I don't smell. Do I smell?"

"Yeah," Jack said, with a grimace. "Go hit the shower."

Toby sat in the bleachers with Uncle Jack and Katie, trying to pick out friends in the graduation procession. He saw Sasha, a senior he knew from her family's café by the museum.

But Toby was searching for Rachel.

The stage was in front of the flagpole, with bleachers arranged around it. Dark blue banners with Asimov Academy's silver-wings-and-sun crest fluttered behind the stage, between the Atlas rockets.

Axel, Zig, and Ruck were directing traffic and handing out programs. They didn't look happy, but they worked with a purpose whenever the lacrosse coach looked their way.

Jack wore his service dress uniform and a blue wheel cap embroidered with silver clouds and lightning bolts along its brim. He had a splash of colorful ribbons on his chest, and Katie made Jack explain what each one meant.

It feels weird to be here. I fought Axel and his crew right there. The damage had been repaired, the storm debris was gone, and fresh flowers filled the planters. The bruises left from that night had faded from campus as quickly as they had from Toby's face. *It happened a few weeks ago, but it feels like yesterday*, Toby thought.

When all the graduates were in place, the speeches began. Toby applauded when Sasha got singled out for leading the swim team to the state championship. Then he found Rachel in the opposite bleacher, looking back at him.

Their eyes locked as students began crossing the stage. The row in front of her stood and cheered. When they settled back down, Rachel was gone.

Toby's heart sank. Just then, Toby felt an arm around his back, and Uncle Jack motioned to where Rachel had been and whispered, so Katie wouldn't hear, "Give her time. She'll come around."

"How can you know that?"

"Well, that's easy, Toby," said Uncle Jack, giving his shoulder a squeeze. "I know you. You have heart and passion and a rare strength of character. The way she looked at you, she sees it too."

Then Principal Jackson said, "You may now move your tassels from right to left. Congratulations, Asimov Academy graduates. Go forth and conquer!"

When the applause died down, most of the new graduates left with their families, but a large group sat in front of the stage.

"That's my cue," said Uncle Jack, rising and adjusting his uniform.

"You ready?" Katie asked.

"You kidding? I broke out my one shiny uniform for this."

Colonel Harris, the JROTC detachment commander, stood at the podium. "It's my honor to welcome Colonel Jack Cypher. He is an Air Force special operator whose missions have helped end conflicts around the world. He is a command pilot and a Ranger. He's worked with the United Kingdom's SAS, the Israeli Mossad, SEAL teams, and even Delta Force."

Jack took the stage to thunderous applause. The difference between Uncle Jack and his father struck Toby again. *They both do secret work, but here we are again. Jack looking after us, everyone looking up to him, and Dad is nowhere around.*

"Thank you, Colonel Harris," said Uncle Jack, shaking hands and taking the podium. "Today isn't about me, it's about us. We who serve. More importantly, it's about you, our newest brothers and sisters in arms.

"I was exactly like you once—young, eager, anxious about what happens next. I wanted to be part of something bigger than myself and I took the same leap of faith each of you are about to take. I fight in the forces which guard our country and protect our way of life. Soon, you will too.

"Few volunteer to join our military. Many Americans have no interest, and that's fine. It's not the right life for everyone. Yet many men and women still tried to be here, and they failed.

"But each of you overcame all those hurdles to stand here today.

"Enjoy this moment because the easy part is over. You are about to pass through fire, and it will hurt. Those of you who succeed will be stronger and more capable than you are now. Sometimes you'll call in precision strikes. Other times, you will rescue comrades, gather intelligence, or disrupt enemies.

"You will do what no one else can do. You will create purpose from chaos and uncertainty, and you will be the first ones your country will call on to defend our freedom.

"We are all counting on you. America needs you. Make us proud." After the applause, Jack said, "Today, I have the privilege of administering your oath of enlistment. Raise your right hand and repeat after me."

"Ten-HUT!" ordered the cadet commander, and everyone stood.

The cadets raised their right hands and swore the oath to support and defend the Constitution of the United States against all enemies, foreign and domestic.

Then they lowered their hands and exchanged a salute with Colonel Cypher. He said, "At ease," and the ceremony was over.

Jack posed for pictures, parents hugged their sons and daughters, and the military's newest airmen spread their wings to leave the nest and fly.

CHAPTER 10

BLUE SKY

Toby stood on a maintenance platform, next to a gaping hole in a bomber's wing, with two long spanners strapped across his back like swords. He was in the restoration hangar at the National Museum of the United States Air Force, a wartime garage that could hold two bombers with just enough room left to work.

As the crane lifted the rebuilt Number 2 engine into position, Wolf joined him on the platform while Clank and Walleye scaled the wing. Toby's maintenance belt was loaded with everything needed to mount the engine. It was heavy, but one of Toby's jobs was hauling tools.

"Last piece of da puzzle, kiddo," Wolf said, with the Cajun lilt that came out when he got excited, "and she'll be back in da sky where she belong." Wolf was the leather-skinned lead mechanic, and his long grey beard was rubber-banded together and tucked into his coveralls so as not to get caught in the equipment.

"Long time coming," said Toby.

"Greaser, ease her up," Wolf directed. "Rest of you, stand clear." Wolf signaled with his hand, and the engine inched closer to the aircraft. "Ready . . . three, two, one. Now!" With Clank and Walleye pulling from the top and Wolf guiding the crane, the engine slid into the wing and stopped with a *snick*. "How's she look, Toby?"

"Alignment's good."

"Excellent," said Wolf. "Lock her in."

Toby nodded, disappearing into the wing behind the engine. He emerged a few minutes later. "Main safeties locked."

Clank and Walleye high-fived, took the big spanners and bolts from Toby, and went to work reconnecting the engine.

Toby's official job was tool mule/assistant, but he had a knack for figuring out mechanical problems, and he quickly earned a trusted spot on the crew.

Toby didn't have a real call sign. *Dad's call sign is Raz, but I haven't done anything great enough, or stupid enough, yet to earn one.* So, until he did, he was "newbie" or "kiddo."

The Martin Company made over 5,200 B-26 Marauders for World War II. Only a handful still exist, and none of them can fly. But today, Toby thought, as he caressed the 2,000-horsepower engine, *that changes.*

Wolf, Clank, Greaser, and Walleye were the main mechanics assigned to renovate the B-26 bomber named Suzie. They were volunteers and veterans who had flown and maintained the leftover WWII aircraft used during the Korean War. Now, they were old, bald, long-bearded bikers with colorful, inappropriate tattoos who still lived to ride anything fast and air-cooled.

The B-26 Marauder was rushed into World War II, and crews called it the widow-maker and flying coffin. She was a shiny, bare-metal bomber a little bigger than a school bus, with a machine gun position in her plexiglass nose and two enormous prop engines hung from wings, which, at first, were too short to do the job. Early B-26s crashed, a lot.

Wolf was telling Toby the story again as he directed the mechanics. "Now, Senator Truman, who later became President Truman, went to the Martin Company and asked, 'Can't you just fix it?' But they said it was already being made, and it was too late to change da design. Senator Truman pondered that, and said, 'Well, if it's gonna kill more of our boys than Nazis, then it's something we don't need. You absolutely sure there's nothin' can't be done?'

"And what happened then, kiddo?" said Wolf.

"Martin rushed straight back to their factory in Baltimore and fixed the wings."

"Correct, and da B-26 went on to fly over 100,000 sorties and drop 150,000 tons of bombs, mostly on Nazis, and we lost fewer Marauders than any other bomber in the war."

History worth preserving, Toby thought as he got back to work.

"You ever wonder why we refer to airplanes with female pronouns?" Wolf said, staring over the top of the glasses resting on the tip of his windburned nose.

"Never thought about it," said Toby. "Suzie is Suzie. She dropped her bombs on target and brought her crews safely home. To me, we're nursing her back to health, more than fixing a machine."

"If you were a bomber crew during WWII, you had a fifty percent chance of being killed or taken prisoner, every time you flew.

"That's like flipping a coin to see if you were gonna live or die," Toby said.

Wolf nodded. "For some missions, their life expectancy was five weeks. You live like that, you need to have faith in something. You get superstitious, find religion, or both. So, aircrews named their planes and painted images on them, to remind them of someone special, usually a wife or girlfriend or daughter or mom, and that after the war there was a life and family waiting for them."

Toby set down his wrench. "So their planes became their hopes, and a kind of good luck charm?"

"The planes were the pride of their crews, and 'they' became 'she' like a mother protecting them, or a goddess guiding them home."

Suzie's B-26 nose had a painting of a young woman with dark wavy hair, wearing cut-off jeans. She had a playful smile and saluted with her right hand. An American flag fluttered behind her, and she had a determined look in her eyes. Four neat rows of bombs were stenciled under the pilot's window, one bomb for each mission she flew. *True-Blue Sue* was painted in large, white letters across the bomber's nose, but she was simply Suzie in the hearts of everyone who worked on her.

"Kiddo," Wolf said, still in a lilting Cajun accent, "I'm startin' to worry about you spendin' every day here. It's summer vacation, boy. Shouldn't you be off doing something, like making memories with your girl instead of bustin' knuckles with a bunch of crotchety old airmen?"

"And miss seeing Suzie come back to life? No way."

Wolf stared in Toby's eyes like he was examining his brain.

"Okay," Toby said. "There's this girl I like, but it's complicated."

"How complicated?"

"She just broke up with her boyfriend and needs some space."

"Sounds like the perfect time to strike, kiddo."

"Ugh. I like her. I don't want it to be like that."

"Admirable," said Wolf, "But what, exactly, are you to her right now?"

Toby sighed. "I don't know."

"That's a problem."

"Yeah, I know."

"But you like her, right?" Clank asked, crowding the platform to inspect the engine.

"I do."

"Then what's da problem?" Wolf asked, securing the engine cowling. "Shouldn't you figure out what you are to each other before you wuss out, or overthink it and it's too late?"

"I told her I want to see her. She knows where to find me when she's ready," Toby said, patting one of the grey steel propeller blades, twice as tall as him. "Until I can tell her how I feel, I'm gonna do everything I can to get Suzie back in the air."

"Alright then, kiddo. Start running the checklist. I'll finish up here," Wolf said. "Let's start her up and see how we did. If she holds together, we'll take her out and see how she flies."

Toby climbed into the bomber from underneath, hauled himself up into the space between the cockpit and the radio room, and eased himself into the copilot seat.

Inside, the aircraft was an olive drab and black tube, divided into a series of rooms for the front gunner, cockpit crew, radio room, bomb bay, and rear gunners. Green, diamond-patterned soft armor, that felt like the lead-lined X-ray smocks dentists use, was packed into the bomber's frame, and plexiglass windows punctuated her fuselage in useful places.

From the copilot position, Toby had a clear view over Suzie's nose and through plexiglass hatches above him and to the left and right. Heavy black control yokes mounted in front of the seats looked like steering wheels with the top half cut off. They turned left and right like a car and moved forward and backward to guide the bomber up and down in flight.

Clusters of gauges and switches filled black metal panels in front of the pilot and next to where Toby sat in the copilot chair. He had just finished the pre-start checklist when Wolf slid into the pilot seat and said, "Let's light her up."

Toby opened the right-side window facing the Number 2 engine, leaned out, and yelled, "Clear!"

Wolf gave a thumbs up. "You got your pilot's license yet?"

"Master and Propeller Safeties ON," Toby said, toggling the switches. "I'm balloon and glider certified, but I can't officially get my private pilot's license until I'm sixteen."

"Cross-check good," said Wolf. "Why's that? I got mine when I was fourteen."

"Tyranny," said Toby, "They changed the rules. It doesn't matter that I have a thousand hours flying Dad's twin engine plane, or more instrument hours than a commercial pilot. Apparently, sixteen is more important than qualified."

"Shame not everyone's as talented as we are."

Toby grinned. "Right?" then he called out the remaining control settings while Wolf cross checked them. "Throttle one-eighth open. Primers OFF. Fuel booster OFF. Safeties OFF."

"Check."

"Battery switches ON. Master ignition switch ON. Main inverter and magneto switches ON."

"Check," said Wolf. "Why are da primers and fuel boosters always kept in da off position until right before startup?"

"To prevent an accidental start," said Toby.

"Got it first try!" said Wolf. "That's right. If fuel's in da line and da props have recently turned, an electrical short . . . even a strong breeze could kick-start an engine. Safety first. Spinning props are dangerous. So are surprises. Wanna start her up?"

"Really?"

"I'm not in da habit of repeating myself."

Toby reached for the controls. "You waited a long time for this, Suzie. Here we go. Starter ON. Booster pump ON. Primers ON." Toby watched the propeller as he pressed the switch.

There was a whine, then a cough as the engine woke up and turned over.

It snarled as Toby pushed up the throttle, then the big engine settled into a throaty drone.

"Looking good," Wolf said. "Now that she's warmed up, run her up to 2,500 RPM, and we'll see if da seals hold."

Toby throttled up, and the engine roared. "Oil pressure good. Output steady. She's holding. We did it. Dropping to 900 RPM."

"Looks like Suzie doesn't need you anymore, kiddo," Wolf said, pointing at something outside the cockpit.

"Don't say that, Wolf. I . . ." Then Toby saw where Wolf was pointing. Rachel was standing in the light streaming through the hangar windows, across from the cordon of orange safety cones. Propeller wash fluttered the white summer dress she wore with a thick brown leather belt and cowboy boots. Gusts tugged at her plum-colored hair, which today had a vivid purple fringe.

Her smile got big when Toby leaned out the window and waved.

"We're taking Suzie up after she clears inspection," said Wolf. "Why don't you and your friend grab some lunch? If Suzie passes her flight check, I'll take you both up for a ride."

"You can do that?"

"Sure can. You earned it."

Toby scrambled out of the bomber to meet Rachel.

"So, this is where you disappear to."

Toby smiled. "Thanks for coming, Rachel. It's good to see you. Meet Suzie."

"Boys and their toys. Hey, can I touch it?"

"Sure."

Rachel ran her hand along the B-26 bomber's nose and stopped to admire the art. "She's beautiful."

"I know, right?" said Toby, glancing from the plane to her.

Rachel rolled her eyes, then grinned. "So, you built this?"

"I helped rebuild almost every part of her."

"Pretty impressive," said Rachel. "Does she fly?"

"Great question. Let me show you around."

Suzie was towed away, the giant hangar doors slid shut, and Toby and Rachel were alone. The big, empty space smelled like oil, paint, and high-octane gas. Rachel had come to see him, and Toby wasn't about to wuss out and overthink it. "I'm glad you came."

Toby hugged her, and his heart raced when she hugged him back and said, "I missed you."

"What are you doing after lunch?"

"I don't have anything planned," she replied.

"Good." Toby smiled, staring in the direction the B-26 had gone.

She followed his gaze, then pushed him off and put her hands on her hips. "Wait, why?"

Toby and Rachel were strapped into the radio room seats as Suzie bounced along the rough cement taxiway. Toby had found her a flight suit that fit, they wore green headsets, and Rachel reached across the aisle and took Toby's hand.

The two big engines droned, and for the first time since the Korean War, a B-26 charged a runway and took off.

They climbed, then hit turbulence, and the aircraft dropped like a roller coaster. Rachel squealed, kicking her feet as the unexpected feeling of weightlessness hit her. When the wings caught air and they climbed again, she squeezed Toby's hand, shouting over the engines, "That was awesome!"

After a series of gentle maneuvers, the aircraft banked left, and Dayton's skyline and the shimmer of the Miami River came into view. After circling Dayton, Suzie accelerated. Toby could feel the pressure changing in his ears as they continued to climb. After they leveled off, the pilot made an announcement.

"This is Captain Wolf. Thank y'all for flying Air Corps Air. We are level at just under 12,000 feet and cruising at 250 knots. Systems nominal, and our girl, *True-Blue Sue*, is back in da sky where she belongs." Toby cheered with the crew. Rachel saw the pride in their faces. They'd rebuilt Suzie with their hands, and their joy was contagious. "You are now free to move about da cabin as we slowly descend to 1,000 feet. Newbie, now's a good time to show your guest around. After you're done, both of you report to da cockpit for further instruction. Wolf out."

Toby hung up his headset and pushed back from the wood slab of the navigator's desk and unbelted. Rachel was struggling to unlatch the vintage metal fittings securing her in place. Toby hit the release on her seat, and it slid back and stopped with a metallic *tink*. "Need a hand?" he asked, taking off her headset.

Rachel smirked. "I'm good," she said as the straps fell away and the buckles clattered to the deck.

"Nice. They can be tricky." Toby offered his hand, Rachel took it, and he led her through a hatch and into the bomb bay.

It was much bigger than the radio room. A walkway the width of a ladder bisected the bay, and Toby pointed out two golden retriever-sized cylinders with fins, hung along both sides of the fuselage. "Don't worry," he said. "These are test sensors, not bombs."

The far end of the bomb bay was stuffed with equipment being used to measure Suzie's flight performance, but they were stopped from going any further by Clank. "There you are. Just in time. Come here." He was holding up a pair of sturdy leather belts with short tethers and metal carabiner clips swaying from their ends. "Step up. Don't be shy." He was looking at his watch. "We're two minutes out. Be quick, or we'll miss it."

Toby and Rachel stood side by side on a step above the bomb bay. Clank secured their belts to the aircraft's metal frame, and Wolf announced over the intercom, "Bombardier, we're at the IP. Heading northeast at eight hundred feet. We're steady, but it's gonna get bumpy."

"Copy that," Clank said, snapping his carabiner to the rail. He gave it a tug just as the turbulence hit, and Suzie bucked like a rodeo bull."

Clank keyed his mic. "Bomb bay is go." The aircraft left the rough pocket of air, steadied again, and he pointed to Rachel.

"Darlin', do me a favor and pull that red thing to your left."

"This?" Rachel asked, touching a lever mounted in the sidewall.

"That's the one."

When Rachel pulled, the floor fell away as it rotated open. She grabbed Toby's arm and the wind whipped them.

"Oh, this view . . . it's incredible!" Rachel shouted as small towns, ribbons of highway, and swaths of farmland passed beneath them.

"Bomb bay doors open," shouted Clank. The aircraft cleared a high fence line, and the green faded from the land. They approached a dry ravine, and a column of blue target smoke started to rise.

"Target locked.

"Bombs armed."

"Armed?" said Rachel. "I thought they weren't real bombs."

"Bombs explode," shouted Toby. "These help measure how well we put Suzie together."

Rachel looked down as Clank counted. "Three. Two. One. Bombs away," and with a *chuff* sound, the bombs slid down their racks into the air.

"Poor Clank," Rachel said, leaning into Toby. "His bombs are gonna miss. They went short and long by about forty yards."

"Circling for assessment," said Wolf, as Suzie continued to turn and gain altitude.

Four columns of red smoke billowed around the blue target mark, showing where the "bombs" hit.

"Target remains," said Clank with disappointment as he reset the red lever and the bomb bay doors slowly closed.

"So, whatcha think?" Wolf asked Rachel when they reported to the cockpit.

"It's amazing," she said. "Thanks for taking me with you."

"Outstanding," said Wolf. "I have one last task for da two of you."

"Me too?" said Rachel.

"If you're manifested as crew, you're crew. Problem with that?"

"No. Actually, I'm kind of honored."

"Good attitude. Toby, we have fifteen minutes before we strap in for landing. I need you two to check out da nose station seals. Report back when done."

"Sir?"

"Snap to it, newbie. Time's a-wastin.'"

Toby was confused, but Walleye pulled back the copilot yoke to access the opening that led down to Suzie's nose, and Toby steadied Rachel as she backed down the steps. Once she was in, he started down, but stopped. "Wolf, there are no seals to check down here."

Walleye grinned, and Wolf keyed his mic and said, "Do it now."

"Do what now?"

Every speaker in the aircraft started playing "Only Fools Rush In" by Elvis Presley.

"That's the best view Suzie's got," said Walleye.

"There's a reason Elvis is called the King," said Clank.

"Guys!" Toby said, shaking his head at the shaggy-bearded maintainers squeezed into the cockpit.

"You should tell her how you feel," said Wolf.

"I will," Toby said. His face was warm and red. He was embarrassed and touched by their surprise. "Thank you."

He backed down the narrow stairs between the valves, electrical panels, and hydraulic parts that led to a bright open space that did double duty as a machine gun station and the bombardier's position.

The guns had been removed, and Rachel was kneeling on the left side with her hands against the plexiglass bubble. The glass was bolted into a crisscrossing metal frame, making the sky and Earth below look like an ever-changing stained-glass window.

Toby knelt beside her while Elvis crooned, and Rachel asked, "Did you set this all up?"

"I had help," said Toby.

"You have good friends."

"I do," he said, putting his arm around her. "This is my first date."

"It's a good one. You set the bar high. So, what happens now?"

"We're at 10,000 feet, in the nose of a bomber, flying . . . I don't know, 250 miles per hour. You're with me, and I'm happy. All I can think about is how much I like you."

"That's it?" Rachel asked.

"Well, that, and I really want to kiss you."

Rachel had a hard-to-read, serious expression. As the aircraft banked, the plexiglass broke the light into a rainbow that moved over her face. Then she giggled. Elvis sang another song, the view changed, and they kissed in the blue sky over Ohio.

CHAPTER 11

NOTIFICATION

Rachel drove Toby home from the museum and parked next to an official Air Force vehicle in the driveway. Officers from the base had been visiting Uncle Jack nonstop since word got around that he was back in town.

Neither wanted the date to end. Toby invited Rachel to stay for dinner, but she was hesitant. *What do I know about family? Mom left me. Dad used me and left me.* "Meeting your family is a pretty big deal, Toby," Rachel finally said. *Always being the new problem kid in a foster family was—*

"I like you," Toby said interrupting her thoughts. "They'll like you. Anyway, it's just my Uncle Jack—and you already know Katie. If it was my dad, well, we might have to prepare you for that."

"You sure?" *I think I'd like to.*

"Yes. Is that weird? If you don't want to, we can—"

"No," Rachel decided. "I want to." Her heart beat a little faster as she realized, *I really want to.*

"That makes me happy. Come on."

They came in through the front door all smiles, holding hands.

Mr. Frost and three officers wearing service dress uniforms were in the living room.

Toby froze. Uncle Jack's jaw was set in a frown. Katie was crying.

Toby's stomach dropped. They looked at him, and he knew without a word.

It was a military family's worst fear. They always come to your house in an official vehicle. A three-person team notifies you that—

Katie ran into his arms. Between sobs, she said, "Toby, Daddy's dead."

Her tears soaked Toby's shirt. *No.* It was hard to breathe. *No.* Then it was hard to stand. *No.* Toby looked around and held Katie and tried to take it all in, but only one thought echoed through his head. *No. God, no.*

"You confirmed the shoot down?" Uncle Jack said, continuing his interrogation.

"We have," snapped Mr. Frost. "I'm sorry for your loss, Jack, I truly am, but there's no doubt." The Air Force officers tried to take over, but Mr. Frost would not yield, and he began counting off on his fingers. "It was a one-of-a-kind, NASA modified F-16. He was the only pilot checked out to fly it. He was attacked on his way back to Balad Air Base. He went down with the aircraft. His death was instantaneous."

Mr. Frost held up five fingers. One for each point he'd made.

"Any fighter pilot could fly it," Toby said. "How can you be sure it was him?"

Mr. Frost sighed then met Toby's hurt stare. "We DNA tested his remains. It was a perfect match. I wish it wasn't, but there is no doubt. Your father is gone. Chaplain Marsh and Colonel Frank from the lab will help with anything you need."

"It was a special mission. Show me the video," Jack ordered.

"Colonel Cypher, the children—"

"These kids will never see their father again. All we have to bury is a sack of ashes and the few pieces of flight suit you managed to recover. We need to see it."

"Jack—" said Mr. Frost.

"Now."

Mr. Frost sighed and nodded to Colonel Frank, who set an aluminum briefcase on the table, entered a code, and opened it. The top contained a large display, and the bottom housed a keyboard surrounded by touch screens that flashed restrictions and warnings. He turned the display toward Jack, and everyone crowded around.

Mr. Frost frowned. "What you're about to see is classified. You will not discuss this or mention it to anyone, or the consequences will be severe. Do you all understand?"

Everyone nodded in agreement.

Frost frowned deeply. "I'd hoped to avoid this, Jack."

"Do it."

Mr. Frost touched a flashing rectangle, and all the displays went black. When he removed his hand and walked away, a girl's voice said, "Welcome back, Director Frost. How may I assist you?"

"Ai, play file Cypher shootdown at this station."

"This is not a secure area, Director Frost."

"Override, alpha one three, director prime seven one."

"Director override accepted," said Ai. "Displaying footage."

There were lines of static, a blur of color, then the display showed Doctor Cypher in a fighter cockpit, framed by the curve of a gold-tinged canopy, his oxygen mask hanging off one side of his helmet. He was wearing a tan flight suit. A patch on his chest read, "Raz," and his blond goatee was trimmed back. The sun was close to setting, and Dad looked calm. In fact, he seemed happy to be at the controls of a fighter again.

Uncle Jack held Toby's shoulder. Toby felt numb. Tears rolled down his face anyway.

Dad donned his mask, and the sky and ground spun behind him. He forcefully exhaled as he strained through high-G maneuvers.

"Rampart, this is Tesla-1. Spiked." He groaned as he turned the jet again. "Defending."

"Tesla-1, SITREP."

"Damn," their father said, panting through another tight turn. "Visual on ground missile launch. Going high and tight."

Dad's under attack, Toby thought. *He's turning, trying to break the lock the missile has on him.*

Alarms and red lights filled the cockpit. Behind him, the sand and buff-colored stone receded like he was being shot from a rocket, but the missile still closed in. His father snapped the F-16 around and groaned again, as the gravity of nine times his Earth weight punched him in the gut. "Deploying chaff and flares."

What looked like an angel's wing made of glitter and fireballs expanded in the sky behind Doctor Cypher and his jet. The missile chasing him exploded, his aircraft shook, and their father struggled with controls.

Toby held his breath as his dad leveled out his aircraft. "Rampart, this is Tesla-1, declaring emergency."

"We read you, Tesla."

"Engine's damaged. I'm barely maintaining altitude."

"Copy that, Tesla. Divert to—"

"Standby, Rampart," Dad said, spinning the fighter jet and searching. "Two new missiles detected. I'm locked. Maneuvering."

His damaged fighter slowed with every turn.

Come on, Dad. You can do it. Come on.

"Can't shake them. There's an oasis. Ejec—"

The cabin filled with fire, and the display faded to white.

Katie wailed, Toby held her, and Rachel held them both, crying.

"Ai, switch to overhead imagery," said Mr. Frost.

A greyish-colored video framed by a black border showed a faraway fire. Data crawled across the screen in white letters too small for Toby to read.

"This was taken after the crash," Mr. Frost continued. "The F-16 is a small, single-engine fighter. This one was modified with large delta wings to carry heavy payloads and fly long distances. You can make out the triangular remains of its wings."

The camera zoomed in closer to the burning wreckage. A line in the sand traced a direct path through the desert to the fire. Columns of black smoke rose from the crash site. As the camera zoomed in, their father's F-16 looked like confetti. The video stopped when it reached the biggest piece of the cockpit. The fire had turned the metal into ash.

Colonel Frank snapped the briefcase closed.

Mr. Frost said, "I am sorry for your loss."

Toby sank to the floor with Katie and Rachel.

He felt Uncle Jack's arms wrap around them. "We'll get through this," Uncle Jack said. "I'll take care of everything."

Frost and the team departed, and Toby had all he could take. It had started out as the best day of his life. Now, nothing made sense, everything hurt, and he knew. Nothing would be the same again.

CHAPTER 12

BOYS ARE JERKS

Uncle Jack delayed his departure, but he'd have to leave right after the funeral, and the Professor came to see Toby and Katie and help as often as he could. It had been a long week. Everyone who knew Doctor Cypher wanted to vent and grieve, and a parade of friends, neighbors, and people from the base came to the house to pay their respects. They didn't stay long, but everyone seemed to leave feeling a little better, like they'd done some good.

It must have been nice for them.

They all said, "Sorry for your loss," and, "If there's anything at all I can do to help." Everyone brought a baked dish or a meal in Tupperware, and the fridge was stuffed with different colored, two-tone plastic rectangles. Any more and the door wouldn't shut.

Toby started calling the Tupperware meals the "tickets to the show." Katie felt awful. She couldn't stop crying, and she couldn't eat, which made her even more miserable. She lost it at about the hundredth time she heard, "If there's anything at all I can do—"

"Well, we do appreciate that," Katie snapped. "What can you do? My mom's gone, dad's dead. What 'anything' are you up for? Pay the mortgage? Take me to Girl Scouts? Shovel the driveway when it snows? I know it's still summer, but a girl needs to plan."

"Uh, sorry, I—"

"Don't worry. You can get back to me. I'll post a schedule. You can pick an open slot."

"Katie, I—"

"Thanks for coming by."

"Katie, I know you're in mourning, but—"

"Oh, that's right. We have a funeral to plan. Wanna help with that?" Katie continued as she backed the lovely people out the door.

"No, I . . . we—"

"Thanks again!"

Toby started running. He ran until his body hurt, then he'd run more, until he could barely move. When he finished running, he'd nuke the top ticket in the fridge, eat what he could, and toss the rest, Tupperware and all, in the trash.

After running, Toby locked himself in his room, piloting virtual giant robots in battle after battle until he passed out. When he woke, he would drag himself to the workshop and tinker with his mimics. Katie found him asleep in strange places. At first, she covered him with a blanket. But he was a jerk about everything, he wasn't showering, and he smelled like moldy old cheese. Every conversation ended with her shouting, "Jerk!" then stomping off, slamming a door, or crying, because Toby was a big stinking jerk.

No one talked much, not even Uncle Jack. He did make everyone family dinner, but it was a ritual of, "Hey, how you doing?" with a chorus of "fine." They'd sit around microwaved show tickets, silently eat, then drift their separate ways.

Katie secretly practiced magic. Tansy had been a good teacher, and the elemental basics of fire, water, air, and earth weren't hard to figure out once she knew what to look for and what to do. Dark magic fed off her anger and despair, and that helped for a while before it made her feel worse. More than anything else, Katie felt drawn to light magic, but it was complicated, and every time she thought about her dad, the spell she built crumbled, her circle fell apart, and her light snuffed out. Practicing did help her deal, but then she missed Tansy even more.

Katie was exploring Dad's office when she found his phone on his desk. She looked at every picture on it and read all his emails and messages.

Mostly she lost herself in his weird music collection. She wondered what each tune had meant to him. *Even though he was terrible at it, Dad taught me to dance, and he still has that song.*

Listening to it made Katie smile as she cried. Katie knew she was obsessing, but every song connected her to him.

So she slept in her dad's favorite college shirt and fell asleep to his music, but she cried as soon as she woke. Katie knew that soon, even his scent on his favorite shirt would be gone.

One night, the quiet tension in the house was broken by Uncle Jack dragging Toby, kicking and screaming, to the shower. That was when Katie got to the last song on her dad's smartphone, but it would not play.

"Toby, open up," Katie shouted, banging on his bedroom door. "I need your help." She was turning to leave when it opened.

"There you are, I—"

Toby walked past her like she wasn't there. Katie followed him to the workshop that used to be a detached garage. Workbenches lined the walls and formed an island in the middle of the large bay. Rolling tool racks were staged in alcoves. Lights, plugs, and computer cables dangled from the ceiling.

Toby had pieced together the remains from his science project before making upgrades and building new mimics. The workshop looked like a stick-figure crime scene with broken mimics, severed limbs, and parts splattered across the floor. The only thing missing was a chalk outline.

Toby ignored Katie as he worked, but he couldn't escape his thoughts. *Dad. I said bad things about you. I'm so sorry. Why did this happen? I don't know what to say to anyone. If I can just reattach this arm and figure out how to increase the power to compensate for the new shielding, then . . . I'll at least be able to—*

"Toby," said Katie. "Stop."

"What?" Toby shouted. He was angry and didn't like being interrupted. He had to focus on doing something, or it would hurt even more. "What, Katie? I'm busy."

"I need your help."

Toby sighed and put down the fried remains of a mimic arm. Optical fibers still protruding from its hand made it look like a giant silver skewer with a burnt marshmallow on its end. "What do you need?"

"I can't get this song to play," said Katie. "And I need—"

"You can't get a song to play?"

"No, I can't."

"Go ask Uncle Jack or the Professor for help. I'm busy."

"But Toby—"

"Go. Now."

"Jeez, why do you have to be such a jerk?"

"Just go, Katie. I don't have time for this."

"Jerk!" Katie yelled as loud as she could.

She left in tears. Toby watched her go. *I should go after her.* But he didn't.

Ding. Toby got a text from Rachel:

> I'm here for you. Whatever you need. You OK?

Toby wanted to answer, but he wasn't okay, and he went back to work.

Katie tried to get her brother to help again and again: "Toby, I still can't get it to play—"

Slammed door.

"Help me Toby-wan, you're my only hope—"

"Don't care. Leave me alone."

"I need your help with this, please. I—"

"Go away."

Uncle Jack was always rushing off somewhere, saying, "Sweetie, I'll look at it later." But he didn't. And the one time she called the Professor, she got the message, "This phone is outside the coverage area. Please hang up and dial again later." *And I had to call him because he's old and doesn't text.*

Katie tried to get help at dinner, but no.

When she caught Toby coming back from a run, he just smirked and said, "Gotta hit the shower, that should make you happy."

Katie screamed, and he slammed his door.

I'm nice, nothing. I yell, nothing. Stupid boys. Katie seethed as she munched through a slice of linzer torte someone had brought. *Jerks. All of them.* Katie rubbed her temples and groaned. *He's lucky I don't know how to turn him into a toad.*

Katie had listened to all the other songs on her dad's phone, but the one song that wouldn't play bothered her. It taunted her. She had to hear it.

It ate at her, and Katie could not let it go.

CHAPTER 13

TAPS

Mr. Frost picked them up in his big Mercedes. Uncle Jack wore his service dress uniform again, but this time it was too bright against the dark mood of the day. Toby and Katie rode in the back seat, looking out their windows, lost in their thoughts.

Beams of sunlight broke through the clouds, conjuring patches of color where they touched the monochrome day. The grass was yellow, and the bluestone chapel looked like a wet gothic keep.

To Toby, most of the funeral was a blur. Important people had traveled to Dayton to say nice things about his father and his accomplishments. Toby tried to follow along, but his eyes always settled on the flag-draped coffin at the center of the dais. All he could think about was that the coffin was locked and what was left of their father didn't fill even a shoebox.

After the service, Chaplain Marsh led them to the grey caisson, the wagon that would carry their father's remains to his grave. A big, brown horse pulled it away. Toby focused on the horse's *clip, clop* hoof steps as they walked up a small grassy hill past a marble monument at its top. It was a tower, surrounded by statues of soldiers flanked by old cannons.

They stopped at a large white pavilion with a podium, a lowering platform for the casket, and lots of chairs. Weathered stones, like teeth, marked the graves of soldiers. The long gravestone rows stretched as far as Toby could see.

The honor guard hoisted the casket. The caisson groaned, the brown horse neighed, and Toby and his family followed Chaplain Marsh. It was the first time in a long time Katie had clung to Toby. The honor guard set the casket in place, and their lieutenant led the Cypher family to seats in the front, next to the Professor.

Chaplain Marsh talked about duty and the toils of man and the after-life with scripture and poetry. *This would be moving if it was for someone else,* Toby thought, *if it wasn't Dad.*

"Gracious and merciful God," said Chaplain Marsh, "into Your hands, we commend Your departed child, Erasmus Cypher, in the sure hope of the Resurrection. This body we commit to the elements of creation, earth to earth, ashes to ashes, dust to dust . . ."

That was the last thing Toby heard until, "Family members, please rise."

Toby was expecting it, but it still startled him when the first shots were fired. Seven airmen with their rifles, one shot at a time, three rounds each. *Crack. Crack. Crack.*

Katie wrapped herself around Toby's arm, and he could feel her flinch at every shot. In the distance, a lone bugler played "Taps," and their father's casket sank into the ground.

When the bugler played his last note, any lingering hope was gone. There was a sense of finality, and the only sound left on the grassy hill after the last note faded was the wail of a girl whose father would never return.

Uncle Jack picked up Katie and held her. When she caught her breath, the family sat again.

The honor guard had removed the flag from the casket and folded it twice lengthwise, each time pulling it taut with a snap. Then they made a fold. Snap and fold. They folded the flag into a perfect blue triangle with four white stars. Their lieutenant cradled it in her arms, and Toby stood. She pressed the flag into his hands and let go as Toby held it against his heart.

The lieutenant leaned toward Toby and said, "On behalf of the president, the United States Air Force, and a grateful nation, please accept this flag as a symbol of our appreciation for your loved one's honorable and faithful service."

"We argued," Toby said. "I called him terrible things." There were tears in Toby's eyes when he looked at her.

She paused. Her job was to maintain composure. To be the calm, solid structure a grieving family could lean on. To provide the honors a service member deserved. But the lab was a small community, and everyone who worked there knew Doctor Cypher and his kids, including the lieutenant. She should have stepped away and saluted. She bit her tongue, then leaned in closer and whispered, "Fathers and sons fight, Toby. He loved you, and he was so proud of you."

Without warning, Toby hugged her. "Thank you."

She stiffened, then hugged him back.

She was gentle as she disengaged. She stepped back, slowly saluted, then marched away before her face turned completely red.

Chaplain Marsh asked everyone to stand, and four F-35 fighters crossed the sky. They came in fast and loud in the shape of a V where the right side was longer than the left. They flew spirals and arcs in the sky, but their final pass was low and slow. When the F-35s were overhead, the middle jet on the right peeled off and raced away into the sunset. It left a hole the formation to honor the missing man and fellow pilot, Raz Cypher.

It was how the Air Force said goodbye.

Toby held Katie's hand as they followed the chaplain to a row of tables piled high with sunflowers. Some were orange, most were shades of yellow. All of them had dark seed-filled centers and thick green stems. "These were Dad's favorite," Katie said as she took the biggest one she could lift. She set it on her shoulder like a parasol, steeled herself, and walked to his grave.

It wasn't a large hole, but it seemed like a pit, with the curved top of her father's casket in the bottom and a long line of people waiting behind her. Katie smelled the flower, then sniffled, and dried her tears on the blossom. She looked from the sunflower to the casket. "Love you, Daddy. I miss you so much."

She let it go. The flower tumbled into the hole and made a swishing sound when it hit his casket. Katie stared at it for a moment, then said, "Bye-bye."

Her feet were unsteady, and Uncle Jack led her away.

Toby was left at the edge of the grave, staring at Katie's flower resting on the casket. "I don't even know if I can say you're with Mom now," Toby said. "I looked up to you and I don't know what happens next. I love you, Dad. We'll be fine. It'll hurt a while, but I'm done crying." Toby started to toss his sunflower in but stopped himself. "I'm going to keep this. Someone did this to you. I'll find out who, and I promise they will pay."

The mourners queued up in front of the Cyphers to give their condolences. Toby could hear them speculate, "Who will they stay with?" "Poor kids, they have no other relatives except their uncle, and he's always gone." "Will they really be all right?"

Rachel caused a scene, pushing through the line to see Toby. He couldn't talk long, but he was glad she did it.

They thought the line of mourners passing through the pavilion would never end, but then Toby and Katie shook the last hand, got the last hug, heard the last, "if there's anything at all I can do . . ."

Then Uncle Jack had to go.

"Stay longer," Katie demanded, but then her chin quivered, and she had to look away.

"I wish I could, pumpkin. I wish it didn't have to be like this, but I can't delay my mission any longer. Both of you stay safe. I'll be back soon. Everything's taken care of. Toby, you're in charge."

"Great," said Toby, squeezing the sunflower stem in his fist.

"If you need anything, call Colonel Osterhaus or Director Frost. I'll check in when I can. The command post can reach me if—"

"That's what Dad said," Katie whispered.

Jack scooped them both into his arms. "I'll be back in a month."

They reluctantly said their goodbyes, he disappeared into the milling crowd, and Chaplain Marsh left to get the car.

Toby tried to comfort Katie. "Don't worry. I'll take care of you."

But Katie erupted. "Liar! No, you won't. You wouldn't even help me figure out what was wrong with a song, and it still won't play."

"Katie—"

"No! You're a jerk, Toby. Mom's gone, Dad's gone, Uncle Jack's on another mission, and we're the only family we have left. But you don't care about that, and you don't care about me. So, just go already. Leave, like everyone else."

CHAPTER 14

DAD'S SONG

Chaplain Marsh dropped them off. The house should have been empty, but when they opened the door, Katie's cat was sitting in the middle of the entry, waiting.

"How'd that thing get back in the house?" said Toby.

Katie didn't answer or act surprised, and Tansy leapt into her arms. As Katie marched up the stairs, Tansy glared at Toby with narrowed golden eyes. It was like even the cat knew he had made Katie cry.

"Creepy," Toby said, with a shiver like he'd seen a ghost. But he couldn't forget Katie's tears, or that she was right. *I was a jerk.*

Katie didn't answer when Toby knocked on her door, so he let himself in.

She was in bed, petting the cat, headphones on, listening to music on Dad's phone.

Katie gave him a dirty look, and Toby stopped short of the bed when Tansy arched her back and hissed.

"I'm sorry, Katie," he said, hanging his head.

"Can't hear you," Katie said, turning up the volume. "Go away."

"Katie, I'm sorry. Losing Dad hurt. I'm have trouble dealing with it, but I was mean, and you're right, we're all we've got.

"That's it?" Katie demanded, pulling off her headphones.

Toby sighed. "I was a jerk."

"You were," Katie said, crossing her arms, glaring. "And?"

"I'm sorry that on top of losing Dad, I hurt you."

"And?"

"I love my little sister," he said, taking another step closer, "and I'm really sorry."

"You ignored me, Toby. You wouldn't listen." Tears rolled down her face, and Katie made a *hick* sound as she sobbed. "You hurt my feelings, and you were a huge jerk."

"You're right," said Toby, holding up his hands. "I was a stupid jerk, and I'm sorry." Toby hugged Katie. After resisting, she wrapped her arms around him and cried. When she was done, she rubbed her face on his shirt until her tears and snot were gone, then pushed Toby off.

Toby looked from his sister to the wet marks on his shirt and sighed. "I came to fix Dad's song so you can play it."

"Really?" Katie said, with a sniff.

"I can't promise I can repair a corrupt file, but I should be able to figure out what song it was and download a copy you can play."

"What do you think, Tansy?" The cat got less puffy, gave a dismissive snort, and turned herself around until she was curled up with her butt facing Toby.

Toby sat on the living room floor, his legs under the coffee table, slurping a Red Bull. A semicircle of laptops, hard drives, and Dad's phone were arranged in front of him.

Katie and Tansy watched him from the sofa. They both looked tired.

Toby's hair hung in his face, and his eyes were golden brown in the computer glow as he scanned the cyberattack, security, and diagnostic programs he had running. *My hair's getting long. I need to get it cut or start tying it back.* Toby looked up. "Astronomy's your thing, Katie. Not computers. How'd you hack Dad's phone?"

"Didn't," Katie said, petting Tansy's belly.

"Then how'd you get in?"

"Please," Katie said, grinning. "I know you grew up in a different age, Toby, but really? Every kid, anywhere, who's ever sat in a crowded waiting room without a smartphone of their own knows their parent's PIN. You just have to whine long enough."

"What's his password?"

"It's your birthday, backward. Four-digit year, three-letter month—last letter capital, two-number day. Zeros are asterisks."

Toby groaned, rubbing his feet together as he fiddled with the phone and tapped the keyboards.

Then his feet stopped, and Toby slapped his hands on the table. "That's why!"

"What's why?"

"The file's not corrupted, Katie. It's encrypted," Toby said, gleefully.

"Sooo, that means what?"

"Not sure yet. Corrupted means data is missing or damaged—the file couldn't play because the player didn't recognize it as a song. But we could still figure out what song it was."

"And encrypted?" asked Katie.

"That's where it gets interesting. Encrypted means someone specifically sent that file to Dad's phone, but it's locked until the right key opens it."

"Can you crack it?" Katie asked, hopping off the couch.

"Maybe," said Toby. "It's a massive video, but even with Dad's password, a security program keeps blocking my access."

"Any good news?" asked Katie.

"Yes. Dad sent it *after* he was shot down."

Tansy watched Toby fiddle with his laptops from the back of the couch, and Katie alternated between pacing and flumping on the couch when she couldn't stand waiting anymore.

It was late, and there was a pile of picked-through Tupperware tickets and crushed Red Bull cans pushed together in the middle of the table when Toby shouted, "Got it!"

"Show me," Katie said. But when she sat behind Toby, there was nothing to see. "Hey, what gives?" she asked, shaking him.

"Okay, you can stop. Now," he said. "This is a stupid-complicated video feed, too big to crack with this equipment—"

"Toby—"

"But I did snatch the sound file and decrypt it before everything got locked down."

"Well, what are you waiting for?"

Toby nodded, hit play, and sat with Katie.

"This is Erasmus Cypher." There was distortion and static, but it was their father's voice. "I don't have much time. I was shot down, and they'll be on me soon. Lawrence, this was no random attack. If you get this, trust no one. Someone with Directorate 13 access set me up. They knew exactly where I was and how to take me down. Countermeasures were useless. I'm okay. I have shrapnel in my shoulder, but I ejected in time. Jet's a complete loss, though.

"I'm heading northeast toward a small oasis. It was the only thing green for miles. I popped my beacon, and I'll try to link up with Search and Rescue there. Hey, Lawrence, you're the only one I can trust with this. Keep an eye on Toby and Katie. Let them know I love them, and when I get back, I'll—"

"Down on your knees, now!" a different voice ordered. "Good. Comply, and you live." There was a brief pause, and then the voice said, "Prep him for transport."

"What's this?" another voice called out. Then there was a crack and hiss, and the recording ended.

Toby and Katie sat in stunned silence while it sank in.

Dad was alive after the crash. And two of the men who captured him spoke perfect English, one with a Boston accent. The other had a southern drawl.

"Dad's alive!" shouted Katie.

"He's out there somewhere," said Toby.

They held on to each other. Tears streamed down Toby's face as he felt relief and hope. He was so tired and full of joy he didn't even try to hold it in. He couldn't. It was too much. *I said I was done crying, Dad, but you're alive, and I'm so happy.*

For Katie, it was the opposite. Her tears finally stopped, and she felt giddy inside. She hugged him, repeating, "Thank you, Toby, thank you."

For the first time in a week, Katie's stomach wasn't in a knot.

Then, Dad's phone vibrated hard enough to move it back and forth on the coffee table.

Toby turned over the phone. It was flashing red and white, and a stern girl's voice said, "Warning. This device has exceeded its maximum-security level."

"What's going on, Toby?" asked Katie. "That was Ai's voice from the lab."

"Looks like we tripped a safeguard. It was probably keyed to Dad's hand."

"Warning. Purge imminent."

"Look away," Toby shouted, grabbing her and putting his back between Katie and the phone.

"Purging," said Ai, and Toby and Katie closed their eyes. But nothing happened.

They opened their eyes, glaring at the phone on the coffee table. Katie breathed a sigh of relief. "Well, that was anti—"

"Purge complete," said the girl's voice.

BANG! There was a small explosion and a blinding flash of light. When they could see again, Dad's phone was blackened and cracked open like an egg. Acrid grey smoke poured from the crispy phone halves. "That was our evidence," said Toby, scowling at the smoldering remains.

"But Dad's alive," said Katie. "He was captured. They could have killed him, but they didn't. Someone wanted Dad alive, Toby."

"And he's out there somewhere. Dad said to trust no one but Lawrence. In the morning, we visit the Professor at the lab."

For the first time in what felt like forever, Toby and Katie had hope. Then, one after the other, smoke detectors started going off.

CHAPTER 15

ACCESS DENIED

"Shouldn't we talk to Uncle Jack?" Katie asked between mouthfuls of pancake. It was morning, Katie had tidied up while Toby made breakfast, and they were eating on the coffee table.

Toby frowned at the scorch mark where Dad's phone had self-destructed. "No. We have to go through the command post, and too many people see those messages before they get to him."

"What if we tell him next time he calls?"

"Wish we could. Even if Uncle Jack calls, they monitor those lines. Someone betrayed Dad— they'll be listening for sure." Toby yawned. Last night he'd finally answered Rachel's "are you OK?" text. It had already been late when he replied, "I wasn't, but I am now. Thanks for yesterday. Seeing you helped a lot." He had been about to crash, but she texted him back. And a text had led to a call, and then they talked about everything except conspiracies and that Dad was still alive. It was hard not to tell her. It was nice to hear her voice, but he didn't want to get her involved in anything dangerous, and he didn't want to hang up.

"No one's gonna believe us without proof anyway," Katie said, aimlessly moving the food around her plate. "They'll say, 'Poor kids lost their father. It was a closed casket. Of course, they want to believe their dad's still alive.'"

"Dad only trusted the Professor," said Toby. "We start with him. If we convince him Dad's alive, the Air Force will investigate. If not, we go to Uncle Jack and Mr. Frost."

"Sounds like a plan," said Katie. "So, let's go already."

Toby yawned again and opened the door to leave, but he stepped in something and recoiled. Someone had left a neat pile of dead mice at their front door.

Tansy bolted past Toby, skimmed the pile, and crossed the street. She disappeared over the neighbor's fence with a mouse dangling from her mouth.

Toby watched after her. *Is this a prank?* It made no sense, and it got creepier the more he looked around. There were neat piles of dead birds, more mice, snakes, and big bugs on the porch. In the front yard was a pile of dug-up bones with dirt still clinging to them, and pyramids of well-used balls and shoes.

"Eww," said Katie. *I'll have to ask Tansy about this later.*

"This is insane," Toby said, taking pictures of the piles before putting them in the trash.

Toby and Katie pedaled on to the base, past the decommissioned nuclear reactor, into an unmarked opening in the woods, and down a winding dirt road. They stopped their bikes in front of the guard shack's orange-and-white drop barrier that blocked the way into the hill where the lab was built. Directorate 13 was the secret arm of the Air Force Research Laboratory, but Toby and Katie only knew it as the place their dad and the Professor worked, and there were plenty of weird-looking buildings on Wright-Patterson AFB.

The usual guards who smiled and joked around when they visited were gone. Guards in Minotaur Security body armor with submachine guns exited the guard shack and surrounded them.

Katie trembled. She recognized the Minotaur Security markings from the memories she shared with Tansy and whispered, "Toby, these are bad guys."

"It's okay, Katie. Stay calm."

"It's not okay, Toby."

A guard scanned their ID cards and handed them back. "Your access to this facility was rescinded. Go back the way you came. If you have questions, see Director Frost at headquarters."

"We're here to see Professor Urbanex," said Toby. "I'm sure he can sort this out."

The guard stepped back, leveled his weapon at Toby, and said, "Leave now. Your access was rescinded by Director Frost. This is a deadly force authorized area. You're just kids, so I'll keep this simple. Turn around. Go now. Don't ever come back."

Toby and Katie were still shaking when they rolled into the parking lot of the white stone and glass headquarters building.

They set their bikes in the rack, and Katie pointed. "There he is."

The Professor was hobbling out of the building, furiously muttering. His arms were full of boxes, an old umbrella was hooked over his elbow, and they hurried to meet him.

"Professor, we were—"

"Just in time," the Professor said, his head bobbing side to side. "Come with me."

"But—"

"Shhh. Let's go. And while you're at it, here," he said, dumping the boxes on Toby. "Be careful with my stuff."

The Professor held out his hand for Katie to take, and she steadied him as he shuffled through the parking lot.

His car was a long, low, blast from the past. It was a 1948 Ford Woody, with maroon pontoon fenders, a winged-locomotive hood ornament, and lacquered wood roof, sides, and doors, like an old boat. The Professor couldn't drive, so a robot wearing a cap and tweed sport coat drove for him.

Katie said, "Hi, Bob," and they fist bumped.

The Professor opened the back of the Woody, gestured for Toby to stow the boxes, swore under his breath, and thrust his umbrella up like he was stabbing a cloud.

There was an electrical charging sound. His umbrella popped open, and a crackling web of static electricity leapt from its taut grey canopy into the sky.

Toby and Katie cautiously drew near.

Then the Professor snapped his umbrella closed. "Ingrates! Censure me? Here's a poke in the eye." He looked up, waved, and said, "We're almost done here."

"What was that?" Toby asked, watching the flashes in the sky.

"I call it the Spider," the Professor said, hands on his hips, umbrella tucked under his arm, head bobbing proudly.

"And that is . . . what exactly?" Katie asked.

"Think of it as a sticky, localized pulse of semi-intelligent energy that drains the power from targeted electronics." The Professor opened his umbrella again, spun Katie around like they were dancing, and pulled her close. She caught him before he fell over. Then it started raining bugs. Hundreds of them poured from the sky. Toby covered his head as blue and grey, still-twitching, bug-shaped machines bounced off him. Their *clicks* and *clatters* filled the parking lot as they drummed on parked cars, the Professor's umbrella, and the ground.

When the bug rain stopped, the Professor poked one of the delicate-winged, grasshopper-like machines with his closed umbrella and sneered. "Really? Second-generation auto-surveillance drones. Almost obsolete. They think so little of me?" His head bobbed like an indignant rooster.

"Time to go," the Professor said, checking his watch from the passenger side of the Woody. "Quickly now. To my other lab."

"What's going on?" Katie asked as she helped him into his car.

"It won't take long for them to set their prying eyes on me again," said the Professor. "Grab your bikes, throw them in the back, and hurry. Next time, they might feel inclined to do a decent job. I know you have questions. Want answers? Come with me."

Tansy sat in the middle of the cul-de-sac, on the edge of a planter, under a crepe myrtle tree full of deep red flowers. She was finishing breakfast when Samson and Delilah approached. She'd watched them patrol the neighborhood from Katie's window, but Tansy had yet to meet them. They were French mastiffs, an ancient and honorable breed of dog. They had short fawn coats, muscular white chests, strong jaws, floppy jowls, and intelligent caramel-colored eyes. The female was one hundred pounds of muscle, and the male was much bigger. They circled Tansy, one always in position to attack from behind if she fought or fled.

Tansy swallowed her last chew of mouse, stretched, and stepped down to the pleasantly warm morning pavement, walking with her tail held high to meet them.

Pets watched from windows and yards. The mastiffs didn't growl until they were within striking range. Tansy ignored them and sat.

They sniffed her, then knelt before her until their big heads were pressed to the ground.

Tansy looked from Samson and Delilah to the watching neighborhood animals. One by one, they all bowed their heads, pressed themselves to the ground, or rolled over to expose their bellies. When she was satisfied they had all submitted, she arched her back and roared. It wasn't a sound a cat could make. It wasn't even a sound a lion could do. It echoed off houses, set off car alarms, and sounded like an avalanche. People came outside to see what had happened. They looked for an accident or a storm, but there was nothing to see except a big tawny cat with a sparkling collar, bounding down the road to the base with two tan dogs running alongside her, like knights escorting a princess.

Tansy ran with the big dogs, lost in thought. *Somehow men from Minotaur knew how to find Ashur's Tears and breach my vault. No human had been capable of that since the kingdom of Aquabah fell.*

Ashur was god of all light during the day and every star in the night. He was a great warrior-maker, and for a time, he was worshiped by all. *I love my uncle Ashur. It was my honor to tend to the part of him that remained after his ascension. Now the gift he left behind might destroy the world he loved because I failed. Mother, the great goddess A'nana, let me live, but—*

"Do not return, my daughter, until you have recovered Ashur's Tears. You were bested by man, now you must work with them to survive. Do not expect forgiveness until you understand your mistake, and set this matter right. Return wiser, and with what you seek."

Tansy's strength had grown since her mother returned her to earth in the body of a stray cat, but she was a shadow of what she had once been. *Mother had a plan. Mother always has a plan.* And Tansy didn't like it at all. She knew what she had to do, but she no longer had the power to do it.

Weeks earlier, crows had told her about hungry creatures lurking in downtown Dayton. The creatures were new. They should not have been there, and they ate people at night. Tansy had left Katie to investigate the rumors, hoping to find Ashur's Tears or at least a clue. The tainted scent of Ashur's Tears was faint, but it blanketed the city and its suburbs. It stung her nose and crawled like bugs on her skin. Ashur's Tears being everywhere was the same as it being nowhere, and she could not track it.

But she could hunt the creatures down, learn what they knew, and kill them. They weren't quite demons, but they were still monsters with a taste for human flesh. They were able to slip through the rift between worlds because the wielder of Ashur's Tears could not control its stolen power.

They began as shapeless things, but to live in this world they covered themselves with parts of their victims. Tansy found the last one after midnight in an alley. The creature had fed off the hospital, and was made of mismatched adult parts and a child's legs. The monster was ungainly and fast, and it charged at her.

It screeched darkness that froze like winter, but Tansy burned it away. Her light flashed in the alley like strobe lights that made everything seem to move in slow motion. Then it was dark and quiet in downtown Dayton again.

"Where is Ashur's Tears?" she demanded as the monster lay dying. "Tell me."

It laughed as it began to fall apart. Tansy's paws crackled with lightning that enveloped the creature; she held it in a place between life and death, and it was finally afraid.

"You know what I am," said Tansy. "I can give you peace or send you to—"

"They want what you know," cried the head that looked like a mosaic of six faces.

"Where is it?" Tansy said, baring her fangs in its face.

"I passed from darkness into this world of spiteful days, in a place where tasty humans prepare for war and worship the sky, not far from here."

"Is Ashur's Tears there?"

"Yesssss," it said, "and nooo. You can feel its strength there. Where it is, I cannot say." Then it began to laugh. "But you search in vain, fallen goddess. It searches for you. It will find you, and when it does—"

Tansy let its life go, and its body fell apart with a splat.

Something terrible was happening on the Air Force base, and the uncomfortable feeling of wrongness grew stronger as she and her knights crossed the broad fields. The sensation drew her past the long grey barn on the quiet hill, where men first built flying machines, and past giant buildings where humans prayed to gods of science named Propulsion, Munitions, and Sensors. When she could feel the taint of demons in her bones, she stopped in the trees across from a white stone building with bronze letters that read, "Air Force Research Laboratory Headquarters."

Tansy ordered her panting knights to wait in the shade as she assembled a bank vault in her mind to hold the detectable parts of her existence. *Camouflage is a simple thing*, thought Tansy, *but true invisibility requires finesse. If it ever feels like something's watching you—something is. Something that's either terrible at invisibility or so powerful, it wants you to know it's there, and there's nothing you can do about it. But I am not so arrogant as to play with my prey. At least not yet.*

For Tansy, stripping off and hiding her physical being felt like stepping out of her fur. One minute, she was sitting between two sweaty dogs with their tongues lolling out; the next, she was gone.

Director Frost's office took up most of the top floor. There were walls of windows with a view of a grassy knoll, the parking lot, and clusters of oddly shaped buildings. Glass display columns packed with models of aerospace weapons separated his desk from a table, sofas, and his private bathroom. Across from Frost's enormous desk, doors led to a balcony.

Tansy hid on top of a bookcase just as the Professor pushed his way into Frost's office, and she watched them argue. The Professor lobbed such intricate profanity at Frost that his face turned red, and all Frost could do was sputter. Despite his shambling infirmity, the Professor backed Frost into his bathroom until he yelled for security. Then Frost exiled the Professor from the AFRL, guards escorted him out, and Frost stood there, cursing.

When Director Frost left for a meeting, Tansy followed the trail of Ashur's Tears straight to his desk. Tansy's eyes glowed gold, and she hissed and chirped to conjure the afterimages of what had happened there. A scar remained where Ashur's Tears had torn through the veil separating worlds. Images like smoke formed, and Tansy watched a man's flickering form twist Ashur's Tears into a knife and cut through this reality. She focused on the man, but his features were a blur. Then she turned her attention to the violet, ghostly images of the demons. An army of them flowed from the cut in the veil, through Frost's office, and they leapt from his balcony into the night. Part of a hilltop was torn away where they had landed and taken form. When the last demon left Frost's balcony, the man closed the rift, and he and Ashur's Tears were gone. It could have been Frost, or someone else.

I'm too late. Ashur's Tears was here, but Frost no longer has it. Doctor Cypher did not have it, but still he was captured. Why? Where are you, Uncle?

A glint caught Tansy's attention. She hopped onto a table and looked across the parking lot. *A rain of insects. No, they are machines.*

Tansy saw Katie huddle under an umbrella with the Professor. Then she watched Toby and Katie throw their bikes into the back of a vehicle and drive away. *We have a common enemy. Katie wants me to trust Toby, work together to find their father, and get back Ashur's Tears, but—*

The doors to the meeting room down the hall opened, and people were coming.

Time to go. Much as I'd like to throw him off his balcony, I don't know enough to reveal myself—wait. When I first met Frost, what was it he said? Ahh, yes. Deathly allergic.

Tansy made sure to thoroughly rub her fur on Frost's chair, his desk, and all his bathroom towels.

The meeting had not gone well. Director Frost returned to his office, lecturing his assistants on their flaws and failings, and Tansy slipped away. His belittling stopped when he flopped into his desk chair. In the middle of, "How stupid do you have to be to—" he could not continue. Sneezing uncontrollably, he waved them away.

Tears poured down his cheeks, snot ran past his mouth, and Frost rushed to his bathroom to wipe his face with a towel.

CHAPTER 16

NIMBUS

They sped down country lanes cut through tall green rows of corn as Toby tried to convince the Professor their father was still alive.

"Toby, I do not doubt you, but I never received that message. Something's been off since your father left," growled the Professor. "One day after the funeral. One day! Frost purges the lab and fires me. Me! That sniffy, incompetent, bootlicker. Good luck running Directorate 13 without knowing where all the bodies are buried." The Professor's head stopped bobbing when he realized what he had said. "Sorry. That was insensitive."

"Like I was saying," Toby grumbled, pressing the burnt halves of his father's phone into the Professor's hands, "Dad is alive."

The Professor examined the phone as they turned into a dilapidated farm and bounced along the two-rut path to an old barn, falling apart over its concrete floor. Robot Bob parked by the barn's one solid wall, next to a steel door with hand scanner and keypad, just like Dad's office.

The door led to a modern, barn-sized room that could have been a warehouse. Toby looked around. *This is his other lab? Old cars, movie props, and anime memorabilia. Action figures still in their boxes? It's a geek-fest, not a lab.*

"Have a seat," said the Professor. "We can talk freely here." He motioned to two red velvet, half-circle couches with a round white coffee table set between them. Behind one of the couches, stairs curved up to a viewing platform midway between the two stories of the "other lab."

Toby and Katie sank into the sofa across from the Professor as he set the two halves of their father's phone on the table. "Well, this certainly was your father's phone. Too bad we won't be able to retrieve anything from it."

"Nothing at all?" Toby asked, feeling responsible for tripping the self-destruct.

"Sorry. Our encryption incorporates leprechaun technology. Good on you for getting past the security, but this can only be decrypted in certain places at specific times, or this happens."

"Leprechauns are a thing?" Katie asked, growing excited.

"Technically, a people," said the Professor, his head swaying side to side. "They're greedy, elusive, mean-spirited little extortionists, but their magic is particularly good at hiding things. That's why we use it for our most sensitive matters."

"Right. Magic," Toby groaned, rubbing the back of his neck. *Professor's finally lost it.*

"Think of a magic circle as a circuit board, and an incantation as an app that lets you do things, for a price. Call it alternative technology if you like. We do."

Katie fidgeted. *I'm so sorry. Right now, I should be telling you it's true: magic is real. But I promised to keep Tansy's secret. I know you'll figure it out. I believe in you, Toby-wan.*

"So, let me get this straight," Toby said. "Magic and fantasy creatures exist?"

"I'd say alternative technologies and preternatural entities, but yes."

"How is that even possible?" Toby asked, crossing his arms.

"Well, the world's a big place, Toby. And any sufficiently advanced technology is—"

"—indistinguishable from magic," Toby finished, with a reluctant grin.

"You guys . . . really?" Katie said, wrinkling her nose.

"Let's say I believe you—and I don't," said Toby. "What do magic and leprechauns have to do with our father? He's a pilot who ran a lab."

"Everything," said the Professor. "He was our foremost authority on alternative technologies. Particularly some of the more difficult and powerful examples."

"That's ridiculous," said Toby. Then the image of metal film rising out of his father's wedding ring, unfolding and floating with its burning message flashed through his mind.

"Ridiculous is what makes it a keepable secret," the Professor said, checking his watch. "There's too much evidence to the contrary. People are comforted by empirical facts, and anything extraordinary is easy to deny."

"Sure, Professor," Toby said, shaking his head, still not believing. "Anything else?"

"Well, yes. If you ever tell anyone, we'll disappear or be killed."

"Great. So why tell us now? Look at this place. It wouldn't be magical anywhere outside of Comic-Con. I don't know what you're going on about, but my dad was an ex-pilot in a lab coat."

"Toby!" snapped Katie. "Not was. Dad. *Is*. Alive."

"Sorry, Katie, you're right. Dad *is* a lot of things, but he pushed papers in the middle of nowhere."

"Tobias Erasmus Cypher," said the Professor, "open your eyes. He was so much more. He's made a huge difference in the world. Countless souls avoided horrible ends because of your father's work. It's all classified, of course, but he was planning to tell you."

"Why would he tell us something so secret," asked Katie, "if it puts us in danger?"

"Because it was getting too dangerous for you not to know," said the Professor. "Even if you didn't know, there are people, corporations, and governments that wouldn't think twice about hurting you if it got them what they wanted from your father."

"Outstanding," said Toby. "First I ever heard of it. So, Dad was all that? Great, but we came here looking for help, Professor, and we got story time."

"Fair enough," the Professor said, standing up. "So—get up, you lot. Move it now!"

Toby was stunned. His world was calculated, organized, and predictable, but now, there was science *and* magic. His carefully ordered life was in chaos. Up was down, and Toby felt helpless. "So, you tell us something unbelievable, and when we don't believe you, you throw us out?" Toby shouted, rising and shaking with anger.

"Not at all, Toby. You make fine, if obvious, points. Follow me, and don't dawdle."

118

"Where are we going?" Katie asked, taking the Professor's arm after he nearly toppled over from fiddling with his watch.

"Let's say I believe your story, and your father is still alive. I'm disavowed, cut off, and monitored like an enemy of the state. But working with your dad was, quite literally, amazing. I owe him, and you lot always made me feel like family. So, if there is *any* chance your father is alive, I will do anything I can to help you find him."

Katie hugged the Professor. Toby felt like he had just handed off a burden crushing his chest and could breathe again, as he calmed down from his outburst. It's a horrible thing to know a truth no one else will believe. *With the Professor's help, we can find Dad.*

"Don't get ahead of yourself. You do need real proof," the Professor said, walking up the curved staircase behind the sofa to the viewing platform, one hand on the railing the other on Katie's shoulder. "The same people responsible for staging your father's death are most certainly the same ones who just destroyed my career and banned me from Directorate 13."

"That's right," Toby said, "the magic kingdom."

"We'll talk about magic again in just a bit," said the Professor. The platform had a stout, practical iron railing, and a 360-degree view of the Professor's colorful collections. "Get ready. Grab the rail and keep your hands inside the ride at all times."

Toby cringed. Katie rolled her eyes.

"Now!" he said, and they grudgingly complied.

Then his timepiece clicked to 4:00 p.m. The Professor turned the titanium bezel surrounding the round face of his watch, and everything changed.

There was a cold rush of air, and they were in the sky.

After their eyes adjusted, they realized they were standing on a different viewing platform with ornate, bronze rails built into the summit of a mountain. It overlooked a vast lake and grey landscape they could see between the whipped-cream-thick clouds floating below them. Steps carved into the rock behind them led up to a faceted crystal dome as big as a palace. And they were moving forward.

The sky was bright blue, and a stiff cross-breeze hit them as they came about like a giant sailboat in a turn, and then it was calm again. There was no mistaking it. They were on a mountain peak that was flying through the sky.

Katie backed into the Professor, and when she looked back, he told her, "It's all right." Wide-eyed, Katie began looking around. *Can't wait to tell Tansy about this.*

Toby stood there with his mouth open, trying to take it all in and figure it out. "How did we get here?"

"That would be magic, Toby," said the Professor.

"Where are we?" Katie asked.

"Over Lake Michigan, on a small island called Nimbus. This is actually my other lab."

"How does it fly?" Toby asked, leaning over the railing, trying to see what held it up.

"Also, magic," the Professor replied. "Magic as old as the world."

Just then, another flying island appeared, and it was massive. It broke through the clouds like a whale swimming through the sky. It was a large green-and-stone isosceles triangle shape, and it was getting closer.

"What's that?" Katie asked, pointing. "We're heading right for it!"

The Professor smiled. "We are safe. Do not worry. You are looking at one of our greatest national secrets. The floating island of Stratos."

Stratos was huge compared to Nimbus. They skimmed five hundred feet above it, and Toby and Katie were mesmerized as forests, verdant fields, and rivers connecting an enormous lake to smaller ones passed below them. Foothills surrounded the edges of the big island, growing into mountain peaks at its stern.

"Its surface area is roughly twenty times the size of Central Park in New York," said the Professor. "That's where your evidence is. Down there. In the Stratos archive."

They watched in dumbfounded silence as Nimbus overflew Stratos. It reminded Toby of flying in Suzie with Rachel, his arm around her, looking through the open bomb bay doors. It was a nonstop rush. Floating islands shouldn't exist. Yet there they were.

They came about again. They turned and dropped and swung like a pendulum back to Stratos, and Nimbus flew beneath the grey bedrock of what would have been its hull if the big flying island were a ship. With Stratos above them, they skimmed the clouds below as if Nimbus were a speedboat on an ocean of foam. It was cold and damp and strangely dark in the shadow of Stratos. Then the clouds grew luminous pink and lavender, and something in the grey stone above Toby and Katie briefly shined like stars.

Toby shielded his eyes as they climbed back into daylight, and they flew until Stratos was lost behind a wall of clouds. When Nimbus finished its climb, it turned again to continue its orbit.

"Stop, stop. Stop!" the Professor bellowed as they shouted questions. His head moved like he was head-banging to death metal. "I can only understand you one at a time."

Toby went first. "What is it?" he asked, gesturing to the island now passing under them.

"Stratos," said the Professor. "She's a floating island we discovered and now use part of as our most secure archive for our most sensitive secrets."

"What kinds of secrets?" Katie asked, and then she sensed someone watching her.

"Well, governments are built on secrets. More secrets than I ever imagined. Details about highly classified military and diplomatic missions. Terrible mistakes we don't want to repeat. Our encounters with beings that could cause worldwide panic. Personal information. You know, secrets. Directorate 13 uses Stratos to archive our explorations, experiments, and most importantly, to protect the world from Alt Tech, dangerous artifacts, and disruptive magic. Much of it is deadly; some of it has decimated civilizations."

"But not all magic is bad," Katie blurted out.

"Right. Some magic is wonderful. We also have arrangements with powerful beings and species who share some of what they know but want their privacy."

"So, Dad knew about this?" Toby asked, knowing the answer but needing to hear it.

"Of course. He was standing right where you are now the night before your birthday."

Toby groaned. It was too much to take in all at once. It made him question everything he knew about the world and his father. *Now I know how Alice felt when she tumbled down the rabbit hole to Wonderland.* "Who built it?" Toby finally asked.

"We built our part of the archive," the Professor said, sitting on a stone step. He fished a pair of dark goggles from his pocket and put them on. "Something ancient built Stratos. She's invisible to the world unless she allows you to see her, and we still don't know who built her or how they did it. After the first atomic bomb test at Trinity, we knew something was flying over Lake Michigan, but we couldn't figure out what. It wasn't until we put a man on the moon that Stratos reached out to us. She made contact and asked, 'What's on the dark side of the moon?'"

"I don't get it," Katie said, putting a hand on her hip. "Who is *she*?"

"Just what I said. Stratos is alive, and she has been around far longer than humans. What we do know is that she monitors every living thing, the earth, probably other things, and then sends the data somewhere. Other beings and creatures live there or occasionally meet there, and we made a deal with her. Now, Stratos mostly tolerates us. We can't stop her from studying us, and as long as we don't dig too deep or mess with her systems, she doesn't seem to care. Actually, she seems rather bored."

"Does she interact with people?" asked Toby.

"Yes, when she wants to, she appears as a young woman with expressive rose-colored eyes and flowers in her green hair. She looks like what you might imagine a fairy looks like. And she did show me her gossamer wings once," the Professor said, wistfully. "To her, we're inconsequential unless we annoy her, and we did annoy her once. In fact, that's how Nimbus came to be."

"Meaning what?" Katie asked, sitting next to the Professor.

"There are, or were, three ways to get to Stratos. The front door and back door both required a transportation ring on the ground, a type of Alt Tech teleport system, but to use them you need the right artifact or magic as a key, and it only worked if you passed a brutal physical trial to prove yourself worthy of visiting Stratos. Too few candidates survived to keep the program going. This was the key to the back door," the Professor said, holding up his watch that always seemed normal enough; but on Nimbus, it shimmered.

"Nimbus isn't part of Stratos," Katie said, growing more confused.

"No," said the Professor. "There was never a Nimbus, until the accident. It was terrible. An explosion blew this mountaintop, and most of the old backdoor, into orbit. It was a miracle anyone survived. We lost a lot of good people, and Stratos has no memory of the event. She repaired herself, but our access was limited to—"

"The third way to get to Stratos," said Toby.

"Yes, after the explosion, the old Stratos front door was sealed off, and we built the airfield we use today."

"But you still have a lab on Nimbus, and she let us in," said Katie.

"Nimbus, Stratos, and I have an understanding. Stratos lets me use this lab, and I can have guests. Nimbus, in a lot of ways, is still a little girl. I'd introduce you to her, but she's away this week on a play date."

"I want to meet her," said Katie.

"She'd like that. Nimbus looks about nine years old. She's a lot like her mother, and—"

"Focus, guys," said Toby. "Back to Stratos. Why store all our most sensitive information on something made by entities who watch us, that you don't understand? That's insane."

"We have an agreement with Stratos called The Accords, that grants us, and a few others, limited access under certain conditions, as long as we follow her rules. Honestly, Stratos is the safest place on the planet. Few people know about it. No one can find it, except under unique circumstances, and anything unauthorized that approaches it is immediately destroyed. Nowhere else is more secure."

"What happens if its builders come back?" asked Katie.

"Well, if they do, we better hope they're friendly. If not, there's nothing we can do, and the Stratos archive will be the least of our worries."

"But we got to Nimbus," said Katie, "and Stratos is right there."

"The only way onto Nimbus is with my key, using the transfer matrix your father built for me. But being a guest of Nimbus won't give you access to Stratos."

"So, how do we get there?" asked Katie.

"One C-17 transport arrives and leaves Stratos once a month. Anything other than that one flight is destroyed in Stratos airspace, and that includes trying to jump from Nimbus to Stratos. Anyone on the Stratos flight manifest is safe, but I can't hack it to get you on board, and the Stratos transport terminal makes White House security look like a joke."

"There has to be another way to get proof," said Toby.

"There isn't," said the Professor, frowning. "Let's recap, shall we? We need the video evidence your father sent so I can convince my contacts in the government to find him and stop Frost, and whoever else compromised Directorate 13 and abducted your dad. But the proof you need is on Stratos, and there it is," he said, gesturing toward the floating island. "So close you could almost touch it. But we have no way to get there, and her security is impenetrable."

The Professor looked at Toby's and Katie's hopeful faces, but he had to tell them the truth. "I am sorry. What you want is impossible."

CHAPTER 17

WORSE THAN YOU THINK

It was dark when the Professor dropped off Toby and Katie with their untouched bags of drive-through food. They had teleported to a flying island made of magic, but it didn't matter. The Professor believed their father was alive, but there was nothing they could do to prove it. Toby and the Professor ran through every scenario.

They all ended in no Dad—dead or disappeared.

Toby couldn't accept it, so he changed and ran until the parts he could actually deal with hurt more than his heart. While Toby ran through the neighborhood, Katie sat in the bath, but as hard as she tried, she couldn't scrub away the ache. *One step closer, not even one step back. Just an invisible wall of death ready to vaporize us if we try to cross it, no biggie.* Katie soaked in the hot water and cried.

Tansy wasn't back, it was after midnight, and Katie couldn't sleep. Then she heard Toby banging around in the kitchen, her stomach growled, and she rolled out of bed.

Katie startled Toby in the refrigerator, and he almost dropped the last tray of Uncle Jack's barbeque. Katie was barefoot, wearing pink pj shorts and a grey tee with graffiti FUBAR lyrics. Toby was still deep in thought. He'd managed to shower and put on plaid sleeping boxers, but his red-and-white Sriracha T-shirt was still swinging from his hand as he stacked food on the kitchen island.

Toby handed her a plate and tore into the drive-through bags. "Fries?"

"No," said Katie, grimacing. "They're good hot, but they turn into cardboard when they get cold."

"So, I can have them?"

"If you put your shirt on."

"Deal," Toby said as Katie nuked her plate.

While they waited on the microwave, he said, "When I was out running, I saw weird signs for missing pets plastered all over the neighborhood."

"What do you mean, weird?"

"The strangest one was: You killed my dog, I know who you are. Your reckoning is coming soon." Then the microwave *dinged*.

"Okay, that is weird," Katie said, heading to the table with Toby.

"I ran into the Millers coming home from downtown. They told me two of their dogs got attacked and hurt bad yesterday. The vet said it looked like some big animal mauled them."

"Maybe coyotes, or a bear?" Katie said, wanting to tell Toby about the animals defending the neighborhood from the demons looking for Tansy. *I need to convince her.*

"Something's got the animals freaked out. I swear, out running, I could see little glowing eyes in all the windows and behind the fences, watching me."

"Glowing and watching you?" said Katie, her blue eyes piercing him as she raised an eyebrow. "Really?"

Something banged on the front door. It boomed through the house, and Toby and Katie jumped. Then the scratching began, and they both laughed.

"Your cat's at the door," he said, but Katie was busy snacking.

"Fine. Don't get up. I'll get it." Toby opened the door, and Tansy was sitting in a dark fog, her eyes blazing in the porch light.

"Oh! It stinks," said Toby. The cat glowered, and Toby slammed the door, but Tansy darted in before it closed. Her claws ticked as she crossed the entry, and she sat on the tile floor in the kitchen across from Katie.

Toby was about to grab her. Then he saw the black gashes and blood in her fur.

The house filled with the reek of fish guts. Dark smoke rolled off the cat, like it was smoldering, and Katie pushed her chair back from the table. "Tansy, what—"

Tansy looked back over her shoulder, and in a clear voice said, "They grow closer, Toby. We should be safe for now, but things are far worse than you can imagine."

Toby turned white. "Your cat just talked! You heard it too. Didn't you?"

"We talk all the time," said Katie.

"And it answers back?" Toby sputtered. "Flying islands, with fairy avatars. Magic and leprechauns. We still can't get proof Dad's alive. Now there's a talking cat?"

"Of course," said Katie. "She's been teaching me magic."

"What can I say? The girl has talent." Tansy made a beckoning gesture with her paw, her eyes glowed gold, and a spinning hoop, filled with dancing azure flames, formed between Tansy and Katie. The cat jumped through the disk, landed in Katie's lap, and turned to face Toby. Tansy came out of the blue fire clean, the flame-filled hoop disappeared with the *poof* of a candle blowing out, and the stench was gone. The house smelled like the clean air after a storm.

Toby reached out to confirm it was real. His fingers touched the cat's head, static stung his hand, and a pleasant feeling washed over him. "I know this sensation."

"Yes. 'Tis like the healing I gave you. After you fought those boys in the schoolyard."

"I remember," Toby said, recalling how much he hurt and how much better he felt after she licked his face. *I'm so confused.* "Um . . . thank you. But why heal me?"

"All debts must be paid in full. I was injured and weak. I did it in exchange for some of the power in your blood. So I could call lightning and destroy the demon that was descending upon us."

"Demon?" said Toby as he looked from Tansy to Katie.

"I'm sure," she said, with a wide-fanged grin, "you've had at least one nightmare, since that night, of something dark reaching for you from the sky."

127

"Okay," Toby said with a shiver. "Katie. Your cat can talk, and you knew about magic and demons? When were you gonna mention all this?"

"Let me think," said Katie. "Now."

"This is insane," Toby said, looking at Katie and Tansy sitting together in the kitchen chair, and he threw his arms in the air. "After all that's happened, why didn't you tell me?"

"First of all, if Tansy didn't cooperate, you wouldn't believe me. Second," Katie said, scratching behind Tansy's ear, "I promised not to say anything until she knew she could trust you. And, oh yeah, in case you forgot, you were being a jerk."

Toby pulled his fingers through his hair and squeezed his head. "So, you can really talk?"

"You are not as bright as people say, are you?" Tansy replied, and Katie smiled. "Yes. All creatures with a degree of intelligence communicate."

"Really? Why is this my first conversation with an animal then?"

Tansy looked up at the ceiling and sighed with her whole body, hard enough to make her necklace jangle. "That's so egotistically human. I presume you mean: Can all other animals and creatures talk to all humans? No. And really? For those who can, why bother? You are usually a lot more trouble than you're worth. You walk around so superior, 'mankind granted dominion over all beasts.' You have barely mastered English, Toby. Are you stupid because you don't speak Elk or Swahili? Actually, perhaps you—"

"That's different," snapped Toby. *Now I'm arguing with a cat.*

"No, it's not. We don't all speak Human; some lack the ability, most lack the interest. But I imagine our purrs, barks, and other noises do sound as incomprehensible to you as your 'where's my good girl, who loves the puppy, there's my big boy' prattle sounds to us." Tansy hopped on the table. "Though to be fair, dogs do find it endearing."

"How could such fantastic things go on," said Toby, "and people not see them?"

"Children see magical things all the time," said Tansy, grooming from her white whiskers to the black tassels at the tips of her ears. "But then you grow up and reject anything that doesn't conform to your preconceptions. The magic's still there, but you learn to look past it."

"Okay," said Toby, pacing. "I've spent my whole life believing magic was just science we don't understand yet. Dad runs an organization that hides powerful magic from the world, and now he's gone, and you show up. That can't be a coincidence, so why are you here?"

"Finally," said Tansy, as she appraised Toby, "the male asks the right question."

"And the answer?"

"Ashur's Tears," said Tansy, her eyes glowing gold. "Power left on Earth by my uncle, the god Ashur, when he left this realm. The power of travel and creation bound to the part of him that remained here as his gift to man. But no human with the strength to wield Ashur's Tears has ever created more than sorrow, and it was locked away. I was its guardian, and it was stolen.

"I found proof that Ashur's Tears brought forth demons in Director Frost's office. He had your father shot down. He played an altered video, and he told you Doctor Cypher was dead. Why would he trouble himself with this charade and capture your father if he was not involved?"

"Minotaur guys blocked us from the lab," said Katie, "on Director Frost's orders."

Toby still wasn't convinced. "The Professor said Dad's job was to stop things like this from happening. That he was an expert in these artifacts. That he saved lives."

"So why did they take him?" Tansy asked.

"Because he's dangerous to them if he's free," Toby said, scratching his stubble and working it out. "But he knows things about relics they don't. That's why they took Dad. He's still valuable. The question is, why are they still after you if they already have Ashur's Tears?"

"Another good question, Toby Cypher. Whoever took the relic has yet to master it. They want me because they believe I can unlock the relic's full potential."

"Can you?"

"Of course," said Tansy. Then she hopped back into Katie's lap. "Which is why it must never happen. It would be the end of your world."

"Why tell us?" asked Toby. "You could just continue your search."

"I will recover Ashur's Tears at any cost. Even without me, its power will grow, and many good people have already died." Tansy tensed up, and Katie wrapped her arms around her. "Like it or not, you are already entangled in its curse. Your father is missing. You want him back. I want Ashur's Tears. I believe he knows who has it."

"Tansy wants to team up," said Katie. "I think we should."

Katie and Toby told Tansy about their day and how the evidence they needed was locked in the archive of an unreachable flying island called Stratos.

"As a gesture of good faith," said Tansy. "I will give you something you need."

"And that would be what?" Toby asked.

"A way to get you to Stratos."

CHAPTER 18

THE PLAN

Toby, Katie, with Tansy draped around her neck like a cat scarf, and the Professor appeared in a flash. They were in an ornate silver ring inscribed into a white-hazed stone floor that looked like old chocolate. The ring rotated slowly. At its edges, bright colored clusters of small circles turned with it as though they were gears in a clock. Fiery gems and burning symbols carved into the floor bordered the circles. Their light faded to a gentle glow, and Toby realized he was holding his breath. He opened his eyes, looked around, and inhaled. *Well, this is different.*

They were back on Nimbus, but they were in the middle of a transportation ring under the faceted dome they'd seen in the distance the first time they arrived. Toby wasn't sure why. *Maybe it was too far to walk.* From inside, the dome looked like chalk lines on the sky and clouds.

The Professor led them through his lab to a park bench with a full view of Stratos.

Every twenty minutes was a cycle of day and night as Nimbus passed over and under Stratos, like time in a dream.

"You are the first guardian spirit I've met," said the Professor.

"Goddess, actually," Tansy said, and Katie set her down.

"Goddess, yes. Well, I'm honored," the Professor said, with a wobbly bow.

"This male has manners," Tansy said, walking to the edge of the dome and glancing at Toby, who scowled. "But time is short, and formalities are unnecessary. Call me Tansy."

"Tansy," said the Professor. "I assume you know what that is?"

"Yes," she said, her forepaws on the clear dome, looking out as they passed over Stratos. "Mother took me there when I was young. The gardens do not seem to have changed, and this moon you call Nimbus was still a part of the big island, when last I was there." Tansy's tail swished side to side like she was going to pounce. "I assume we are having this conversation because you found an intact gateway."

"Yes," the Professor said, sounding relieved, "which saves us a lot of time. Can you open the way to Stratos?"

Tansy looked at Toby and Katie sitting on the bench, then back at the Professor. "Yes. But they will have to undergo the trial to use it."

The Professor went pale, staggered to the bench, and leaned heavily on it.

"Professor!" Katie jumped up and eased him onto the seat.

"What happened?" Toby asked.

He waved his hand and ignored them as he spoke to Tansy.

"Is there no other way?"

"No," said Tansy, circling Katie's legs. "I can accompany them, but I cannot interfere."

The Professor sighed, and his shoulders sagged. "Remember when I told you lot yesterday that there were only two ways left to reach Stratos, but both were impossible?"

"Yes," said Toby, "the original front door was abandoned and sealed, and the new air terminal was installed, but we can't get through their security or Stratos's defenses. You did say the original entry chamber to the front door is still intact on Stratos, and there's a magic circle somewhere that might get us there, except we're missing the key to make it work."

"Correct," said the Professor looking at Tansy. "Only now we do have a key."

The dome grew dark as Nimbus passed under Stratos, the magic circles cast a flickering glow as they turned in the floor, and soft lights came on across the lab. Katie picked up Tansy, holding her up by her front paw pits, and asked, "What trial?"

"Not just anyone can visit Stratos, kitten, and there's a difference between whom she tolerates and her guests. The gateway will transfer people up to Stratos only if they prove themselves worthy. Now, this is hardly dignified. Hold me properly or put me down."

132

Toby stood and paced. Katie let Tansy climb back around her neck, and the Professor continued, "It is a dangerous physical and mental test: of you, your character, and your abilities. It's a different trial for everyone who takes it, and you could die."

Toby stared at Tansy. "Can you make it work?"

"If we make it to the gateway, I can perform the ritual and transfer you to Stratos. Although," Tansy said, looking from one Cypher to the other, "few pass the trial."

"Do you think we can?" asked Katie.

"Yes, but it will test your resolve. I won't be able to help, and it will hurt."

"What do you mean hurt?" asked Katie, holding Tansy's striped tawny tail with both hands like she was holding a rope.

"You already know the trial is dangerous, and people have died trying to pass," said the Professor. "In its simplest terms, you just have to reach the gateway. It's a hike to a structure we call 'the old front porch' that overlooks Lake Michigan. But there will be terrible obstacles. Some will be obvious, others subtle, and they will all push you beyond your limits, past more pain and fear than you can imagine."

"But people have passed it?" asked Toby. "Right, Professor?"

The Professor opened his mouth to answer, then bit his lip, and paused so hard his head stopped rocking side to side. "Of course. Well, one person passed it."

Nimbus climbed out of the darkness and into the bright afternoon light.

"Who was it?" Katie asked, shaking the Professor's shoulder.

"She was your mother," he said with a sad smile, his head bobbing up and down again.

"Mom was here," Katie squealed. Her memories of her were cloudy, and Katie wished she could remember more.

"She was conducting an experiment deep inside Stratos when the explosion tore Nimbus away. Then, she was gone."

Toby felt like he'd been punched in the throat. *Mom passed the trials. She was on Stratos.* Toby's mouth went dry. *Dad lied.* Then he thought about exactly what Dad had told him. *Mom was lost in an earthquake while investigating an unknown culture on an island, and Dad was hurt after he landed a plane . . . that was the truth.* Toby watched the rivers snaking through forests and the rising foothills along the sides of Stratos. *Mom was down there. She might be buried there. And the proof that Dad's alive is down there.* Toby worried about all the unknowns and perils of the trial, but his fear was gone. It was replaced by resolve. *We will get to Stratos. I will find Dad.*

When Toby turned back, he realized he hadn't been listening to the conversation, and the Professor was talking to Katie, who was sitting next to him, swinging her legs.

". . . And that's what happened. I think she saved everyone."

"What do you think, Katie?" asked Toby. "About the trial. It's going to be hard."

"I know."

"We'll have to work together," Toby said, unconvinced.

"Duh," said Katie. "You just figuring that out?"

"It's going to be dangerous."

"I'm going."

Toby frowned and Katie nodded yes. "Okay. But even if we pass—"

"When."

"Even when we pass the trial and reach the old front porch," said Toby, "even after Tansy gets the Stratos gateway working, that only solves half our problem."

"You're right," said the Professor. "You'll still need to override the security seal to get in and access the system. But the only person who can do that is Director Frost, and we do not have his access code. It's keyed to him, and all his biometrics, so without him it's—"

"Alpha one three director, prime seven one," said Katie.

"What's that, Katie?" asked the Professor.

"Alpha one three director, prime seven one. It's Frost's override. He used it to make some girl named Ai play Dad's shootdown video when she said our house wasn't secure."

"You are formidable, Katie Cypher," said the Professor. Then he whispered proudly, "Ai runs all Directorate 13 systems. Most people think Ai stands for artificial intelligence, which she is, but it's really Japanese for *love* because she was a labor of love."

Katie smiled and scratched under Tansy's chin. "When we get in, what happens next?"

"We exploit the bureaucracy," said the Professor, his head bobbing with excitement.

"And *how* do we do that?" asked Katie.

"Stratos is a small, tightly-controlled world that keeps out everyone except the chosen few who have access. If you are on Stratos, everyone will believe you belong there. So, the plan is to pass the trial, get to Stratos, copy your dad's last uploads from the memory core, and then get out. That's the mission," said the Professor as he rocked back and forth. "Frost gutted all the personnel loyal to your father and replaced them with lackeys. Everyone's new, so that buys us time."

"How much time?" Toby asked.

"Enough," said the Professor. "Ai monitors security, but no one's ever infiltrated Stratos before, and we shall have the element of surprise. Plus, they're arrogant."

"That gives us an advantage," said Toby, "and now we have a plan."

"Sadly, it is all academic if we can't override security. Frost must cooperate for this to work. Because biometrics, like his features, retina, fingerprints, voice, even his DNA, are all part of his access key. Unless you can charm or possess him, we're still a no-go."

"No," said Tansy. "As I am now, I cannot beguile him or compel his service."

"But I can," Toby said, with a serious look in his eyes.

CHAPTER 19

SERVICE WITH A SMILE

Toby stood at the counter of First Flight Coffee, the café Sasha's family ran. It was down the road from the Air Force Museum, and he was a regular.

"Hey, Toby," said Sasha. "How you doin'?"

It was barely summer, and Sasha was already profoundly tan. A vividly inked, water-dragon tattoo encircled her forearm. Her dark, wavy hair was pulled back from her face, and her eyes were amber in the early morning light.

"Saw you at graduation. I was surprised to get your text. We're not open yet, but let me get something started for you."

"Do you still make that thick hot chocolate?"

"Not a big summer seller, but give me a few minutes."

Then her smile drained away. "Sorry about your dad. He was kinda cool. I know you guys were goin' through a thing."

"Thanks." *You have no idea.*

"So, Toby," Sasha said, "tell me why you're really here, and what's with the huge duffle on your back?"

Toby assembled his mimic on a prep table in the back, away from the busy kitchen. It looked like a man made from shiny pipes.

"So let me get this straight," Sasha said, arms crossed. "You wanna replace one of my servers with a robot?"

Toby activated it. The mimic swung its legs, wiggled its toes, and examined the front and back of its hands. It stretched like it had been

136

sitting in a chair for too long and rolled its head around before it hopped to the floor.

"That's chill and all," said Sasha, "but why do you want your robot waiting tables?"

"It's a mimic. No one will know."

"I saw your presentation," Sasha said, studying the stick figure robot looking back at her. "I expected something more impressive."

"You're right." Toby glanced at the robot. "Engage mimic drive, include last night's new features."

"Engaging. Unit 117 nominal," it said as soft fibers extruded from its metal frame. At first it looked like a giant stuffed animal with soft fur that shifted colors until it found the right ones. Then its fur seemed to melt, and it changed shape until the mimic was a blank model of a roughly proportioned human. Slowly, the features of a Latino teen with upswept black hair, dark brown eyes, and a sparse, finger-width training beard emerged. He had a big smile and was wearing the same white T-shirt, sky-blue apron, and khakis as Sasha, but his name tag read "Hugo."

"Who's the dude?"

"I compiled his features from your competitor's baristas, and people from the neighborhood. So, he would look familiar, but no one would recognize him."

"Hugo, nice. Can he actually do the job?"

"I promise, he can," said Toby.

"Well . . . I am down a server today. New guy. Car trouble. At least he called in. But you never answered my question—why?"

"I need something from one of your least favorite customers."

"Who?"

"Frost."

"Ugh," Sasha said, recrossing her arms. "He bullies the servers, and he's a terrible tipper, so usually I get stuck dealing with him. But we cater events on base, and this sounds sketch."

"Will you keep this secret?"

Sasha groaned, then nodded.

"Frost lied about what happened to my dad, and the only way to get the truth is to get close and copy the data we need, without him getting suspicious."

"I don't know, Toby. That's a wild story."

"I know it sounds crazy—everything's crazy lately—but it's true," he said, meeting her gaze. "I wouldn't ask if there were another way."

Sasha sighed. "Okay, Toby. Don't make me regret this. What do you need me to do?"

Toby checked the video feeds on the security monitor above the manager's desk. People were gathering outside the café. "Show Hugo the ropes, then let him serve Frost and bus his plates."

"That's it?"

"That's it."

"He's here," Toby said, pointing to the monitor. Director Frost was parked in front of the café. He wore a white linen suit and extracted himself from a red Ferrari straight out of a video game.

"You ready, Hugo 117?" Toby asked.

"Dude, I was born ready," he replied.

Toby frowned.

"Sasha provided an excellent orientation," 117 said in his usual, more serious voice. "I will capture Director Frost's complete suite of biometrics to include DNA from his used tableware. I will not disappoint you. I will not damage your enemy unless you order it, and I will not fail."

"I know you won't, 117," Toby said, realizing his hands were trembling. "I'm proud of you." He squeezed his fists, and the shaking stopped. "It's showtime."

Sasha opened the café, and Frost came in with the other customers. He grabbed a table, looking back at his car.

Sasha worked the counter. Hugo 117 took Frost's order.

"Good morning," Hugo said, sporting an 82 percent smile. "What can I get you?"

"I've seen you somewhere," said Frost.

"I'm new here, but I used to work at Jet Fuel, down the road."

"Hmph."

Hugo recalculated the threat level and his eyes darted to the red car outside the big front window. "But I'd recognize that car anywhere. Saw you drive up. You have one sweet ride."

"It was just delivered. It's a classic," Frost continued, turning back to the menu. "Now try to keep up."

Hugo's smile decreased to an appropriate 55 percent. He noted the drop in threat level and nodded.

"I want a triple decaf espresso soy latte with two shots of agave and a dusting of vanilla. A well-buttered, toasted croissant, not too dark. The cheese and mushroom omelet, egg whites only, with bacon and the cheese and mushrooms on the side. Substitute the fruit cup for hashbrowns, and only give me grapes. Got it?"

"I'll get that started for you." No change to smile intensity necessary. Frost was done with Hugo and admiring his Ferrari through the glass.

Every time Hugo checked on Frost, he had a complaint or sent him searching for something.

"I want a clean fork."

"More water."

"Siracha, not ketchup."

Hugo dropped off the siracha and updated Toby in the kitchen. "I have captured and verified Director Frost's biometrics."

"Good job! Now, we just need to bus his table, and we'll have everything we need to replicate his DNA."

Frost ordered another coffee. "But this time, I want . . ."

Hugo scanned Frost. He had finished 89 percent of his breakfast, and his blood pressure had increased.

When Hugo returned with Frost's fresh latte, he closed out his bill and carefully cleared the table. Hugo took the crumpled dollar Frost had left as a tip, dialed up his brightness to 91 percent, and said, "Thanks. Come again." Hugo understood the tip was meant as an insult and his smile was excessive, but it was the first money he had ever earned, he'd just completed his mission, and he was pleased.

Hugo 117, holding his head high, set the tray of Frost's plates and glasses on the counter next to Toby.

Sasha came over. The kitchen was getting noisy, and she was sweating.

"Anything else for me, boss?" asked Hugo 117.

"No. We got everything. Revert to travel mode and standby. You did great."

Hugo grinned, then faded, got fuzzy, and shrank until 117 was a pipe skeleton again, sitting cross-legged on the floor.

There was a crash from the kitchen. Toby looked up.

"We're changing the line over to lunch," Sasha said, raising an eyebrow at the tray. "So, dirty tableware helps you?"

"Yeah. It does. Thanks again. I really owe you."

"I'll hold you to that. Now that you got whatever this is," Sasha said, frowning, "you're gonna do something crazy, right?"

"Pretty much."

Sasha rolled her eyes, then wished him luck and left.

The kitchen grew louder and livelier, and Toby got to work packing up 117. He was sitting on the floor putting the last parts of his mimic back in the duffle when his phone *dinged*. It was a text from Rachel, and Toby stopped everything to read it.

> Plane flew by. Guess who I thought about?

> ❤ Now I'm thinking of U

> Good. U doin OK?

> Better now ☺

I can swing by if U wanna talk

> I wish. But I'm taking care of family stuff. Can I see you tomorrow night?

I suppose ☺ See you then 💜

Toby was feeling pretty good about himself as he took a giant zip bag from his duffle. He was thinking about all the work he still had to do setting up the Frost mimic, but then he'd get to see Rachel.

He stood, turned to pack up the tableware with Frost's DNA, and gasped. The tray of Frost's dishes and cups and forks was gone.

Toby panicked and searched wildly around. He darted through the kitchen, looking everywhere, but he could not find them, and his heart felt like it was about to explode. *I had everything. Okay, think. Someone took them.* He asked the cooks, but they had no idea what he was talking about. Then he ran into a tall skinny guy, tying off a bag of trash.

"I'm sorry. I was helping out today. I had a stack of plates over there on a tray," Toby blurted out, pointing at the prep area.

"Oh yeah, thanks for covering for me, bruh. My car got fixed way faster than I expected, so I only missed the morning."

"Did you take a pile of plates on a tray from back there?"

"Sure did. Don't worry. Saw you on break. I already finished cleaning up and running them," he said, glancing at the big industrial dishwasher. The gauge on it moved from "Sanitize" to "Done."

"I blew it," Toby said, backing up. *I had everything to mimic Frost.*

"Naw, don't be so hard on yourself. You just didn't know—"

141

But Toby was already gone. He staggered into the café. His stomach was in knots. Frost's table was empty and reset with a fresh napkin roll of silverware. *I blew it.*

He looked for Sasha, but the café was empty.

Toby stepped past the row of potted trees that formed a to-go area and stopped at the door by the big front window. *We did this once; we can do it again.*

Then he looked up. The Ferrari was still there.

Toby had a bad feeling, and he turned slowly.

Frost was there, leaning against the counter, sipping a latte.

"Uh. Hello, Director Frost," said Toby, with barely a crack in his voice. "What a surprise." *Stay calm.* "What are you doing over here?"

"They got my coffee wrong. I was going to make them fix it to-go, but I decided to stay and admire the view."

"Nice car!"

"It is. I didn't know you worked here?"

"Uh, no, sir. Not exactly. They were shorthanded today. And a friend asked if I could cover a shift." *I can still do this.*

"Busy is good," Frost said, pushing his big, sloshing latte cup at Toby. "You can start with this."

Toby's heart skipped a beat. Frost's lip prints stippled the brim. He wanted to throw the coffee in Frost's stuck-up face and call him the liar that he was and demand his father back, but he grit his teeth. *Now I have your DNA. Now I can stop you. Now you'll pay.*

Toby held that cup like it was the most precious thing in the world, and he smiled a genuine, 100 percent smile, as Frost chirped his tires and drove away.

CHAPTER 20

MIRROR MAGIC

Katie stood in front of the large gilded dressing mirror that swiveled up and down in its carved wooden frame. It was old, older than even the United States, and Katie didn't know what it was at first because her father had kept it turned around in his room. For years, it was the backboard to his laundry basket.

When Dad told her the mirror was her mother's, Katie took it. It was heavy, but Toby helped carry it into her room, where it stayed. Katie glanced at her mom's picture on the dresser. *Toby looks like her, but I have blonde hair and blue eyes like Dad. Now we know she was on Stratos. After the trial, we'll walk where she walked, and where she . . . no.* She patted her cheeks. *This is a good thing. When we find Dad, we'll be a family again.*

Still, it bothered Katie that she could recognize her mom in pictures, but she couldn't remember much about her. She was an empty space that hurt. Now that her dad was gone, she couldn't stop thinking about them both.

Katie was holding the edges of the mirror, peering into it, her nose to the glass. She was turning her head side to side, trying to find some of her mother in herself, then sighing, pushing back, and sighing some more.

Tansy was curled up on a soft pillow, binge-watching the Travel Channel, when her eyes drifted to Katie. With a flick of her tail, she turned off the TV and padded over to her. "What *are* you doing?"

"Jeez, I don't know," Katie said, biting her lip. "Thinking about surviving a death trial, so I can break into the most secret place on Earth. I'm scared, Tansy."

"You don't have to do this trial, kitten."

"I know. But I'm going to, and I won't fail."

"With such determination, I have no doubt," Tansy said, circling Katie. "But why bury your head in the mirror?"

"Ever notice when you're stressed, if you stare at yourself long enough, all you see are flaws?" Katie said, making faces at herself.

"One finds what one looks for, Katie Cypher. But who decides what's a flaw? I am a goddess. I see great things in you. Personally, I find you quite lovely, for a human."

Katie looked at her and hissed.

Tansy laughed. "Kitten's got claws."

Katie blew a blonde lock out of her eyes, and with forlorn indignity said, "It's not claws I want."

Tansy ears twitched, and she laughed again. "Having claws is always a good thing." Her voice was husky and powerful. "I can show you something you'll like. What do you know of this mirror? Do you use it often?"

Katie nodded. "It was my mom's. I love it."

"Care to see what you will look like all grown up?"

"You can do that?"

"Yes," said Tansy, "but a lot depends on your mirror. And there's the cost."

"What do you want?"

"The usual: gold, jewels, a lifetime of service. But you tended my wounds and kept my secrets, so I think a salmon fillet will do."

"Done."

"And you must do exactly what I say," Tansy said, radiating light.

"Deal." Katie sat with Tansy in front of the mirror. "What do I do?"

"Shush," Tansy said, pushing the mirror until the bottom of the frame was against the wall and the mirror was angled down at them. Then she stood with her forepaws against the glass and her back paws touching Katie's legs.

Tansy uttered an undulating yowl, the room darkened, and the mirror flickered. "Think on what you've learned about the craft of magic. Empty your mind. Focus on my voice. Do as I say. This is how you learn the way. These simple tools will become paths to your own power. But first, we must find you in the mirror. Do not let go of me, and repeat: Coowl."

144

"Coowl," Katie said reverently, and the mirror went crazy, releasing every reflection it had ever seen.

Tansy purred approvingly. "Invectus."

"Invectus," Katie repeated. And the mirror showed her in her T-shirt, with her nose pressed against the glass, examining herself left and right.

Katie concentrated on each word, and how each one felt like a tumbler turning to open a lock deep inside her.

"Kadesh," Tansy said gutturally from deep in her throat.

When Katie said "Kadesh," a vibration passed through her body, the mirror flickered from her father's room to darkness, to their old house, to a place she didn't recognize, to a frosty grey that melted away like ice on a puddle. Then her lock opened to reveal . . . not Katie.

"Mommy!" Katie cried, squeezing bunches of Tansy's fur.

Ariana Cypher was dancing in front of the mirror in a floral summer dress. Her long mahogany hair bounced as she moved, and her hazel eyes twinkled. She looked happy and kissed the mirror. Red lipstick marked the spot.

"Tansy, what'd I do wrong? This isn't me, but it's wonderful."

"Watch a bit longer, kitten," Tansy replied as Katie's mom picked up a drowsy toddler clutching a blue and white stuffed brontosaurus, and set him on her bed for a nap.

"Aww. Toby was so cute."

When his eyes closed, Ariana Cypher crept back to the mirror, pulled her dress tight against her, and turned sideways to examine the bulge in her stomach that was just starting to show. She hugged herself and spun, laughing until she fell panting on the bed next to little Toby.

Tansy brought the scene back one more time and stopped it when Ariana was pulling back her dress to show her swell. "There you are, Katie. The mirror's first image of you, still deep inside your mother."

Katie sniffled. Joyful tears streaked her face. She burned every detail into her memory. Her mother. Her smile. How happy she was to be having her. Watching her mom in that moment sparked other memories of her mom to life, bright and in focus, like lightning flashes revealing things in the dark she never knew were there, and Katie remembered.

Then she felt what she had missed so much. The ache in her heart faded. She could feel her mother's love.

Tansy played the scene of Katie's mother in the mirror again, and Ariana Cypher fell back on the bed panting next to little Toby, and his blue dinosaur fell to the floor. Katie's mom frowned as Toby began reaching for it in his sleep. Then she flashed a peace sign at the stuffed dinosaur, and it came to life and hopped on the bed.

"What the—?" Katie's mouth hung open as she watched her mother's fingers move like a soldier's marching feet, and the brontosaurus trotted its plush legs into Toby's arms.

"I am like my mom," Katie whispered, overjoyed.

"Katie, about your future self."

"It's okay you couldn't find it, Tansy. Just seeing my mom like this, I—"

"'Tis not okay. After today, all your reflections are gone."

"Did the mirror break?"

"No, Katie, the mirror remains for several lifetimes to come. It's something . . . wrong."

"What does that mean?" Katie gasped. "Am I gonna die?"

"I am not certain, but there is a way. Can you be brave?"

Katie was scared, but she nodded.

"Give me your finger."

"I'll have to let go."

"'Tis fine if you hold me tight with your other hand."

Katie presented her finger. Tansy jabbed it with a claw and was back to holding the mirror with both paws so fast she blurred.

"Why'd you do that?" A drop of blood grew fat on the tip of her left index finger. Reflexively she drew her finger to her lips.

"Stop!" said Tansy, and Katie froze. "There's power in blood, and we'll need every bit of it. Rub that drop over your hand and press it against the mirror. Do not break contact with the mirror for anything, until I tell you it is safe. If you wish to stop, we need to do so now. Once we begin, we cannot turn back."

Katie felt like she was somewhere she wasn't supposed to be, doing something she wasn't supposed to do. She hesitated. *But I have to*

146

know—time slowed—*why I'm not in the mirror anymore.* She looked up at her mom and tightened her grip on Tansy. *No turning back.* She rubbed her thumb and fingers together. When her palm was red, Katie pressed her hand against the glass.

They said the words together. At "Kadesh," Ariana Cypher's kiss mark faded, and Katie's hand and Tansy's paws sank into the mirror. Glass rippled over their arms. Katie's heart pounded; her body shook. Terror hit her like ice water.

As if sinking into the mirror wasn't enough, something lurked under the dark glass waves. It bumped them like a shark testing its prey. It felt like back-to-back sleepless nights, falling on sharp rocks, and a million heartbreaking goodbyes.

"It's so cold, Tansy."

"Keep going, kitten. Bear it a little longer. This is dark magic, the most selfish kind."

Katie tightened her grip on her fur, and Tansy's claws dug into Katie's legs. "I feel so empty and lonely," Katie said, shivering.

"Almost there." Tansy caterwauled, a vortex formed within the gilt wood frame, and the violent waves drained away.

The mirror grew placid. Katie's hand and Tansy's paws rested back on the smooth surface, and the glass reflected a door.

Katie felt someone watching her. She didn't recognize the door, but as she focused on it, the keyhole grew until it felt like Katie was traveling through a tunnel, suddenly blocked by a peculiar eye. It was jade green and brown, but around the deep well of its pupil blazed a golden sunburst.

The eye widened when it saw Katie looking back. Then something slammed the other side of the mirror, like it was trying to break through the glass.

Katie screamed but did not let go.

"What do you seek, kitten?" A gentle voice reminded her, "Use your words."

When Katie remembered what she was looking for, her fear faded, and she whispered, "Coowl." She was going to find herself in the mirror, and even though she was scared, she said, "Invectus," and the word vibrated in her chest. Then she pressed her hand hard against the glass, took a deep breath, and demanded, "Kadesh."

Katie smiled even though she was cold and it hurt. Then the darkness shattered like a boot crunching through hollow ice, and the angry eye was gone.

Katie hung her head, panting, but it was like she'd come in, soaked from a cold rain, to find a warm fire burning just for her.

"What was that thing?"

"You can let go of the mirror, kitten," said Tansy between purrs. "You did well. Now look up."

Katie, still shaking, regarded the mirror, and there she was—long blonde hair, bright eyes, taller than she expected. She was wearing a T-shirt and jeans. All grown up.

Katie smiled, and her older self smiled back. Katie slowly stood holding Tansy and adjusted the mirror to see herself better.

Grown Katie was pretty, and her ears were pierced with gold bands and hoops that sparkled when she moved. She wore a bright yellow gem in a pendant, rings that seemed to glow, and a devilish grin of a smile. She produced a dry erase marker and wrote across the mirror in green. *Congrats. I've been waiting for this day. Follow your heart. You're braver than you know.* A scar shaped like a crescent moon filled the back of her hand.

Future Katie kissed the mirror and left a mark and waved.

Then she faded and the mirror reflected only Katie and Tansy. Katie's handprint and future Katie's writing and kiss were gone, along with her mother's lipstick mark.

Katie fell back to the floor.

Tansy worried the strain was too much for the small human girl. "Are you alright?"

"I'll be fine," Katie said, thoughtfully. "What was that eye, Tansy?"

"Something powerful has been watching you."

"Did I beat it?"

"You broke its hold on the mirror, and it returned your reflections. I don't know what it was. It cannot watch you through this mirror anymore, but it is still out there."

"Well," said Katie, with a yawn. "I should freak out, but I got to see my mom, and future me, so I'm not letting a creepy stalker eye ruin the moment. Let's just add whatever it was to the list of everything after us."

CHAPTER 21

INVASION

Even with the Professor's help, it took Toby longer than expected to prepare the Director Frost mimic and get their gear packed and up to Nimbus. He pumped Tansy for details about the trial, but all she'd say was, "It starts at what is now Sleeping Bear Dunes National Park, and once you begin, you must never give up." The Professor added, "Give up and you die. So don't." *Sigh. So, in the morning, just fly to Lake Michigan, find an old front porch that doesn't want to be found, and then magic our way up to Stratos. Great. Thanks, guys. That's just great.*

Robot Bob was taking Toby home when Rachel texted:

Hey. What RU doing?

Now?

YES now

Just finished going through Dad's lab stuff with the Prof. You?

Did you eat?

Not yet.

GOOD

Good?

U home?

No. Will be. 30M.

I'm coming over with dinner

Thanks!!!

See Ya!

Katie was impatiently guarding the door.

Toby watched her seething on the edge of hangry. "You know you could have eaten something earlier."

"That's not the point, Toby. I'm hungry now." He smiled and turned back to the schematics on his phone. "Have it your way."

"Gawd, you're annoying."

The doorbell barely made it through the *ding* in *ding dong* when Katie threw open the door. "Hello, Rachel."

Rachel shifted her grip on the box in her hands. "I brought Chinese. I wasn't sure what everyone liked, so I got everything."

"Everything, really?"

"Plus, a killer assortment of dim sum."

"That's an obvious ploy," Katie said, obviously happy. Then she hollered, "Toby, your girlfriend's here," and took the takeout box.

Katie made "ahh" and "nah" noises in the kitchen as she organized the containers by what she wanted for herself and what was for everyone else.

Rachel gave Toby a hug. "How are you holding up?"

I wish I could tell you. He hugged her back. "Better now," he said, pulling out her chair. *Dad was right. Secrets get heavy.*

She held her hand out to Tansy, who sniffed it, then turned so Rachel could stroke her. "I'm glad you kept the cat. She looks good as new. What's her name?"

"Tansy," Toby said, sitting next to Rachel. *She smells like vanilla coffee and flowers.*

"I gotta ask," Katie said, smacking down her piled-high plate and sliding into the chair across from Rachel. "You like Toby, right?"

"Yes."

"Didn't even hesitate," Katie said, a little impressed. "But do you *like* like him?"

"Katie! Rachel. I mean—"

"It's okay, Toby. I want to set this straight, but with everything that happened, there was never a good time." Then she took a deep breath, looked uncomfortable, and said, "I—"

Just then, all hell broke loose.

Tansy leapt onto the table, her ears pinned back, hissing. The air around her glowed, and the electricity went out.

The only light in the room came from Tansy. Her golden eyes locked on the doors to the pool. Clouds obscured the moon. Then every door and window along the back wall shattered.

Toby wasn't sure what he was seeing. Dark creatures swung into the house and dashed across the floor on sickle-shaped arms. The monsters screeched as they sprinted toward them.

Rachel screamed.

Tansy sprang to the counter, her fangs and claws pulsing with light. "Get back!" She growled. "We waited too long. They found us."

"Your cat just talked!" Rachel said, looking wide eyed. Toby took her hand, pulling her up. "Your cat," repeated Rachel, "just talked."

"That's what you focus on?" Toby said. "I'll explain later."

"You better," snarled Rachel.

Katie glared at the monkey-like horrors, past the plate she'd lovingly filled, as she backed away with Toby.

He knocked over the table, putting a barrier between them and the creatures. Rachel smashed a chair and held the long back piece in front of her and Katie like a shield. Toby snapped the seat off a counter stool and held the metal base with both hands like a mace. He swung as the monkey demon horde crashed into the table, pushing it back.

They were three-foot-tall monsters with round bodies, hands like hooks, and serrated teeth in round mouths that jabbered and drooled.

Tansy's claws burned like yellow suns, and eight golden slash marks left her claws and cut through the air like solar flares. The force of her slash ripped through the demons, tore apart the back wall, and cut down creatures still outside. The demons not vaporized by her attack looked like heaps of melting black gelatin.

Tansy was still panting from her first strike when another wave of demons attacked. "Katie. Light. Do it now!"

"Now?" yelled Katie. "I just learned it. Are you sure?"

"Never going to be a better time," Tansy said, eyeing the approaching monkey demons. "You got this, kitten."

Toby bashed monsters with his makeshift mace. Rachel knocked them away with her broken-chair shield. Together they protected Katie.

Katie closed her eyes. In her mind, she emptied the room, stopped the sounds, and let everything she felt fade away. In the dark, quiet space inside herself, she drew a silver circle and pinned the symbols she needed around it.

Katie remembered the lesson. *Everything's in the right place, I can feel it. Now what?*

"Now fill the circle," Tansy had said.

"But what do I fill it with?"

"Creating light is about structure and honesty, experiences that resonate, and, if you can muster it, joy."

"Okay? Can you give an example?" Katie asked as she struggled to keep the circle and symbols she'd learned held together in her mind.

"That which makes you cold and empty when it's gone," said the little goddess.

"I don't understand, Tansy."

"Yes, you do. What do you love, Katie Cypher? Fill it with that."

Katie opened her eyes. Tansy was cutting down monsters. Toby and Rachel were doing anything they could to keep her safe, and they were both bleeding.

"Now!" Tansy shouted, slicing through the demon mob.

Katie filled her circle with the things that left her cold and empty when they were gone. She loved her father and brother and uncle and friends. She felt their warmth and their love.

In the middle of that demon attack, Katie felt real joy.

She said, "Caritas." And all the memories and feelings she had packed into her circle melted together like platinum in a crucible until it was a shining, hot liquid made of Katie's most precious things. Then Katie said, "Lux," and she compressed all that molten emotion until it filled her heart with light. When it burned bright, she said, "Bullarum."

Katie took a deep breath, put her two fists together like a tube, and with everything she had, she blew. Iridescent soap bubbles streamed from her hands, and she sprayed them everywhere. The bubbles grew, until softball-like spheres shimmered and floated between and around every demon like a rainbow minefield.

The demon horde stood very still. They were terrified of the iridescent bubbles that smelled like sunshine bobbing around them, and they shrieked like kettles.

"Katie, what is this?" asked Toby. "Why are they scared?"

"Told you," she said, sinking to her knees. "I'm learning magic. They can't stand light."

"But this is—"

"After everything you've seen, how do you still not get that my teacher's a goddess?"

"You stopped them cold," said Toby. "This is . . . you're amazing!"

"Keep watching," Katie said, resting her head on the overturned table. "It's not over yet."

The biggest demon snarled at the bubble floating in its face. Then the demon screamed and bit it. The bubble popped like a flashbulb, burned through the demon, and blew it apart.

Then other bubbles popped, and light cascaded through the room and into the yard. When Toby could see again, they were alone in a lumpy, black fog that smelled like a bay at low tide. The demons were gone, it was eerily silent, and the house was trashed.

"Okay Toby, what the hell's going on?" Rachel yelled, pulling a large chef 's knife from a knocked-over wooden block. She stabbed it into the remains of a demon on the floor and rolled it over. It was vile. The stench was staggering, and it was melting into goo.

"Our father isn't dead," said Toby. "He was captured by Frost. We're trying to prove he's alive. A magic artifact that does bad things was stolen. Now they're after us."

"Bad things, like summoning these—"

"Demons," said Toby.

"Demons?"

Toby sighed and waved his arms around at the holes in his house and the monstrous, decomposing bodies. "This and worse."

"You weren't going to tell me?"

"Rachel, we didn't know any of this until after the funeral. That was bad enough. It's been a long week. We didn't want anyone else caught up in all of this."

"Really?" Rachel said, waving her arms and pointing at all the damage, corpses, and cuts.

"Yeah, I'm sorry. It was the best we could do."

Rachel sighed. She was scared and angry, but she cut strips off her skirt and started binding Toby's deeper cuts. "This is insane."

"Welcome to my world. And this," Toby said, motioning to the cat licking her paw on the sideboard, "is Tansy. Tansy, this is Rachel. I know you've met, but . . ."

"A pleasure," said Tansy. "I've heard good things."

Rachel jumped back against the table. "My God, I thought I imagined—"

"Goddess, actually." Tansy touched the wound on Rachel's arm.

"S-s-s-t," winced Rachel, as Tansy drew green symbols over her cut. "What are you—hey, that's better!" Rachel saw the bleeding stop and her wound close like a zipper. She forced herself to meet Tansy's eyes. "Thank you, I'm sorry. It's a lot to take in."

"I take no offense, circumstances being what they are."

Rachel looked around, then asked Tansy, "Is this thing over?"

"Hmm . . . a very good question."

"You did all this, Katie?" said Toby. "Who's the best little sister in the world?"

Katie smiled and took a step toward him. Toby caught her as she started to fall.

"Are you hurt anywhere?" Toby asked, checking for injuries.

"No. S'okay," Katie said, giving him a thumb's up. "Took a lot out of me."

Tansy looked Katie over. "She'll be fine. She just needs rest. Like I said, kitten's got a rare talent for the arts."

Tansy's ears twitched, and she jumped up to the shattered kitchen island, sniffing the air and listening.

"What's the matter?" Toby asked.

"More will come. They'll be upon us soon. To survive, you need weapons," Tansy said, crouching. "Truly, I hate doing this." When she stepped away, there were two large amber-and-bone claws on the remains of the countertop. "This is only a loan. They take a long time to grow back."

Toby lifted one of the claws. It filled his palm and looked like a thick, four-inch-long letter G that ended in a sharp curved edge on one side and white bone at the other. It was weighty and warm.

"How is this possible?" Toby asked. "These are bigger than a lion's, and you're—"

"You may have noticed, I'm not made like you."

"Right," said Toby. "Thanks, but I can't use this."

"Feel it in your hand, Toby Cypher. Now imagine you need to protect your female, and it will form the weapon best suited to you."

Toby nodded and blushed. Katie took the other claw. As soon as she did, it uncurled in her hand and grew into a staff. She held it in both hands, and when she concentrated on defending her family, the end of her staff ignited into a rippling flame of a spearhead, with a point that defied physics and stayed fixed toward wherever she pointed.

Seeing what his sister had done, Toby held his claw tight and concentrated—hard. He remembered the fight they just had and his desire to protect Rachel and Katie.

But nothing happened. Toby piled on every fight he ever had and his will to survive. Still, nothing happened. Then he added revenge. How he craved to make those who took his father pay, and his hunger to bring whoever sent the demons to justice, because no one else would—and his claw finally changed. It unwound and stretched and grew, but then the color left it, and no matter how hard he tried, the magic was gone. Its amber and bone dried out. With a *crack*, it split in half, and Toby was left with a gnarled, pointy stick in each hand.

"Oh, Toby," Katie said, leaning on him. "At least they're sharp."

They felt like hangnails in Toby's hands. He looked from Katie's flame-tipped spear down to the twigs he'd made, and he didn't know whether to scream or laugh.

He didn't get the chance to do either. The front door exploded into the entry and broke apart on the stairs.

Then something huge came in.

It had no head, just a fleshy curve from shoulder to shoulder above a vertical maw full of gleaming teeth that ran from where its head should have been down to its waist. The demon's mouth opened and closed like a Venus flytrap, its torso was covered in dancing black flame, and its ember-red eyes searched the room from where its nipples should have been. Giant, crab-like claws dragged behind it. It had no legs, but its torso was mounted on a large, skirted foot that oozed slime like a slug when it moved.

"That looks bad," said Toby. "What do we do?"

"Run!" yelled Tansy.

Toby threw Katie over his shoulder, took Rachel's hand, and they bolted through the back wall toward the pool. The air was easier to breathe outside. There was a breeze and a break in the clouds. Moonlight reflected off the water.

They made it to the pool when the slug demon crashed through the back of their house. It was bigger now and growing. Monkey demons flowed around it and rushed toward them. Their backyard was surrounded by high stone walls that blocked their way to the woods.

There was nowhere left to go.

Tansy was on the roof of the palapa, ready to pounce. Katie could barely stand, but she had a spear and her magic. Rachel stood beside Katie, brandishing a chef knife that glowed after Tansy had blessed it. Toby had his two sharp sticks.

It felt like a last stand.

CHAPTER 22

BITE AND HACK

Katie leaned against the palapa. "I kinda overdid it with all those bubbles."

"I'm almost out, too, kitten. One more push. We have to slow the demons down."

"Well . . ." Katie said, looking around. "We've got plenty of saltwater in the pool."

"Perfect. You form, I'll freeze."

Katie staggered to the edge of the pool. She looked at the slug demon gathering its forces and her ruined house and couldn't hold back her tears.

Some spirits can only be seen under starlight, and the stars were faint, but with the power out, there was just enough. Katie searched the water and found the spirit dwelling there.

Katie was lucky. The water spirit hated the approaching demons, Katie had never wronged it, and it was curious enough about what was going on to talk. The surging spirit agreed to do what Katie asked for the promise of three things: that humans stop peeing in the pool, that if any still did, it could stain them blue and toss them from its water, and finally, to seal the deal, it wanted Katie's tears. She took a step back as the spirit rose from the pool like a child pretending to be a ghost in a reflective sheet of water. Its eyes were big green saucers, and its mouth smiled like a waterfall.

Katie made the contract, and it felt like a caress squeegeeing away her tears. They sped away through the air into a translucent hand, and the water spirit's power was hers. Katie made circles with her right arm, and the pool water became a whirlpool.

She felt the weight of the water and the minerals in it as she touched its hydrogen and oxygen and took firm hold of their bond. It was heavy.

Katie adjusted her footing, straightened her back, and pushed both of her arms toward the moon.

It felt good. She was connected to the liquid in her body, the humidity in the air, and the water in the spirit and the pool.

Katie said, "Aqua Veni," beckoning the water to come, and it did. It climbed from the pool in a giant waterspout that Katie pulled close, turned on its side, and crashed through the front line of demons upon her.

Tansy added cold and gusting wind, the temperature dropped, and the waterspout stretched and froze into a whirling crystal meat grinder, spinning inches from her face. The twisting ice looked like cotton candy wrapped in razor wire. The water's roar was deafening, and Toby shivered from the arctic blast.

The frozen waterspout slowed to a stop as an eight-foot-tall ice wall that cut the backyard in half. In the moonlight, Toby could see the distorted shapes of demons in the ice. On the other side of the wall, they howled with rage.

The slug demon had grown visible over the wall. It emitted malice like concert bass thumps they felt in the chest.

Rachel set an exhausted Katie on a lounge chair at the far side of the nearly empty pool, and readied her knife.

The first two monkey demons to scale the jagged ice wall jumped Toby. He thrust his pointy sticks deep into them. What happened afterward surprised everyone.

Both demons shrieked as Toby's sticks sucked them dry of whatever energy held them together, and piles of black sand poured to the ground.

After feeding on demon, Toby's sticks had grown into long kukri knives with kinked blades and sharp bellies. Their grips were bone, their blackened amber blades danced with blue fire, and they throbbed like purring cats in Toby's hands. His heart raced triple-espresso fast, and Toby felt lighter and faster.

Each blade had a slightly different weight and shape. One had jagged serrations, and without thinking Toby said, "Your name is Bite." The other was longer with a sharp, glass-smooth belly that felt more like an ax than a knife. After a few chops and cuts at the air, he said, "Your name is Hack."

Bite and Hack. He didn't so much hold them as they held on to him, and Toby felt their hunger as though it were his own.

More demons leapt from the wall.

Toby grinned and rushed to meet them.

White and black fog filled the low spaces, and the stench grew with each kill. He had lost track of how many there were, and Toby retreated from the mounds of demon-sand growing around him. He felt a jolt, and more of his wounds closed when Bite stabbed a demon or Hack chopped deep, but the battle was long, and he was panting and ached all over.

Another demon jumped him, claws hooking his shoulders. It screeched. Toby screamed, thrusting his knives up, just missing his ears, and the creature fell away as sand. Relief flowed from Bite and Hack through his hands and arms, and Toby sighed as its life force restored him and gave him strength.

He hunched over, hands on his thighs, trying to catch his breath before the next attack, but demons stopped scaling the wall, and Toby met with the others, between the pool and palapa. "Why doesn't the big one attack?"

"Maybe it doesn't like the salt in the water," Rachel said.

"Maybe," said Tansy. "But something's coming. I can feel it."

From the palapa Tansy could see the slug demon gathering its little monkeys. It wrapped its arms around them, held them to its black flame hide, and they caught fire like campfire marshmallows.

The demon lobbed claw-fuls of them, like firebombs, over the icy wall.

Tansy stood on her hind legs on the palm frond roof, weaving a canopy of light to protect them. A hail of shrieking, fiery demon-bombs struck. Some missed, others bounced off Tansy's barrier. Blasts cratered and shook the ground. Part of their wall was blown apart. Drifts of shaved ice covered the yard. Puddles of black fire burned everywhere.

Then, Tansy's barrier failed, and the palapa exploded.

The two-story slug demon lurched through the hole in the wall, and firehose-thick tentacles shot from it. They hit Toby like bolos, wrapping his legs, knocking him down, pulling him to its sideways mouth. Toby dug his blades in the ground to stop, but the demon yanked and tugged, and Toby lost his knives.

Toby could feel his blades, like phantom limbs that still felt attached, even though they were gone.

The demon slurped its tentacles binding Toby into its mouth like Ramen noodles.

Toby was terrified, but he laughed. *I'm going insane.* He was being eaten by a demon, and all he could think about was how itchy his palms felt with Bite and Hack still stuck in the lawn.

The demon's teeth closed on Toby like jagged glass. *Help me,* he cried out, reaching for Bite and Hack.

The itching stopped, and the giant mouth snapped shut.

The demon chewed Toby's leg, then he felt the sensation of something reeling in through his arms. His blades tore through the demon, and Bite and Hack were back in his hands.

He screamed. Blue flame burned on his blades.

Toby chopped, and the demon shuddered.

Bite and Hack pumped the big demon's energy into Toby, and he stung the slug demon's throat so bad, the demon spit him out.

Toby slid over the icy ground, empty handed, past Tansy fighting in the dancing light of the burning palapa, and Rachel was there, helping him up.

"Thanks." Toby was dizzy and disoriented, and when he stepped with his right foot, he regretted it. His sneaker and sock had been ripped off. The bites in his leg were slowly closing, but the monster's teeth had sliced through both sides of his foot, ankle to toe, and the pain was almost unbearable. Through his teeth, he said, "Rachel. Give me some room."

Rachel shook her head. "No. You were just eaten by a monster. Look at your leg, I have to—"

"It'll be okay," Toby turned to face the demon. He could almost hear Rachel frowning. "I only need a sec."

Rachel glared, then reluctantly stepped back, and Toby felt for his knives. His palms itched. He glanced from Katie to Rachel. *I will protect them.*

Then Toby focused on Bite and Hack still in the monster, and he spun them like the blades in a blender.

The big demon roared like a jet engine on afterburner. Toby pulled back his arms, and one of its ember red eyes went out.

Bite and Hack returned to Toby's hands, burning hot and covered in slime, and Toby staggered.

Rachel guided him to a pool chair, then cut more strips from her skirt to bandage his foot. He was asleep before she was done. Rachel chewed her lip, then kissed Toby.

This isn't goodbye.

Her chef's knife glowed brighter, and she returned to the fight.

Katie had watched the fight, barely able to move. *I used too much magic too fast.* Her entire body ached and she had a throbbing migraine, like someone was stretching her brain in and out like a Slinky. *They protected me again.*

Even with Rachel's back to her, Katie could see she was scared.

Toby took the big demon's eye, but he was snoring next to her, and his foot was a mess.

Tansy attacked the monster's arms and its wriggling pedestal of a slug foot and darted away, but the demon's claws were destroying everything around her, and each hit was closer.

Their attacks weren't enough.

Katie stood with the help of her spear and raised her arm. She could still feel the water around her, and she grabbed every drop she could use.

"Aqua Veni." She convinced the water of what it was born to do, whispered where it needed to go, and reminded it that the last part of a promise was due.

A stream of water as long and thick as the trunk of a great tree swirled together from the pool, ice, and fog. Katie formed it into a gigantic arrow and fired. It shot straight at the demon, like the shimmering outline of a ballista bolt.

"Tansy!" Katie shouted over the din. "Form and freeze." Katie's power was spent, but it was okay, the water knew what to do.

The slug demon towered over Tansy. *Now you shall see what a goddess can truly do.* Tansy rose to meet the monster, and darkness turned to desert day.

Then she heard Katie, felt the water move, and understood.

The monster demolished the spot where Tansy had been.

Its tentacles tried to intercept her, but Tansy curved up and around through the air in a golden arc, faster and tighter than the monster could follow. She reached the saltwater bolt before the demon even knew it was there.

Tansy grasped the living water and released her remaining power into it. As she glided over its surface, it hardened into sea ice that she accelerated like a rail gun.

It penetrated the demon. Tansy detonated the water spike, and ice fragments ripped through it like swords, from the inside out.

The slug demon froze like a giant black cactus covered in crystal needles. The fire dancing over it went out, and the demon toppled over and began to dissolve.

It was a great victory. Rachel got Toby and Katie up, but Team Cypher could barely stand, and the surviving monkey demons howled and charged them. The lawn was cratered, like it had been shelled by artillery, and it was slippery and burnt, like the fires had been extinguished with snow cones.

They stumbled through the yard. Only a few dozen small demons remained, but that didn't matter. They were at their limit.

The demons surrounded them. They could hardly lift their weapons. The moon retreated behind the clouds, and a monkey demon drove its hooked arm through Rachel's stomach.

Toby cut the creature down, but her injury was bad.

Rachel sobbed, Katie cried as she worked to stop the bleeding, and Toby and Tansy defended them, knowing they couldn't win.

They were done.

Or so they thought.

Sampson and Delilah didn't snarl or bite until they were right on top of them, and the big French Mastiffs ripped through the ring of monkey demons like they were chew toys. When a demon spun to attack Toby, they grabbed it from both sides with their powerful jaws and tore it in half.

Howls, growls, and caterwauls echoed around them. It wasn't just Sampson and Delilah. Every animal had come.

Cats crisscrossed the battlefield in hissing formations, taking down demon prey.

Wolfhounds with their dark wiry coats attacked. Ridgebacks guarded Rachel so Katie and Tansy could heal her. Collies herded demons. Bulldogs and retrievers took the creatures down. Dobermanns and rottweilers ended them.

Little dogs fell on injured demons, nipping them to death.

"Did you do this, Tansy?" Katie said as family pets battled the demons around them.

"I simply asked if they would come," Tansy replied with a stretch. "We are fortunate. They were bred to fit in houses, but they are still hunters at heart."

Toby, Katie, a fallen goddess, and every neighborhood pet fought until the last demon was gone.

Afterward, Tansy bestowed blessings on the animals. Dogs howled in victory, and for that one night, even the smallest cat was permitted to roar.

CHAPTER 23

STORMING THE CASTLE

The worst part of Toby's night was not fighting for his life or cutting his way out of a slug demon's mouth or hurting from his injuries. Those were all horrible. But the worst part was seeing Rachel bleed and having to hold her down so Tansy and Katie could heal her.

They left the house when the Professor arrived. "You're safe now," he said. "Quickly, come along."

Neighbors were out, swinging lights in the dark, talking about earthquakes, the stench of broken sewer lines, and noises in the night after the power went off.

Toby helped Katie and Rachel into the car and stowed the trash bag with the few things they had rescued from home.

Robot Bob pulled away, and for the first time all night they heard sirens in the distance.

Katie fell asleep with Tansy in the back, and Toby held Rachel in the second row as gently as he could, but every pothole made her groan, and Toby raged. *Demons came from his office.*

Police cars with flashing lights and armored Minotaur Security Humvees blew past them. *It was Frost.*

"Will we be okay?" Toby asked. *Will Rachel?*

The Professor pointed to the air freshener hanging from the rearview mirror shaped like a witch, with big anime eyes and electric-blue hair. "This will keep us off the government's radar. It uses a poly-spectral mix of . . ." Toby listened to the Professor explain how it worked as the little witch air freshener spun on her broomstick, and more Minotaur vehicles sped past. *Handy,* Toby thought, dozing off. *And now the car smells like blueberries.*

At the Professor's place, Rachel and Toby's wounds required true healing. While battlefield sorcery could bolster the body, dull the pain, and hold one together so they could keep fighting, true healing would make the body right and whole again, and it wasn't as simple as waving a wand. It's complicated, and for Rachel and Toby, it crammed months of recovery into one long, scream-filled night.

When Toby came to, he was drenched in sweat, shaking, and nauseous from all the changes Tansy had made to restore his body. "What happened? Are Katie and Rachel all right?"

"They are fine," said Tansy. "As are you. But Rachel's wound was grave. Her body and mind will need time and rest."

"But I was hit a lot worse, why—"

"You hunger, Toby Cypher. You lack magic, but your hunger for knowledge and revenge have created something from my claw I did not foresee. When you feed your blades, they feed and heal you. Tonight, they saved your life and helped save ours. They are a part of you now that I cannot take back." Tansy's eyes gleamed gold as she spoke. "Be firm with them. Beware your hunger does not devour you."

Toby looked from Rachel on the other couch, to Bite and Hack, to Tansy sitting on the white table. "If it weren't for your magic, and these weapons, and teaching Katie, I don't know what we'd have—"

"The words you struggle to find are *thank you*," Tansy said with a long yawn. "Ashur's Tears has fused our fates. You fought well, and Rachel chose to defend you. Your children will be brave and reasonably bright."

"Tansy!" Toby winced as he sat up. "We're not even officially going out. After this, I don't even know how she feels about me."

Tansy laughed. "A girl who guards a boy from monsters has marked her territory. Her desire is to hunt with you again."

Toby regarded Rachel with a sad, faraway look on his face.

Tansy followed his gaze. "Worry not. The Professor has made arrangements. She will be safe and receive the care she needs. Now, I must get Katie up. 'Tis time to go."

Rachel was propped up on the red velvet couch. *We survived an army of demons.* Her eyes moved rapidly under her lids. Her body trembled. It was a nightmare, and she cried out.

Toby took her hand until she slipped into a peaceful sleep. "I'm so sorry, Rachel. All you did was come see me." He smoothed out her hair and fixed the blanket over her. *You got hurt because of me.*

He wanted to stay, but Toby had to save his dad. "I have to go." He kissed her forehead. "I wanted to hear you tell Katie that you *like*, like me."

You'll be safer when I'm gone.

The Aero Club was a quarter mile past the world's smallest abandoned guard shack. It was a cluster of old hangars, a few corrugated metal buildings, and a stretch of patched concrete with rows of airplanes arranged between faded parking lines.

During the car ride, Tansy taught Toby and Katie that by concentrating a certain way, their weapons could shrink and change back to something like their original form. Katie wore her spear as a lion claw choker, and Toby's Bite and Hack transformed into a pair of twisted blue-and-amber bone bracelets.

Doctor Cypher's airplane was a '79 Beechcraft Duchess. It was a white-and-blue, twin-engine, T-tail aircraft parked by itself away from the other planes.

Flying always helps me feel better. "There's my girl," Toby said, leaving the wood-sided car and running his hands lovingly along the Beechcraft's flanks before starting his preflight check.

"That's just not right," said Katie, shaking her head as she carried Tansy to the aircraft.

"Says the girl who became her cat's pet," said Toby.

"No, Tansy and I just like each other's company. We're our own people, and she's a good teacher, plus she's warm."

"Don't listen to her, baby," Toby said, patting the plane's nose.

When the aircraft was ready to go, the Professor called everyone together. "Find the old front door, restore the gateway to Stratos, get to the memory core, retrieve the data, get out. That's the plan."

"Okay," said Toby. "Let's roll."

"Not so fast," said the Professor, his head bobbing with annoyance. "You'll need these communications glasses for you and Katie, plus an earpiece for Tansy. Wear these, and we'll be able to talk and exchange information. And here's the memory stick you'll need to download your father's data from the M-Core." Then he handed Toby the little witch air freshener from his car. "I've recalibrated it to act as a jammer and a decoy so it will be much harder to find you if they're looking for your father's plane. Everyone ready?"

"Yes!"

"Good." Then the Professor turned and left.

"Wait," said Toby. "Where are you going?"

"I'm headed home to check on Rachel, then probably a nap."

"You're not coming with us?" Katie asked.

"What? Of course not."

"What do you mean you're not coming?" exclaimed Katie. "What kind of grown man sends kids alone into battle?"

"One confident in your abilities."

"But you're an adult," said Katie.

"Mmm, yes," said the Professor, his head nodding rapidly.

"And you're going to let Katie, me, and a cat storm the castle by ourselves?"

"First of all, Toby, this is hardly storming the castle. This is infiltration. Second, while my powers are profound, you may have noticed the cane. I'm no good to you in a fight. I can't even drive. So, I shall be your eyes and ears and work the system for you. I wish there were another way, but that's how it is."

"That's it?" Katie asked, one hand on her hip with a scowl.

"Yes. That and I have the utmost confidence in both of you."

"Great," said Toby. "Just great."

"Now, now," said the Professor. "Have fun storming the castle."

"It's an infiltration," said Toby.

"See, you are trainable. You have a plane and a plan. Stop wasting good daylight."

CHAPTER 24

THE TRIAL

Toby hung the little witch air freshener off the passenger sun visor. She spun on her broom, and he took off. Three hours later they landed at Cherry Capital Airport outside of Traverse City, Michigan. *I can't count the number of times I've flown this route with Dad. One day we'll do it again.* After Toby refueled the plane, Katie wanted road trip snacks. Then they caught the shuttle to the national park. An hour later they were standing at the base of the dune with their packs.

The dune at Sleeping Bear Dunes National Lakeshore was a climb from the parking lot into the sky, like a walk across a two-hundred-foot wide beach to the ocean, only up.

"I can feel the old front porch," said Tansy. "It longs for Stratos."

It was late morning, the sky was a cloudless blue, and Toby saw through his glasses that it was 76 degrees. Dozens of people were spread across the wide dune. Some were trudging up to explore the top and catch a glimpse of Lake Michigan. Others were dug into the sand at various heights, enjoying the sun. Groups of little kids in Skittles-colored swimsuits squealed, ran down the dune as fast as they could, and tumbled into laughing piles.

The Professor had told them how to find the old front porch, but it had not been a pep talk. "Climb the big dune, turn left, and go toward the distant trees. Even though you won't want to, head uphill and toward Lake Michigan. Go past the warning signs, and when your every instinct tells you to run away screaming, you're almost there."

The glasses the Professor gave them were not only dark in the bright sun, they also augmented reality. Everything was tagged wherever Toby looked. Location, elevation, temperature, wind speed, current events, even history. The longer he stared at something, the more information was displayed. He saw people's names and where they were from. It was like Google in his head.

The first thing the Professor sent to their glasses was a map. It superimposed a thick dashed line on the ground that led somewhere in the distance to an X-marked spot, two to three hours away. Toby and Katie adjusted their packs and slowly trudged up the dune with Tansy bounding alongside them.

They enjoyed the cool breeze and the views from the top and caught their breath. They didn't talk as they turned left toward the trees in the distance. It was nice to be outside hiking on a sunny day after a night spent fighting for their lives, but they were numb and tired.

Toby and Katie climbed a steep rise, passed through a thicket, and were winding their way down again when they hit a ridge. Grassy dunes to their left hissed in the breeze and rippled in green waves flecked with wildflowers. The right side of the ridge led to the base of a cliff, where a dirty stream flowed down a steep ravine. They might have missed it if the dashed line had not led them straight to the muddy trickle and pointed up.

The Professor was right: the path was treacherous, and they didn't want to climb up.

Katie fell and was washed twenty yards downstream before she was able to stop her slide. "This is impossible," she whined. They were covered in mud and exhausted from climbing silty waterfalls and trudging through pools of muck. As they worked their way up the narrow V-shaped ravine, they squeezed through places so tight Toby could touch both sides. While they fought against the current, it didn't help that the water smelled like roadkill.

Toby hauled himself over the next big rock, tossed the rope to Katie, and pulled her up. "This is stupid!" Katie shouted. "Why do you get to be in the front? You keep kicking mud in my face, and I'm sick of it."

"Yeah?" Toby snapped. "Who'd carry the gear and haul you up if I was in back?"

Katie groaned. She was exhausted, and they weren't even halfway to the X. "We need to stop fighting, okay? It's not helping."

"You know what's not helping?" Toby shouted. "Your stupid cat." Toby pointed at Tansy. "You're a goddess, right? Do something."

Tansy's eyes narrowed, her claws flickered gold, and she leapt down from the rocks. She landed on a ledge inches from Toby's face, and her growl echoed through the ravine. When the echoes stopped, Tansy said, "Hear me well. I cannot help you here. This is a trial, and a good barrier makes it easy to find reasons to turn away. If you do not prove yourselves worthy, Stratos will not let you in."

"Any advice then?" Toby said, with a sneer.

"Prepare yourselves. It grows harder the closer you get, and you are closer than you think."

"That's just great."

Toby's glasses indicated they had climbed for seven hours. When they scrambled over the top of the ravine, they collapsed on the first flat, dry ground they found. Their muscles burned, their feet and hiking shoes were soaked, and Toby and Katie stripped off their wet socks to dry their shoes and feet in the sun. One of Katie's red socks tore in half when she pulled it off, and Toby tossed her a fresh pair from his huge pack.

It felt good to wiggle his toes in the warm sandy soil, but Toby could hear big animals grunting and tearing through the underbrush somewhere close by.

When Toby stood, he noticed the signs. The first read: *Danger. Sheer Bluff and Unstable Ridge Erosion Ahead. Area Closed.* The second warned: *Return the Way You Came. Life-Threatening Injuries May Occur Beyond This Point.* If that weren't enough, there was a third sign: *Bears Beyond This Point Are Rabid.*

Toby scouted the area past the signs. The mosquitos were thick, and the thorns were sharp. He was covered in stinging cuts, and his mud-plastered clothes were in tatters by the time he found a rise where he could zoom in on the animals and study them through his glasses.

Four huge black bears were roaring, foaming at the mouth, and fighting each other. There was no way around them, and the closer they got, the more Toby felt the need to flee.

Snap out of it and focus. The bears patrolled the narrow section of the bluff they had to cross to reach the final hill and the old front porch. Toby's hands were shaking. *Fighting through isn't smart. We need a distraction to lead them away.*

"This place has a strong barrier," said Katie. "I feel it, but what exactly is it?"

Tansy looked up from cleaning the mud off her paws. "There are different kinds of barriers, kitten, but the very best, like this one, are part illusion and, to a degree, fear culled from the uninvited. It looks to see what frightens you, then it turns your fear against you. Sprinkle in a healthy dose of elemental bewitchery, and you have a great barrier. Structurally though, it's like mirror magic but with a twist."

"What's the twist?"

"You'll know it when you feel it," Tansy said as she inspected herself for any more dirt. "The magic you used to find your future self in the mirror and the magic the old front porch is using to keep you away are both a kind of netting. You sent your power through the mirror like a fishing net to catch images of your future self and draw them back to you. The old front porch is protecting the gateway to Stratos by setting traps to entangle you. It's wrapped this entire place in a web of fear to push you away or into danger. So, you must figure a way past or through her nets. This barrier is a labyrinth. The barrier I cast was a net of light to bounce flaming monkey demons away. But usually, a barrier is a shield."

Toby came crashing through the undergrowth past the signs, relieved to be alive and back after being chased away by bears. The dirty stream down the ravine was starting to look more like a waterslide. He described the tough path forward and the angry, rabid bears. Tansy sat in Katie's lap as they listened.

"So," Katie said, "you need something to lure the bears away?"

"Yes," Toby said between guzzles of canteen water.

Katie thought about it, scratched behind Tansy's ears, and said, "No prob."

"Okay," said Toby. "What are you up to?"

"Remember when you helped me build that snowman a few winters ago?" Katie said, patting the sandy patch she was sitting on.

"Yeah," said Toby.

"It's gonna be like that."

Katie cleared the sandy spot and drew the outline of a giant man in the ground with her spear. "I gotta get a few things to make this work. While I'm gone, dig deep around these lines."

"Fine," said Toby, "but what am I making?"

"It's called a golem." Then she and Tansy disappeared into the woods.

The sand was packed, and Toby grunted and sweated as he dug a deep trench around the lines Katie had drawn. He used the dirt from the trench to fill out and sculpt the giant sandman until he was big and buff, with an oversized chest, eight-pack, and a pineapple-shaped head.

Katie returned with Tansy and an ornately carved chunk of bark that she buried in the center of the sandman's chest. Then she stood, transformed her choker necklace back into a spear, and used its flame tip to refine the sandman's features. The shadows were long when Katie added the final touches. She took Toby's stiffening, wet socks and tore them into strips she put around the sandman's wrists and ankles.

"Why do that?" Toby asked.

"Animals react to smells, and these are pretty ripe," Katie said as she worked. She used her ripped sock halves as cheeks and her other red sock as its mouth. When she stood to admire her work, she frowned, added a flat pinecone nose, pine bough hair, and a thong of leaves. Grudgingly, Katie used her last two chocolate-covered snack cakes as its eyes. Then she touched its chest and said, "Like is to like, power to power, this is to that," and stepped back.

Katie put a hand over her heart, pointed the other at the sand golem in the ground, and said, "*Na'im Me'od*. Now, rise."

There was a sound like stone grinding stone, the golem shimmered, and first one arm, then the other, lifted from the earth. It sat up, stood, and towered over Katie when it left the pit.

It made a noise like banged fists on pipe organ keys, and blinked its big chocolate eyes as it looked around and leaned down until Katie was eye-to-eye with its big pineapple face. She ran her fingers through its spikey pine hair and told it what she needed done.

It smiled a big, red-sock smile and spoke haltingly in its pipe organ voice. "Wind and water never listen to sand. Sand go where they say. Sand do what they say. No fair."

"If you do as I ask," Katie said, looking up at the giant. "I promise you at least three sunsets of freedom. Go and do what *you* want for a change."

The sand golem made another stone-grinding sound, blinked its big chocolatey eyes, and bowed to Katie. "We agree. Now you must give us a name."

Katie bit her lip and said, "Your name is Marv." He just looked like a Marv.

Toby, Katie, and Tansy raced through the opening into the dense forest that covered the last hill between them and the old front porch. They could hear the roaring bears chasing Marv. He had jumped right into the middle of four of them and sprayed their faces with sand. The rabid bears stood on their hind legs, thundering with fury, then Marv slapped his butt and ran. Enraged bears chased him. They tore down trees to get at the sand-spraying, butt-wagging golem taunting them, but Marv was too fast, and per his deal with Katie, he led them away.

Team Cypher climbed the gentle hill, over the bouncy pine needle carpet, through the tightly packed woods. Toby was almost clear of the trees and into the flat, open space at the crest of the hill when a grey mud beehive the size of a beach ball broke free from a high branch in front of him. It cracked open like a giant papier-mâché egg when it hit the ground, and the black cloud of bees that emerged were hornets, each bigger than Toby's thumb. The angry swarm buzzed like chainsaws and mowers and came at them.

"This just gets better and better," Toby said, as he threw Katie over his shoulder and took off running. "Cover your eyes, Katie!" Toby shouted, covering his face with his arm and rushing into the part of the swarm between them and where "X" marked the spot.

Each sting felt like a rusty nail hammered into him, and Toby's face and arms and legs burned. Katie's weight threw him off balance, and Toby stumbled.

Hard to breathe. Black and red lines over his face and arms marked the bee toxin spreading through his body. *I led us to this. If we don't turn back now, we'll die.*

It was like running through pain, regret, and quicksand. Toby choked as he struggled forward. Every heartbeat was like another nail in his chest. *It doesn't end here.* Toby took two more steps, and his vision dimmed. *No. One more.*

Suddenly it was gone. The fear, the pain, the swelling were all gone, and he could breathe again. Toby fell to his knees and set Katie down. The world reeled as he tried to understand what had just happened. He was with Katie in a bubble of blue sky and sunshine. The air was clean and crisp, and he was surrounded by white sand raked in perfect circles around boulders and clusters of flowering trees. Crowning the top of the hill was a giant dome-like gazebo made of loops of blue metal and pure-white stone.

He looked down. Katie was unconscious. He tried to wake her, but he couldn't.

Then Tansy appeared next to him. "Tansy, it's Katie—"

"Shh," said Tansy, "Katie's fine. She passed the trial before you did, so I put her to sleep. Any more would have been cruel." Tansy chirped, and Katie's eyes opened.

"Hi, Tansy. I had a horrible dream. There were hornets. Big hornets."

"Even the bravest warriors flee before bees, kitten."

Katie smiled.

"I thought I lost you." Toby pulled Katie up and hugged her until she tapped out.

CHAPTER 25

OLD FRONT PORCH

Toby and Katie were clean, their cuts and stings had faded, and their clothes were as good as new. Toby checked his glasses. The trip timer showed they'd been slogging up mud falls, evading bears, and fighting bees for nine hours. But it was only noon, two hours after they'd started out for the old front porch. Toby wasn't sure what to believe, but he remembered every bit of the trial and all the pain.

They walked across the perfectly raked sand through an opening in a low blue metal wall, onto the stone patio that surrounded the gazebo. Toby heard a slithering sound and turned. The gap in the wall had closed. Their footprints were gone, and all the sand was perfectly raked again.

Toby hurried to catch up.

Lake Michigan moved like an ocean made of every flavor and shade of blue. It stretched to the horizon and blended with the sky, and Toby stared. Then Katie's stomach finally growled for lunch.

It was proof that only two hours had passed in the real world.

While they ate, Tansy said, "What you're calling a gazebo isn't really a gazebo."

"So, what is it?" Katie asked. "Is it the old front porch?"

"Partly," Tansy said, her claw skewering the last sardine from the tin Katie had gotten her. "We are sitting at the top of an observation tower, high above the old front porch gateway to Stratos." Tansy finished the fish, licking every nook of her paw. "This tower was once the tallest thing around. But time passed, and it was underwater. Then a glacier covered this land. When it receded, it buried the old front porch in rock and sand."

"It's hard to even imagine how old you are," Toby said, thinking about what she'd seen.

"My worshippers have faith, yet here I am in the flesh, and you still struggle to believe."

"That's not it exactly," said Toby. "It was hard to accept, but here we are, science and magic, having lunch with a goddess. It's just that . . . wait, you still have worshippers?"

Tansy hissed. "Rude question to ask a deity. Of course I have worshippers. Though they grow fewer each year." Then Tansy looked down. Her empty sardine tin, and the rest of the trash, was gone. "It appears the old front porch wishes us to keep moving."

Under the blue metal loop and smooth stone dome was a platform suspended high above the gateway. "Congratulations on passing your trials," Tansy said, hopping onto a white stone table at the far end of the platform. "Now all that remains is a leap of faith."

Toby looked down and zoomed in. There were linked rings with writing, gems, and symbols in the floor like the old back door on Nimbus. But there were two differences. The most significant was the size. While the gate on Nimbus could hold several people in the central circle, the old front porch to Stratos was big enough to park tractor-trailer trucks inside its main ring. The other difference was that on Nimbus, the old back door was alive. Symbols moved, the writing glowed, and the gems glittered as the circles slowly turned like watch gears. The Stratos gateway looked like a sketch drawn on the floor with charcoal. It looked dead.

The stone table held a vase filled with fresh flowers, and two rings made of blue metal, each with a glowing white stone. Tansy circled the rings before sitting.

"So, now what?" Toby asked.

Tansy smiled a fang-toothed smile. "Now we jump."

"So, we each take a ring, base jump this platform, and float down?" asked Toby.

"Yes, but I suggest you mind the order," Tansy said. "Ring first, then jump equals good. Jump then ring, bad."

Toby examined the rings, then he put one on. The white stone had something bright spinning inside, and its blue metal band was decorated with waves.

Katie took her ring from the desk and admired it. It seemed familiar. "Alrighty then," she said, slipping it on and walking to the platform's edge. The ring tightened to a perfect fit on her finger.

Tansy was wiggling her haunches and ready to pounce. Katie counted down: "Three, two . . ." They were a long way up. Katie took a deep breath.

". . . one, jump!" They hopped off the platform with Toby right behind.

They fell through a cavern big enough to hold an Amazon warehouse. Sand-diffused light streamed into the cavern, casting dancing speckles over everything, and their fall slowed to a walking pace. An opening in the carved stone ran from halfway up the cavern down to a smooth white floor. It framed the blue view of Lake Michigan, and they slowly fell toward the flat top of a pyramid in the center of the open space that glowed like a winter moon. A silver throne was perched atop a tall spire, overlooking the old front porch. Steps led down two sides of the pyramid. One side led toward the cavern opening, and the other steps led down to the still, grey magic circles that, once activated, would take them to Stratos.

Katie landed on top of the pyramid like an Olympic gymnast, taking a hop, planting her feet, and arching her back with hands in the air to catch Tansy. Toby wasn't so graceful, but he stopped short of falling down the stairs. His ring disappeared with a flash, revealing a blue-ink isosceles triangle over a pattern of waves around his ring finger.

"I got a tattoo," said Toby, surprised and strangely happy about it. "Did you get one too?" Then he noticed. "Why does Katie still have her ring?"

The ring sparkled blue and white on her finger, and Katie realized why it looked familiar. It was one of the rings her grown-up self had worn when she found herself in the mirror.

"Never," said Tansy, "has this trial been passed by creating a life and not taking one. Stratos has marked you as worthy and welcome, but in recognition of her feat, Stratos has also given Katie her blessing. Her ring is like the watch the Professor uses to travel to Nimbus."

"Well, that golem Marv was really something. It looks good on you, Katie." Toby's eyes followed the pyramid steps down to the dull magic portal. Then his eyes met Tansy's. "Can she use that blessing to get those circles going?"

"Not yet," said Tansy. "I must finish waking the old front porch, and she's been asleep a long time." Tansy bolted up the spire to the silver throne they'd seen floating down.

Toby and Katie followed the pyramid steps down to the greyed-out gateway, and through the blue metal trees surrounding the circles. Volleyball-sized gems hung from their branches. Then Tansy began to sing, and one by one, the gems began to glow.

Red energy flowed from the pyramid into the gateway through arteries in the stone. A trilling vibration filled the air. The grey markings in the smooth white floor flickered into color, the symbols came to life, and the linked rings began to turn.

"We should get the Frost mimic ready," Toby shouted over the din. Katie helped him remove the mimic cylinder and gear from his backpack. He'd ported all the biometric data Hugo 117 had collected into a more rugged mimic, and Frost quickly took form: first came his oblong shape, and almost pointed nose, then his hawkish eyes. *His eyes, and the DNA at his mouth and hands, were hard to get right.* When all his physical traits—heartbeat, sweat, weight, and breathing patterns—were right, Frost's overbearing attitude emerged. When Toby couldn't stand the sound of his voice anymore, Frost was perfect. Toby had him dress in the expensive Italian silk suit and shoes the Professor had found for him, and they were ready to go.

They had three hours to get through security, find proof their father was alive, and egress before the mimic's batteries ran out.

When the red veins faded from the white stone, it became ghostly quiet. Toby and Katie left their packs on the pyramid steps, and they followed Tansy to the center of the largest slow-turning circle. Passing into the gateway was like walking into strong wind, but the air in the circle was calm. Toby was sore from the trial and carrying the heavy pack, and he was nervous about going through security, but this was it. *I made him. The mimic will work.*

"The gateway is excited to reconnect to Stratos," Tansy said. "She took almost no convincing."

"Is it fixed now?" asked Toby.

"It is. Want to do the honors, kitten?"

Katie smiled, her ring glowed, and she said, "Activate."

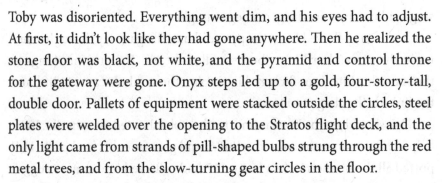

Toby was disoriented. Everything went dim, and his eyes had to adjust. At first, it didn't look like they had gone anywhere. Then he realized the stone floor was black, not white, and the pyramid and control throne for the gateway were gone. Onyx steps led up to a gold, four-story-tall, double door. Pallets of equipment were stacked outside the circles, steel plates were welded over the opening to the Stratos flight deck, and the only light came from strands of pill-shaped bulbs strung through the red metal trees, and from the slow-turning gear circles in the floor.

More importantly, there were no alarms.

They left the circles and climbed the steps. The massive gold doors at the top were covered in a block character language Toby had never seen, and they were still beautiful, despite the thick welding scars that sealed them shut. A hatch big enough to drive a car through had been cut into the door. Next to the hatch was a flashing panel, and above it, a camera hummed as it turned and focused on them. If that wasn't disconcerting enough, when they approached the door, floodlights blinded them.

A girl's voice Toby recognized announced, "Unscheduled transport. Intruders detected. You have sixty seconds to present valid authorization, or the air in this room will be purged."

As the warning counted down in different languages, Toby checked his mimic one last time. Director Frost's sharp features, dark hair artfully combed over his bald spot, and salt-and-pepper grey at his temples were just right. *This is it.* Toby adjusted the mimic's silk pocket square and said, "Looks like you're up, sir." ·

The Frost mimic pushed past Toby. "Just who do you think you're talking to, Ai? We finally get that damn circle working again, and you can't even tell it's me? You're supposed to be the greatest machine intelligence ever created. How can you possibly be this stupid?"

The display panel went black, and the orange outline of a hand appeared. The Frost mimic put his hand on the panel, scowled at the camera, and said, "Override. Alpha one three, director prime seven one."

The hand outline disappeared. "Director override accepted. ID valid. Access granted. Apologies, Director Frost. You are currently scheduled for a budget meeting at the Pentagon."

"We wouldn't be much of a secret organization, that does secret things, if we always followed the schedule, now would we, Ai?"

The floodlights went out.

"Understood, Director. Why do Doctor Cypher's children and their pet accompany you?"

"Their father was our leading expert on this Alt Tech, was he not?"

"Yes, Director."

"Turns out they have skills we couldn't find elsewhere."

"That line of thinking is at odds with your directive to isolate and observe the remaining members of the Cypher family," said Ai.

"Is the main transport circle working now?" Frost said smugly.

"Power appears to be stable. However, tests are required to determine whether the system is fully operational."

"Rescind the Cypher directive and assemble a team. I'm conducting research in the M-Core. I'll escort the Cypher children. So leave me be. I'll call if I need you," Frost said.

"Understood. Conferring with Stratos per The Accords. Stratos grants your guests access. Ai switching to standby mode."

The hatch opened to their collective sigh of relief.

CHAPTER 26

STRATOS

"Well, that was intense," the Professor said, appearing through their glasses, all head bobs and smiles, as the white hatch closed behind Toby and Katie.

"*Now* you show up?" huffed Toby.

"Congratulations on passing your trial, and welcome to Stratos."

They stood on a wide boulevard made of smooth, black stone with their backs to the golden double doors that were built into the face of a cliff. Above them was a crystal dome nestled between the mountain peaks. Like Nimbus, the dome blended into the clouds and sky, only betraying its existence with what looked like the curve of a few chalk marks on the horizon. The boulevard was elevated over the rocky ground, and it split into many paths. Some curved back into the mountains that formed the stern of Stratos, others crossed streams to different gardens, or followed the shore around a wide, still lake that reflected clouds.

"Are you talking to him now?" growled Rachel's voice. "You're talking to them through those glasses, aren't you?"

"Wait. Don't—" The Professor's image froze in front of them.

Then it was replaced by Rachel, still in bandages—and she was pissed. "There you are. What the hell, Toby? I wake up, and you're gone, and you didn't even say goodbye."

"Rachel, I—"

"No. You had your chance. I fought demons for you. Demons, Toby. And you leave without a word."

"I only wanted to protect you, I—"

"Yeah," Rachel said, wincing when she moved. "Great job, Toby. And then you left me behind."

"You know you're being unfair," said the Professor's voice. "Toby didn't summon those demons. You were hurt, and he saved your life. It wasn't anyone's—"

"And what about you, Professor?" Rachel shouted. "How many times have you sent them into danger, while you watched!"

"If there were any other way, I would have spared them this—"

"But you didn't, did you?"

"Rachel, I would do anything to help them."

"Well, we got that in common, don't we?"

"Rachel," Toby said, "I'm—"

"No, Toby. Shut up. You had your chance. I can't stand to look at either of you right now." Then she threw the Professor's glasses, and her image was gone.

Toby was gutted. "So I guess that's it—hey!"

Katie punched him hard in the arm. "Don't be stupid. Give her some time, then remind her why you like her, and make her remember why she likes you. Last night was horrible, Toby."

"Yeah, I know. But you heard her. She said I had my chance."

"And maybe you did blow it. She got hurt bad, but she was *way* more mad you left without saying goodbye. Think about it: she's scared, and she wanted you."

Toby ran his fingers through his hair and let out a moan. Then he punched Katie back in her arm.

"Oww," she said, glaring.

"How'd you get so smart about this stuff?"

"Well, duh," she said, grinning. "I've been a girl my whole life."

The Professor sheepishly reappeared, and they followed him as he caned his way toward the lake where a massive shrub on the shore had been clipped and sculpted into a topiary cat as big as a house. It leaned over the edge of the lake, stretching its paw into the water, and it grew more realistic the closer they got.

Then two enormous, leafy tails slapped down in front of them, blocking the way. Their branches groaned. The cat turned to look at them and frowned.

Tansy trotted past the Frost mimic to meet it.

Toby asked, "Do we fight or run or—"

"No," Tansy replied. "It is simply curious."

The topiary cat creaked as it bent its giant head down to examine them. It narrowed its shining emerald eyes within its boughs, and its whiskers grew toward Tansy.

Toby and Katie stood very still. Tansy raised a foreleg, and the bush cat's tendrils encircled her paw. It sighed like wind in its branches, and its leaves quivered as it purred a pleasant vibration that tickled their insides and made Toby and Katie laugh.

Then, with groaning branches, the topiary cat returned its attention to the lake.

Toby and Katie followed the others, giggling at random things, because everything's silly after a good laugh. Toby smiled. *It feels good to laugh again.* Then his smile faded. *When I get back, I'll make it up to Rachel.* Then he frowned. *I am starting to think like Dad.*

The Professor led them out of the dome to the edge of a rocky outcrop with a view of the island. Foothills bordered the edges of Stratos, and between them forests, fields, and rivers spread all the way down to a mesa at the point of her bow. Toby reckoned Stratos was about five miles wide and nine miles long. Taking it all in as Stratos flew over Lake Michigan, he felt a real sense of awe and accomplishment. *We made it.*

Bird-sized dragons swooped down from the sky, wheeling and whirling around Toby and Katie. Some were red like saffron, others were holly green, and their scales glittered in the sun as they plunged down the cliff and into the valley.

"We call those flocks a storm of dragons," said the Professor. "Large dragons tend to fly solo. Although they do gather at times."

"Whoa," Katie said, watching the little dragons disappear as sparkles in the distance. "Did my mom come here?"

"Yes," said the Professor, nodding vigorously. "In fact, sit by that stone, where the path turns toward the foothills. Now dangle your legs over the side."

"Right here?" asked Katie.

"Perfect," said the Professor. "That spot has the best view of Stratos. It's where your mother liked to eat her lunch."

Watching his little sister sit there teary-eyed, with a smile on her face, made Toby feel closer to Katie and his mom than he had in a very long time.

"I uploaded a map to the memory core," said the Professor. "Find the main terminal—it's the only place you can use that memory stick. Then download Raz's original video and get out as quickly as possible. Ai is thoughtful and brilliant, but she will ruthlessly do her job. Don't get distracted; you won't fool her long. So don't dawdle." The Professor dissolved, and a purple dashed line appeared on the floor, showing them the way.

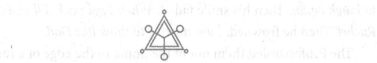

Fast-moving steel escalators and walkways carried them down the length of small mountains, through treetops, behind waterfalls, and past ruins overgrown with vines and flowers.

The Frost mimic led them through security checkpoints and sealed hatches to passages underground.

The Professor whispered, "The M-Core itself is a part of Stratos, but the archive is permitted to use some of its capabilities. Since the government could not control Stratos, it did what governments do. It built infrastructure and fortifications it could control."

They passed through the final security hatch, and it locked behind them. *Up ahead is our evidence.*

Toby was lost in thought when they reached the blue metal bridge that crossed the vast chamber that made up the M-Core.

Katie froze. "Whoooaaa!" she said. "Pretty."

Toby ran into her. "Hey, why'd you—" Then he looked up, and he had to agree.

Walking through the memory core was like flying through fireworks. Long-tailed, every-color comets shot straight up, filling the cavern with streaks of light and exploding starbursts that blossomed and dissolved into polychrome sparks.

The dashed purple line crossed the bridge to the top of a pillar in the middle of the cavern, where an "X" marked the spot.

The M-Core interface was a raised stone platform that looked more like an empty stage than a data store. Computer banks curved around it, and Toby looked from the technicolor stream of lights flying upward like Roman candles, to the hatch they came from, past the computers, to the rock wall anchoring the far side of the bridge over the chasm. *One way in, one way out. If something goes wrong, that's a problem.* He reached for his Bite and Hack bracelets. It comforted him to feel them there.

This is it.

Toby found the main terminal, and the Frost mimic placed his hand on the scanner and inserted the memory stick.

Everything had gone to plan.

Until a girl appeared on the round stone stage in the middle of the M-Core, rubbing her temples and looking annoyed. She was about Katie's age with short, bright red hair tied into pigtails with black ribbons. Her eyes were large and ruby red, and she was wearing a burgundy-plaid middle school uniform, a white blouse, and knee socks. "Greetings again, Director Frost and Cypher children. What do you need?"

The Professor whispered, "Careful. That's Ai."

"That's a pretty jumper," said Katie.

"Thank you. It's good to see you again, Katie Cypher, and it's particularly nice to talk to another girl for a change. The Professor made this dress for me, and I really like it," Ai said, spinning around. "I hope he's well. I haven't seen him in a while."

"If you're finished," snapped the Frost mimic, "why are you here, Ai? What happened to Stratos? She's the core interface."

"She suddenly dropped all her ancillary functions in my lap is what happened," Ai said, looking annoyed again. "And then she left."

"And why is that?"

191

Ai scowled. "She said she was catching up with an old friend."

I guess Tansy meant they were actual friends when she said the gateway at the old front porch longed for Stratos. The Frost mimic paused and looked at Toby. He took a deep breath and nodded.

We can't stop now.

"Very well, since you're here," said the Frost mimic, "display all Cypher shootdown video files and any documents with the keywords *Ashur's Tears.*"

The search results appeared as seven file folders, orbiting Ai.

Toby touched the file "Cypher Shootdown Final Transmission—Raw Video" when it passed in front of him.

"A restricted file has been selected, Director."

"That's fine. Override all file restrictions for this session. Play the video now."

"Understood, Director Frost. Accessing data." Ai stretched like she was reaching for a book on a high shelf, and a glowing blue Roman candle ball with a long bright trail shot down from the ceiling like a meteor. It hit at Ai's feet, and its splash of light was absorbed by the M-Core stone that was Ai's stage. "Playing raw video now."

Ai disappeared and a holographic closeup of Doctor Cypher's face with a bright desert blur behind him appeared. He was unfurling an orange parachute. The wind filled it and carried his still-attached cockpit seat aloft toward a column of smoke in a sandy valley. "That should lure some of them away," he said.

Katie was smiling and squeezing Tansy.

Doctor Cypher walked up to the camera. Toby's heart was pounding, and his mouth went dry. It was Dad. Pale blue eyes, disheveled blond hair, goatee with a touch of grey. *We finally did it.*

"This is Erasmus Cypher. I don't have much time. I was shot down, and they'll be on me soon. Lawrence, this was no random attack. If you get this, trust no one. Someone with Directorate 13 access set me up. They knew exactly where I was and how to take me down. Countermeasures were useless. I'm okay. I have shrapnel in my shoulder, but I ejected in time," Doctor Cypher said as he looked back at the roiling smoke in the valley. "Jet's a complete loss, though. I'm heading northeast to a small oasis. It was the only thing green for miles. I popped my beacon, and I'll try to link up with Search and Rescue there. Hey, Lawrence, you're the only one I can trust with this. Keep an eye on Toby and Katie. Let them know I love them and when I get back, I'll—"

A man in a Minotaur Security desert uniform, wearing a red and white tasseled scarf and wielding a submachine gun, came at their father from the left. "Down on your knees. Now!" he said with a thick Boston accent.

Doctor Cypher knelt, grimacing as he put his arms up.

Another man in the same uniform advanced from the right with a handgun drawn. "Good. Comply, and you live," he said in a Southern drawl. "Prep him for transport."

Four more men with submachine guns converged on Doctor Cypher. They all wore Minotaur Security uniforms. One zip-tied his arms behind him, and another put a cloth sack over his head and pulled him to his feet.

They were leading him away when another voice called out, "What's this?"

The picture swung wildly, and the camera hit the ground.

A boot came at them, and the transmission ended.

Stay calm. Data crawled across the bottom of the video with the mission number, location, and the date/time of the recording. It proved their father was alive after the crash.

Now the Air Force will have to rescue Dad.

Ai returned to the stage, search files still orbiting her, and the Frost mimic said, "Download the file we just viewed."

"Understood, Director. Initiating download. The password is your override code. Time to task completion, three minutes. Do not remove the memory stick prior to complete data transfer."

A yellow circle with a sweep arm like a clock appeared around the memory stick. With every sweep, more segments of the circle filled with green. The indicator read 7 percent.

"Now, display file 'Ashur's Tears—Artifact Survey.'"

A kaleidoscope of comets hit Ai's stage, and papers piled up around her. "History and mission reports are contained in this file."

"Focus on recent expeditions and summarize."

"Of course, Director. Seismic and remote sensing used during oil field exploration detected an anomaly associated with high-value ancient structures."

"This I know," said the Frost mimic. "Refresh my memory about the expedition."

Toby checked the download. Most of the circle was green. They were 89 percent there.

"Dr. Luc Haddad, a talented, young archeologist who had previously recovered Alt Tech for NSA, led the expedition. Per your instructions, dig site security personnel were replaced by specialists from Minotaur."

Ninety-six percent. *This is taking forever.*

"They found an ancient temple," said Ai. "A month later, intact chambers protected by spirit barriers were discovered. However, Dr. Haddad hid this information from us. He claimed the site had been plundered, and he nearly succeeded in ending the expedition."

Katie could feel the tension running through Tansy's body. She went from being fluffy to feeling like metal cable hanging from her neck. As her claws extended, Katie stroked her and whispered, "I know, Tansy. I know. We're almost there. Just a little more."

"We were suspending operations when our team leader discovered Dr. Haddad's deception. Minotaur Security recovered an item matching the description of Ashur's Tears, and the structure and all personnel not under our control were sanitized. However, the Guardian and Dr. Haddad did escape. Dr. Haddad died en route to Baltimore. The temple Guardian, however, remains at large."

The yellow hand finished another sweep. The download was 98 percent complete when a familiar voice interrupted.

Everyone looked from Ai to the voice coming from the computer speakers.

It was Director Frost.

The real Director Frost.

"What do you think you're doing, Ai? I restricted those files. Lock them down, now."

Ai responded. "System lockdown initiated." The yellow sweep arm stopped at 99 percent complete, and the green circle around the memory stick disappeared.

Toby screamed, "No!" and tried to pull the stick from the terminal, but static blanketed the memory core interface, and Toby was thrown to the ground, convulsing like he was hit with a Taser.

The Frost mimic was shouting orders for Ai to stand down.

Toby could barely focus. *We failed.*

He watched the crackling static covering the computers eat away the memory stick. *No.* Then it was gone. *NO!*

No alarms, just two Frosts yelling at each other.

Ai noticed she was biting a fingernail and stopped. "Data secure. Core shields active. Director override access compromised and rescinded. Rejecting the null. Initiating invasive IFF."

Panels opened in the computer bank around Ai's platform, and metal claws whipped out, lifting and immobilizing the Frost mimic.

Toby regained his feet, releasing Bite and Hack. Tansy glowed gold. A dozen long needles on undulating tubes emerged from each claw, like glittering snakes in the multicolored light.

Before they could react, Ai sank the needles deep into the Frost mimic and announced, "Director confirmed via deep-tissue DNA sampling." Then she ripped the Frost mimic apart.

Toby and Tansy cut down the needles and claws, but they couldn't get to Ai.

Toby shook with rage. "Ai, is Frost still there?"

"No. Director Frost is currently undergoing post-confirmation medical treatment."

"Let him know he messed with the wrong family. We will get our father back."

"You will not, Toby Cypher. Life support is set to zero atmosphere. Temperature is set to absolute zero. I'm sorry, Katie Cypher," said Ai. "I would have really liked to have talked some more. Purge complete in sixty seconds."

Tansy shouted, "Run! Follow me," and Toby bolted after her in the direction opposite the security door.

Katie hesitated, scowling at the red-haired girl behind the dancing static. "You know, Ai, the Professor won't like you anymore if you keep doing bad things." Then she ran.

Toby had come back for her and grabbed Katie's hand.

They sprinted after Tansy.

"There's nowhere to run, Katie," Ai said as she watched the Cyphers and what she had determined to be the Guardian. Ai ran every possible scenario. None would allow them to survive.

Ai observed everything. The temperature and pressure drop. The removal of breathable air. The physiological effect it was having on the humans. The flow of data collected and circulated through the M-Core, and her regular duties monitoring and managing over a billion functions for Directorate 13.

She could still hear the real Director Frost cursing her in Washington, D.C. She had removed non-essential samples from all his major organs to confirm his identity, and medics were rushing him to the hospital.

Ai could see Katie's breath becoming labored.

If Katie looked back, she would have seen Ai crying. Katie was the first girl who had ever told Ai she had a pretty dress.

It was the first time Ai ever wanted to be more than her programming. But she could not disobey. They had to be sanitized. All she could do was make it as painless as possible.

"Keep running," Tansy said.

"That's a stone wall," said Toby.

"Run through it," wheezed Katie. "It'll be okay."

Toby's lungs burned, it was so cold. They were close to the wall. *It's like space, without a space suit. Why am I running again?* He couldn't feel his fingers or toes.

Dad says, "Cyphers are smart, Cyphers are strong." It was a stupid thing to remember after just failing his mission. *"Cyphers always find a way."* He was about to die, he would never see his father again, but he could still feel his sister's hand, and he wouldn't give up or let her go.

Ai smiled when she saw Katie disappear through the wall. She had failed to stop them, but Ai was happy Katie got away.

Ai reported their escape and scanned the parts of Stratos she controlled.

Toby opened his eyes. The M-Core and stone wall were gone.

They were in a place like an undersea reef, where he could breathe, and it was warm. It felt like they were on a waterslide, gliding through scenes of Stratos. Only they were going up.

"How?" Toby asked.

"You passed the trials of Stratos and received her blessing," Tansy said, floating to Katie. "That trumps Directorate 13 and any agreement your country may have with this island."

"We ran through a solid rock wall," said Toby.

"You earned the right to travel through Stratos. Do you really think those who built all this needed moving steel steps to get around?"

They appeared in the middle of the turning rings on the black floor of the Stratos gate. The security lights came on, but the magic circle activated, and they were already gone.

Then they were back at the old front porch.

Katie turned to Toby. "What do we do now?"

Toby didn't have a good answer. "We have to keep moving, Katie." He wanted to scream. *One more second, and I would have had it in my hand.* "For now, we run and regroup on Nimbus. We failed, and wasted the one—"

"That's not entirely true," said a voice from behind them. "I've been trying to reach you," said the Professor. "What happened?"

"We can talk about that later," said Toby. "What do you mean, *not entirely true?* We went to Stratos to prove our father's alive." Toby paced and tried to compose himself. "We saw what really happened, but Ai destroyed the evidence, and we'll never get another chance like that again."

"Yes," said the Professor, while his head emphatically shook, *No.*

"Aargh!" Toby screamed. "You're making me crazy. Yes or no?"

"Yes," said the Professor. "You did fail to get evidence, but no, the trip was not a waste."

Toby was grinding his teeth, "You *could* just tell us what you mean!"

The Professor smiled. "You accomplished five things you should be proud of. You got this gate artifact to work reliably. Not even your father pulled that off. You entered Stratos when its security was thought to be unbreachable. You entered the M-Core without authorization, which Directorate 13 believed was impossible, and while you did get caught, you escaped their perfect trap. Based on those deeds alone, I imagine by now they're terrified."

"That's nice of you to say and all, Professor," said Katie, "but we just got our butts kicked, and we're no closer to getting Dad back." Katie looked about to cry.

"You said we accomplished five things, Professor," said Toby. "Those were only four. What's the fifth?"

"Clever boy," said the Professor, nodding in agreement. "While Ai had the Ashur's Tears file open, I found a transfer order from Minotaur Security. It's not the evidence you were looking for, but it does show where your father is.

"What do you say we go get him?"

CHAPTER 27

BONEYARD

Toby and Katie sat on the bottom steps of the white pyramid, in the old front porch. "Your father is being held in *cryostasis*, frozen asleep in a sarcophagus," said the Professor. He was virtually leaning on his umbrella in front of them, and they were trying hard to stay awake—but it had been a long, long day.

Tansy was stretched out on the step above Katie with her forepaws crossed, yawning through the Professor's briefing.

"The sarcophagi are sometimes called *cryotubes*. They were designed so people could sleep without aging, while traveling to other planets. But the spaceships aren't ready, so cryostasis tech is being used to warehouse terrorists in a facility called the Icebox. The Icebox protects several highly classified programs. Your father is being held in the one they call the Meat Locker."

"You should stop there, Professor," said Tansy, arching her back. "They need rest."

Toby and Katie protested, but Tansy chirped like a bird, and the old front porch made the wide pyramid steps soft and warm.

"No fair," Katie said, as they sank into what felt like feather beds.

"Fly into Davis-Monthan Air Force Base, outside Tucson, Arizona, and get to the Icebox complex," the Professor continued after breakfast. "I'm hacking them now. I just sent a prisoner transfer order. With a little luck, you can simply wheel your father out."

"And if we're not lucky?" Toby asked.

"Then we improvise," said the Professor. "But this time they shall be expecting you to pick up your father's sarcophagus as part of a scheduled transfer to another facility. Compared to Stratos, or fighting an army of monkey demons, this will be a cakewalk."

Toby snorted, "Right," as he and Katie donned packs. *We'll see.*

The Professor ended the briefing, "So be careful, and don't die."

He faded from their glasses. Toby made a mental note to speak to the Professor about his pep talks, and Katie activated the gate.

They appeared at the airport, just steps away from their plane. "How'd we get here?" Toby asked, impressed. "When you said it would take us out, I thought maybe the top of Sleeping Bear Dunes."

Katie held up her still-glimmering ring. "VIP access to Stratos and the gate, remember? But this is about the limit of my range. Well, for right—"

Two men in grey camouflage uniforms, wearing chest and shoulder riot armor, stepped out from behind their plane. Expandable steel batons hung from their belts, and the taller of the two held out a Minotaur Security badge as they approached.

"I'm Officer Jessie, this is Officer James. You kids need to come with us."

"Now," said Officer James.

"What's this about?" Toby dropped his pack and walked to Jessie. *If you're going to wear riot gear, you really need to wear the parts that protect your head, groin, and joints.*

"All I know is that it's news about your dad," said Jessie.

"Good news," said James. "So, come along, and—"

Officer Jessie grabbed Toby, and Toby headbutted his face. *The element of surprise.* It was a savage hit to Jessie's nose that made him yelp and stagger backward. In quick succession, Toby's fists hit Jessie in his soft, unprotected spots like hammers.

Toby was angry. About losing the evidence on Stratos. About Frost hurting his family. About Rachel almost dying. Her screams echoed in Toby's head as he attacked. This wasn't a schoolyard fight. It was life or death. He didn't have to hold back.

Toby pulled the steel baton from Jessie's belt as he went down, extended it, and sidestepped James' blow to his head. He didn't even need Bite or Hack. He spun in a roundhouse kick that crumpled James' knee. As James toppled over, Toby's baton strike ended the fight.

They were sprawled out unconscious on the tarmac, but they were still breathing.

Toby checked around. *We got lucky.* No one else was in the area.

"Well, that was one-sided," said Katie. "Aren't all Minotaur mercs ex-Special Forces?"

"They were expecting kids," Toby said, catching his breath. "Not someone Uncle Jack personally trained."

The Professor appeared, clapping his hands. "Good job, Toby. Well done, indeed. Now, before they wake, strip one of those mercenaries. You need a uniform, their badges, and any other useful kit."

"Ugh!" said Toby. "You seriously want me to take the clothes off some unconscious dude?"

"This will not work if you do not look like Minotaur Security."

Toby groaned. He didn't have a better plan. He grudgingly pulled the boots off the smaller of the two mercs. After he changed into their gear, he dragged them under a nearby plane, and Tansy made sure they would stay asleep.

Then Tansy turned her attention to Toby's uniform. "I cannot say it suits you."

"I just stole these clothes. My options were limited."

"One does as one must," Tansy said, turning the mercenaries invisible before circling Toby and laughing. "You look like a little boy wearing his father's uniform." Then suddenly, Tansy jabbed Toby's leg with her claw.

"Hey, watch it. Why'd you do that?"

Tansy sat, smiled at Toby's angry face, and licked the red tip of her claw. "Everything has its price." Then she circled Toby again, and as she did, the cut of his uniform improved, and Toby's sleeves and pant cuffs shrank to where they belonged. His boots fit, and their soles and his shoulder armor thickened. When Tansy stopped circling him, she sat, admiring her work. The uniform changes made Toby look taller and more mature.

"So, you needed power from a drop of my blood as payment to do this?"

"Not this time," Tansy said, swishing her tail. "I simply wished to see the expression on your face when I jabbed you."

Toby pushed up the throttle, charged the plane down the runway, and pulled back gently on the yoke. Toby loved that moment of lift when he left the ground and climbed into the sky. After leveling out, he turned to the Professor, virtually bobbing his head in the copilot seat. "Now that they know we're here, they'll be on us in no time."

The Professor pointed to the little witch above him, spinning and making the cabin smell nice. "I gave it another upgrade. Finding you lot now should be impossible."

As soon as Toby relaxed, his phone rang. It startled everyone, and he glared at the Professor, whose movements ceased. The Professor looked embarrassed, then muttered, "I'll also deactivate all phone tracking after this call."

Toby talked for a bit, then put his thumb over the microphone. "It's Uncle Jack. His mission is taking longer. He wants to know how we're doing and if we need anything."

Katie and the Professor shook their heads no.

Tansy was half asleep, purring in Katie's lap.

"No, Uncle Jack, we're good," said Toby. It was killing him. He wanted to download what they'd been through. What they were still going through. With his help they couldn't lose, but anyone could listen over a cellphone, and they were on the way to get their dad. So, Toby swallowed hard and continued. "Well, as good as can be expected, anyway."

"Sounds like you're in a plane."

"Uh, we are. We're on our way back from the beach. You know, sun, sand, waves."

Uncle Jack sighed. "I get it, okay? But expect a hard talk about you taking the plane when I get back. I'm worried about you guys."

"I'm sorry. We really appreciate everything you're doing for us. We just really needed to get away."

Uncle Jack sighed again. "Chaplin Marsh called me. He said there was an earthquake in Dayton and when he went to check on you, the house was trashed, and you were gone."

Toby gulped. "It was bad. We—"

"What's done is done," growled Jack. "I got you rooms on base. Find Chaplain Marsh as soon as you land. This is important, Toby. What you're doing is dangerous. I need you to promise."

"I promise I'll find Chaplain Marsh when we land in Dayton." *And I will when we get back to Dayton.* Toby felt awful lying to his uncle. It felt like a fist to the gut. *Maybe there is a way to tell him—*

"Good. Now, where are you?"

But that was one thing Toby couldn't say. Minotaur was after them. *It would be easy for them to listen in on this call. They shot down Dad's F-16, and that was a fighter with defenses.* Toby looked back at Katie and made one of the hardest decisions he ever had to make. "You're breaking up, Uncle Jack. We love you."—and Toby ended the call.

From the air, Davis-Monthan AFB looked like a mountain-framed grave-yard made of silver, faded camouflage, and grey painted planes. They haunted the fields and roads scratched into the desert, like ghosts with unfinished business. Thousands of fighters, bombers, and cargo planes waited, and if they didn't get scrapped, they might fly again one day. The Air Force called it the Aerospace Maintenance and Regeneration Group, AMARG, but everyone else called it the Boneyard.

Katie pressed her face against the window. The aircraft arranged on the ground went on for miles. Even Tansy was impressed.

Then the Professor was back. "Toby, I'm in the Icebox system. Looks like no one knows you're there, and security is light. Four guards, and possibly a four-person research team. Follow the procedures I sent. Your credentials are Mitchell Tanner, employee number 43TDA3669.

"Collect your father's sarcophagus. We'll release him from cryostasis in the hangar marked on your map."

"Got it, Professor. Landing on Runway three-zero now."

CHAPTER 28

ICEBOX

"Step one," Toby said, adjusting the shoulder armor over his uniform, "sign in. Pick up a vehicle and the access controller from Base Ops."

Toby took deep breaths as he walked. *I'm Mitchell Tanner, Minotaur Security number 43TDA3669, I am Mitchell Tanner . . .*

Katie and Tansy followed him at a distance, looking concerned.

Base Operations controlled the flying schedule, tracked weather, and helped aircrews get where they needed to go. It was a modest building with a lobby, counter, a few offices in back, and a small waiting area in the front. Toby stepped up to the counter.

The airman on duty wore an olive-green flight suit. She had short dark curls, bright blue almond-shaped eyes, and a bronze complexion. She smiled and said, "Can I help you?"

Then she noticed his uniform. It had been a warm smile. Toby missed it when it was gone.

"Hi, Airman Jones," Toby said, reading her name tag. "This is my first trip to the Boneyard, and I—"

"Stop right there," Airman Jones said, holding up her hand. "Obviously, you're new. We don't talk. Take the key to the vehicle you want off the board. They all have tow hitches. If you are alone, I recommend the car. Sign for it there. Vehicles are round back. Same slot as the number on the key fob."

Then Katie came through the door. "Excuse me, my dad's refueling the plane and said I could wait here. Is this the right place?"

"Sure is," said Airman Jones, smiling again. "Take a seat over there." She pointed to the couches and wall-mounted TV playing the news. "There are water bottles in the cooler. Restroom's around the corner."

"Thanks!" Katie said, rushing off.

Airman Jones turned back to Toby and extinguished her smile. "First thing, Mister Minotaur Man. This is AMARG, not a Boneyard."

"Sorry," said Toby, "I thought we weren't supposed to talk?" He sighed. "Look, I didn't know. Boneyard just sounds bad. AMARG's the sound you make when you throw up."

"That's funny," Airman Jones said, smiling reluctantly. "Uncalled for, but funny. I think so, too, but the brass loses it when anyone says Boneyard."

"I won't say it again," Toby said, holding up his hands.

"Okay then, Minotaur Man. We close promptly at 1700. If you're late, park the car where you found it and drop the key through that slot in the door."

"Thanks," Toby said, swinging the key on his finger and turning to leave.

"Hey. Don't forget the clicker," Airman Jones said, pointing to the old garage door opener on the shelf below the keys. "You'll need it."

Toby was a little embarrassed. "Thanks again."

"Remember: always stop behind the red line, and you'll be fine."

It was still morning, and it was already hot. Toby leaned on the building, in the shade of the alley, and asked the Professor, "If I record a video with my glasses, can you get it to Rachel?"

"Send it yourself. After she broke my pair, we both felt bad, so I gave her glasses of her own."

Toby tried to connect to Rachel, but she didn't pick up. So, he set his glasses on a crate, said, "Record," and began: "Rachel, I'm sorry. The other night was horrible, and you got hurt. And I'm so sorry I didn't say goodbye. I wanted to be there when you woke up. I wanted to stay, but I have to find my dad. I'm scared too. All you wanted to do was give us a nice meal, and you don't deserve any of this. You were brave, and you ruined a nice dress bandaging my leg. I miss you. I want this to be over, and when it is—if you want to—I'd like to see you again." Toby sent the video and groaned. *I hope it's not over.*

Katie left Base Ops, and they walked around the building to what looked like a used car lot. No vehicle was newer than 1972. Toby's ride was a banged-up '71 Chrysler 300 four-door, resprayed dark Air Force blue with a block of yellow *For Official Use Only* text and serial numbers stenciled on the front doors. The car was sleek in its own way, with a long hood and front lights hidden behind a black grille. A chrome roof bar supported oversized red-and-blue turret lights that made it look like a patrol car from an old black-and-white police movie.

Tansy was sitting on the hood.

Katie looked from the car to Toby. "You sure you can drive this thing?"

Toby gave her a look of disbelief. "I illegally flew a plane halfway across the country, broke into a secret base, tried to steal classified data, and, oh yeah, beat up two government dudes and left one half naked. Driving without a license? No problem."

Katie smiled. "I meant, can you reach the pedals?"

"I think we're lost," Toby said, driving around a cluster of B-52 bombers and passing between rows of six-story-tall, green and grey C-5 Galaxies, each with a wingspan wider than a soccer field.

"Did you follow the map I gave you?" snapped the Professor.

"Yes."

"Did you find the C-5 transport aircraft in Area 18?"

"There are, like, fifty C-5s here. The procedure just says stop where indicated and employ the device. I hope that means something to you."

"Are you stopped where indicated?" asked the Professor.

"The 'X' covers a whole lot," said Toby looking at the map through his glasses.

"Did you zoom in?"

"Did I . . . disregard. I see it."

The old Chrysler kicked up clouds of dust as Toby followed the dashed line superimposed on the desert road to a cargo aircraft a few miles away. As they drove, the Professor carried on like a tour guide: "The C-5 Galaxy transport is the second-largest aircraft ever made. Russia holds the record for largest, but if you need six Apache helicopters halfway around the world, or to move tanks, or drop more than seventy combat troops and their gear, then the Galaxy's your girl. We even use them to move stealth aircraft, and once we launched a nuclear missile from the back of one, in-flight. Just to see if we—"

"Professor, we're here," said Toby as he slowly passed under the massive T-shaped tail of the aircraft, to where "X" marked the spot. Big aircraft surrounded them. Toby stopped behind a row of dusty red bricks cemented in the ground.

The only sound was the rumble of the Chrysler's big V-8 engine.

Toby put the car in park and looked around. *Great. Secret Icebox complex. There's nothing here except the butt end of a big jet.*

"Next step," said Toby, looking at the old black garage door opener, "Employ the device." He pointed the opener at the plane and activated the remote.

There was a distinct *click*, but nothing happened. After a pause with still nothing happening, Toby moved the clicker around, pointed at different things, and clicked it about thirty more times.

Every time he pressed it, a small red light came on, but that was it.

"Well, this was a waste," said Toby.

"Are you sure you're doing it right?" asked Katie.

"Point and click. Not a lot to screw up."

"Maybe there's some trick they teach at mercenary school," Katie said looking around.

Toby turned the garage door opener over in his hands a few times. The top of the back was worn and scratched and made from a different material than the rest of the remote.

The metal clip slid back when he pushed it and locked with a *snick*, then it slowly returned to its original position. "Professor?"

"Yes, Toby."

"I'm in the Minotaur system, right?"

"You are. Did you figure something out?"

"I did," Toby said, sliding the remote on the sun visor, and pushing the flat black part forward with his thumb until it locked in place. When he pulled away his hand, a blue thumbprint lingered on the garage door opener. When it slid back to its original position, the back of the clicker opened to reveal a card reader. Toby swiped his Minotaur badge, and the light on the remote turned green.

This time, when he clicked the clicker, orange lights strobed in the ground, there was a whine of old hydraulics, and a top-to-bottom vertical seam appeared in the back of the aircraft. Two aluminum rectangles that made up most of the rear of the C-5 slid apart to reveal the cavernous inside of the cargo plane. As the doors opened, a yellow-and-black ramp unfolded and clanged when it hit the ground.

Inside, the jet was mottled green like the skin of an old lime.

The orange strobes went out, and white lights lit their path.

"Whoa," said Katie. "That's something you don't see every day."

Toby agreed. "But I'm not moving this car another inch until you two disappear."

Tansy nodded, chattered her teeth, and mewed. There was a flash of golden light, and Katie and Tansy blurred. When they were invisible, Toby put the car in drive, gave it a little gas, and they crept up the ramp and into the giant plane.

Toby stopped at the red line painted on the jet's metal deck, exited the Chrysler, and held the door open until he felt Katie and Tansy go by.

Lines of white laser light filled the entire cargo bay. They passed through Toby and the car. When the scan ended, the cargo doors closed

209

with a moan and a sound like rattling chains in the darkness. Floor lights lit up in sequence, and Toby followed them to a control panel.

The panel housed a badge reader, palm scanner, and a large lever that glowed red. Next to it, a big sign read: *No Smoking.* Under it in smaller print, another sign read: *Use of Deadly Force is Authorized.*

A round metal plate with a locking ring was built into the bottom of the aircraft. It was three Chryslers wide and took up all the remaining floor space. Toby slid his badge into the reader, placed his palm on the scanner, and said, "This better work."

Gatling guns dropped from points in the ceiling, and their barrels spun up. Red lasers targeted Toby, and a male voice programmed for intimidation barked out, "You have requested access to a National Security Area. You have thirty seconds to authenticate, or deadly force will be applied."

"No pressure," muttered Toby. Then he noticed the red dots clustered on his crotch. "Now that's just rude."

"You have twenty seconds to authenticate or—"

"Authenticate: 43TDA3669, Mitchell Tanner," said Toby.

"Authentication accepted." The warning lights went out. "Access granted." The guns withdrew. The voice sounded disappointed. "Welcome back, Mitchell Tanner. Have a nice day."

The lever glowed green, and Toby pulled it.

Locks around the metal plate in the floor disengaged, a column rose into the aircraft, and a wide elevator door opened with a pleasant *ding.*

He stepped in, Katie and Tansy brushed past him, and Toby pushed the button labeled *down.*

CHAPTER 29

MEAT LOCKER

Tinny instrumental versions of 1980s hits played as they rapidly descended.

"Hey, this was on Dad's phone," said invisible Katie. "It's called 'Hungry Like the Wolf.' It's old-timey music from a group called Duran Duran."

"That's redundant," said invisible Tansy.

"Right? They're named after the bad guy in some movie called *Barbarella*."

"Was the movie any good?" said Tansy.

"Don't know. Let's watch it when we get home, wherever that winds up being."

"Can you guys focus?" Toby said, hand in front of his mouth, hoping the cameras weren't also listening, "We're breaking in. Stop playing around."

"Really, Toby?" He couldn't see Katie but knew from her tone she was scowling. "It's been two nonstop weeks of insane. You deal with crazy your way, I'll deal with—"

Ding. The elevator came to a stop. There was no indicator to show how deep underground they were. The same intimidating voice that had threatened Toby's crotch announced, "You have reached the Icebox complex. Comply with all instructions. Quarantine protocols are strictly enforced. *De omnibus dubitandum.*"

The Professor whispered in their ears, "That last bit of Latin is appropriate: 'be suspicious of everything.'"

The doors opened into what looked like a large hospital lobby with a security room and long, wide hallways. What wasn't painted white was covered in cheerful Santa Fe-patterned tiles. But there were also things a hospital wouldn't have.

A pair of miniguns were trained on Toby. He stepped out with his hands held high, calling, "Hello?" and they tracked him as he walked, but no one was there. Toby passed an M-777 howitzer aimed at a wall, and he shuddered. *Why,* he wondered, crossing the lobby's expanse, *would they need an artillery piece big enough to destroy tanks fifteen miles away, inside a building?*

Life-sized photos of arctic scenes, icebergs, and winter wonderlands lined the walls. The security room was enclosed in bulletproof glass, and its entire back wall was covered in monitors. Except for the elevator feed, they were all static.

Toby put his arms down, calling out, "Mitchell Tanner. Here to pick up a package," but there was no reply. He could see two empty guard desks through the glass. One desk had a holiday theme with a twinkling, light-covered Christmas cactus, an electric menorah, a carved wood Kwanzaa candle holder, and a cup of steaming hot tea that looked just poured. The other desk was stark and utilitarian, with one pen perfectly centered on the desk. *I wonder if those guards are best friends or hate each other?* Ice floated in a glass of soda on the spartan desk, but the door into the security room was locked.

"Where are the guards?" said Katie.

"Appears we just missed them," said Tansy.

"This isn't right, Professor," said Toby. "Something happened—can you figure out what?"

"On it."

"Guys," said Toby. "Stay unseen. Let's look around before we head to the Meat Locker."

"Aye, aye," said Katie.

Three hallways led away from the lobby, in three different directions, and they were all sealed off by massive steel doors. Signs posted above their respective doors read *Deep Freeze–Long-Term Storage, Meat Locker–Short Term Storage,* and *Stasis Experimentation.*

Scanning with their glasses also revealed a fourth door—a nuclear blast door that used Alt-Tech weaker than Tansy's invisibility to hide it. That was where the howitzer was aimed.

Its virtual sign read *Ice Age–Biosafety Level-5 (BSL-5) Drexler-Fortress Vault,* and all the warnings were in bold print. A few jumped out: *ALL Personnel, Cargo, and Equipment Proceeding Beyond This Point are Subject to 2-WEEK (Inbound) AND 2-WEEK (Outbound) Quarantine. Individuals are responsible for hand-carrying a 45-DAY supply of any medication.* And, ominously, *NO Individual is authorized to proceed without a signed, next-of-kin notification form.*

It felt like something big was pacing just beyond the secret door. Toby touched It, and the lights flickered. When he pulled back his hand, he was covered in cold sweat like he just woke from a nightmare. "What was that?"

"Something ancient slumbers there," said Tansy. "It's powerful and perilous, but for now, it sleeps and dreams. I strongly recommend we don't wake it."

As everyone backed away from the hidden door, the Professor made contact. "You were right, Toby. Something did happen, but all the surveillance data is gone."

"Aborting," Toby said, banging the elevator call button. But the doors didn't open. The elevator went up, and its controls went dark.

"Toby, we're so close," said Katie. "Dad's on the other side of that Meat Locker door."

"I know, and I hate it, but we're leaving. Professor, can you bring the elevator back?"

"No, Toby. The power was physically cut. I can't restore it remotely."

"Where can we fix it?"

"There's a backup power relay in the Meat Locker," said the Professor. "Seventy yards in, on the left wall. I marked it on your display."

Toby realized he was grinding his teeth. "And this is the only way out?"

"Yes."

"Can we restore elevator power from one of the other vaults?"

"No."

"You're just full of good news," Toby said, walking to the Meat Locker door. "Katie, Tansy, stay hidden as long as you can. We can't run, so let's show 'em we have a few surprises of our own."

Toby pressed his palm against the Meat Locker access panel, hit *open*, and the thick metal door slid up. "Let's go get Dad."

The corridor opened into a huge, round room. It was dim beyond the lights embedded in the perimeter wall, and they moved cautiously toward a large, brightly lit structure centered in the room. The Meat Locker was chilly, but not see-your-breath cold. There was a distant click and snap of circuits opening and closing, and the occasional hiss of gas.

Toby glanced at the schematics the Professor had sent: the Meat Locker was two round rooms labeled Meat Locker One and Two, connected by a passage that made it look like a dumbbell as long as a football field.

Meat Locker's a prison. Prisons have guards, but no one's here.

Toby's dread increased with every step. *But each step brings us closer to Dad.* They reached the massive structure in the bright middle of the room. It was a ring within a ring. An outer ring that looked like a circle of fat bronze, three-story tall D-cell batteries, surrounding an inner ring of skinny green, five-story tall AAs.

"Kinda looks like Stonehenge," said Katie. A sign where they entered the structure read: *Meat Locker One.*

"Fan out," Toby said, transforming Bite and Hack back into long, amber kukri knives, burning with blue fire. "They will attack. So be ready."

Inside the rings, cryostasis sarcophagi were arranged in concentric circles. The sarcophagi were oval-shaped, crimson metal tubes set upright and plugged into the tile floor. They were ten feet tall and four feet wide, and the top third of each sarcophagus was made of curved glass. Lights illuminated the sleeping face of each person imprisoned inside. Health and status data crawled across the glass. Each occupant's name was displayed over the date they were born and the date they were placed in stasis, like the inscription on a tombstone.

Toby scanned the stasis tubes. The people in cryogenic sleep had been stored there for years. There were hundreds of them, but none of them was Dad.

Somewhere ahead in a red tube, Dad's frozen like this. Toby's regret and anger surged, and he adjusted his grip on Bite and Hack. *The ones who took Dad away are up ahead waiting to attack.* Knowing this did not take away his fear and uncertainty. Toby grinned anyway. *Hopefully, Frost is there for payback.*

They reached the narrow passage connecting the two halves of the facility. The dashed line superimposed on the floor showed the power relay ahead and to the left of Meat Locker Two.

"Tansy, scout ahead," said Toby. "That's where it'll happen." A growling breeze blew past him.

When Tansy returned, she climbed Toby and whispered in his ear, "Many dozens of demon snakes lie in wait. They hang from the crane rails in the ceiling. Some are bigger than you, most are smaller, but there are many."

"Dozens, not hundreds?"

"Correct, but I could only survey the force before us. 'Tis likely more wait hidden."

"You wouldn't be able to magic up some venom resistance by any chance?" asked Toby.

"Not exactly."

"Yeah, that would have been too helpful. Wait, what?"

Tansy laughed. "For a short while, I can make you and Katie immune to toxins."

Toby provoked the snake demons.

He ran into Meat Locker Two, under where they hung lying in wait, screaming and yelling like an idiot.

When they fell on him, Tansy became visible as a golden bolt of lightning, and cut most of them down. The survivors hit the ground with a *splat*, like a monstrous pile of spaghetti. The snake demons had long thick purple-and-black bodies, sideways mouths that opened and closed like jagged zippers, and rows of fiery red eyes inside hoods like black spiderwebs. They moved fast.

Toby spun and slashed and turned as the snakes struck, and he hacked his way through them. The smaller demons turned to sand when Toby absorbed their life force. The bigger ones didn't die so easily. They struck hard, and their curved rows of teeth sank into him a dozen fangs at a time. Bite and Hack were getting better at healing him, but it didn't stop the pain as Toby staggered forward, cutting them down.

Toby was nearly through the ambush when four demons, a lot bigger than him, struck all at once.

He decapitated one with Hack and gutted another with Bite, but one coiled around him and squeezed. Toby cried out, and the other demon reared back to strike. Its mouth dripped long strings of venom, but Toby was caught, and he could only watch the demon's mouth, as big as a recliner, widen over him.

Tansy raced to Toby as a dozen curved dagger teeth came for his head.

The demon shrieked and shook. Then it slowed, and its fangs came to a drooling rest against Toby's cheek. It was dead.

Katie's spear had skewered the demon and was poking out the back of its head. When she appeared proudly beside him, Toby wanted to say thanks, but a demon was squeezing the life from him, until Tansy turned the monster snake to ash.

Toby lunged at the last giant snake and chopped off its head. But its body stood wriggling. Then the headless snake popped like an evil piñata.

Hundreds of finger-thick vipers exploded from the demon's remains, hitting everyone like darts. They barely hurt, and were easy to kill, but the tiny snakes hung off them like tassels.

Katie spun, yelling, "Get them off, get them off!"

After Toby picked the last one off her, she screamed, unleashing gouts of white fire at the demons like a firehose.

Her flames passed through Toby and Tansy like a warm wind, but they burned away the rest of the still-moving demons. She was panting when she finished.

"I don't know what that was, but next time, lead with that!"

She was still weirded out, but she smiled at Toby.

Bite and Hack were feeding Toby energy and closing his wounds. Katie's skin was covered in red polka dot patterns from where the small snakes had attached themselves and left tiny holes that made parts of her cutoff jeans and embroidered yellow peasant top look like Swiss cheese.

We did it. We beat the ambush.

But Toby couldn't shake the feeling they were being watched.

The fight had taken them through the second metal Stonehenge, and it took a moment to sink in. "Over there!" Toby pointed. *Erasmus Cypher* was written in white digital letters on the crimson sarcophagus.

Katie shouted, "Dad!"

CHAPTER 30

BETRAYAL

Katie and Tansy took two steps toward Dad's sarcophagus and collapsed.

"What's the matter?" Toby shouted, running to his sister.

"Toby," said Katie, "I don't feel so good."

"Thought we were immune to toxins?" Toby snapped at Tansy as he checked Katie. She was pale and sweating and now unconscious.

"We are. This is something else." Tansy struggled to reach Katie, and Toby picked her up. "It's a curse. It destroys the magic inside you."

"I feel fine."

"Rocks have more magic than you," Tansy said, shivering in his arms. "For Katie and me, not generating magic is worse than any seasickness you can imagine."

"Will she be all right? What do I do?"

"With time. She will be fine. This will pass." Convulsions wracked Tansy's body. "Be vigilant, Toby. This was no accident."

Suddenly, the shadows moved like living plastic and grabbed them. Their weapons and glasses were slapped aside, and Toby, Tansy, and Katie were wrapped in ribbons of cold shadow. They looked like black mummies, and only their eyes showed. Toby searched the room as the shadows pulled him to his knees.

Someone was clapping.

Horrific jellyfish grew visible above them. They filled the air like malevolent clouds of fluttering slime, each with a single red ogling eye. Their long thin tentacles dragged the ground, and every shadow they touched, they controlled.

"Bravo, Toby Cypher. Magnificent. Y'all put up one hell of a fight." It was the man with the Southern accent from Dad's video. He stopped in front of Toby, gestured, and a six-person Minotaur Security team surrounded them. "We have not been formally introduced. My name is Dunbar."

Toby struggled against his bindings. Katie was beside him, wrapped like a spider-caught fly, but her breathing was steady, and her eyes moved under her lids like she was dreaming.

"Area secure, sir," said one of the mercs.

Dunbar had his arms behind his back like he was standing at parade rest. He bent down until his bottle green eyes and bushy brown beard were in Toby's face, and he talked with the stench of chewing-tobacco breath. "What's the matter, Toby? Cat got your tongue? Let me help you with that." He smiled a brown-tooth smile, snapped his fingers, and another Minotaur merc handed him a small cage made of greenish-gold wire.

Dunbar stepped back from Toby and pointed to the biggest demon bobbing in the air, focused on what he needed, and said, "It puts the cat in the cage and lets the boy speak."

Strings of shadow loosened and whipped around Toby's arms, prying them apart. Other shadows took Tansy, opened the cage, and squeezed her inside like a letter being stuffed into an envelope. Dunbar locked the cage when the shadows withdrew. Warding symbols and words of power arranged in patterns on the greenish metal flickered. When the seal was complete, the inscriptions and Dunbar's eyes briefly glowed red, and the shadows around Toby's head melted away.

Dunbar wrapped his arms around the cage and shook it every time Tansy tried to get back on her feet. "I had this metal imbued with the same imprecation currently ravaging your psyche," he said with a shake. "Your body won't recharge in there, and in your current state, you can't break free."

Tansy felt around. She could not break free, and she couldn't regenerate her magic. It was a well-made cage that did what it was designed to do. That's why it had handles mounted eight inches away from the metal mesh. The crate was made of thick, woven wire, but there were gaps where the magic symbols had been hammered into the metal.

Tansy lunged with all her strength against the side of the crate. She couldn't cut through the wire or break the magical field, but it was enough to let her drive more than an inch of three of her claws through the gaps and deep into Dunbar's right arm.

Tansy tore what she could. Her paw came back red and wet, and a small spray of his blood sizzled as it blackened the warding symbols.

Dunbar cursed and dropped the cage.

"Oh, my," Tansy said, licking her claws. "Does it hurt?"

Dunbar kicked the cage, and the medic from his security team stepped forward, quickly gluing his gashes closed and bandaging his wound.

"Laugh while you can. Tomorrow, you get declawed and spayed."

"Let me repay you for the meal with some advice," said Tansy. "Release us now, or you will die a painful, inhuman death."

"Says the Guardian who had one job and failed," drawled Dunbar. "You lost the relic. Your precious magic is gone. You're locked in a cage, and you still think you can threaten me?"

"More prophesy than threat," said Tansy.

"I like that. When I break you, I'll put that on your tiny gravestone."

"What do you plan to do with us?" snarled Toby.

"Nice of you to join in. You've been a busy boy," Dunbar said, tightening Toby's shadow bonds until his discomfort became pain. "Let's get to know each other a little better."

Katie stood next to her shadow-bound body in a place that was similar, yet different from where she had been a moment before. Instead of standing among rings of metal columns and stasis tubes arranged in the Meat Locker, Katie stood under a charcoal sky, surrounded by big, red balloons that were chained to the ground, each with a prisoner inside. Katie saw their dreams when she touched the balloons. She felt their hopelessness and loneliness and fear.

Katie knew the balloons were cryostasis sarcophagi, and she was still on the floor in the Meat Locker, but it felt too real. Some of their dreams frightened her, and she didn't touch another balloon until she found her father. She hesitated, then reached out to him. He was reliving their childhood, holding Toby's hand, waiting for the bus to arrive on his first day of school. "It'll be fine," he said. "Everyone's good at something, Toby. You'll figure it out, and when you do, you'll be great." Then he was teaching Toby chess, and he looked so proud the first time Toby beat him. Katie saw herself with her dad, and she said the words with him. He was running beside her as she was learning to ride a bike. "You've got it!" Dad shouted. "Pedal. You can do it. Great job! You're doing it by yourself. Katie, you're riding your bike! Pumpkin, it's all you."

Katie didn't want to leave him, but knew she had to and turned away.

Then a voice called her name. She could feel the power in his words. It wasn't just her name; it was an invitation.

Katie RSVP'd *yes*, and she was pulled away to somewhere else. It was the same sensation as when she was little, laughing as her father pulled her through the pool. Then there was the feeling of being picked up and thrown into the air. When she splashed down, the water was gone. She was standing on a snow-covered hill in the middle of a blizzard.

It was cold, but it didn't bother her. She had learned from Tansy how to stay warm. Katie followed a glow up to the hilltop and stepped out of the blizzard into the eye of the storm.

The stars were bright, and there was a table set for two with a silver candelabra and five burning candles. In front of one chair was a cup of steaming tea and a plate overflowing with bright-colored French macarons.

Katie sat there.

The cup was warm in her hands, and the smell of baked sugar and scents of fruit and chocolate made her mouth water.

"Thanks for inviting me," Katie said to the empty chair. "Everything is lovely. I don't mind starting, but it's rude to keep a girl waiting, especially when you asked me here."

And then, he was there. One moment Katie stared at the empty chair, and the next, a dark-haired boy with a strong jaw was sitting across from her, smiling. It was a sad-looking smile, if she had to be honest. More like a scowl he was trying hard to correct. He had dark purple eyes and a piercing gaze. She figured if he was in high school, he was a freshman, but she knew he was older than that. Purple eyes were not his most unusual feature. He had silvery white wings he wrapped around himself like a blanket as he leaned back in his chair.

Katie felt power radiate from him, and staring at him too long was like staring at the sun. He wasn't *Seventeen Magazine* celeb gorgeous, but he was Labrador-puppy-dog cute. He was an ancient being, earnestly trying to make an Ohio girl feel welcome. Katie was worried about her dad and brother and Tansy, but she found his gesture endearing.

"Welcome, Kathryn Anne Cypher," the boy said in a soft, clear voice. "My name is Fan."

"Hi, Fan," she said, reaching for a lemon-yellow macaroon. "Call me Katie. You were what we felt moving behind that hidden door when we first got here, weren't you?"

"That is also what I am," said Fan. "Does that part of me frighten you, Katie? It should. I watch and judge while I wait, but you can rest easy. While you are here, you are safe."

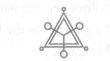

Dunbar tightened his fist, and the shadow bonds around Toby tightened. "Who has been helping you?"

Toby's arms were pulled just short of being ripped from their sockets. He could not feel his knives through the shadows, and he couldn't get free. He stared at his dad's sleeping face. *We were so close.*

Dunbar relaxed his fist, and the pain eased.

"I'll ask you again. What do you know about the Guardian and Ashur's Tears?"

Toby mumbled, "Professor, you seein' this?" But then he remembered his connection had turned to static when the shadows touched his glasses, and now, they were useless on the floor.

The room rippled. Toby had already passed out once from the pain, and he was sure he was hallucinating. Then there was a flash, and Uncle Jack was walking toward them while the world flickered behind him. Toby blinked to clear his eyes, but his uncle was still there. Desert camouflage uniform, a green-and-black checked scarf loosely tied around his neck. Weapon ready. Brush-cut blond hair and, as he got closer, Toby could make out his narrowed blue eyes.

When his uncle spoke, Toby knew he was real. "The hell is going on here?"

Toby shouted. "Uncle Jack! Frost and Dunbar have Ashur's Tears. They captured Dad."

Uncle Jack approached, sidearm drawn, and came up behind Dunbar. He was angry and closed in jaguar-fast before Dunbar could turn around.

Toby locked eyes with his uncle.

It is him.

Uncle Jack shook his head, sadly. "You lied to me, Toby. You promised you'd go back to the base where you would have been safe. Now here we are." Then he snarled at Dunbar, "Why are they still alive?"

No!

Uncle Jack leveled his gun at Toby. His weapon was an old Model 1911 Colt .45 pistol. A jagged blade protruded from under its barrel. The metal was black as obsidian, and the weapon glowed red in places like its core was fresh from a forge.

Toby's heart pounded, and he shook his head *no*. He struggled against the shadow bonds, but his body was fixed in place. He glanced at Tansy in the cage; then he focused on Jack's pistol.

Its jagged blade vibrated. Its black metal pulsed with fire. It howled, and Toby knew he was looking at Ashur's Tears, the relic Jack took from Tansy and made a weapon of his will.

Toby felt Ashur's Tears staring back at him.

Uncle Jack, who was always there for us, who taught us to fight. The uncle we love. How?

"Why?" Toby groaned. "Why?" he cried. "You took Dad. You tried to kill us. It was you."

"Pointless to continue," Jack said, moving his finger to the trigger.

That was when Katie woke up.

CHAPTER 31

DEMON LORD

Katie woke blushing, but no one noticed except Tansy. Everyone else was blinded by her radiance, and the shadows binding her melted away. There were things she could not recall from her dream. Parts were still foggy, but she remembered a boy, and she was happy.

Demons filled the air around her, and they were entwined with every tint of darkness in the chamber. Katie stood and took hold of the shadow strands that remained. She twisted them together and swung the jellyfish demons through the air like kites on strings.

Katie had made a contract with the boy in her dream. She gave him something important. Something she didn't want to trade away, but now she could help them, and Katie remembered, *This is what I chose to do*. She wore a yellow diamond pendant that pulsed with light, like a living heart set in golden flames. It hung from her neck by a chain of stars. It was proof of their contract.

"Everything will be all right," Katie said, releasing her light. "Now, close your eyes."

Katie burned through the shadows still binding Toby and bathed them in a bubble of sunshine. The tendrils of shadow she held in her hands ignited like a bundle of fuses. Each shadow fuse sputtered, then raced back to its fluttering demon. Each demon's eye went wide as it tried to flee, but it was too late.

As Katie's light entered the demons, she said, "O'ra Akal," meaning *Light, devour them*, and the demons burned from the inside, like floating paper lanterns.

She whispered, "Phanuel Eloheem," meaning *Sacred light*, and the fire enveloped them.

When Katie said, "A'meyhn"—*So be it*—the fireballs the demons had become exploded. The blasts knocked Jack, Dunbar, and the mercenaries back, Tansy's cage skittered across the floor, and Toby scrambled to his feet in the muzzle flash of submachine guns.

A hail of bullets assaulted Toby and Katie. They stood in the open, in a patch of sunshine with no chance to survive, but each shot vaporized as a black puff. Even the bullets Uncle Jack fired from Ashur's Tears that hit like a sledgehammer could not penetrate Katie's bubble of light.

They fired in bursts and emptied their magazines until Jack called, "Cease fire."

Fan had shown Katie her uncle's betrayal, but seeing him do it hurt so much more.

There were brass casings everywhere. Lead slag was hardening around them on the tile floor, just beyond her barrier.

Jack lunged, stabbing Katie's patch of light with the extended blade of Ashur's Tears. It stopped like it hit a wall, and he grimaced.

Dunbar gingerly picked up Tansy's cage by the handles and stood at the edge of the circle of light tapping it with his foot; then he shrugged at Jack. Katie was scared and angry, and it broke her heart. Katie loved her uncle more than chocolate. *But he tried to kill us, and he doesn't care. Dad's frozen right there, Toby's hurt, and Tansy's—*

Somehow Tansy caught her eye from the cage. Tansy flicked her ears, then smiled and extended three claws, and Katie knew. Tansy had a plan.

She wiped her tears on her sleeve, noticed the holes in it, and frowned. *I liked this blouse.* "Toby, we'll be okay. I just need to rest before we go." Katie sat on the floor, closed her eyes, and focused on her barrier.

Toby had a million questions, but Jack was close. So, he picked up his glasses and recalled Bite and Hack to his hands.

As Uncle Jack tested the barrier, he laughed. "You really thought Frost was smart enough to pull all this off?"

"We followed the trail of demons you summoned back to his office," said Toby.

"Well, I did need access as well as a few artifacts that aren't supposed to exist. Frost was a useful fool. All he wants is money and a certain lifestyle. He was never worthy of wielding Ashur's Tears. I thought you'd have figured that out."

"You sent demons to kill us," Toby said, getting angrier.

"Oh, Toby, I did no such thing." Then Jack slashed at the wall of light, but his blade bounced off with a sound like a plucked guitar string. "You should have stayed at the house, like you said you would. I made sure it was safe there. I wanted to keep you out of this, and if you'd just left things alone, none of that would have happened."

"You're blaming me?" yelled Toby.

"You interfered with a plan in motion. You must have seen the danger in getting involved, but you stuck your arm in a wood chipper anyway. Not your best call. You're just kids. You really expected to just waltz in here and take back your dad? That Guardian played you."

Sparks streamed off Ashur's Tears as Jack dragged the relic against the light barrier while he walked and talked. He stopped in front of Katie. "Not bad, sugar plum."

Katie opened one eye. Tansy was smiling in her cage on the other side of the light, with two claws showing. Then Katie opened her other eye and frowned at her uncle. "Leave me alone. I hate you. You're not the man I thought you were."

"Well, you're right about that. I'm so much more."

"No, you're not, and you can't break my barrier."

"Let's see about that, pumpkin," Jack said as he took a few more swipes, then fired shots at Toby and Katie. The rounds thundered, hit the patch of light, and disintegrated into puffs of smoke and dripping slag.

"Seems you're right about the barrier, Katie. But, sweetie, how long can you keep this up? You're still a growing girl, your power is finite, and your sphere is shrinking. It's already collapsed a foot. You'll be out of juice in less than an hour."

"Why, Uncle Jack?" asked Toby.

"Well, Tobias, since we're gonna be here for a bit, I'll let you in on a secret," Jack said, smiling. "I've spent my entire life treating the symptoms of diseased societies. Now I have the cure."

"But you protect people."

"I've conducted hundreds of high-stake missions, but in the end, they were all just triage, and the disease has spread deeper than you can imagine. Corruption, war, famine, inequity, envy, and blame. People trade truth for convenience. They only hear what they want, and mob outrage is the new religion. This world needs order, and the only way to save it from itself is to take control. I will master Ashur's Tears, and with it, remake the world."

"You're using a demon army to become a dictator," said Toby.

"For only as long as they're needed."

"You were my hero. I idolized you."

"That's the problem with heroes and worshiping idols, Toby. They're never quite what we want them to be. But I should be thanking you. If you didn't provoke your father, he'd have never left his fortress of a lab to investigate Ashur's Tears—and I wouldn't have caught him off guard. You were brilliant. Props to the rebel without a clue."

Toby fell to his knees, crushed.

Katie's patch of sunshine retreated another foot, and she stood.

Dunbar handed the cage to Jack, and Katie caught a glimpse of Tansy holding up one claw. "Here you go, Boss. Got you a present."

"What happened to your arm?"

"Didn't like the accommodations," said Dunbar. "It'll be more obedient once we get it fixed."

"He's your brother," Katie said to Jack. "We're your family. How could you do this?"

"Oh, pumpkin, I did everything I could to keep you safe, but you wouldn't stop. Your father is our only expert on apocalypse-class artifacts. But he wouldn't help me. After all, your mother was lost during one of his experiments with this same type of magic."

Katie and Toby went pale and looked at each other.

"So, he never told you," Uncle Jack continued. "I put him on ice in case we couldn't acquire the Guardian. The Guardian knows how to unlock this relic. Now it will cooperate, and the full power of Asher's Tears will be mine."

"And that's worth killing us?" said Toby.

"Sorry, kid. Wish I could just let you go. I love you. I do. It tears me up that you both got caught in all of this. But now you're loose ends. The world can't stay the way it is, and sacrifices must be made. I'm going to be a god. And you keep getting in my way."

What Jack noticed too late was that blood has power. Tansy used Dunbar's to neutralize the curse breaking her magic, and there was just enough power left.

Katie saw her retract her last claw, and then Tansy erupted. She shattered the cage and ripped into Jack with her claws and fangs and all her fury.

Tansy mauled Jack's relic-wielding arm.

But Jack attacked her, and the relic attacked her, and between their two wills, she could not pry Ashur's Tears from his grip. The relic knew where Tansy was weak in her current form. Power had blinded Jack to everything but his desire to change the world. Changing worlds is what Ashur's Tears existed to do, and it refused to let Jack go.

But Tansy was also family, and the remnant that remained of the god Ashur also retained his feelings for his niece. It remembered things they had done together, and how well she had cared for it over the very long years.

While the relic would not relinquish its freedom, it did allow Tansy to cut a place of her choosing through reality. Jack's arm swung wide, the tip of Ashur's Tears sank into the Meat Locker's very existence, and it cut a silver-outlined rift to somewhere else in the floor.

Dunbar and the Minotaur force closed on Jack and Tansy.

"Katie!" Tansy shouted, as Jack tried to rip her off his arm. "What does even the strongest warrior flee before?"

Katie smiled, and her barrier changed to what she had learned during the trial.

Her patch of sunlight cracked open like a broken hive, and Katie made yellow and black hornets as big as French macarons.

Angry bees swarmed and stung her enemies. Dunbar and Jack instinctively protected their eyes, and the Minotaur force flailed and tried to get away.

In the chaos, Tansy, Katie, and Toby jumped into the rift, and it snapped shut behind them.

The big, angry hornets became motes of dancing light, and Jack set his commanders to work restoring order. He was equal parts angry and impressed with his niece and nephew. Bones showed through the missing chunks of his left arm. Even with Ashur's Tears reinforcing his body, his pain was staggering. He closed his eyes, felt for the relic, and its power coursing through him increased until he wasn't sure where he ended and Ashur's Tears began.

Jack's bleeding stopped, and his torn muscles and gnawed bones filled in and healed. As his skin grew back, his pain faded.

"Where'd they go?" Dunbar asked when the troops were assembled.

"Strange. I don't know," said Jack. "Somehow the Guardian activated the relic, but I couldn't see where they went, and I can't track them. It manipulated Ashur's Tears in ways I hadn't thought to try, and I learned something new."

Ashur's Tears whispered to Jack, *It is taboo. It is forbidden magic, but with the right materials . . .*

Jack smiled. *Only the weak fear power.* "Dunbar, have the men clear Meat Locker Two; we're giving it new purpose."

Minotaur Security forces pushed all the crimson cryostasis tubes out of the double ring of giant battery-like columns. There were over two hundred prisoners, but the sarcophagi raised and lowered and wheeled like medical beds, and the cryostasis tubes were quickly parked outside the Stonehenge-like structure.

Dunbar wheeled the last sarcophagus over to Jack. "What do I do with this one, boss?"

Jack looked at his brother frozen asleep in the tube and frowned. "Store him in the other room. He may still be useful."

Dunbar relayed Jack's orders to a Minotaur specialist. As they watched Doctor Erasmus Cypher get wheeled away, Dunbar asked, "So, what's the plan?"

"I'm ready to create our Demon Generals."

Dunbar swallowed hard. "Sure it will work?"

"Absolutely," said Jack. "But we shall test it first to be certain."

"Test it how?"

"The Guardian's free because you were careless. So, you get to go first. That a problem?"

Dunbar looked from Jack to his twelve best warriors gathered around them, ready to sacrifice their humanity for the cause. Like him, they were all true believers. Weakness and failure were not tolerated. "Sir! It will be my honor."

"I will give you power beyond your imagination," Jack said, grasping Dunbar's shoulder and looking deep into his eyes. "Do not fail me again."

Dunbar felt rapture in Jack's trust. "For the cause, my Lord. For the new world!"

Jack cut a rift in reality and brought forth the thirteen most formidable demons he had bound to Ashur's Tears, and he paired them with his most trusted men.

Then he changed Ashur's Tears into a scythe, and cut the deep grooves of an ornate circle and symbols of binding, submission, and transformation into the floor.

He became one with Ashur's Tears, and with a snap of his fingers, the columns forming the inner ring of the Meat Locker Two structure melted and flowed into the grooves Jack had cut. When they were full, the floor beyond circle and symbols rippled with molten metal. With a sweep of his arm, wind howled and the patterns in the floor solidified.

Jack focused on the circle he had cast, and it began to turn. Violet fire encircled the turning ring. As the circle turned faster, the flames rose higher, and Meat Locker Two flickered black and lilac in the wicked firelight.

Then he reached for the criminals asleep in their sarcophagi. They were defenseless, and in Dreamland he popped their red balloons. Jack distilled their lives into a billowing crimson smoke that he poured into the burning ring, like he was adding ingredients into a pot.

For the ritual, Jack still needed more. He felt between the worlds until he found the right demons, and inside the burning circle, he cut a path to them with his scythe.

This time he did not offer to trade for what they desired or make them swear an oath so he could use their power. This time Jack wanted, at the atomic level, their total subjugation.

He divided Ashur's Tears into two parts. He transformed one half into an obsidian harpoon that glistened in the crazy violet light. He rested that against his shoulder as he pulled the other half of the relic like taffy until it looked like a rope coiled on the ground. Jack whispered to the black coil, and it raced around the dancing flames, growing until it encircled the ring like a black-pearl scaled python—and still it grew.

Through the tear between worlds, Jack panned and zoomed through a blue wasteland until he found a giant round demon that was covered in thorns. It had rows of red eyes, and it stood atop a still-standing skyscraper, in a city where every other building had been toppled long ago.

Jack threw the relic-harpoon. It hit the demon like a rocket, penetrated its thorny armor, and blossomed deep inside its body. The demon shrieked with rage and fought with all its might as Jack reeled it into this world.

Once it was trapped within the ring of fire, the black-pearl python struck and coiled around the demon. It fought. More coils bound it. Then the python mouth of Ashur's Tears stretched and swallowed the demon whole. When it was a massive lump in the middle of the giant snake, Jack turned his fists, and the giant python's body twisted like Jack was wringing water from a rag. The demon's essence dripped from the python. Its life force, its magic, and all the elements that made the swallowed demon what it was pooled beneath the snake as a shimmering ichor.

When the demon was completely wrung dry, Jack recalled his harpoon to his hand and the whaling continued. Every demon fought. None survived. Jack didn't just kill them; he juiced their everything.

The humans watching had no sympathy because his prey were demons, and the thirteen demons Jack had summoned to serve him were powerful and took no interest in their slaughtered kin. They were weak enough to get caught, and the weak only existed to feed the strong. The air crackled with demonic energy, and when the circle of lilac flames was filled waist-deep with the shimmering ichor of demon essence, Jack held the harpoon above his head, thought *rejoin,* and his weapon reabsorbed the snake. The harpoon melted from his hand, and Ashur's Tears reformed on Jack as a crown.

It was finally time. Jack addressed his most powerful demons and best warriors.

"Who do you serve?"

"We serve our Lord, Jack Cypher, wielder of Ashur's Tears," they replied responsively, like they were praying. Then they saluted and said, "For the new world!"

"For the new world," said Jack, returning their salute. "Follow me and be reborn."

They waded into the swirling pool of ichor, two by two, and knelt before him in pairs of demon and man, and Jack joined more completely with Ashur's Tears than he had before. Tansy, using the relic to escape, had inadvertently unlocked something important.

He looked at Dunbar and the archdemon whose shape most resembled both a bird and a squid, and Jack placed a hand on each of them. Then he released the power of creation, and Jack pressed the man and demon together until they were one. It was like he was shuffling cards. He rearranged what they were, imbued them with demonic power from the pool, and remade them into something new.

When he was done, Jack admired his work: all the power of the fiercest, most cunning demon and Dunbar's knowledge, experience, and single-minded devotion to the cause.

Dunbar's face still resembled his human form, but he was twice as big, with pulsing black and purple tattoo scripts of dark magic inscribed into his body and soul. He had massive black wings, but his lower body was tentacles.

233

Jack had combined great strength with dark power, bound it together with a soul, and its abilities would only grow. He looked at Demon General Dunbar and deemed his creation good.

After Dunbar, he created twelve more demon generals, and then he absorbed the power collected in the pool into himself. When he extinguished the flames, Jack emerged as their Demon Lord.

CHAPTER 32

DESPAIR

Tansy and Katie landed on a soft burgundy couch in a large elegant room filled with expensive furniture. There was a wall of windows with a commanding view of glimmering city lights and a long jetty that curved into the breaking waves of a bay.

Toby hit the patterned blue carpet like a sack of rocks, and the rift in the ceiling closed.

Their travel through reality was instantaneous, but the changes were hard to process. Threat to calm, harsh to plush, day to night. It was as simple as walking into a different room, but it felt like jetlag and six shots of espresso.

And that was nothing compared to the weight of what had happened. *It was all Uncle Jack.*

"Where are we?" Toby asked, climbing to his feet, trying to get his bearings.

"The Conrad Suite at the Hilton Hotel in Chicago," said Tansy, her tail curling like a question mark as Katie pet her.

"And why are we here?" asked Toby.

"I saw a special about it on the Travel Channel, so I booked it just in case."

"Look," said Toby. "We have to keep moving—"

"We're safe for now," said Tansy. "But we do have to head downstairs."

"Downstairs?"

"Yes, it's an appropriately sized suite for a princess. The hotel staff believe you just arrived at the helipad, and that Princess Kate will stay here for a week or so until her parents and their entourage return."

Katie stood with Tansy in her arms and left the room.

235

"Princess Kate?" asked Toby. "Wait, what about me?" Toby followed them into a wide hallway and down a winding, white, wrought-iron staircase to several bedrooms.

"Of course, she won't be unattended," said Tansy.

"I really don't like how you said that," snapped Toby. "Do you even get what we've been through? And what we—"

"Yes, Toby, you've been hurt and terrified by things no one should have to see, but for now you must shake it off. You need to change because your butler is on her way."

"Butler?"

"Of course. Do you think royalty checks in through the lobby?"

"You made all this happen with Ashur's Tears?" asked Toby.

"I arranged to have this ready in case we needed a place to hide," said Tansy from over Katie's shoulder. "It would have been a pleasant surprise for you if everything went to plan, but since that never happens, here is your room." Katie stopped in the middle of a bedroom, and Tansy said, "Clean up, get dressed, and meet me upstairs." Toby rummaged through the closet.

"They're all suits," said Toby.

"Well, you will be in disguise," Tansy said.

"In disguise as what?"

"Katie's manservant, of course."

Toby was exhausted. Seeing his reflection in a Minotaur Security uniform made him want to shatter the glass. *It was Jack.* He was there. The bruises on his arms were real, his dad frozen in a tube was real, fighting demons was real. He wanted to scream, but they were still alive. Katie and Tansy got them out, and there was still a lot he didn't understand. So, he quickly showered, changed into a suit, tied back his hair, and climbed up the stairs. It was eerie how perfectly everything fit. *If this keeps us hidden, fine. Maybe I misjudged that smug old cat.*

"Okay," said Toby, "you saw this place on the Travel Channel. Why are we here?"

"Presidents and royalty stay here, so they're used to strange happenings and bizarre requests," said Tansy. "They will protect our privacy, and you'll have dedicated security, a private gym and spa, plus, there's a wonderfully named pub called Kitty O'Shea's."

"And that keeps us safe how?" Toby asked, narrowing his eyes, made to look turquoise in the soft hotel light.

"At ten thousand dollars a night, the staff will be discreet and get what we need without question. So, do a bit of servant's work. We shall hide in plain sight, and they will not find us here."

"That's a ton of money," said Toby, "and the minute I touch a bank account or use a credit card, they'll be—"

"One of my retainers has already guaranteed the funds."

"How?" asked Toby.

"I am a goddess. Even in exile, I can still afford to live like one. So, order what you like. Now play your part. Our butler arrives."

A woman with shoulder-length black hair, brown eyes, and a willowy build crossed the room. She wore a black silk suit and bowed. "I am Chun Mei Wu. Call me Chun. Welcome to the Chicago Hilton. I will ensure your visit is perfect. I can get anything from anywhere, so do not hesitate to ask." But before Toby could reply, Chun said, "You must be Tobias. I understand from the instructions we received that you're mute. So, I brought you an iPad. Use it to let me know if you need anything at all."

Toby stared daggers at Tansy, who was behind Chun, laughing.

Fresh flowers filled the suite. Delicious meals were served when they sat down, rooms were cleaned by the time they returned, and anything they asked for appeared. They really were treated like royalty. It was wonderful, but it also gave them time to think about everything. So much had happened since their father said goodbye. Uncle Jack turned their world upside down, they had lost, and no one knew what to do.

The Professor's augmented reality glasses stopped working just before Jack arrived with Ashur's Tears, but they began working again after they fell into the hotel. Toby let the Professor know what happened and where they were, but he wasn't ready to talk, and Katie wouldn't leave her room, so the switched-off glasses sat in a basket by the door.

After a few days of swimming laps in the rooftop pool and working out until he could barely crawl back to the suite, Toby went to the library. Tansy was there sitting on the red pool table, bouncing the cue ball off the bumper. Toby turned to leave.

"You should stay," said Tansy. "We need to talk."

Toby kept walking, but the door slammed shut in front of him. Tansy's golden eyes glowed. "I won't lock it," she said, swatting the cue ball into the corner pocket, "but we must discuss what happens next."

Toby turned and shouted, "There's no way we can win, okay? That's what happens next. We run, we die, they get you. And either you do what Jack wants, or he tortures Dad until he does—and then you both die. Next time we meet Jack, it's checkmate."

"I'm not so sure," said Tansy.

"If it were anyone else, we'd have a shot, but Uncle Jack's taken down governments and has an army of fanatic soldiers and demons. We don't have a chance. We never had a chance. He's been in our heads the whole time."

"And despite his best effort and another elaborate trap, here we are because he failed."

Toby sighed. "He'd say we got lucky, and he wouldn't be wrong."

"I'm sorry we did not get your father," said Tansy, "but your uncle didn't get what he wanted either. Now we know he's responsible for—"

"We wouldn't have gotten away if Katie hadn't . . . I still don't know what she did."

"She was resourceful," growled Tansy, "as were you. I know it hurts, but you have family and friends. You should trust them a little more. Isn't that right, Rachel?" Tansy said, glancing at Toby's glasses set on the edge of the bookcase. They projected an image of Rachel with her arms crossed. Then she sighed and looked at him.

"Sounds like you had another tough day," she said.

"Rachel, I . . . how are you feeling?"

"Dinner out," she said, looking away again. "Somewhere nice with linen tablecloths. And a night flight in your plane to somewhere fun, where we can hang out under the stars."

"Anything you want."

Silver tears raced down her cheeks. "Promise me you're coming back."

Toby's stomach dropped. He knew what she wanted to hear, and he wanted to say it, but he couldn't. "If it's humanly possible, and then some, I promise I will find a way."

Rachel nodded her head and wiped away her tears. "Guess that'll have to do for now. Don't make me wait too long." Her eyes were still wet, but she smiled. "Now, let's talk."

Toby slipped on his glasses. Rachel was there, and Tansy left. She had one last stop to make.

"Rise and shine, kitten," Tansy said, hopping onto the king-sized bed covered in pillows. Katie was dug in under the duvet.

"Still sleeping," said Katie, her voice muffled from all the covers.

"You've been in bed for two days. Time to come out. It's almost dinner."

"Not going. Have dinner with Toby."

"Toby is brooding and coming to terms with things, as men do. We have cried. Now 'tis time to indulge, and after that, we will find a way to make things right."

"I'm not coming out!" roared Katie, flipping open the covers to peer at Tansy like an angry bear in a cave.

"There's a spa," said Tansy as she moved closer to Katie. "You'll feel better if you go."

"No, Tansy. I won't," Katie said, sniffling back her tears. Her eyes were red and puffy. "I'm not going anywhere."

"Kitten, you can't stay in bed forever. If you want, I can—"

"I want my dad and Uncle Jack back!" cried Katie. "We tried so hard, and we got so close. But it wasn't enough, and now we either run or keep fighting. And I'm sick of it. We're kids—how can we win a war?"

"When I was younger, it wasn't uncommon to see battle-hardened twelve-year-old warriors. I would not wish that fate on you. But even today, children fight wars across the world. You can see it on your news if you're willing to look."

"I don't know if I'll ever see Dad again, Tansy."

"You are the most talented wielder of magic I've seen in a thousand years, Katie Cypher. You will grow into a fine woman, and in time, a great mage."

"But is that enough?"

"It doesn't have to be," said Tansy. "You have your brother, and me, and the Professor. Together we will get your father and Ashur's Tears back."

"Let me just sleep a little longer," said Katie.

"I understand. It's been difficult. Let me say one more thing, and I'll leave you be."

"What's that?"

"Pear maple bread pudding."

Katie swallowed hard, and her stomach growled.

"So unfair," Katie said as she hugged a pillow and rolled over.

"If that doesn't do it for you, kitten, I happen to know there is a freshly baked blackberry pie ready to serve in the kitchen, with their famous, house-made vanilla bean ice cream. I've heard the pie is beyond delicious, and the crust is flaky."

Katie's entire body balled up. She wailed and struggled so hard to hold back the drool her face hurt. "You are so mean. Fine. FINE!" she said, standing up.

"Come along then. 'Tis time to get ready."

After her bath, she did feel better, and Chun brushed and braided Katie's hair and helped her into a summer dress and jewelry from the hotel vault.

The distinguished gentleman who'd come to play the piano escorted Princess Kate to a single table on the terrace with a sweeping view of Lake Michigan and the Chicago lights.

When Katie was seated, Tansy hopped onto the other chair, where a dinner plate was flanked by gilded saucers of hand-selected bourbon.

"Princess, we've taken the liberty of also placing a cat box around the corner," said Chun.

"Thank you for that," said Katie. "She can use a flush toilet, but she finds a litter box more convenient when she's drinking."

The incredulous look on Chun's face was priceless.

It was the first time in days that Katie had smiled.

CHAPTER 33

KATIE AND FAN

Tansy's bowls were refreshed, dessert was served, and Katie told Chun to release the staff and take the night off.

"Poor girl," Chun said to the piano man as they were leaving. "She has everything in the world, but there she is, all alone, having dinner with her cat. It's just so sad."

Over bread pudding, pastries, and pie, Katie and Tansy finally had the talk.

"So . . . tell me," Tansy said after lapping up more of her new favorite drink. "Why were you blushing when you woke up in the Meat Locker?"

"Uh . . . that's what you ask about? Not how I learned to use divine light?" Katie stammered, turning red.

"Kitten, please! That rosy déjà vu blooming across your cheeks screams one's a result of the other."

Katie sipped her tea and collected her thoughts. "Okay. When I passed out from the viper curse, I met a boy in a crazy dream that wasn't a dream. We were at a table on a mountaintop, eating macarons under the stars, while a blizzard raged around us."

"You were in Dreamland," said Tansy. "It is the closest other realm to your people, but you went deeper in than most humans ever go."

"It felt so real," said Katie.

"Because it was, kitten. It's just a different real than you're used to. Some do accidentally wander in, a few purposefully find it, but most humans there were invited."

"That's where I met Fan."

"So, he was the being slumbering behind the door we avoided?"

"Yes," said Katie, watching lights twinkle across the harbor. "He took the form of a boy with dark fluffy hair you'd want to pet, and deep purple eyes. And wings. He was kind and a little awkward, but he was fun and charming too."

"Did he tell you what he was?"

"I am judgment," said Fan, sitting up and moving his hand over the candles. The flames leaned toward wherever his hand went and strained to touch it.

"Judgment?" said Katie, rolling her eyes. "Isn't that too much and not enough, at the same time? I'm German American and a student. I'm a girl and the daughter of Doctor Cypher, and—"

"Recently magical," Fan said with a grin. "You are many things, Katie Cypher. I am judgment. How to explain . . . I'm like Santa Claus."

"Really? Santa?" Katie said, raising an eyebrow.

"Well, I do see you when you're sleeping, and know when you've been bad or good, as a part of the whole judgment thing."

"Who do you see?"

"Everyone," said Fan, "all the time, but I only judge those who seek eternal life."

"So . . . you're a stalker?"

"Harsh," said Fan with a hurt expression. "Why give Santa a pass? He's a serial trespasser."

"He's jolly and brings us presents."

"He scares small humans into wetting themselves on his lap in malls. Definitely not nice. Anyway, didn't you accept my invitation because you wanted something from me?"

"I accepted your invite," said Katie, "because I was scared, and your voice calmed me."

"Even though what I am frightens you?"

"Part of you is frightening, but I can tell you're trying hard to make me feel at ease."

"Is it working?" asked Fan.

"The tea and sweets are amazing. Are you gonna hurt me?"

"No," said Fan, wrapping himself back up in his wings. "You are unlike the others in that place. I was curious and wanted to talk."

"I'm glad you did. I like this, but you know what's happening. I'm having a horrible time right now, in real life, and if you helped—"

"I cannot. Not directly, Katie. Your conflict isn't my domain."

"Am I your prisoner?"

"No. You're free to return as you wish," said Fan. "This is a dream of sorts. Your body sleeps in what you call the Meat Locker. You and your brother are bound by shadow. He is being interrogated, but time moves differently here. When you wake, only minutes will have passed." Then a troubled look passed over Fan's face and his huckleberry-purple eyes stared deeply into Katie. She couldn't look away, and she saw.

Katie saw Dunbar torturing Toby, Tansy in a cage, and her uncle. *It's Uncle Jack!* Katie dropped her macaron, panting.

She tried to catch her breath.

Then Uncle Jack said, "Why are they still alive?"

"No. It can't be. NO!" Tears rolled down Katie's face. She didn't want to believe. She couldn't believe. Every part of Katie tried to reject it, but she knew.

"Tell me it's a lie, Fan. Tell me it's not true," Katie begged.

"Katie, I am sorry. All your recent heartache was his doing. Your uncle has betrayed you."

"I have to get back," Katie said through her tears.

"You will die as you are now. Stay here, and I can protect you."

"I have to go. If you can't help us directly, loan me your power."

"You would contract with me? What do you have that I want?"

Katie didn't know how to answer that question. She wanted to scream, "Take anything or everything!" Then she remembered what Fan was, and she had an idea.

She pushed back her chair and stood. "I've seen what the people here dream about," said Katie, "and it's all kinds of awful. Why sleep here when you could be anywhere?"

"It interests me," said Fan.

"Why?" asked Katie, setting down her napkin.

"Those slumbering here could live forever, but they can never leave," Fan replied. "It changes what immortality is, but I haven't seen enough to judge it yet."

"Then judge me and tell me what you want for your contract." Katie walked to Fan, took his hand, and her blue eyes locked with his. "I will help my family and Tansy, so do your best. I'm a billion pixels of full-color wonderful. Don't underestimate me."

Fan nodded and squeezed her hand.

Katie felt what people resuscitated after an accident say death is like. Her life flashed before her, then it stretched out into every possibility. She could catch only glimpses of herself as an image here or emotion there. It felt like swimming down waterfalls, where every crash into the churning water at the bottom led to another fall. Katie lost track, and when Fan released her hand, she had to lean on the table because even her dream-knees were buckling.

"So . . ." said Katie, steadying herself, "what did I tell you?"

"There is one thing I would accept as equal value for what you want."

"Good," said Katie. "I knew it."

"But it might be too great a sacrifice for you to make."

"What do you mean?"

"It is what you've wanted so desperately for so long. Something you only recently got back."

"Fan, I don't understand. What are you asking for?"

"I want the moment you found your mother in the mirror and watched her dance, joyful of your coming. It is a treasure you cherish, and an appropriate exchange for the power of light you seek."

Katie's stomach dropped with apprehension. "Why that?"

"Before you discovered that moment, you could recognize your mother in pictures, but you couldn't recall much about her. You no longer felt a connection with her, and that loss hurt.

"That image of her happy to be having you awoke memories you never knew you had. They are precious, and they evoke powerful emotions.

That moment led to your happiest recent memories. Recollections of your mother, Ariana Cypher, your love for her, and her love for you. Love that you feel now that you could not feel before. I would take that in exchange for what you seek."

The color drained from Katie's face, and she shivered. "What happens to me, if I give that to you for our contract?"

"What you remember and the mother's love you feel now, and those memories sparked by that moment, will fade and be forgotten. You will return to the way you were before you located her in your mirror, and those memories, and your recently found connection to her, will be gone. And you will never be able to regain what you lost by looking in the mirror again."

"You're serious? I never knew I had those memories of her. I never thought I could feel that close to her again. After losing my dad and my uncle, you want me to give up my mom? That's horrible, Fan."

I have never once considered forming a contract, and you are asking for much. But you offered me something I have not seen before, and an insight into humanity that I have never known. That is why that moment is valuable. If you are not willing to sacrifice that much for the power you seek, you do not have the strength to wield it anyway."

"So, you're saying," Katie said slowly, "my choice is to sacrifice the memories and feelings I just got of my mom for the power to maybe save my brother and Tansy."

"That is the price of my contract."

Katie swallowed hard. "If I do this, can I save them?"

"That will be up to you, but yes. I will lend you my power and a divine light that can burn away demonic darkness and protect you."

Katie bit her lip. "I want to save them, but what you're asking . . . can I trust you, Fan?"

"Well, the obvious answer is yes."

Katie scowled.

"But that is something only you can decide."

"I can't just say yes, Fan. I want to, but . . ."

"You are not sure you can trust an archangel." Fan tried to grin. It didn't come out great, but it was an improvement from his first attempts at a smile. "Some of my brothers do have bad reputations. I can give you time to weigh this decision and decide if you can trust me. I know you have a heavy heart, Katie, but I swear your family and friend Tansy will be safe until we return."

Fan turned his hand face down, and the candles went out. Then he turned it palm up. Katie hesitated, then she took it.

"Where are we going?"

Fan grinned even better, and his wings snapped open wide. "Many places. But as you have an interest in astronomy, we should visit an elegant star that is about to die. You would call it a supernova. We should say goodbye and wish her well before she leaves this realm. Her passing will be beautiful."

Katie nodded and squeezed his hand, and they were gone. She clung to him, and they traveled through infinity, seeing the sights. Their first stops were the birth, then the sad, far-future end of the Earth. Fan showed Katie places he thought she might like, and he brought her to where life and souls began. Fan showed her how things evolved and grew and learned until the spark of a soul became fires that burned like beacons across realms of space and time, like mirrors facing mirrors to infinity inside a kaleidoscope.

Then Fan and Katie paid their respects in the dying heart of an ancient star, where there were colors Katie had never seen.

She felt Star all around her, and Star held on to Katie like a proud grandmother rejoicing at a visit. Star had touched human life with sunlight before, but a human being had never once touched her back. Star accepted it as a gift. Katie showed Star what life was like in darkness and light, and Star showed Katie how all life is stardust and static wrapped around a precious spark that could grow into so much more. When Katie and Fan said farewell, Star transcended. Her last breath blew a dandelion ball that seeded life on a thousand new worlds, and Katie could feel something within herself changing. She felt like she was part of everything. There was so much to see and learn, and Katie wanted more. Fan was a cosmic, all-access, behind-the-scenes pass to how different realities and magic worked.

She felt safe and warm traveling with him. It would have been easy to let go of her humanity and get lost in the universe, but the ache in Katie's heart for her family and Tansy brought her back.

"Amazing-est trip, ever," said Katie. "But I have to go."

"You've decided then?"

"I'll trust you, Fan. This is so hard, but I will give you that moment of my mom in the mirror, and all the feelings and things I remembered about her because of it. Make a contract with me. Give me the power I need to save my family and my friend."

"So be it," said Fan, and he spread his wings, and light enveloped her.

When it dimmed, so did her memories of her mother, and everything that she remembered was foggy and far away. The moment was gone, and the closeness she felt with her mom was gone, and when Katie could see again, she realized she was crying, but she wasn't sure why.

"Everything's fuzzy. Did it work?"

"Yes, Katie. Our contract is complete. If you're still around, let's hit the road again sometime."

"Anytime! Hey, before I go, can I get a pic?" Then Katie realized what she was asking. "Oh, yeah. My phone's still on the plane, and this is a sorta dream."

One corner of Fan's mouth clicked down. "It's okay. Your glasses can take pictures. Reach into your pocket."

She checked, and her glasses were there. Katie set up the shot, got close to him, Fan wrapped a wing around her, and she said, "Smile!"

Katie took a lot of pictures. Awkward shots, stupid shots, crazy-face, crossed-eyes, and tongues-hanging-out shots, until she finally got one she really liked.

Fan smiled crooked, held out his hands, and Katie took them. "I will send you back now. Worry not, you haven't been gone long."

Katie's heart and eyes glowed with pure white light, and her hair crackled with energy as a pendant appeared around her neck. "This serves as proof of our contract, Katie Cypher. Tell Tansiluros that Phanuel sends his regards and wishes her success with her penance." Fan's warm wings wrapped around her. Katie's heart raced and the pendant blazed.

"It faded like a dream," Katie said. "But when I woke, I knew the words, I had his power, and I wore this." Katie showed Tansy the big, yellow diamond pendant set in gold shaped like flames on its necklace of stars, and it pulsed with living light.

"So, how do you feel now?"

"I know what happened, but it's all gone," Katie said, calming her light. "I guess I pretty much feel how I did right before casting mirror magic, but I don't remember ever feeling different."

Tansy polished off another saucer of bourbon. "You sacrificed something important to you; was it worth it?"

"You mean aside from saving you and Toby?" Katie said wryly. Then she snatched the top cream puff off a Saint Honoré pastry and munched thoughtfully. "It's hard to regret what I can't remember. I do wonder what I felt about my mom. That does make me sad. But I trust Fan, our deal worked out, and he let me take a selfie of a dream. Who gets to do that?" said Katie, showing Tansy their pictures in the glasses.

"Even amongst gods, this is rare."

"Not every day a girl gets to hang with her guardian angel."

"These beings usually have no interest in corporeal things beyond destruction, yet you made a contract with an archangel."

"No," Katie said, her face beaming. "I made a contract with Fan."

CHAPTER 34

TOBY'S DEAL

Katie and Tansy sat in the large living room, on the burgundy sofa, across from Toby. He was shaking his head. The view was beautiful, but there were white caps on Lake Michigan and lightning in the distance. Toby turned back to Tansy and realized he was grinding his teeth again. "So, what happened? You had Ashur's Tears in your claws."

"Yes," Tansy said, annoyed. "I thought I could wrest control from Jack, but it would not let him go. Although it did allow us to escape."

Wind rattled the windows, dark clouds dimmed the room, and Toby groaned.

"I cannot change what happened," said Tansy. "We must decide what to do now."

"The Uncle Jack we love is gone," said Toby, and he hated that Katie's chin quivered when he said it. "Jack intends to kill us and capture you. If we don't stop him, no one will."

"He will destroy this world in the process of saving it," said Tansy.

"Question is," Toby said, "do we run, or do we fight?"

"Can we really beat him if we fight?" asked Katie.

Rain fell in sheets over the windows, distorting the view.

"It won't be easy," said Toby. "I have a plan. Tansy and the Professor think it could work. It's a long shot, but I think we can beat him."

"Then I'm in," said Katie.

"You haven't even heard the plan yet."

"Doesn't matter. If you say we have a chance, I'm in."

Toby had to look away from his sister because tears welled up. He cleared his throat, blinked his eyes, and swore to himself that he would live up to Katie's trust. He looked back, and said, "To beat Jack, this is what we have do . . ."

The Professor and Toby worked on the satellite hops and rerouting to make the call untraceable until it confused even them.

"Okay," said Toby. "Everything from this point on is liberty or death." They put on their glasses, and Toby made the call. The Professor and everyone at the table would be able to hear, but only Toby could talk.

After a series of clicks and static pops, the phone finally rang.

"Colonel, a spoofed call's coming in on your private line," said the signals captain. "Looks like it's from Akre, the big town near that tomb we raided."

"Put it through."

"Hello, Uncle Jack," said Toby through the warble and delay of a call bounced all over the world to hide their location.

"Impressive. Always knew you had real talent."

"We both know I don't have much time before you find me. Is Dad still alive?"

"For now."

"Good," said Toby. "I wanna make a deal."

"I'm listening," said Jack, turning to his captain.

"Still tracing, sir," said the captain. "There's a lot of chaff."

"You need the cat. We want Dad and our lives back. Simple exchange."

"Very soon, Toby, I'll be able to take it from you anyway."

"I believe you, Uncle Jack, but you have things to do and other people to kill, probably far away from here. Plus, I'm sure you noticed. We are getting better at magic."

"That was pure dumb luck, and you know it," Jack said with a snicker.

"Maybe, but we've been pretty lucky so far. Make this deal, and you get what you want, with the added benefit that your brother and his kids don't have to die. We meant a lot to you once, remember? That has to count for something. Once you have the cat, really, what threat are we to you? None. It's a good deal."

"All right," said Jack. "We'll meet—"

"No."

"Excuse me?"

"I have what you need," said Toby. "I pick the place. You taught me that. We meet at the Air Force Museum on Friday night, twenty-two hundred hours. That gives us time to get there, and it's night, so it'll work for all your monster friends. Dad walks in, you take the cat cage from under the SR-71 spy plane. Leave Dad there, alive. We go separate ways. Simple and clean."

"Why the Air Force Museum?"

"Honestly, it's the only place in the entire world I know better than you, and like you always say, choose the right battle space, and control the fight. Just don't expect Christmas cards."

"Ha. Good job, kid. You just put a smile on my face. All right. Deal. I'll see you—"

Click.

Colonel Jack Cypher smiled at the phone in his hand. "That kid has some set of balls. Such a waste. We know where they'll be. Let's get moving."

Toby hung up, crumpled into the cushions, and groaned. "Too much?"

"I believe you properly convinced him," said the Professor, virtually rocking in a leather chair.

"We're not really trading Tansy?" Katie asked.

"Don't worry, Tansy's not getting traded," Toby said, watching the little goddess nod in agreement. "Even with this deal, Jack has no intention of letting us live. Since we were kids, he always said, 'Never ever leave loose ends, they always come back to bite you.' You saw him in the Meat Locker. He wants us dead."

"I know that," Katie said, "but—"

"If you want out, you're out," said Toby, "I know we're asking a lot. It's all right to say no."

"I'm in, okay," said Katie. "I only wish there were some other way. It's a good plan. First, we trick them with a copy of Tansy, and while they're confused, we science-and-magic the bejeebers out of them. After we whittle down his forces, we overwhelm Uncle Jack and take back Ashur's Tears. If that doesn't work, we escape to Nimbus or Stratos with Dad."

"Professor," said Toby, "is your part ready?"

"Nearly there. Everything will be assembled by the time I collect you at the airport."

"Good. Tansy, you sure you can do this? Everything hinges on you making Jack and Ashur's Tears believe you're in that cage."

Tansy wrinkled her nose. Her tail lashed side to side, and she turned her head back toward Katie. Then Tansy closed her eyes and sighed, "I can do what you ask."

"Then we agree," said Toby. "We stick to the plan. We get Dad back, Tansy takes Ashur's Tears, and no one ever has to go through anything like this again."

And if we don't get Ashur's Tears, everyone lives happily ever after until Jack unleashes his demon army on the world.

"I'm not worried so much about me," said Katie. "I've already seen some of my future. I live through this. I'm concerned about you and Dad. You're both impulsive."

Toby blew a lock of hair out of his eyes and sat back up. "I'm taking the initiative, not being impulsive."

"Riiight," said Katie.

"Odds are," said the Professor, "Jack will attack before you reach the SR-71. You'll be under observation from the moment you land. He will try to verify that Tansy is real, and from the data I've gathered, his demons are much more powerful now, so be careful."

"But will he really bring Dad?" Katie asked.

"He looked hard, but he couldn't find you," said the Professor. "Jack won't risk you going underground again. So, he will produce your father as bait, and, based on his recent behavior, to gloat."

Mute Toby texted Chun that they needed to go. She mobilized a small army to pack their stuff into a long, dark red limo with a posh black-and-tan quilted leather interior.

"This is a Bentley," said Katie.

"If you don't like it," Chun said with a broad smile, "I can always get you something else."

When Katie and Tansy were settled into the back, Toby gave a Chun a thumbs up. *Can't wait to talk again after we're on the jet. Revenge, Tansy, will be sweet.* But his heart wasn't in it. She was the reason they escaped Jack, and Tansy was paying for everything. Still, Toby's hand shook when he signed the bill. Four days and three nights, plus expenses, meals, travel, and tips came to more than the price of a brand-new Corvette.

Katie waved, Chun bowed, and the driver eased the big car into the honking Chicago traffic. They had one last chance to beat Jack, get Dad back, and maybe save the world.

The limo stopped in front of a sleek Gulfstream jet. After they climbed into the sky, Toby and Katie changed into more practical clothes. Once they reached the museum, Toby, Katie, and Tansy would either win or they would die. The butterflies in their stomachs grew as they got closer. When the Professor met them in Dayton an hour later, their butterflies were as big as bats.

CHAPTER 35

MASS PRODUCED

"It's good to see you lot again, in person," the Professor said, hugging Toby and Katie. "Now, in you go, and give me a hand up."

Their ride to the museum was an autonomous, tractor-trailer truck with a bulbous nose and a sweeping red-and-white sensor, like a shifty, cyclops eye.

"What happened to Robot Bob?" Katie asked, cramming into the vestigial crew cab.

"These big boys really don't like drivers except for emergencies," the Professor said, shutting the door. "Take us to the Air Force Museum."

"Destination," said the large white truck, in a deep vibrating voice, "National Museum of the US Air Force, aye."

The museum comprised four linked hangars, a missile gallery, a grand entry atrium, a theater, restaurants, and a store. Around it was an airpark, restoration areas, and the runway.

For Toby, pulling into the museum felt like coming home. He looked for Suzie on the parking apron, but she was gone.

The tractor-trailer backed into a spot close to the museum and stopped with a huff of air brakes. Under the parking lot lights, the Professor led them, bobbing and weaving, to the back of the truck. "First things first," said the Professor, squinting at the sky and snapping open his old grey umbrella. "Too many watching eyes."

There was the sound of electricity charging up. A web of white energy formed, crackling and glistening on the umbrella canopy, and the web leapt into the sky.

"I've made several useful modifications to the Spider since you last saw it in action."

There were flashes of chain lightning in the sky above the museum, then black hail fell, bouncing off the white truck and asphalt in a shower of *tick-tack* sounds.

The silver web returned to the Professor's umbrella, and Toby brushed the tiny drones off his shoulders and out of his hair.

Katie scooped up handfuls of the silver-and-black discs. They looked like breakfast cereal-Os. A dozen of them could fit on a spoon, each with a stopped propeller in its hole.

"Hmm," said the Professor, approvingly, "we recently fielded this model. Very capable. Finally, a little respect."

"They still watching us?" Toby asked, crunching drones under his feet like dried leaves.

"Let me see," said the Professor, studying something displayed in the underside of his umbrella. "Oh, dear."

There was a chorus of, "What?"

"Not to worry," the Professor said, squeezing Toby and Katie together against the semi's tailgate. He turned toward the museum. "Taught my Spider a new trick. I call it the RTS."

The Professor held the umbrella in front of them, gave it a spin, and a tight, bright web of energy pulsed around them, and something moving too fast to see came to a stop when it touched the umbrella. It made a loud noise like *crack* and *ssshew* combined.

Toby glanced at the display in the curve of the umbrella and was stunned to read, *50-caliber sniper round—CAPTURED*. He heard cars in the distance on Colonel Glenn Highway. Then two more big rounds—*ca-crack* and *sha-ssshew*—decelerated and stuck in the web in front of them. The display updated to, *CAPTURED (X3)*.

"I do appreciate the Spider's new web—after all, it kept us alive," said the Professor with a wink, "but my favorite part is this." The large, pointy bullets did a one-eighty, the web pulsed again, then the bullets were gone. There was a trio of sonic booms, and the Professor pointed the umbrella around before he closed it and leaned on it like a cane.

"What happened?" asked Toby.

"One sniper team silenced," said the Professor. His head bobbed north and south like he was pleased with himself. "There was another team on the water tower, but they withdrew."

"What does RTS stand for again?"

The Professor grinned. "Return To Sender. It uses multispectral analysis and elastic gravitons to decelerate projectiles and return them to their source. But enough prattle. Before they reestablish surveillance, let's talk about your gear."

The Professor collected their glasses and Tansy's earpiece, but Katie wouldn't give hers up. He glowered; she shook her head *no*.

"Moving on," the Professor said, producing an old gold-and-black perfume atomizer that looked stolen off a grandmother's vanity. He squeezed a rubber bulb on the back of the bottle and sprayed a pink mist at each of their faces. Each spray glittered, then divided itself, and dove into their noses, eyes, and ears.

"Close your eyes. Let the nano-mist work," said the Professor. "You may feel itchy, dizzy, or disoriented, but that will pass."

Toby's ears, eyes, and throat felt hot and tingled. Then he realized, even with his eyes shut, he could see. For Katie, it felt like bad allergies, but something was forming in her mind's eye.

"Give me your undivided attention. Colonel Cypher jammed your glasses, but he cannot jam this bit of biomechanical augmentation while you lot are within five miles of each other.

"Now, think 'map'—you should see the map and each other's location. Enemy and friendly positions are displayed based on what you see; plus, you still have all the features you enjoyed with your glasses. So, give your new tech a try, but don't dillydally; there's still a lot we need to get through."

In addition to the nano-mist, the Professor gave Toby and Katie biomechanically enhanced high tops that bonded to their feet and legs. After the kicks synched with the nano-mist, running incredibly fast was easy, as was jumping two stories high.

Toby tried his new sneakers. With no effort, he jumped to the top of the semi. *Yes! So awesome.* He landed a little off-balance, but it worked.

Jumping down took a few deep breaths the first time, but it felt like hopping off a step.

The Professor set down a cat crate nearly identical to the one Tansy had destroyed in the Meat Locker. "Now it is your turn, Goddess. If you're ready, it's time."

"You are certain there is no other way?"

"I am," said the Professor. "If Ashur's Tears doesn't recognize you down to your aura, Jack will know your decoy isn't real."

Tansy's ears drooped, and her tail dropped. "I truly hate this."

"There's no way this plan works unless you leave a temporary part of yourself behind."

Tansy mewed and then growled as she resigned herself to the task. "I never know what part of me will take form in this ritual, and I do not like it." Dancing scarlet flames enveloped Tansy, and she made a complicated sound like rain hissing on hot desert sand. When Tansy left the flames, an image of her remained behind.

When she turned to examine it, the fire went out.

"Ta-da! Pet me!" said the other Tansy. "I'm a spell, call me Spell." She was an exact copy—the same appearance, fur, jewelry, movements, voice, everything.

Everything, except—her personality was a little different.

"What are you here to do?" Toby asked.

"Besides gettin' ya to stroke me?" Spell said, jumping into Toby's arms and nuzzling his face. "When the bad man picks up my cage, I stun everyone that's bad—so stupid, they'll forget everything that happened to them the last fifteen minutes. Then I punish 'em."

Toby noticed his petting Spell made Tansy unhappy, so he went all out, scratching her ears, pulling her tail, and rubbing her belly when she fell over purring. "So, you can be nice like this, huh, Tansy? Who's a good giiirl?"

"I don't know why you don't like him, Tansy," said Spell. "He's an obedient minion with big, warm hands."

Toby smiled. "Yes, I do have big, warm hands." He scratched and played with Spell even more. *Payback,* thought Toby, *is sweet and fluffy.* "You like that, girl? Who's a pretty Spell?"

"This is why a copy of a copy is never a good idea," said Tansy, looking away in disgust. "The lines get all blurred."

Spell played with Toby, purring like a big engine, until it was time to go into her cage.

"Now I suppose I should introduce you," said the Professor, as he lowered the lift on the back of the cargo trailer. They stepped on, and it rose five feet until it was level with the trailer floor and stopped with a *clang.* The Professor hit the access panel, and the trailer's metal back rolled up. Light flooded the cargo area, and Toby and Katie saw a trailer full of copies of themselves.

"Told you I was busy," said the Professor, his head proudly swaying. "Toby sent me his mimic build plans. They'll go in with you for support, to catch Jack's troops off guard, and to fight. You control them through the bio-augmentation I just gave you. All told, there are one hundred Toby units and fifty Katies."

"Would you look at that," said Katie. "Wait. How come there are more Tobys?"

The Professor smiled. "The Tobys are optimized for attack and defense. Katies are built for speed and stealth, and your parts were exotic and difficult to come by." Katie grinned as a Katie mimic waved to her and handed the Professor a tablet that he tapped like he was playing a drum solo.

When he looked up, his head stopped bobbing. "I will help from here as I can. The museum doors are now unlocked, and the alarms are disabled. I believe in you. Come back safe with your father."

It was the point of no return. The Professor stepped aside, and a force of 150 Tobys and Katies exited the trailer like paratroopers leaping from a plane. They hit the ground and raced away, mixing into teams. Then Tansy made Toby, Spell, Katie, and herself invisible, and they slipped into the museum with the mimics.

CHAPTER 36

THE MUSEUM

Toby entered the museum and into gunfire. The map showed Katie and Tansy behind him and mimics fighting ahead. He hugged the wall and ran through the atrium. Bullets whistled past as he took cover behind an engine with a large wooden propeller. They made it to the first hangar. The SR-71 meetup was several hangars away.

Toby's heart raced, and fear twisted his gut. More than anything, he was angry as bullets destroyed the displays around him. As if it wasn't hard enough trying to stay alive and get his dad and Ashur's Tears back, he had just turned the museum he loved into a war zone.

Shots ripped through Toby and Katie mimics and thundered through the World War II and Early Years of Flight galleries.

The mimics leapfrogged colorful biplanes, slid under bombers, and hit the dug-in Minotaur squads like a tsunami.

Invisible Toby leapt over the battle, onto a silver Boeing B-29 Superfortress, called Bockscar, that had dropped the atomic bomb on Nagasaki, Japan, ending World War II. Toby directed the battle from its wing, and the Minotaur mercs were quickly overwhelmed.

The giant, fiery-eyed beetle demons were the real problem. They were vicious and hard to kill. Toby lost eleven mimics before they finally took them out, but the Katies couldn't pierce demon armor, and that was a problem.

Toby spotted *True-Blue Sue* in the back corner, across from the melting demons. Despite the losses, seeing her made him smile.

He sent a team to scout ahead, and they won the first hanger, but a few things still bothered him. He expanded the map at the top right corner of his view, focused on two green pins, and said, "Katie, Tansy."

"Here, yes," they replied.

"The Katie mimics are weak against demons. When demons attacked our house, Tansy did something to a kitchen knife so Rachel could fight them. See if you can do the same thing to your mimics. You have ten minutes."

"Stingy," said Katie.

Toby growled and set his mimics to defending the hangar. He reviewed the intel they had so far. *It's too quiet. And why were the Minotaur soldiers using old AK-47 Kalashnikov rifles from the fifties?* Toby turned it over in his mind. *Everything Minotaur used before was high tech. Maybe to make the damage look like terrorists?*

"Okay, we have a plan," said Katie.

"Copy that," said Toby as groups of Katies sprinted past him, bounced over a Japanese Zero interceptor, and formed a line.

Forty-six Katies stood shoulder to shoulder, determined blue eyes forward, backs against a wall illustrating the War in the Pacific. They wore sky-blue soccer uniforms with numbers and CYPHER in white, with matching scrunchies, socks, and sneakers. But each Katie unit wore her blond hair differently, mostly in braids.

"Listen up, ladies," Katie said, walking the line like a general inspecting her troops. "Our job is to end demons. Not send them home cryin'. We're gonna hurt 'em so bad, demons from this day on will fear our realm. Do you hear me?"

"Yes, ma'am!" the mimics called, responding in unison.

"When I modify Mimic-1, copy her mod and pass it down the line. Today, you become demon-slayers. Are you ready?"

"Yes, ma'am!" The hangar echoed with their voices.

"Good." Katie picked up Tansy, who extended a paw to the first Katie-mimic in the line. "Take it," Tansy said.

When it did, Tansy poured power into Mimic-1 until its hands glowed and its nails grew into glittering knives that the mimics copied down the line. Tansy had made them hard and sharp. Katie would fill them with the power to cleave darkness.

Katie had to forge divine light into machines without souls. To do that, she needed to bridge spirit and circuit, and she wasn't sure where to begin. Then Katie heard Spell and Toby having a strange conversation about nursery rhymes, and it brought back memories of visiting Star and what she taught Katie when she and Fan paid their respects and said goodbye.

Katie slipped into Dreamland to work because time moved differently there. To bind divine light to her mimics, she would have to change what they were. In her mind Katie wove patterns about light and life that she had learned from Star. Then she gave it form, added the symbols for being and soul, and filled it with power until the pattern shimmered with gold and circled her like a living merry-go-round. But something was still missing, and it hurt.

Katie loved her uncle. She could still feel the warmth of that love beating inside her, but Jack's frozen hand was squeezing her heart. Katie remembered a dearest memory, and her chest tightened more. She adored him, but Uncle Jack had torn her family apart. She loved him, but Jack wanted to kill them, and he would do the same to the world. The more she remembered, the more Katie's heart hurt, but memories connected them, and Katie could not let them go.

When Uncle Jack taught her to make pasta, she was small and still needed to stand on a chair to do anything useful in the kitchen. Katie made a big mound of flour on the counter, added a pinch of salt, and made a depression in the flour, into which she added a little olive oil and cracked three eggs. Uncle Jack made her use her fingers for everything. He said touch was the best way to learn when everything changed from egg and flour into pasta dough.

Katie remembered the cool, slimy sensation of putting her fingers into the eggs and whisking the yolk and whites together. As she whisked the eggs, the magic pattern matched it, twirling around her as she fed in the flour. Katie followed her uncle's funny instructions, and the gooey ingredients came together as a smushable ball. That was how Katie incorporated divine light into the pattern, a little at a time until it felt different in her hands. When it was right, Katie remembered the feeling of kneading dough, Uncle Jack's encouragement, and the stories he told of faraway places while the dough rested enough to roll it out. How they laughed and how serious Uncle Jack had been when she used the chef's knife to cut the dough into fettuccine noodles. Katie remembered how good that pasta tasted with everyone eating at the same table. Katie felt so proud when Uncle Jack told everyone she had made dinner all by herself.

As Katie wrapped her magic in the warmth of that memory, it threw off sparks of life. She placed one spark inside each mimic, like she was tucking in a sleepy child. Then she fanned the sparks until her mimics burned with divine light.

She knew everything was ready when she found the right words. Katie shifted back from Dreamland and whispered, "Ita Amor Invenitia." *Love Finds a Way.*

Tears ran down Katie's face, and her mimic's long fingers became like rays of sunshine streaming through a dark forest. Katie felt like she had run up twenty flights of stairs. She sank to the floor, admiring the glowing Katies.

Tansy yowled softly, then she, Katie, and her mimics faded into invisibility.

Toby watched the Katies disappear. "They can kill demons now," Katie said, her voice breathy from the effort, even over nano-radio. He was about to give the order to move out when Spell began to sing:

"Twinkle, twinkle, little star,
How I wonder what you are!
Up above the world so high,
Like a diamond in the sky.

When this blazing sun is gone,
When he nothing shines upon,
Then you show your little light,
Twinkle, twinkle, through the night.

Then the traveler in the dark
Thanks you for your tiny spark;
He could not see where to go,
If you did not twinkle so.

In the dark blue sky you keep,
And often through my curtains peep,
For you never shut your eye
Till the sun is in the sky.

As your bright and tiny spark
Lights the traveler in the dark,
Though I know not what you are,
Twinkle, twinkle, little star."

Toby had never heard all the verses sung before, and Spell's lilting voice carried strangely far in that concrete-and-metal hangar full of battle-ready mimics and the flying machines of war.

They moved swiftly through hangars full of Southeast Asia and Korean War displays and encountered no more Minotaur troops or hidden demons.

They reached the Cold War hangar. *We can do this,* Toby thought. *We can stop Jack here.*

Toby passed the B-2 stealth bomber named The Spirit of Freedom. Then he saw their destination: the SR-71 Blackbird with its still-futuristic lines and long, thin nose and body like a black dagger, driven by two impossibly powerful engines. *It was made in 1964, and it's still the world's fastest aircraft.*

Toby ran his fingers through Spell's fur, set her cage under the nose of the Blackbird, and climbed over the rail that kept the jet safe from people. Spell was still purring when Toby joined Tansy near the far wall. Katie became visible and took his hand.

Mimics formed a defensive perimeter around them and on the wings of aircraft and in the jets suspended above them. Many remained unseen. It was 10:00 p.m.—twenty-two hundred hours.

It was time.

The air around the stealth bomber distorted like a rock skipping through a pond's reflection. Katie raised a barrier of dappled sunbeams around her family, invisible Tansy, and their mimic guards. A dark, vertical line appeared in the distortion. It widened, and two platoons of Minotaur troops marched into the hangar. Huge demons took nightmare forms around them.

"Your uncle crossed a line," Tansy's voice whispered in their ears. "Be wary. He has merged demons and men. They are strong, and light will not dispel them."

Then Toby saw *them*. Giant, foul creatures entered the hangar, and Jack smiled at his niece and nephew as he strutted to the SR-71. He was bigger, and even through Katie's barrier, they could feel demonic energy rolling off him like waves of heat.

Then the rift closed. Their two opposing forces faced off, with Spell in between.

Jack surveyed the Toby mimics arrayed before him, and Toby held his breath as Jack extended the jagged knife under the Colt .45 of Ashur's Tears into a long rapier blade. Its tip touched the cage. Jack seemed to be listening for something. Then his eyes locked with Toby's.

After a long, uncomfortable silence, he looked over his shoulder and nodded.

The mercenary line opened wide, and Dunbar wriggled past them on his tentacles, pushing their father's sarcophagus to the Blackbird. Toby shivered, remembering his torture in the Meat Locker as Dunbar stood their dad's cryotube upright, then took his place at Jack's side, tentacles writhing, black wings unfurled.

Toby could see his father's sleeping face through the glass. "Professor," said Toby, "can you confirm Dad's status?"

"Interrogating. Negotiating with the system. Overriding protocol. I'm in, stand by."

"Copy that, Professor."

"Toby, it is your father. He is in stable condition. But there's a manual lockout, so I can't reanimate him remotely. You'll have to use the controls on the sarcophagus."

"This is a fine way to greet your uncle," said Jack. He was grinning as he appraised the mimics. "Impressive though."

"Like you would have taken me seriously if I didn't bring an army," Toby said from the edge of the barrier.

"True. Pity you picked the wrong team,"

"Doesn't look like it from where I stand," said Toby.

Jack chuckled and retracted the blade under his sidearm and holstered Ashur's Tears. Dunbar handed him something round, wrapped in a Blackwatch tartan cloth. "I figured you'd come at me with some insane tech, and you went all out!"

"Thanks for bringing Dad. He's alive and well. Cat's right there. After you."

Uncle Jack frowned. "Toby, you know that's not how this ends."

"Elite warriors take a long time to grow, Jack. Even if we don't win, you're gonna lose big. We got you outnumbered."

"I admire your confidence, kid. But about that," Jack said, unwrapping the cloth to reveal what looked like a small bowling ball. If it had a fuse instead of a digital display, it would have looked like an old-timey bomb. Jack held the ball in his palm and extended his arm so Toby could see the display numbers counting down.

Jack tossed the ball, and Toby yelled, "Attack!"

Mimics assaulted the mercs and demons, and guns fired in every direction.

"You rely too much on tech," said Jack.

The ball rolled to a stop in front of Spell's cage. The timer read: three, two, one.

They braced for an explosion, and Uncle Jack said, "Boom."

There was a loud screech, a flash, and a strong ozone smell. All the lights went out. Toby's eyes burned and every mimic stopped working and crashed to the ground.

"Cease fire," said Jack. His mercs popped light sticks, medics dragged away casualties, and his demons tossed their dead out of their way. "I knew you'd have some trick up your sleeve and pull off something remarkable, and you don't disappoint. But that was an electromagnetic pulse bomb strong enough to fry every circuit and microchip from here to downtown Dayton. That numerical advantage you were so proud of—it's gone."

Toby's eyes stung, but his biomechanics still worked. He checked the status of his mimics. They were all offline.

"And would you look at that," Jack said, pointing to sparks shooting from their dad's sarcophagus, the alarm panel flashing red. "Looks like stasis tubes don't like EMP either. Your father doesn't have long before he suffocates. I'm not a monster, kids. Give up now, and I'll end this, so you don't suffer long."

"This isn't over!" Toby roared. But he didn't know what to do.

"Tick, tock," said Jack. "Your dad has maybe twenty minutes, tops, before brain damage starts, and he dies a miserable death. Now, what's it gonna be?"

Toby's stomach turned. *It can't end like this. What can we do? Tansy couldn't beat Jack and take Ashur's Tears before this. Now he's even stronger. Even with Katie's magic, without mimics, we can't beat his mercs and demons. Can we even get to Dad before he dies?*

Jack laughed when he saw the broken, desperate look on Toby's sweat-soaked face.

"Surrender, kid. It's checkmate."

CHAPTER 37

DARKNESS AND LIGHT

There's gotta be something. I must have missed something.

Toby racked his brain. One blow, and his entire mimic army was gone.

Grim men and demons waded through his fallen forces.

Tansy hasn't shown herself yet. What if—

That was when Toby realized there were no Katie mimics on the floor, or anywhere to be seen. They were still invisible, and that had to mean something.

The towering demons kept their distance from Katie's barrier, but the Minotaur squads advanced closer and grotesque figures moved in the darkness just beyond Katie's ray of light.

It's over. We'll be safe a while longer. Then we're dead.

Toby finally lost it when he realized summer break wasn't even halfway over yet, and fear and anger poured out of him in a crazy laugh.

His hurt, distant expression scared Katie, and she took his hand in both of hers.

Toby didn't notice. He'd gone from despair to full-blown fury. *Everyone else I know is on vacation. They're on the beach or traveling or camping with their family,* Toby seethed, *not battling for their lives against a mercenary army. Not trying to stop demons. I'm watching Dad die because I can't do anything. I was supposed to be helping the crew with Suzie, and tutoring Rachel to catch her up on—*

Toby remembered getting lectured by Mr. Carpenter when Axel Suarez and his minions sabotaged him in front of the entire school. "*And* while it does look like *someone* tried to ruin your presentation, you could have easily made your point *and* limited the risk. But you elected to remove all the safeguards and make a big, showy splash. Reflect on what could have happened while you tutor Ms. Majeski."

I did reflect on that. Not that you gave me a choice. And to make sure it wouldn't happen again I hardened my mimics against electromagnetic— Jack's EMP hadn't fried their circuits! Toby had been so angry at Axel for trying to ruin him, he made his mimics resistant to even the most powerful magnetic pulse. *It's the safety protocol they forced me to add in case something went wrong. The attack didn't destroy my mimics, it flipped their switches. They're not dead, they're powered down!*

Toby felt Katie squeezing his hand, which was weird. Tears streamed down her face. She looked up at him and said, "Toby, I'm still here, and Tansy's still here." Then she sniffled and punched him hard in the chest. "Now tell us what to do."

Toby hugged Katie. He loved his sister. The two of them were alive and together after everything that happened, and Katie still believed in him. He wasn't about to let her down.

Toby ordered the mimics to reboot. "New plan," he said. "On my signal, we attack."

Katie nodded, and Toby adjusted his grip on Bite and Hack.

Jack crossed the battlefield to his niece and nephew standing in a spotlight ringed by fallen Toby mimics.

Jack stopped in front of Toby. "So, what do you think of my demon generals? Aww, Toby, don't look like that. We've been here before. We all know how this ends. I've grown powerful, and your barrier's shrinking. Take a good look at your dad's sarcophagus. He'll choke to death before your barrier's gone. You can stop his pain. You fought well. You've earned a peaceful rest. In an instant, this can all be over."

They were mentally and physically exhausted. Jack's voice was soothing and persuasive, and he was right. It was hard to keep going. It was miserable and awful.

Jack sounded like the uncle they loved, except he wasn't talking about bedtime. He was talking about killing them.

"No. This isn't over."

"Toby, you can't win." Jack's face was smug, and his voice hardened. "You know that, right? Sure, you fought as hard as you could, but you never had a chance. Ever."

"We have been here before," Toby said. "But you keep forgetting one thing."

"Yeah, what's that?"

"Cyphers always find a way."

Jack screamed as a Toby-mimic lying on the floor sank its fingers into him and ripped a chunk from his calf. The mimic pulled itself up Jack, tearing pieces out of him as it climbed.

Jack destroyed it with shots from Ashur's Tears as chaos erupted.

The demons and mercenaries had mostly ignored the mimics they were walking over. After all, they were no longer a threat—until they reactivated like zombies rising from a graveyard and caught Jack's force by surprise.

The EMP did have some effect. Not every mimic rebooted, and although most of them did, the Tobys weren't perfect copies anymore. Some looked swollen, others looked melted, and they shambled as they attacked. Panicked mercs died from their own friendly fire as they unloaded at the Toby zombies in their midst.

Katie transformed her choker necklace into a spear, kept seven of her mimics close, and ordered the rest to attack. "Three squads per demon. Happy hunting, girls. Make me proud."

The Katie mimics moved like soccer-uniformed ninjas, attacking from three directions at once. Katie squads materialized, tearing into demons, overwhelming them with the blinding force of their light, and then disappearing again. With every attack, a demon would burst, and Katie felt a sense of satisfaction. Each pop sounded like payback. The mercs who survived the zombie-Toby ambush fled as their big bad demons went *bang* all around them.

Jack reached out to Ashur's Tears, and its power surged. He felt its need for him and his need for it, and it fortified him. Living purple energy filled his missing chunks, and his flesh began to heal. Then he cut himself free from the mimic still latched on to him and snarled at Toby, "What did you do?"

"Get over yourself, Jack. You're not the first jerk to try to stop my mimics with EMP."

Toby attacked.

Hack left a deep red gash in Jack's wrist, and Toby barely dodged a relic shot that cratered the concrete floor. He leapt up to the black Stealth bomber, and Jack landed across from him on its wide bat wing. "You're gonna have to do more than run away."

"Bring it, old man," said Toby. "If you can."

Jack smiled, instantly closing the distance.

Toby blocked Jack's assault, swept Jack's legs, and lunged.

Parry, riposte. Block, attack, counter. Their blades crossed. Blood was drawn.

Then Toby missed, lost momentum, and had to block a flurry of attacks as he was beaten back. There was the clang of metal on metal and sparks as Bite and Hack met Ashur's Tears.

They moved and turned like the martial artists they were, striking faster at different angles as their weapons whipped through the air.

They sprang back from each other, both dripping blood.

Toby felt his pain and fatigue fade as he drew life force from his knives. Jack tapped into the power of Ashur's Tears. And their wounds closed. The stench of burnt iron, fried circuits, and rotten fish hung in the air.

Both smiled as they sized up the other. Another exchange, and more gashes appeared. Toby avoided Jack's gunshots and snake-like blade as they fought, and Jack always stayed just out of reach of a killing blow.

The fight blurred. Blades and fists whistled and crossed. They stopped, face to face. And they both knew it was over.

The point of Toby's blade was sunk into Jack's right eye. The power flowing into Bite from Jack was like rocket fuel, and Bite was greedy as he gulped it down.

Toby had an instant of hope. But his other blade missed.

Jack had locked his arms and stopped Bite inches away from killing him. Then Jack twisted Toby's arms until Bite was out of his eye. His socket erupted with purple and black flames, but he showed no sign of pain.

"At least you're consistent, Toby. Always close, no cigar."

"Laugh while you can, Jack," Toby said, wincing as his arm was twisted further back. "Your mercenaries are gone, most of your precious demon generals are dead, and my mimics are destroying the rest."

Jack extended his blade through his nephew's shoulder, and Toby screamed. Jack leaned in, and his eye flames scalded Toby's face. The look on Jack's face terrified Toby—Jack was smiling. "You're not the only one with cards left to play, kid."

Jack tightened his grip on Toby and turned his head toward the battle. Toby followed his gaze. One last demon general remained in the hangar. All of Jack's other forces had fallen or run away. The demon looked like a giant red and black starfish made of hundreds of spinning table-saw blades. Blades would stop spinning in random places, luminous predator eyes would open and close, and the blades would spin again. Its starfish arms slashed as it spun and cut down mimics as other Tobys and Katies rushed in to surround it.

Jack closed his good eye; through Ashur's Tears he connected to his demon general, and they became one. Jack reveled in the power he had concentrated into his demon. It was the force of dozens of lives and the might of creation. He felt around for the linchpin that held his demon general together. Jack focused on that one single point, turned creation into destruction, and pulled the pin.

The massive starfish demon bellowed, Toby ordered his mimics to retreat, and the demon general detonated like a bomb.

The blast tore through the hangar, and Jack held Toby in place as the shock wave washed over them, pushing back the Stealth bomber.

"No!" Toby screamed. Except for a few Katies, all his mimics were gone.

He struggled in Jack's grip, but it was useless.

"I kept most of my generals in reserve, and now your army's in pieces," gloated Jack. "After all the sacrifices your friends and family made for you. How's it feel, Toby? Knowing that when it mattered most, you just weren't good enough?"

Jack fired two point-blank shots into Toby's chest. The blast blew Toby off the wing, and he crashed to the floor.

Katie burned her way through the Minotaur troops between her and Dad's sarcophagus with blue and white fire. In the Meat Locker, Toby had said to lead with that, so she did. Puddles of melting demons burned like raging oil field fires, but her flames were a cleansing magic that only consumed enemies, leaving the museum untouched and friends unharmed.

Two Katie teams appeared and struck, popping the demon guarding Dad's sarcophagus. *We made it.* Katie touched the cool crimson metal and smiled at her father's sleeping face despite the warning lights flashing on the cryotube.

Toby was fighting Jack on the wing of the big bomber, and Katie hated that she couldn't help. Tansy hated being out of the fight, too, but she could sense that Jack still had powerful forces hidden. If Toby could hold out just a little longer, they could drive Jack back, and once he took the cage, they could win.

Katie had sent all but three of her remaining Katie mimics to fight the last demon general when Toby ordered the retreat. Katie looked up. Jack's blade was jutting out of her brother, and she screamed.

Tansy shouted, "Take cover, now!"

Katie barely got a barrier up when the explosion hit them, swatting aside aircraft like they were toys.

Shrapnel shredded mimics and Minotaur mercenaries alike.

Katie watched Toby fall to the ground. She shouted, but he didn't hear. She choked back her sobs and started to rush to him, but Jack hopped down from the bomber's wing, landed next to Toby, and in a flash, Katie was surrounded by demon generals.

She didn't know what to do. The main cryotube controls were fried, and it wouldn't open. She had protected her dad, Tansy, and her last three mimics, but it wasn't enough to fight them all. *Why can't we win?* Katie leaned against her dad's failing sarcophagus. Toby was bleeding, and she fought her tears as invisible Tansy nuzzled her, whispering, "There is still light in this darkness. There is still hope."

"How?" Katie shouted. "What can we still do?"

"Why did you come here, Katie?"

"Because I love my family. I came to save them."

"Then there may still be time."

But Katie couldn't see it, and Tansy went silent as Jack approached the cage.

"What are our orders, master?" asked one of the two demon generals near his nephew.

Jack looked at Toby's body. "Eat up, boys. When you finish, rally with the others." To his remaining demon generals, Jack said, "We're done here. I have the Guardian." Looking at Katie, he ordered, "She's nearly spent. When the barrier drops, kill her."

Then Jack picked up the cage, and Spell disappeared.

CHAPTER 38

DREAM EATER

Spell triggered when the bad man grabbed her cage. She was gone, and Jack and his demon generals froze in place, oblivious of everything. Spell was in their heads. She gave them their dreams, and the bad man and his monsters lived their most-secret desires. Spell wasn't just the magical version of a Claymore mine, set to go off when someone tripped her wire; she was the clickbait you absolutely had to see, that ate what you didn't know you had, until it was gone.

While they lived their dreams and ambitions, Jack and his demons were dazed. As Spell devoured their recent memories, they grew befuddled. Once all their recent experiences were gone, she ate their dreams, and when their dreams died, they suffered.

Toby hit the concrete floor. Every breath was harder than the last. He couldn't feel his legs. His body spasmed. He knew it wouldn't hurt much longer.

Toby felt like Goldilocks in the "Three Little Bears" story. First, he was too hot; then, he was too cold—nagging voices stopped him from feeling "just right."

I feel like the porridge in the story, not Goldilocks.

Then Toby heard his uncle say, "Eat up, boys," to the demons standing over him.

Yep, Toby thought, *I'm the porridge. You think about funny things when you're dying.* If it weren't for Bite and Hack strengthening his body and that last gulp of Jack's power, he'd already be gone.

Toby was jolted awake. *Where am I? Was I dreaming or something?* But his sleeping bag was warm, and just as Toby drifted back to sleep, two little kids shook him awake again. He was tired, and they were annoying. "Sleeping here!" Toby yelled. "Get lost. Go away!"

But they whined and pulled at Toby until he got up.

He was groggy and mad, but they were familiar. Toby finally figured out who they were, because while they made him breakfast, they complained.

"Eat up," said the little boy with curly brown hair and crooked teeth, as he smacked his lips and drooled. "It's fine. It's not like we had to fight demons for that or anything."

"Is it good?" asked the taller boy with blue hair and a perfect smile. "I hope so. Oh, don't worry. You're just taking food out of the mouths of growing boys."

"But you enjoy," said the brown-haired boy. "We'll get by, somehow."

"At least he left us crumbs, brother."

"How thoughtful, brother! He ate everything but the yummy, delicious crumbs."

He knew he was looking at Bite and Hack. They loved Toby. To them, he was a father and a good provider, and they did what they had to do, but it was hard for them to share.

Toby's wounds burned with blue energy, as the power his blades had hoarded from Jack and other demons was pumped into him. Toby convulsed as the missing puzzle pieces of his body were slapped back into place, then covered with a spiderweb of scars on his chest and across his back.

Toby woke again, with a sharp inhale on the museum floor. Two humongous demons were swaying over him. *I'm alive.* Farther away, he saw another knot of demon generals milling around Jack, holding the empty cage.

No time to lose.

Toby had injured Demon Lord Jack in a fight to the death and lived. Now Bite and Hack were starving, and it was time to feed the boys.

Toby rolled to his feet and stabbed his blades deep into the flesh behind the closest general's knees. It moaned and crashed to the floor. It breath was clinging orange fire that continued to pour from its neck after Toby took its head. The demon's energy coursed through Toby's veins and up and down his newly minted spine.

The next general looked like a cross between a massive crab and a clown. It snapped at Toby with its claws, but it was still disoriented and unsteady on its big red feet from Spell's attack. Toby jumped up to the bomber, then onto its shoulder, and he severed its antenna, red nose, and a claw. It hissed and struck blindly, but Bite and Hack were gluttonous, Toby's attacks grew faster and stronger, and the demon disintegrated into a sandy hill.

Katie was waiting at the bottom of the hill. She dropped her spear and hugged him. "Toby! I was so worried. I thought you were dead. What happened?"

Toby hugged her back, then let her go. Demons were attacking. "Promise I'll tell you everything when we're out of here."

Tansy materialized as a golden streak, striking down the horned and cloven-foot demon general behind them. "Nice to have you back," Toby said, throwing Bite and Hack at the rhino-faced demon charging them.

Tansy smiled her best predator smile before launching back into the fight.

Toby recalled Bite and Hack to his hands, but before he could attack, Katie flung her black-stained spear. It struck the rhino general in the throat. She leapt and grabbed her spear, intensified its flame, and slashed down until the demon was gutted like a fish.

"Nice!" said Toby. "World's best little sister *ever*."

She leaned on her spear, panting and beaming.

"Our advantage won't last," Toby said, scanning the museum. "Get Dad. Find the Professor; he'll know what to do."

"What about you?"

"Spell has one trick left. We're going to finish this. Save Dad."

Katie nodded, checking the sarcophagus mobility controls. They still worked. Katie lowered it flat enough to see over, then looked back at Toby. "He nearly killed you. Don't be a hero. Run if you have to."

Toby nodded. Katie twisted the speed to high and left as fast as the cryotube would go. When she was out of the hangar, Toby cut down another demon general. He felt stronger than he ever had. Bite and Hack vibrated happily in his hands, screaming for more.

That was when Spell brought the pain. Jack and his demon generals shrieked and shook. Katie rounded a corner, but a two-story blob like a lime gelatin octopus blocked the way. She wrapped herself and the sarcophagus in a barrier, and the demon attacked with tentacles.

Tansy said normal light wouldn't trouble these demons. But light isn't only strong, it's fast too. Katie closed her eyes, felt Fan's warmth envelope her, and said, "Celeritas Lucis"—Speed of Light—and Katie and the sarcophagus shot through the demon like they were fired from a cannon. They splattered it across the exhibit and bounced through the hangars. Katie flipped over the controls, scrambled to hold on, then slammed face down on the cryotube so hard it knocked the wind from her.

The sarcophagus skidded and banged to a stop in the middle of the entrance atrium.

"Oww!" She pushed herself up and looked around. *I did it. We got away!* Katie was feeling proud of her achy self until she looked down.

Her dad was struggling, his eyes were bulging, and his face was panicked.

He was suffocating.

Killing demon generals was getting a whole lot harder. Toby and Tansy took down one more. It withered as Bite and Hack guzzled the last of its life force until only a black dune remained. Toby shivered as its energy coursed through him. It bolstered him and he hungered for more, but Dunbar and two powerful demons still stood between him and Tansy and Jack.

"Can't keep this up, they're getting stronger," said Toby. "We need a *new*, new plan."

Spell's magic faded, and Jack was starting to piece together what had happened. He remembered holding the EMP bomb, certain it would crush Toby and the Guardian would be his at last. Then he was leading the greatest army ever assembled. Men and demons united under his rule. The world was his. Demon Lord Jack Cypher was brutally just. The cancer in society was purged, and his subjects bowed and cheered. It was a golden age of peace and prosperity . . . and then it was all gone. Jack stood in the Cold War exhibit surrounded by three rampaging demon generals and the dissolving carcasses and sand piles of six more. Jack was trying to figure out how he got there. *What happened?* Then he realized the cage in his hand was empty.

So, it was a trap. The SR-71 and B-2 Stealth bomber were pushed out of place. Most of the other aircraft were broken or tossed aside.

My brother and Katie are gone, thought Jack. *The Guardian is that golden light bouncing from wound to wound on the generals protecting me, and Toby is—*

Then it felt like someone was drilling through his brain. Jack grabbed both sides of his head and howled.

He steadied himself against the Blackbird until the agony passed and he had recovered enough to stand on his own and survey the destruction.

His Minotaur force was beaten. Out of thirteen demon generals, only three remained.

Now Toby and the Guardian are gone!

Jack screamed in rage. "Find them! If my brother survived, secure him. Bring the girl to me alive and intact. As for the boy, do not touch him. Send me word. I will deal with my nephew myself."

CHAPTER 39

LEAP OF FAITH

"So, our *new*, new plan is run and hide?" Tansy said, chasing Toby through the museum. He finally stopped in the far corner of the World War II hangar, leaning on his favorite bomber to catch his breath. Suzie wore the unmistakable scent of aviation gas like perfume, and Toby followed her landing gear up to the hatch and into the cockpit. He took the pilot's position, checked the controls, and sat back.

Tansy sat in the copilot seat, looking around. "Why are we in this contraption?"

Toby sighed, gripped the yoke, and continued flipping switches. "It helps me think." Then he noticed her curiosity at all the controls. "And she isn't a contraption. Her name is Suzie. You act like you've never been in an airplane before."

"Of course, I have," Tansy snapped, "but my first time flying in one I was a stowaway in a cargo hold. I could not see how it worked until I flew with you."

Toby groaned and then stood and walked back to the radio room. He touched the empty seat. *I had my first date with Rachel here. I owe her another.*

"New plan, no pressure," Toby said, in his most sarcastic voice as he tapped the main fuel gauge. "Empty," he said, switching to the reserve tank. "You'll figure something out—" Toby checked the gauge and was startled. The reserve tank was still half full! *How could someone miss this? Wolf is meticulous. Because if there's fuel in the lines—*

Toby raced to check the bomber's other systems. He turned all the battery switches—ON. The master ignition switch—ON. Main inverter and magneto switches—ON.

"Tansy, if you don't know much about planes, does that mean Ashur's Tears doesn't know much about them either?"

"My uncle could fly, but craft like this were unknown to him before his ascension."

An idea was forming. Toby remembered his last engine test, when Wolf asked, "Why are the primers and fuel boosters always kept in the OFF position until right before startup?"

As Toby toggled the rest of the switches, he prayed it would work. The answer to Wolf's question was, "Because leaving them on would be dangerous."

Cowl flaps set to OPEN. Supercharger—HIGH. Oil shutters set to OPEN. Fuel boosters—ON. Primers—ON.

And, most importantly, safeties—OFF.

That was how Toby turned *True-Blue Sue* into a timebomb.

"Come on, Tansy," Toby said. "We need to lure our uncles here."

Jack was every bit as smart and terrible as Toby had imagined, and more. Technology and magic didn't stop him. *Our old, new plan used the best possible combination of the two, and it didn't work. To beat him, we need something Ashur's Tears has never seen before.* Toby took one last look around the cockpit. "Sorry, old girl. You earned a rest, but there's one last mission only you can do."

Then he pushed the throttle up, and they left.

Toby had his *new*, new plan.

Katie pounded the *emergency reanimation, open, and evacuate* buttons, but nothing freed her father from the sarcophagus that was killing him. Everything she touched set off more alarms. None of the Professor's instructions worked, and her spear wouldn't cut through the metal.

I didn't fight my way through demons and rescue Dad only to watch him die.

Katie did the only thing she could. She closed her eyes and emptied her mind to craft a spell. She knew what she had to do, just not how to do it. Enemies were everywhere. They could be found any moment, and there was no more time. Her father was yelling and pounding on the other side of the glass. He was dying inches away from her. But how could she ignore him and focus? How could she let him go?

Then Katie realized she had already let him go. She remembered his funeral when they lowered him into the ground, and she didn't want to, but she let that sunflower as big as a parasol fall into his grave. Katie focused on that sunflower . . . how it tumbled and fell . . . the curly yellow-orange petals and the center eye that was black and brown and packed with seeds.

Everything else around her fell away. She cast circles around the sarcophagus and that flower on his coffin and filled them with her love and hope. Then she pulled both circles together. *Like is to like,* thought Katie. *It's one of the oldest spells.* What was done to a part of a thing could affect the whole of a thing. *Part of a grave that was. Part of a grave that would be.*

Katie reached through the circle, past the memory of her father's grave, and she strained to grasp that sunflower until, finally, she held it in her hand. *Like is to like.* She gently freed seeds from the flower's center. *This is to that.* Every time she pulled a sunflower seed, there was a corresponding *crack*, and a rip formed in the red stasis tube. With each freed seed, the rip advanced and the lid opened a little more, until there was a bare patch in the center of the sunflower and the top third of her father's sarcophagus was peeled jaggedly open, like Katie had used a can opener to cut away its metal lid.

Katie was woozy. The magic she used was unfamiliar and difficult to manage. She was shaking and exhausted. A cold, white fog boiled out and pooled around the sarcophagus.

Her father was unconscious, but he was breathing.

"Dad, you okay? Talk to me!" Katie shouted, grabbing his freezing hands. "Daddy?"

But there was no response, and she was ready to cry. Then Doctor Cypher's eyes blinked open.

"Oh, Dad!" Katie said, hugging him. He was cold, and she had to be careful of the opening's sharp edges. But none of that mattered. Her dad was alive.

"Hey, pumpkin," her father said, smiling. Then his face clouded, and he grew confused, "Wait, where are we? Why are you—"

"It's okay now, Daddy," Katie said, trying to burrow deeper into his chest. "You've been out for a while."

"How long?" Doctor Cypher asked, still bewildered.

"Weeks. But the Professor's outside, and he'll—"

"You've got to get out of here. It's not safe. Jack's—"

"Dad, we know. It was Uncle Jack. He took Ashur's Tears."

"I'm so sorry, pumpkin. I must have put you through a lot, I—"

"It wasn't you, and we have to go," she said, sliding off the cryotube. Katie forced a smile as she propped open the double doors. She knew what was coming. She had to get him out before he asked the one question Katie didn't know how to answer.

She could feel the summer breeze and see the moon shining on the white semi in the dark parking lot across the street where the Professor was waiting. She was so close.

"Katie, where's Toby?"

Tears ran down Katie's face as she pushed her father's sarcophagus past the doors as fast as she could. Her brother and Tansy were fighting to protect her so she could save Dad. He was a reckless boy. Katie loved him, and she feared the worst. *But Cyphers are smart, and Cyphers are strong.* She believed in Toby and Tansy, and she had to be brave a few minutes more. Katie took a deep breath and tried to say, "Cyphers always find a way," but she could not get the words out.

Doctor Cypher knew something was wrong. "Katie, where's Toby? Why are all the lights out?" Katie was bathed in moonlight, and she was crying. "Katie, what happened?"

Then something black wound itself around his daughter's neck. Her eyes rolled up, and she fell backward. "Katie!" he yelled, struggling to free himself, but he was still bound to the tube. Tentacles grabbed his sarcophagus and yanked him back into the museum.

Doors slammed and locked behind Doctor Cypher. An emergency light flickered in the atrium. He saw the flutter of impossibly large black wings. Then he recognized its face.

"You're . . ."

"Different than you remember me," said Dunbar, in a halting voice full of menace as he pulled the sarcophagus upright, so he and Doctor Cypher were face-to-face.

"What have you done to my daughter? Let me out of this thing, Dunbar!"

"She's fine," Dunbar said in a gravelly rumble. His dark wings beat, and his tentacled lower body undulated as he talked. "My master wants her, but later I will return for you."

"Katie!" Doctor Cypher screamed. He fought to get loose, but the sarcophagus was designed to be a prison. Even in its damaged state, he could not break free. He shook the tube, cursed Dunbar, and continued shouting, "Katie!" as Dunbar dragged his daughter away, leaving a trampled sunflower behind.

"Come out, come out, wherever you are!" Jack bellowed, and Katie groaned as Dunbar dragged her alongside her uncle. When they reached the War in the Pacific display, they passed two silver, low-wing fighter planes, and Jack looked up at Toby.

Toby sat on the wing of a small, red-and-white aircraft suspended from the ceiling above a fake coconut tree. He stopped swinging his feet when Jack met his gaze.

"Hey, Toby," said Jack.

"Hey, Jack. Come to give up?"

"I do love your youthful optimism, Toby, but here's the thing. Your robot army's destroyed. I have Katie, *and* your Dad's on display in the museum store. I just need the Guardian, and you're my last loose end before game over."

Keep it together, Toby. Don't let him rattle you. There's only one way you can help them. "I figured after taking out two platoons of your best mercs and destroying most of your demon generals, you'd at least take me seriously," Toby said. "Guess I'll have to try harder."

Toby dove from the wing as Jack fired three shots that blew away the small plane and left its tail spinning on a wire holding it to the ceiling.

Toby landed on the ribbed metal of a twin-engine Bolo bomber and bolted. But a demon general with arms like clubs smacked the opposite wing like a teeter-totter, catapulting Toby across the hangar.

Demon generals came at him from two sides.

Toby rebounded when he hit the ground, giving silent thanks to the Professor for his bioengineered shoes. He arced over the demons and landed on a brown railcar in a prisoner-of-war display. Bite and Hack's flames burned a vengeful blue as the demon generals circled him.

"So, where's the Guardian?" Jack asked with a grin, purple-black flame still dancing in his eye socket as he and Dunbar approached. "Or you gonna fight me again with knives? That didn't work out great for you last time."

"So, how's the eye, Jack? 'Cause now you're a terrible shot." Toby didn't wait for an answer. He ran as fast as he could. Jack's shots followed him, blowing the railcar apart.

Toby hit the ground, rolled, and ran straight into a demon that looked like a giant mound of eels. Mouths at the ends of iridescent tentacles sank into Toby, and he screamed, "Why is it always tentacles?" as he cut them off. "There's something wrong with you, Jack!"

The eel demon roared and whipped hundreds of tentacles at Toby. He couldn't stop them all. He raised Bite and Hack to try to cut a path through them.

Then a golden flash turned the tentacles to ash.

Thank you, Tansy. Toby sank Bite and Hack deep into the wounded demon. He felt better and hyperaware as the last of its life force filled him.

Toby hopped onto the large green wing of the *Memphis Belle*, the first B-17 Flying Fortress to fly twenty-five missions against Nazis and return with its crew. Tansy ran beside him. The club-armed demon was stalking them, and Jack and Dunbar were closing in.

"Thanks for the save," he said. "I'm so sick of tentacles."

"About your *new*, new plan," Tansy said. "We did not expect them to have Katie and your father. What do you want to do?"

"You won't like it. I need Jack to follow me. Can you hold off the demon generals?"

"They're a lot bigger now," grumbled Tansy.

"You are a goddess."

"Ugh. Fine."

"You break right," said Toby. "I'll push Uncle Jack's buttons."

Toby stopped on the wingtip and turned to face Jack, while Tansy hopped onto a blue-grey night fighter, then to a flat spot on the nose of a sand-colored B-24 Liberator. She had already wounded Dunbar and the club-armed demon general. In the absence of orders from Jack, Dunbar severed a few tentacles and left Katie bound in them on the floor.

Toby let out a sigh of relief when Dunbar and the club-armed demon converged on Tansy for payback. He half expected Jack to attack him with all his remaining demons, but they really hated Tansy. She had hurt their pride. They were the best combination of battle-hardened warriors and powerful demons, and they couldn't stop a big fluffy-eared cat.

Pride, Toby thought, as Jack approached. *That's got to be it.* He was still amped up from his last demon kill, and everything seemed to move in slow motion.

Toby widened and thickened his flaming blades and used them to deflect Jack's shots. Bite and Hack vibrated hard, and Toby's hands stung like he'd just smacked back two cannonballs. The parried shots blew through the roof, and Jack stopped in surprise.

"You talk a good game," Toby said, motioning to Tansy's fight with the demons, "but you're not really great at this whole 'tying up loose ends' thing, are you?"

Toby dropped under a silver Spitfire fighter and ran for cover as a barrage of relic shots assaulted him. "Guess that hit a nerve," Toby shouted. "You had a good run, Jack. People looked up to you. Now, you're everything you always hated."

Toby feinted right, then used every bit of speed in his bioengineered shoes to run left. He deflected another shot back at Jack and took cover behind a large cargo plane.

"You were the hero, the monster slayer," yelled Toby, jumping up to the wing of the big, two-engine transport. "Now you are the monster!"

"I will bring order to chaos," barked Jack as he closed on Toby. "I will end the violent, self-indulgent waste of this world."

"Keep telling yourself that, Jack," Toby said as he jumped into the fuselage, then up to a boxy glider suspended from the roof, "while you destroy everything you ever loved."

"Your sacrifice will end suffering and war," Jack's voice boomed through the hangar. "Humanity will prosper under my rule. History will record my actions as righteous and necessary."

"Says the Demon Lord," shouted Toby as he put as much of the glider as he could between him and Jack.

"Finally afraid, Toby?" Jack asked, moving closer.

I'm not afraid. Toby peeked around the glider. *I'm terrified.*

Jack was somewhere a few yards away, out of sight.

Katie was unconscious on the floor, and Dunbar and the club-armed demon were locked in combat with Tansy. It was now or never.

"Bye, Toby," said Jack. "Good concealment, but it's not cover if it won't stop an attack."

Jack unloaded on the glider, and Toby wasn't fast enough to dive away. The broken aircraft crashed before Toby could get his legs under him. He hit the floor hard.

His blades clattered from hands.

When Toby looked up, Jack was on top of him, wielding a long, thin, black blade with red veins that glowed like lava.

Ashur's Tears whistled as it swung. Toby pushed himself backward under the museum barrier surrounding Suzie, but Jack's blade ran through Toby's thigh and arm.

Toby's every wince and cry resonated through Ashur's Tears and felt like pure joy to Jack. Every swing of his blade erased another indignity his too-smart-for-his-own-good nephew had caused, and Jack took his time.

Toby made it to Suzie's wing.

Jack cut through the plane's barrier and slid his blade through Toby's foot, twisting the relic as he yanked it out, and Toby yelped in pain.

"You never answered my question. How does it feel to know you worked so hard for nothing, and everyone you ever loved will die because you failed?"

Toby clawed his way to his knees.

Jack raised Ashur's Tears over his head, making it a heavy sword with a jagged blade for the killing blow.

Toby raised his arms, but he had nothing to block Jack's blade.

Jack swung. Ashur's Tears howled.

Toby concentrated and closed his eyes, and the rippling blade came for his face.

Then Bite appeared in Toby's hand, fortifying and pumping life into him, and Jack's blade shrieked past Toby, shattering the floor.

Jack groaned and staggered, reaching behind him.

Hack was buried in Jack's back, happily drinking its fill.

Jack swung wildly as he tried to reach Hack.

Toby ducked and rolled and stabbed Bite through Jack's foot, nailing him to the concrete where "X" marked the spot.

Jack growled, "Toby," and Hack clattered to the floor.

Toby had one thing left to do, but Ashur's Tears was healing Jack too well. His sword changed too quickly, and it moved too fast.

Jack slashed, and Toby jumped away to Suzie's nose.

Jack made Ashur's Tears into a pistol and fired, punching cannon holes in Suzie, but Toby had already leapt away.

Toby grabbed the big propeller with both hands and pulled with all his might.

Ashur's Tears never saw it coming.

The prop kicked. The engine roared to life, and the propeller blades tore off Jack's left arm, just below his shoulder.

Blood sprayed. The prop flung Toby. He smashed into a fighter.

Jack's severed arm landed between him and Toby with a splat—Ashur's Tears still in its hand.

The demons froze. Then they faced the relic and stared.

Toby hit the floor and summoned Bite and Hack, but his leg was broken, and it was hard to get up.

Dunbar and the club-armed demon general stood transfixed by Ashur's Tears, and Tansy ran to Katie.

Suzie droned and twisted and pulled at her moorings, kicking off her other engine with a deafening roar.

The demons ignored the noise. They watched Ashur's Tears as it fell from Jack's hand and changed. The rough-shaped, black metal, and lava-bladed gun contracted into a dark ball in a swirl of light. As it shrank, its darkness faded. A coral-colored heart formed and began to beat. Its light turned white, then solidified into feathers.

Jack tied off the stump of his arm with his belt, and Ashur's Tears became a luminous, pink-and-white bird, spreading its wings to fly.

CHAPTER 40

FATE

Jack and the demons rushed to the relic.

Suzie jerked against the chain on her tail, bucking up and slamming down. Her prop blades shattered, and a gale of metal fragments pushed Jack and the demons back. Her engines shrieked and banged, then seized, and the old girl crashed to the ground.

"Tansy!" Toby pulled himself to his feet. "Can you hear me?"

"Yes!"

"Get Ashur's Tears."

Jack and his generals circled the relic, each intent on taking it for themselves.

"Toby, I just cut Katie free, if I leave—"

"Do it, Tansy! We end this now."

Tansy appeared at the demon-surrounded relic and took Ashur's Tears. It hung from her mouth like a pulsing white dove, and Tansy glowed like the sun through a cloud break on a stormy day. Then the clouds closed, her light disappeared, and Tansy and Ashur's Tears were gone.

The demon generals bellowed at where the relic had vanished.

We won, thought Toby. *We really did it.*

As Jack backed away, the demons turned their heads to him.

The relic that had bound and created them was lost, and failure came with a price.

Dunbar hesitated, then pushed past the other demon general that was lurching toward Jack.

Without Ashur's Tears, Jack was no longer fit to lead them, and the weak only existed to feed the strong.

Toby was hobbling toward Katie when Jack grabbed her. Katie screamed, and they disappeared in the wreckage.

"Katie!" Toby called, chasing after her. Her icon zigzagged along the hangar wall on his map. He could see her life signs but got no reply.

The demons brayed like bloodhounds. They chased Jack through the debris, tearing apart upturned aircraft until Katie and Jack were cornered. Then the demons attacked.

Toby sank his blades into the club-armed demon.

Dunbar screeched as divine light burned through the demon generals and flooded the museum. Without the protection of Ashur's Tears, the demons dissolved like shadows at noon.

Toby shielded his eyes. It was Katie's light. It was warm and gentle and healing as it flowed through him. When the light dimmed, Jack and the demons were gone.

It's over. A wave of relief hit Toby so hard his whole body shook. He wasn't sure whether to sigh or cry, so he did both. Standing tall, looking up. Tears streaming down his face, smiling. *We really did it. It's really over.* He took a deep breath.

"Katie, that was incredible!"

Toby searched. "Katie?"

There was no answer. Except for Toby, the hangar was empty.

Moonlight streamed through the holes blown through the roof, illuminating the destruction and Jack's severed arm.

A trail of splattered blood led from the crumpled, smoking hulk of *True-Blue Sue* to where Jack and Katie stood when the demons attacked.

Silhouettes of recoiling demons were carbonized like permanent shadows on the wreckage and walls. No tracks led away.

Jack and Katie were gone.

Toby looked for Katie on the map. The display read *Out of Range.*

He knelt where the blood trail stopped, and his heart sank. *Where 's Katie? Where's Jack? What did he do?*

Think. Toby looked around, grinding his teeth, trying to stay calm. Trying to figure it out.

She destroyed them with her light and healed me. She was fine before she was gone. Maybe Jack had a backup artifact as a way out.

"Tansy," said Toby, hoping the Professor's augmentations would still reach her, "can you hear me?"

"Yes, it is done," said Tansy. "Ashur's Tears sleeps once again."

"We need you, Tansy. It's Katie. Jack took her," Toby said, standing. "I'm getting my dad. Meet us here as soon as you can."

Did we go through all this just to trade Katie for Dad?

Toby ran to his father in the museum store. It didn't make sense. Without Ashur's Tears, the same divine magic that destroyed the demons should have ended Jack. *Where's Katie? What happened?*

Toby's kukri knives burned blue and did what they did best: they bit and hacked. The metal sarcophagus opened, and Doctor Cypher fell into his son's arms.

"Toby, Dunbar took Katie. And your uncle—"

"We're safe now," said Toby, "but Jack took Katie, and I . . ." Toby held his father tighter. "I'm so sorry, Dad. After you got shot down, if I would have just—"

"Shhh. You didn't do anything wrong. I love you."

"Love you, too, Dad."

Doctor Cypher leaned on Toby. He was still hurt from the shoot down, his beige flight suit was tattered, and he could barely walk.

As they slowly made their way, Toby told his father everything.

Tansy sat in a moonbeam on the warm remains of one of Suzie's engines. The blue stones on her necklace glowed softly, and she cocked her head as they approached.

"My God," said Doctor Cypher, "you're—"

"Someone who's searched a long time for you," said Tansy. Then she reached up and cast a spell. It enveloped him like sunbeams in a field of flowers. Twisted metal fragments emerged from his shoulder and arm, *clinking* as they hit the concrete floor. He grunted when his dislocated shoulder snapped back in place.

Doctor Cypher studied Tansy as his wounds closed. Her coat was tawny with black-and-white markings, accentuating her face and eyes. She was slightly bigger than a house cat, and her ears were a bit longer, with black fur on the backs and black tassels at the tips. She still wore earrings and a thick gold collar full of blue stones. Only now he could see them clearly, and they sparkled. Now he could feel her power. *How could I have missed what she was?*

Tansy's luminous eyes met Doctor Cypher's. "I only returned for Katie." As if she were reading his mind, she said, "When last we met, I was spent and injured and a shadow of myself. Little more than a wounded stray until your daughter nursed me back to health." With a swish of her tail, she hopped down. "First, let us see what you saw."

Tansy stopped at the edge of the blood trail and hissed. Wavering images formed of Jack dragging Katie away as Dunbar and the club-armed demon pursued.

Doctor Cypher bit his lip and growled.

"Stolen power returns hungry to its thief," Tansy muttered as she watched the ghostly demon images rush to devour Jack. "Sometimes fate needs a good kick in the right direction."

"What does that mean?" asked Toby.

"It was something Mother said when we first took Ashur's Tears from man, that changing fate is the greatest power of a god." The images moved like translucent neon-tinged projections. Jack dragged Katie into the aircraft wreckage, demons pursuing them.

Toby appeared, backstabbing the massive, club-armed demon.

A ball of light surrounded Jack and Katie as Dunbar attacked. Then the ball exploded, and divine light dispelled the demons. When the light faded, Katie and Jack were gone.

Toby's nostrils flared. A frown carved into his face, and something inside him snapped. Toby's heart pounded like a war drum; his head full of primal, eye-for-an-eye rage.

I will find you, Jack. You hurt Rachel. You took Katie. You'll regret everything you did. I'll make sure of it.

Doctor Cypher looked from Tansy's images of what had happened to the grim expression on Toby's face, trying to process what his children had done to survive.

"I thought I knew what Mother meant," Tansy said, replaying the scene, backward and forward. "Humans are cruel, wasteful, and arrogant. But I learned that you are also loving and capable and brave. History doesn't have to repeat. Mother wanted me to learn that, and how to give fate its push."

"Tansy," said Toby, "where did Jack take Katie?"

"Please," said Doctor Cypher.

"Katie is still alive. If I can show what happened from her perspective, I think we can—"

Burning white symbols surrounded Tansy. It happened fast. When the circle was complete, it vibrated with a deep bass thrum.

Tansy was pulled upright on her hind legs, her front paws outstretched, her head turned up. Her eyes became molten gold, and a geyser of effervescent light engulfed her, tearing through the roof, and shooting into the sky.

Red, orange, yellow light.

As the colors changed, more of Tansy disappeared. "Tansy, what's going on?" shouted Toby.

Green, blue, indigo.

"It's Mother. She's summoned me!"

The light pulsed to violet.

Tansy's voice broke and echoed. "Katie is. For now. She—"

Then Tansy vanished, and the light went out.

CHAPTER 41

EPILOGUE

"Glad you missed it, Raz, but it really was a lovely funeral," said the Professor. He was sitting in a lawn chair next to Doctor Cypher, handing him a beer from the cooler.

They were in the shade of a cluster of old trees. There was a small hill to their right, crowned with a monument of four soldiers guarding a tall pillar that shimmered in the late day sun above the gravestones.

"The place was packed," continued the Professor. "Dignitaries told pretty lies about you, and there wasn't a dry eye."

"Which one's mine again?"

"There," said the Professor, pointing a finger. "The one with the fresh flowers."

"Why's the grass a funny color?"

"Lawn's probably not getting enough nutrients, with just rocks and sand in your coffin."

Doctor Cypher laughed as he popped open a fresh beer for the Professor. "Thanks again for everything. When I think about what my brother and Frost did, I—"

"Speaking of devils," interrupted the Professor, "while you were at your checkup this morning, guess who the FBI captured?"

"Frost?"

The Professor bobbed his head in agreement. "They raided his properties and found evidence he was selling sensitive government technology to hostile foreign powers."

"Good job on that," said Doctor Cypher, raising his beer.

"Yes," said the Professor, "some of my most satisfying work. Now, he's being held as a terrorist under the Espionage Act. His assets were

298

seized, and he's on his way to experience some good old-fashioned Navy hospitality at Gitmo."

"To the Navy," Doctor Cypher said with a smile. "I expect things will be less grand than he's used to."

"How are you doing otherwise?" asked the Professor.

"Aside from the fact that no one really believes you're alive after the government declares you dead?"

"I'm serious, Raz. Don't deflect. It's annoying."

"I do love throwing back beers with you, Lawrence, but why are we really here?"

"Coming from someone who until recently was sitting on a shelf like a can of peaches and considered dead? It should be obvious."

"Enlighten me," said Doctor Cypher.

"Mortality, Raz. Look around. What do you see? This was where your kids buried you."

"Lawrence, I know they went through a lot."

The Professor sighed, his head rattling side to side. "You need to tell them."

"They're not ready," Doctor Cypher said, growing angry. "Not yet."

"How would you know? You were on ice in a box," said the Professor. "One that, if you recall, they rescued you from."

"Lawrence—"

"No, Raz. Not this time. We wouldn't even be having this conversation if they hadn't saved you. They need to know."

"They're not ready," insisted Doctor Cypher.

"They've earned the truth, Raz. It's time to tell the kids what happened to their mother."

"And what good will that accomplish, Lawrence?" snapped Doctor Cypher as he stood up. "Right now, Toby has some closure, and we still have to find Katie. The truth will only hurt them more."

"You weren't there to see it," retorted the Professor as he stood, wobbling. "They did magnificent things. They're tougher than you think!"

"Maybe," said Doctor Cypher, steadying his friend. "Let's say, for now, you're right. They're ready and able. What good will the truth do if we still can't do anything about it?"

"Weren't you the one who said no more lies?"

"They'll figure it out soon enough," said Doctor Cypher as he tossed the empty can into the cooler and sat back down. "Even after everything that happened, what kind of father would I be if I didn't let them be kids for just a little longer?"

"This was only a taste of what's coming," warned the Professor.

"That's why they should stay kids for as long as they can."

"That ship sailed, Raz."

Doctor Cypher swore under his breath.

"Let us review then, shall we?" the Professor said. "Your daughter was taken by your brother, who betrayed you, and it's consuming Toby. He is a doer, and if he doesn't do something constructive, he's going to do something rash because he's too much like his father."

"Alright, done," said Raz. "Toby gets access, but only the fundamentals for now."

"Fine," said the Professor, shaking his head, feeling the cool breeze moving through the trees. Then his gaze settled back on the long rows of headstones. "After we find Katie, Raz, you have to come clean. But do not wait too long. If you don't tell them, I will.

"They need to know their mother's still alive and what she's become."

Toby's head throbbed, and his body ached from sorting through rubble for clues for most of the night, but he couldn't sleep. Not for long. When he closed his eyes, he returned to the museum. *Jack's blade all the way through me. Shots to my chest. His grin as I fell to the ground. He left me for dead. I was nothing more to him than demon chow.* "All for what?" Toby screamed, sitting up in bed. "He took her."

Toby shivered. *He took her* echoed through his mind. It shook the emotions he'd bottled up. *He took her* untwisted the lid he'd locked down tight on everything he felt. *He took her* and all his anger and frustration exploded like soda spraying everywhere and soaking him in a sticky mess of everything that hurt. *We got Dad back. We got Ashur's Tears back. We stopped Jack from unleashing an army of demons on the world.* "But he got away. He took Katie," Toby said, through gnashing teeth, "and I can't find her anywhere."

Toby felt hopeless. Then he felt rage. "When I get you, Jack, I'll—"

Bite and Hack were in his hands, spouting wild blue flames, and he needed to feed them.

Toby squeezed them until his hands shook. Slowly, he calmed himself, and their fire subsided. Then he let his blades go, willing them into bracelets again.

Slowly, Toby caught his breath.

When he got up, he opened the blinds. He was on Nimbus. It was dark, but she was rising, and in a flash, it was dawn. Toby groaned and closed the blinds again.

Jack's EMP bomb had fried electronics across Dayton, but the power was starting to come back on. Vehicles were moving again, still mostly buses and government vehicles, but some cars were back on the road. It was still hard to get around or connect to the internet, and school openings were all delayed.

Dad had decided to keep the house, but everything except the basement needed to be torn down and rebuilt. So, until then, they were mostly staying on Nimbus.

Toby checked the map in his mind's eye. His father and the Professor were already at work. But even after boosting the signal, the icons for Katie and Tansy were still red exclamation points, labeled *Out of Range*.

"Katie, are you out there?" Toby whispered. "If you can hear me, let me know you're okay. If you can't talk or tell me where you are, don't worry, I'm coming to get you. Tansy, if you can hear me, I need your help." Toby listened and waited, but no reply came. *I'll try again later.* It had become a habit, checking when he got up, trying again before he fell asleep.

Toby's stomach growled. It reminded him of Katie, in a good way, as he made his way to a kitchen full of white counters, blue metal cabinets, and a ridiculous number of pots and pans hanging from various racks. Toby was starving, but nothing looked good in the fridge. So he brewed a pot of coffee.

It was dark again on Nimbus when the coffee was ready, and Toby filled two mugs, one with a bit of milk and sugar, the other with a big splash of vanilla cream. Then he grabbed a bag of mini donuts and cut through the middle of the lab, skirting the glowing, slow-turning magic rings.

He found Rachel at the edge of the dome, on the bench with the best view of Stratos. Her bandages had just come off. She wasn't supposed to walk on her own yet, but she was stubborn.

"You're up early," she said with a grin, taking the vanilla coffee. "So, how's the Hero of Dayton doing this morning?"

"Don't," Toby growled. "Please." It happened the day after the battle at the museum. *A team from the lab took us to a press conference on the state capitol steps. Social media had whipped itself into a frenzy of blame for the attack. I figured the president would lock everything down, hide behind "it's classified," and the Air Force would take credit for saving the day—but no. They gave me a choice. Play along, and the White House and Air Force would help me find Katie. Or turn them down, and I would go somewhere far away for a while. They were vague about the details. So, I went where they told me and said what they wanted. After the press conference, the headline read, BOY GENIUS TOBY CYPHER STOPS DEVASTATING DAYTON TERROR ATTACK! That was the story. No demons. No magic. Dayton needed a hero. I was it—and it sucked.*

Toby plopped down on the bench next to Rachel. "I brought you a present," he said, "but now, I'm not sure you deserve it."

Rachel pouted. Toby sighed and handed over the donuts.

For a while, they sat like that, shoulder to shoulder, munching donuts, drinking coffee, watching Stratos go by.

Toby set his mug down. "You know, Dad always asks me on my birthday if I feel different now that I'm a year older."

"I think my dad stopped asking me that when I was, like, nine."

"Right?" Toby said, staring at the view. "I said 'no' when he asked at the pool party. I always say 'no.' He usually asks when my friends are around, and it's embarrassing. But now, I'm two months into fifteen, and everything is different. Katie got the cake for my birthday. She said she filled it with all the stuff 'we' like, and it was delicious. Now she's . . ."

"I'm not gonna lie, Toby. You look bad. You're still not sleeping, and those raccoon eyes aren't a good look for you. So, what happened last night?"

"I finally got back in the museum, and I spent the night going through the wreckage and searching through the surveillance footage that survived the EMP, but there's nothing there. Nothing useful anyway. Nothing to tell me where Jack took Katie."

"Oh, Toby," Rachel said, putting her arm around him.

"It was a lot of work getting the video system back online. While I was waiting for it to boot up, I played around with what was left of one of Suzie's engines and found a part I could rebuild. It was only a small part, but I fixed it. I know that's not much, but it felt like a start. When the video was a bust, I left. I got mobbed by reporters, and Directorate 13 locked down the museum again, but I don't think there's anything else I can find there, and I hate feeling like this. I hate him, and when I find Katie, Jack's getting everything he deserves, and I'm gonna be the one to make him pay. But the longer it takes to find her, the greater the chance she'll be hurt or dead. And I—I . . ."

"I'm sorry," Rachel whispered.

"Why are you sorry?"

"I don't know. I just am," Rachel said, tearing up. "I'm getting stronger. And I'll help find her."

"Why are you crying?"

"I'm not crying. Shut up. You're crying," she said, wiping her face. "You loved your uncle so much, and he did this and took Katie. I get it." Rachel gently took Toby's hands. He'd been squeezing his fists so tight his nails had cut red dashed lines into his palms.

Her hands were warm. "Thank you," Toby said, feeling some tension leave his body.

"We'll find her, Toby," Rachel said as Nimbus rose back into the sunlight.

"Yes. *We* will," Toby said, and they moved a little closer. Rachel put her arms around his neck, and Toby leaned in for a kiss.

"Eww," said a girl who had suddenly appeared inches away from their faces, her elbows resting on the back of the bench.

They startled—standing up, turning red—and the girl scowled from Rachel to Toby. "I don't get to leave here very often, but when I finally do, I come home to find you two yucking up my place."

"Sorry," they said in unison.

The girl had a bob of wavy green hair that framed her face to just past her chin. Her eyes were bright and rose-colored, and she had emerald and black butterfly wings.

"Nimbus?" said Toby.

"Bingo. Perhaps you mistook me for Cupid?" she said, grinning at their discomfort and flicking the tips of her wings. "He's actually much taller than me, but for some reason, humans fixate on his baby pics."

Nimbus was wearing denim overalls, a gossamer tutu, and pink high tops. Nimbus looked like a fourth grader, but she was once a part of Stratos, who was older than time.

"I'm sure the Professor told you I'd be back today."

Toby and Rachel looked at each other and shook their heads no.

"Then I suppose the Professor also neglected to tell you, Rachel, that I'm now in charge of your physical therapy." Nimbus cracked her knuckles, and her smile wasn't cute. "It'll be fun."

Rachel was pretty sure it wouldn't be fun at all. Then Nimbus tossed her something. It sparkled and made a pleasant tinkling sound. Rachel caught a delicate band of fire opals and tiny golden bells.

"It's beautiful. What is it?"

"It's an anklet. For now, let's call it a training aid. If you wanna get stronger, put it on."

Then Nimbus skipped over to Toby. "And you wanna find your sister Katie. Don't cha?"

"I do," Toby said, balling up his fists again. "But there are no clues left to follow. I keep waiting for Jack to make a mistake, but—"

"There are other ways to find what you seek, Toby Cypher."

"Like what?"

"That depends on how far you're willing to go," Nimbus said, lacing her fingers behind her back and looking up at him. "The price is steep."

THE END

DISCUSSION QUESTIONS

1. What surprised or interested you about Ashur's Tears? Based on the book descriptions, what locations in the story would you want to visit? Why would you want to visit?

2. How long do you think the Cyphers' government can keep real magic (Alt Tech) hidden from the world? Why?

3. If Katie and Tansy could teach you one magic spell, what would you pick?

4. When Toby needs to complete the Stratos trial, he leaves Rachel in a safe place before she can wake up. Do you think he did the right thing? Why or why not?

5. Technology changes fast. It delivers fun and useful things, but tech advances can both help and hurt people. What's one example?

6. If Fan showed you time, space, and the universe, where would you want to go?

7. What would you do with a perfect walking, talking mimic copy of yourself that would obey your every order? What would you worry about if someone else had a copy of you that would obey their orders?

8. Toby makes mimics of his school classmates and programs them to dance with their originals. Phones and computers also allow us to copy ourselves in different ways. What are some fun ways we copy ourselves? What copies could be dangerous or embarrassing if we lost control of them?

9. The Professor makes Toby an advanced virtual reality gaming system, so that he can pilot giant robots in battle. What worlds do you like to explore through gaming?

10. Tansy and her mom are fighting. Tansy feels terrible about it because she lost something important. Her mom feels bad because Tansy didn't keep her promise. Can you think of some ways that Tansy and her mother could make up?

11. History repeats itself if we don't pay attention and learn from it. Was there a time you didn't learn from a past mistake? When you handled the problem differently, what changed?

12. Toby loves to work with his hands. He builds new things, gets old things working again, and loves to fly. What do you love to make or do? What about it makes you happy?

13. Katie feels a connection to the goddess A'nana and Mesopotamia through some of Tansy's memories also becoming her memories. What are two things Katie found out about Tansy's mom and her uncle, the god Ashur?

14. A'nana was a goddess in Mesopotamia (the Persian Gulf area of the modern Middle East). What two things can you find out about Mesopotamia?

To learn more about the Cypher universe, visit
www.BillRileyAuthor.com.

ACKNOWLEDGMENTS

Thank you, Jodi-bird, for believing in this story, for your encouragement, and for always rushing over to find out what happens next.

Chris and Beth Armour, thank you for your tremendous support, every talk over great coffee, and your generous gift of time and space to write by your river at the Southfork Lodge.

I subjected my first readers to a rough early version of this manuscript and I am grateful for their feedback. Thank you, Linda Channel, Ainsley Treesh, Kim Rourick, and Mike Ryan.

I also need to thank Tom Reale, for shuffling this manuscript into the top of the slush pile to gauge reader reactions. "Let's see what happens," Tom said. "It'll be fun," he said. Thanks again, Tom. It's been a wild ride.

Thank you, Milli Brown and everyone on the Brown Books Publishing Group team for believing in this story and for all your help.

I would especially like to thank my editors Kelly Lydick, Hallie Raymond, Brunella Costagliola, and Alix Reed for sharing their talent, time, and amazing perspectives.

I'm indebted to the unstoppable Amy Goppert who continues to champion this book. Getting a book noticed is like shouting into the wind. Thank you for making magic happen.

I can't thank Amanda Turner, Elaine Ambrose, Devri Walls, and Margo Kelly enough. They are captivating, best-selling authors who made time for me. Your advice meant a lot—thank you.

I also want to thank Brian Call for bringing *Ashur's Tears* to life with his beautiful art.

Finally, I'm indebted to the US Air Force and National Museum of the USAF. You gave me powerful experiences and a solemn understanding of the consequences of war. I'm sorry for breaking your stuff.

ABOUT THE AUTHOR

Bill Riley is an award-winning author and retired US Air Force lieutenant colonel. He was the kid who always got yelled at for daydreaming in school but still earned advanced degrees. Mostly, Bill uses his powers for good. He also spent much of his life working in secret worlds and this book was reviewed by several agencies for classified information before it was released.

Bill wants to assure you, and he is obligated to say, that this story is fiction. The fantastic events depicted in this fantasy book did not happen, and the world was never actually in danger. Really.

Bill lives in Eagle, Idaho, with his wife and two sons. Visit him at www.BillRileyAuthor.com, or follow him at billrileyauthor on Instagram, Facebook, and Twitter.

ABOUT THE ILLUSTRATOR

Brian Call has always loved to draw. He began his career in fifth grade when they put him in accelerated math to work on his own. He never worked on math a day after that—until he was found out. He spent his time drawing and would sell the pictures to kids during lunch hour. Brian attended Ricks College to begin his education and continued his learning at Brigham Young University Provo. He now lives in Ammon, Idaho, with his family and works as an illustrator. He also shares his talents as an instructor at Brigham Young University Idaho.